the DAMNED and DIVINE

BOOK THREE *of* REVIVAL OF THE FALL

STELLA HOPE

Print ISBN: 979-8-9918400-4-0

Ebook ISBN: 979-8-9918400-5-7

Book Cover by MiblArt

Copy editing by Laura Josephsen

First edition.

PRONUNCIATION GUIDE

Characters

Cerys: "Kehr-ihz"

Creiddylad: "Cree-thil-ahd"

Glais: "Glice"; rhymes with "slice"

Guillermo: "Gee-yair-moh"; Will's full given name

Gwyn: "Gwen"

Gwythyr: "Gwenth-yere"

Llefelys: "Th-vel-as"

Nudd Llaw Eraint: "Nee-th"; the "th" sound is soft. "Thau-Errent"

Creatures

Afanc: "Avank"

Dullahan: "Dule-a-han"

Gwyllgi: "Gwith-gi"

Leshy: "Lesh-ee"; rhymes with "slushy"

Nguruvilu: "Nuh-j-oo-ruh-v-oo-l-oo"

Púca: "Poo-ka"

Other

Arawn: "Arr-own," close to saying "Our own," the king of the Otherworld in Welsh mythology

Annwn: "An-noon," the Otherworld in Welsh mythology

Sláinte: "Slawn-che," Irish way of saying "Cheers!"

CONTENT WARNINGS

This book contains material that some readers may find disturbing or triggering. Please review the following content warnings before proceeding:

- Fantasy violence typical of the genre

- Profanity

- Physical assault (**non-sexual**)

- Loss of control over one's body by force (magical)

- Depictions of depression and mental health struggles

- Sexual content (spice level 1.5 out of 5)

- Dissociative episodes

- Death of a character

Please proceed with caution. Your mental health is incredibly important!

CONTENTS

CHAPTER ONE

NIGHTMARE MORNING

Esme

Esme was trembling. Not with fear, sadness, or fatigue—all of which would be fitting for the night she'd just experienced. No. Esme was shaking with fury, hot and burning like the infernal power she was barely restraining. It wanted to take her over, to infuse every inch of her body with its violence.

It wanted to change her.

"Is it true?" She bit down on the last word so hard she heard her molars groan in protest.

"Is what true, lovely?" Miles stood in her living room, his tuxedo still covered in jorōgumo guts, chestnut brown hair even wilder than normal. A faint black mark, a lingering trace of the venom his magic had purged from his body, stained his cheek near the scar that served as a reminder of his first encounter with a malevolent.

Even in disarray, he was as handsome as ever. It was like he had his own gravitational pull, irresistibly drawing her closer to him.

That she was drawn to him, even after everything he'd done, only infuriated her more.

"Are you patronizing me right now?" Her voice, a high-pitched shriek that cut through the silence, was filled with disbelief and horror. "You didn't even talk to me about it. The notion that I'm too emotional to handle murder is a worn-out trope. Been there, done that."

A barely perceptible downward turn of the corners of his mouth revealed the truth. Even through his short-cropped beard, she saw it. Miles knew exactly what she was talking about.

His head tilted to the side, mirroring Lily, his massive Irish wolfhound, who had settled in to rest at his heels. "What is this about, lovely?"

Esme wanted to reach out and snatch that term of endearment from the air. She wanted to bury it six feet under in her tiny backyard.

"Leon." The next word struggled to break free from her mouth, sounding constricted and strained. "Sylas."

Miles blinked, his left hand tensing ever so slightly, while his prosthetic right remained motionless. He nodded once. "That was not your Sylas. He disappeared a long time ago, Esme." Like a statue, he stood perfectly still, not a muscle twitching.

But Esme barely heard him. Her heartbeat roared in her ears, matching the furious rhythm of the molten anger simmering within her. By her next breath, the room was suffocatingly cramped, with the walls closing in on her. Infernal power, familiar but unsettling in its intensity, welled up within her.

"Why?" she spat. She could feel herself detaching from reality, bit by bit. His betrayal was like salt in an open wound, raw and searing in its intensity.

Miles met her eyes then. His green eyes reflected the hardness in her own. "I had to protect you and everyone else."

Esme's voice was flat, emotionless, a monotone. "You don't get to decide that." Her words hung in the air.

Miles opened his mouth to say something, but Esme didn't hear it. A jolting, unbearable pain ripped through her skull, making her breath hitch and her head feel as if it was being torn apart. She gasped, clutching her head as her vision blurred.

Esme doubled over, her nails scraping the ground as she fell to her knees. A deep, burning ache spread from her temples down her spine.

She screamed.

It was finally happening. The battle with her inner demon had finally tipped all the way over in its favor.

A sickening crack split her skull as two small horns protruded from her forehead, their points aimed defiantly skyward. Her hands shot up to her head a second time, encountering a rough texture that felt too real, too solid. She gasped for air, her chest heaving in ragged gasps.

Miles reached out toward her, but she stepped back. Esme spoke in a low, guttural voice that was hardly recognizable as her own. "Don't come near me."

"Esme..." For a moment, just a moment, something inside her softened at the sound of his voice saying her name. But it was a fleeting thing. Her fury was a raging inferno, obliterating any other emotion in its path.

"Embrace it," something old and terrible, but still familiar and welcoming, whispered softly in her ear.

Esme awoke, but not with a gasp or sobs but silently, eyes still eclipsed. She barely saw the walls of her bedroom or heard the soft sounds of the man sleeping beside her. Sweat covered her body, and her hands trembled.

For what seemed like an eternity, she did nothing but breathe, her hands clutching the sheets with a clammy grip. They shook as she reached up to feel her forehead. The slight movement sent the waiting beads of sweat trickling down her face. Over and over, she fought to banish all thoughts of the dream and the future it predicted. But each time, she failed.

Maybe the dream had been caused by the ancient, probably expired, sleeping draft she'd taken the previous night to avoid confronting the reality of Miles coming home. Perhaps she'd come down with the flu. Or maybe she was slowly transforming into the very creature that was always simmering inside.

She wiped at the sweat on her face again and moved to sit up. In his deep slumber, Miles seemed blissfully unaware of any troubles, his face untouched by the torment she experienced. She stared at him, the man she loved, the man she trusted with her body, heart, and soul.

How could he sleep so soundly after what he'd done?

Even with him unconscious, she already knew his answer. He thought what he'd done was right. He thought he was protecting them, protecting her.

And then, before she could stop it, doubt crept in—doubt about Miles, about every aspect of their relationship. And for a moment, she thought her doubts might change her mind about him.

The terror of that revelation made her push off the covers and grab her phone. She either needed to find peace with what Miles had done or do something about it.

Esme's breath plumed in the frosty December air as she walked through Pioneer Square's early morning streets. The nostalgic scent of pine and cedar from the festive decorations almost made her forget about her dream.

It was the last morning the Sanctuary of Spirits would be open for nine days, so she only had one shift to slog through before her extended break. It was the yearly post-gala brunch celebration. Hair-of-the-dog remedies and laughter would be on tap. Considering the amount of sparkling apple juice she'd drunk the night before, she didn't need the former and would try her damndest for the latter.

Sylas, her Sylas, wouldn't want her to stop everything to mourn. He would want her to smile and put on a brave face, then come to talk to him about it all later. That last step wasn't available now, so while Esme prepared the bar for opening, she'd do what she could to find a bit of peace in his absence, even if it did mean talking to his killer.

As she switched on the fairy lights her trolls had hung a few days prior to add a festive touch, the hidden entrance magically announced the assassin's arrival with a familiar buzz on her skin.

Leon walked in, his usual thick-rimmed glasses conspicuously absent. Somehow he remained effortlessly polished: tall, with sharp east Asian features, and an air of casual confidence. He was wearing black jeans and a black jacket that covered a black T-shirt. The ensemble was like something Gwyn would choose to wear, adding one more thing to her list of reasons she suspected their shared origin. He was also carrying two travel cups of coffee.

"Hel-lo, beautiful," Leon greeted as he approached. "You're up and at 'em early! Your call has completely brightened my morning. I'm surprised you have any energy left after those late-night shenanigans." He grinned, holding one cup out to her.

"Which you had no small part in causing," Esme muttered, grabbing the cup on autopilot. Thinking better of it, she immediately set it down. She massaged her temples, trying but failing to release a bit of the tension that had built up since yesterday. It didn't help that she'd only had a few hours of sleep.

She should be afraid of Leon. Last night she'd been terrified of him, but in the daylight, he seemed much more normal, more approachable—as if his hands weren't stained with the blood of someone she'd loved.

He gestured at the drink. "Full-fat latte, extra shot of espresso. Thought you could use it."

"How do you know my—" Surprised, she leaned over the cup and took a sniff. "Oh, wait, I forgot. You're a total creeper. This isn't drugged or poisoned, is it?"

Leon looked at her like she was the crazy one. "Who drugs or poisons people, seriously?"

"... People." Time to redirect from that uncomfortable reminder of Miles' tactics. "You're not secretly Fae, right? I can say thank you?"

He laughed. "I'm human, well... at least ninety percent human." With that, he voluntarily eclipsed his eyes.

Esme let out a soft whistle. "Damn. You have *got* to teach me how to do that."

She took a sip of her latte, hoping it would settle her.

It didn't. She fidgeted, tapping her nails on the side of the cup. If Miles knew she was alone with Leon, he'd be against her taking that risk.

"Thanks for coming. I couldn't sleep because I wanted to know more about what you said last night. How... how did all that come about? You taking the job and all."

Her hands trembled slightly as she arranged the oranges, the knife slipping once before she steadied herself. The familiar motion of slicing garnishes shouldn't be this hard, but her body was operating on wonky autopilot while her mind raced.

"Yeah, you look wiped." Leon shifted forward slightly, scrutinizing her.

"Thanks for the wholly unnecessary commentary on my appearance. Just answer the question," Esme shot back, though her tone lacked bite.

"I did call you beautiful the moment I walked through the door." He shrugged. "It was Gwyn who contacted me, actually. He approached me in the library downtown, offered me a contract. Payment came directly from the Corded Brotherhood."

Esme's stomach sank. "So Jacob was involved."

Leon nodded slowly. "It... uh, is his job to deal with malevolents..." Leon hesitated, as if searching for a delicate phrase. "And, well, you know what happened at the last Assembly meeting."

Esme leaned forward over the bar that separated them. "Why are you so interested in Gwyn, anyway? Besides you sharing the same dead language thing. Yes, I've figured out by now you're like him. You popped out of one of those malevolent prisons too, didn't you?"

The only thing keeping her from pointing an accusing finger at him was how many oranges she needed to slice.

Leon smirked, folding his hands across his chest. "I shall neither confirm nor deny these allegations."

"Don't play coy," she said. Bantering came naturally to her, making it difficult for her to refrain even with him. She didn't forget his failure to answer her question about his interest in Gwyn. But she wouldn't press it.

"Sorry." Leon didn't appear the least bit apologetic. "*Yes* to the malevolent prison. I've been trying to make that obvious." Leon's smirk softened into something that might be genuine. "You've got more questions burning in you; I know it."

Esme hesitated, then forced herself to speak through a throat that wanted to close in rebellion. "Did Sylas deserve it?"

Leon's expression shifted, growing thoughtful. After a long pause, he answered simply, "Yes, Esmeralda. He did."

Her throat constricted, and she swallowed hard, the dry lump catching in her throat. Before she could respond, Leon reached across the bar and lightly touched her arm. Warmth radiated from the contact—not fiery or oppressive, but soothing. It was almost identical Miles' magic.

Esme finally cleared the hesitation from her throat, withdrawing from his touch. "Did he suffer?" The question came out as barely more than a whisper. She hated how small her voice sounded, how vulnerable she felt asking her friend's murderer for comfort.

Leon showed no change in his expression. He answered her evenly, "He didn't even know it happened. I promise you that."

A mixture of relief and something heavier weighed on Esme as she ceased her work on the celebratory brunch's rosemary and cranberry sprigs. It took a herculean effort to keep going because she wanted to curl up into a ball, but she managed to transfer the garnishes to their bins.

The door pulsed its magical warning again, shaking her out of her growing melancholy. Will stumbled in, looking even more tired than Esme, walking next to a far too energetic Finn.

Will's voice sounded almost petulant as he walked toward the kitchen. "Frickin' A, Esme, are you trying to kill me? Constantly bringing gorgeous men into this bar." His whining ceased, replaced by a wry tone. "That outfit could use some serious work, though, bro. I can tell by the way those pants fit that we're working with a full dinner plate, but you're only serving up a snack."

If Leon was blushing through his glamour, it didn't show. Finn glared at Leon from the sidelines. Esme thought he probably had his Fae "ignore me" charm in effect.

Leon glanced down at himself. "What's wrong with my clothes?"

Will snorted derisively. "This is like 'brooding emo man-boy' and yet you could so easily pull off 'take-me-now dragon daddy' instead."

It dawned on Esme that Will and Leon had never met. To avoid where Will's big mouth could lead them, she cut in. "Will, this is Leon. The guy who helped Jacob. Leon probably has absolutely no idea what you're talking about because he's weird like Gwyn. He was explaining a few things to me, but he's leaving now."

The subtle upward curve of Leon's lips told her he'd gotten the message. "If you want to learn more about our kind, you know how to contact me. I'm also here to help with the malevolent problem. So call me if you need help with one of them."

She spoke the one hope she had for this man, this killer, into the universe. "I'd rather have you help us stop them from coming back altogether."

Leon paused mid-movement, considering. With a dramatic sigh, he said, "Guess you'll have to keep me around to find out what I can do."

With a sudden deliberate movement, Finn planted himself squarely in Leon's path as he began to turn away. The stillness that followed made the leprechaun's unexpected behavior all the more startling. "Seems our demoness has gone and found herself another stray. Guess she has a soft spot for vagrants with the whiff of malevolent magic about 'em."

Leon chuckled, a low, velvety sound that didn't match the tension in his posture. "That nose of yours sure is busy."

Finn clapped a hand to his chest, mock-wounded. "*Ouch.* And here I thought we were gettin' along famously." He stepped back, narrowing his eyes with a playful glint. "Now, don't get me wrong. I'm not judgin', just curious. I like to know things."

Finn performed a passable replica of the courtly bow she'd seen Gwyn execute perfectly before, bending over slightly lower than Gwyn had. While Leon gaped at him, Finn strolled over to the bar and leaned on it. "The nose knows! And remember—"

Finn straightened up, paused theatrically, and put on a mask of seriousness. "I've actually forgotten what I was sayin'. But it was going to be very profound and slightly threatenin'."

Though clearly exaggerated, the leprechaun's wink at Leon was a bizarre mixture of playful and subtly menacing. Though Finn often acted catty, Esme wondered about the hidden meaning in his last remark.

With a wicked glint in his eyes and a playful scowl, Leon turned away from Finn. As he walked out the door, he left Esme standing there with the lingering tingle of his magic on her skin, an unbidden smile on her face, and a pit of worry in her stomach.

Miles

"Stop!" Nudd shouted. The sound was so loud within Miles' mind that he worried he might have bleeding ears come morning. He found himself back in the dream he had fallen into while unconscious from the jorōgumo venom.

His dreams weren't sequential, ever. Miles mentally sat up, paying closer attention to the story playing out before his eyes—not that he really had a say in whether or not he watched it.

Startled, the man in the black robes and hood stalking the feasting hall snapped his attention toward the king.

"My people will not be your feast!" Nudd Llaw Eraint roared. "This is beyond insult, brother. This is... unforgivable!"

Be his feast? The king's choice of words made no sense to Miles. Had the magic that fueled his dreams suffered a translation error for the first time? Or was his Brythonic simply not as good as he thought it was?

Nudd's brother tenderly caressed the braid of Elena's hair he held, exactly as he had in the prior dream. The gesture was almost obscene.

Miles could feel the tension in Nudd's jaw as his teeth were clenched so tightly they seemed about to shatter. "Neither is she for the taking—as feast or bed sport. Begone or fight! This will not stand."

There was that word again—brother.

Nudd's brother, whether the invader was Llefelys or Nynniaw—Miles was uncertain—argued, "You would attack your own? Fratricide? I have done nothing!"

Nudd gestured at the room, filled with his people asleep at the tables they'd been feasting at minutes earlier. "There is no one here to watch your performance. Let go of any pretense and be who you truly are—a plague on everyone around you, a leech."

The intruder finally removed his hood but didn't drop Elena's hair. Nudd's brother looked like the reflection Miles saw in the mirror every day. The intruder's skin was more olive toned in complexion, his hair black like Gwyn's, but his face was nearly a match for Miles' own. The expression he wore, however, was ugly. His smirk held a palpable sense of disdain, a clear message of disrespect, and a challenge to Nudd.

With his silver hand, Nudd raised his sword, pointing it at his brother. "Why are you in Wales? You should be with your new wife."

The intruder stroked the braid again, staring at it as he spoke. "Not much to my liking." Each word dripped with scorn. "This, however..." His words trailed off.

"Since when has power over so many lives not been to your liking?" Nudd asked. Miles could practically feel the king's mind spinning.

The intruder finally peeled his eyes away from the braid. Turning his attention back to Nudd, still standing at the raised dais, he shouted, "I'd rather take what should be mine than act as consort to a horse-faced bitch."

With a decisive motion, Nudd's brother unsheathed his sword, its blade reflecting the fire in the great hearth at the center of the feasting hall. He charged.

Miles woke up slowly, groggy from the fight against the jorōgumo and his fitful dream. He reached out, the stump of his right arm encountering only cold sheets where the body of the woman he loved should have been.

Maybe the fact that he'd entered the same dream a third time was nothing but a strange coincidence, unrelated to his unique magic. Maybe the dream was simply a stress response to the fight or an aftereffect of the venom. Miles had far too many reality-based problems to face before he started delving into the surreal ones that disappeared with the sun.

Miles had had a lot on his plate currently, so it shouldn't have been a surprise to him that his dreams reflected that. David Abington, his former mentor and puppeteer, had traveled to Seattle to take over the Assembly. On top of that, Jacob had asked him last night to oversee Corded Brotherhood operations while he was abroad. And he had a backlog of patients at the hospital.

Problem after problem. With David Abington now residing in Seattle, he had to figure out how to handle all the baggage that came along with him. His old mentor would use and abuse Miles' power and time at any given opportunity. If Miles didn't give in, David would find subtle ways to torture him for it. Leon was also out there somewhere with a bank account full of Corded Brotherhood funds and the mystery of his strange magic trailing behind him. Gwyn had become so entangled with Abby and the Corded Brotherhood that Miles now wondered if cutting him loose would ever truly be an option.

And Esme... If she discovered his and Gwyn's secret arrangement with Leon, her grief would ignite into an infernal fury—aimed directly at him. He could handle failing at everything, but losing her would shatter him completely.

CHAPTER TWO

GOOD MORNING, GWYN

Gwyn

Gwyn's new apartment was little more than a narrow rectangle with only three doors. It came with unimaginative, sparse furnishings, but the fridge was stocked and the space was *his*.

It was his reward for helping the Corded Brotherhood, the undercover combative arm of the magical community, in their fight against the returning malevolents. Gwyn hadn't exactly put a dagger to Miles' throat when the promise for his new space was made, but the memory of the dagger's grip in his palm had still been fresh when the deal had been sealed.

Unable to shake the habit of rising with the sun, even after nearly a year of enjoying the luxuries of central heating and blackout blinds, Gwyn had woken far too early after the abysmal night before. Now that he was awake, he had to deal with the conundrum of how to make a sleeping Abigail coffee when the foot of his bed was barely more than a meter from his kitchen counter.

A light knock on the door spared him from making a decision. Cerys had been nothing short of focused when the nguruvilu arrived at Miles' front door. Yet this visitor disturbed her to a far greater extent than the large malevolent had. Unease pricked at him—her instincts were rarely wrong. She bared her teeth and even growled—a behavior uncommon for hellhounds. From what he could recall, they communicated within the pack by either howling or barking. Growling was a threatening sound, and gwyllgi usually skipped over threatening to attack immediately.

Sitting at the edge of the bed, he looked back to see if the disturbance had awoken Abigail. Because she hadn't moved, he was confident that he could address the interruption at the door without her stirring.

To calm the hellhound out of her fight-ready state, Gwyn had to pull hard on their connection as he petted her. He conveyed the image of a hellhound guarding the sleeper and, on top of this, he layered the emotions of gratitude and pack. Cerys' mind swiftly grasped this idea, and she positioned herself as a guard, putting herself between the bed and the door. Taking this as a good sign, Gwyn tiptoed over and opened it quietly.

Miles had called the man in the doorway a "bastard" more times than Gwyn could count this past week. He'd always meant it as an insult, and now Gwyn understood the modern meaning. Being a bastard wasn't about birth anymore. It was about being disagreeable—and Leon fit the term perfectly.

His and Miles' deal with the assassin had specifically required Leon's discretion, and yet they had received a deliberate display of grotesquery. Dropping the leshy's head at their feet, right on the heels of their battle against hundreds of spiders, had been nothing short of calculated. He simply hadn't figured out Leon's reasons for it yet.

Gwyn briefly considered shutting the door in his face, partially because he wasn't wearing a shirt and partially because he deplored the man, but Gwyn stopped himself. If Leon was here, maybe Gwyn could finally get some answers. Without a word, Gwyn shut the door behind him, leaving him and Leon alone in a deserted hallway for the second time.

In low, sharp Brythonic, Gwyn asked, "Here to crow about your victory? Your delivery was revolting. But I'll give you this—the cut was clean."

A single compliment, especially when given at the end, could soften the sting of insults, making it easier for a proud man to accept.

"More importantly, my delivery was on time." Leon deigned to match his tone, unlike at the library in the past. Every time they met, he sported the same glamour as a fit east Asian man in his thirties, complete with thick glasses and an ever-present wide grin.

"On time?" Gwyn rocked back on his heels. "The clock showed past midnight. By all rights, you should forfeit half your payment."

"Brother"—the paid assassin put on a show of appearing offended—"the solstice lasts until the sunrise."

Gwyn didn't want to hear his excuses. Leon's ability to conceal his magic from him only heightened his frustration. "That is not how these people think, and you know it... Why do you constantly test me?"

It was high time for Gwyn to begin asking direct questions.

Leon barely concealed a withering gaze but shifted tactics before the expression could fully take root. Speaking in English again, he said, "No, I'm here to ask why *she* didn't know."

Behind him, Gwyn heard the soft creak of the door opening. Abigail was wearing one of his hoodies and a pair of his sleeping trousers that she'd rolled up the legs on.

She looked at Gwyn with a puzzled expression, silently seeking answers. Her eyes were still fatigued from the strain of the night before, but she was a woman who recovered from any setback quickly. "She didn't know what?"

She added, "I had to use some bacon I found in the fridge and a little bit of magic to convince Cerys that hanging out in the bathroom was a good idea. She was... tense."

Gwyn tore his eyes away from her long enough to notice Leon's lingering gaze on her. Aware of Gwyn's scrutiny, Leon gave Abigail one of his too frequent, too deliberate smiles that cracked at the edges.

"Hello." Leon gave her every ounce of his attention. At least he wasn't trying to charm Abigail like he had Esmeralda. "I don't think we've been formally introduced. I'm Leon, and you must be... Abigail, correct?"

Abigail offered her hand to shake his, but Gwyn quickly pushed it down with an accompanying shake of his head. After what he'd seen the other mage do to Jacob with a simple touch, he didn't want her anywhere near him. She narrowed her eyes, disapproving of his action.

Leon, to Gwyn's surprise, chuckled and flashed another dazzling smile. He was clearly trying to charm her. "Oh, yes, your boyfriend does have the right of it, Abby. Best not to offer up your hand to those with magic that you don't trust—yet."

Thrown off for a moment, Abigail shrugged. She repeated, "She didn't know what? Are we talking about me?"

Leon mumbled, "I'm getting the sense that the answer is 'also, yes.'"

Gwyn hissed, low but direct in Brythonic, "Answer that question and I will remove your jaw from your skull with a blade or my bare hands, whichever time allows."

As Gwyn spoke, Leon's fingers twitched at his sides, a gesture so quick it might have been imagined if Gwyn hadn't spent most of his life on the lookout for the threat of a hidden blade. Perhaps Gwyn wasn't the only one battling against ancient habits in this modern world.

Leon did not escalate the argument with petty defiance. He raised both palms in the air in a gesture of surrender, something he was quite good at pretending, and widened his eyes in false shock.

"Apparently, I am not at liberty to say. It seems that I have already erred in coming here. Gwyn, you have my number. We should talk because you're about to walk into a very messy situation. Well, two very messy situations, one with your friends... The other..." He grimaced as if he'd smelled something horrible.

Gwyn's patience snapped. "You should leave."

Leon smirked, glancing at Abigail. "It was lovely meeting you, Abby. I'm sure we'll see each other again soon. Oh, one more thing: check your trunk. It's handled, mostly. But you'll need to deal with the rest. I... didn't know what to do with it on short notice with the sun coming up."

"My car?" Abigail seemed more confused than anything else.

Leon grimaced again. "The mess. I covered it with a trash bag. I don't have the contacts you two do to finish the job—sorry. I'm happy to pay the cleaning bill. Gwyn knows how to contact me. I know you'll forgive me when you see it," Leon said with a shrug that seemed practiced.

Doesn't have connections? Gwyn wondered why someone so powerful would deliberately maintain such distance from the magical community.

"Okay..." But before Abby could utter a word of protest or question, Leon gave them a little wave and mist walked to the other end of the hallway, blatantly shirking mage law. They saw him again as he stepped through the door leading out, waving again in their direction.

"I can't decide if he's an ass or if I like him," Abby muttered.

"It's to be determined," Gwyn said, "but I'm leaning heavily toward 'asshole,' as you Americans say."

Abby sniggered but quickly sobered. "What was he talking about, Gwyn?"

Gwyn rubbed her shoulders through the fabric of his hoodie, practically begging, "Cariad, please allow me to explain inside."

"Cariad, huh? I'll take it." She arched a brow. "But if this conversation's going to piss me off, I need caffeine and for you to finish the massage you started. Please tell me you have a coffee pot."

Striking a delicate balance, he confessed his recent sins to the woman he was growing to care for deeply. He needed to make her understand his actions had stemmed from his deep affection for her and his friendship with Esmeralda. Unfortunately, that took longer than he'd anticipated, and she was growing impatient.

"Okay, Gwyn, you've reminded me how magical beings inclined toward morally gray areas risk losing themselves to the dark side—in detail. *I get it.* What does this have to do with Leon?"

"Abigail, I love your brilliant mind."

Though she was amused, a silent challenge flickered in her eyes. "Thanks, Gwyn. You can shower me with compliments later, all day even, but right now, I really want to know what Leon was doing here."

"I'm avoiding the truth because I don't want to hurt you. The truth is... Sylas was lost to us weeks ago."

"Okay...?" she questioned, her face clouding over with caution.

"Malevolent magic twisted him too far. By the solstice, the man you grew up with had... died, for lack of a better term. He was replaced by something else. Abigail, the changes in Sylas were irreversible. He could never go back to being the man you grew up with, the man who helped train you."

Gwyn dropped to his knees, grasping both of her hands, pleading with her to understand. "Jacob, Miles, and I took all of this into account in making our decision. Sylas had already attacked Jacob. The result of which could have been his death, had Leon not come along. Sylas was planning to take more lives... He wouldn't have stopped until Esmeralda was dead."

"Gwyn, I already don't like where this is going."

"Cariad, we truly had no choice. The choice was between the walking remains of your dear friend or the living, breathing presence of your loved ones. Leon helped us remove the threat."

Her voice was flat, but not accusatory. "Did you have Leon assassinate Sylas?"

"Yes."

Abigail did not react in the way he'd expected her to. With her eyes closed, she tilted her head back, inhaling deeply. Gwyn was certain she was about to cry. Instead, sharp enough that her voice probably carried through his apartment's paper-thin walls, she yelled, "Fuck!"

After a moment of stunned silence, he kissed her knuckles, hoping it wouldn't be the last time his lips could touch her skin. "I'm so sorry."

Abigail pursed her lips, shaking her head angrily, her blonde curls bouncing with the movement. "Esme is going to lose her mind, Gwyn."

"I fear that is what Leon was suggesting when he questioned why she hadn't known earlier. That may be the mess we will have to walk into..."

Desperate for an answer, almost as desperate as his body was for his next breath, he asked, "Do you understand why we did it?"

A look of icy disapproval settled on her face—one he'd rather not receive again. Her serious tone left no doubt about her feelings. "Yes, but never lie or hide something this important from me again or we're done."

In times like this, the simple, unadulterated truth was best. "Then let us not begin the 'us' with a lie. Abigail, I will do my best."

"No promises?" Her expression hovered on the edge of scorn, her eyebrows furrowed and lips curled slightly. His harpy clearly disliked their decision, but her logical mind stopped her from rejecting their reasoning or him outright.

"I have learned from some past mistakes that I will only make promises to you I know I can keep. Abigail, if it protects you, or Esme, or even Finn, I will do whatever it takes, even if it means leaving out important details."

She puffed out her cheeks, blowing out an aggrieved breath. "*Fine.*" She sighed with the word. "You make moral ambiguity sound so damn logical. I've begun grieving, but I think I want to—no, I need to—be with Esme. We both need the closure... Plus, convincing her not to leave Miles after this will require some serious effort on my part."

Although the talk had gone far better than expected, he didn't assume Esmeralda would react in the same manner. She was far more emotional by nature, and her connection to Sylas had been deeper. Despite their current discord, Abigail's family was all alive and maintained, from his perspective, good relationships. In contrast, Esme had lost all of her family by blood and had since taken to finding one for herself. Sylas and Jacob were both clearly in those ranks. If Esme had already found out what they had done, it would be a challenge.

He nearly asked if she really had to try to save Miles and Esme's relationship, but he held his tongue. Abigail wrapped her arms around him, something Gwyn didn't know his confidence needed until he received it. She snuggled into his chest and murmured conspiratorially, "Let's go see what that viper left in my trunk."

Gwyn fully concurred with her assessment of Leon's forked-tongue nature.

The building only had one small elevator, so after they both changed into their daytime attire, they took the stairs down to the parking garage. When they reached Abigail's small blue car, what she had referred to as a "Beetle," Gwyn cautioned her. "Please allow me to open the trunk. I do not trust Leon."

She stood with her hands on her hips, ready for a verbal spar. "I can create a weak personal aegis if needed."

"Abigail... *please* allow me to do this." She'd reduced a prince to a beggar, but he had smiled more since relinquishing his title than during the entirety of his family's reign. A fair trade, he supposed.

On the verge of pouting, she conceded, "Fine. I guess I don't have another change of clothes here anyway. He said 'messy.' Gods, I hope it doesn't stink! I have to drive home before the family therapy session later."

He released the door latch to find something rather large concealed in a plastic garbage bag. Regrettably, it emitted a foul odor.

Abby groaned. "I spoke too soon."

He turned to her. "I am going to open it now. Agreed?"

"Well, it doesn't seem to be moving at least. Yes, just get it over with."

Whatever was inside was warmer than the ambient air. He carefully untied the string at the top of the bag. Peeking inside, he saw reddish brown hair. By all the magic, Gwyn hoped that the rogue mage hadn't harmed a child. He would rip him apart with his bare hands.

As Gwyn opened the bag all the way, the blood pooling at its opening caught his attention first. The sight of all-too-human pale skin followed.

"What is it?" Abby pressed.

Gwyn braced himself for the worst-case scenario. Seeing the creature's wrinkled, craggy face and the red hat clinging to its head brought him immense relief that mixed with stirring trepidation. He removed his hands from the plastic and sighed. "Our forked-tongued friend has left us with the still-warm corpse of a redcap."

Her hands flew to her mouth, her eyes wide with shock. "In Seattle? Gods below, where there's one, there's six!"

Gwyn nodded. He wasn't certain if they returned from their malevolent prisons in pairs or groups, but in his time, the gnomes were a nasty bit of work when encountered in numbers. Indiscriminate, they would just as soon strip the meat from a living, kicking horse as devour an infant human child. The idea of hunting such creatures in a city the size of Seattle was daunting, but it had to be done.

It was time for another malevolent hunt. Following that, he'd hunt the human serpent responsible for the mess—someone who clearly saw their destructive handiwork as something to be proud of. Perhaps Leon had spared them the effort of killing this creature, but Gwyn's gut feeling warned him against trusting Leon.

Still, Gwyn had made a promise to speak with the assassin after the solstice, and Gwyn kept his promises. His damaged memory was a persistent fog, obscuring the clarity of his past. Their shared history suggested that Leon might be able to help him remember more.

Though Leon swore he desired an alliance, his actions and strange behavior lent his words a ring of falsehood. When they next met, Gwyn would bring an abundance of caution *and* his sword.

CHAPTER THREE

A BLOODY HELLO

Abby

The parking lot was full of cars that hadn't moved in over a week. It made sense—the holidays were in full swing, and Gwyn's apartment complex was the kind of place filled with young single people off visiting their families during the break.

Abby wasn't happy about the mess Leon had left in her car, but she figured a mess was preferable to a live redcap. A little blood seeped from the garbage bag, ruining the trunk's pristine upholstery and causing her to wrinkle her nose in disgust. "Gods, I hope we're not at risk of catching something from that thing. How about we go inside and take a nice long shower together? Since we're missing brunch at the Sanctuary, let's make breakfast. I'm sure Jacob has already called a meeting anyway. I haven't had a chance to check my phone yet this morning."

Gwyn smiled at her, his eyes warm with affection, as they headed into the building. "Abigail, you have the best ideas."

But her cozy morning in was doomed to failure. A sudden sharp wave of nausea ripped through Abby's stomach. The queasy feeling wasn't hunger or fear. The miasma of foul malevolent magic crept up on her from behind to overwhelm her senses.

Still unaware of the danger lurking somewhere nearby, Gwyn reached for the handle of the stairwell's door.

Her hand shot out, gripping his arm tighter than was polite. Abby whispered, "Malevolent magic. It's not coming from my car."

Gwyn must've sensed the dark power before she even spoke. In one swift motion, she found herself shoved through the open door and into the stairwell. He followed silently, pulling the door shut behind them.

"You can open the trunk remotely? Do it!" he urged, voice held low, careful not to let it echo through the concrete walls.

Her hands shook as she fished the keys from her pocket and held down the button to unlock the trunk. "What do you think it is?"

He was already climbing the stairs two at a time. "Abigail, I need my sword. Stay with me!"

"Should we get Cerys?" They'd left the gwyllgi inside. Concerns had arisen before his move-in about Cerys being able to live with him permanently, given the challenges of concealing her true nature with a glamour. But recently Gwyn had improved markedly at having his illusions stick to the hellhound long enough for them to take her on a walk.

"Not for this fight."

Thank the gods Abby had taken up practicing sprint intervals after the Dullahan attack. From start to finish, she stayed right behind him until they reached the fifth floor. She was gasping for air by the time they reached the hallway.

Before she could ask what their next move was and what the hell he thought was out there, Gwyn ran at a full sprint, stopping only once he was in front of his door. A small burst of magic that made the door hit the adjacent wall proved that he'd skipped using his keys. By the time she made it down the hall, he reemerged with his sword in hand.

An ominous whisper replaced his normal tone. "The edict may have to bend."

"What do you think it is?" The exertion had caused her body to heat up, but not all the perspiration trickling down her back could be blamed on the sprint. His reaction to whatever was down there had terrified her.

"I'd bet everything on it being the dead redcap's friends. I asked you to open the trunk to distract them long enough for us to prepare."

Abby understood now. Legends told that they needed to keep their hats constantly soaked in blood or they'd die.

Damnit, almost anything would be better than mur-der-gnomes. Their cozy morning was turning into a nightmare, but hunting redcaps was infinitely better than running into them. Abby groaned, realization sinking all the way in. "And we have to kill them now before they hurt someone."

Gwyn gave her a grim nod and said in his matter-of-fact manner, "Yes."

"Do you have another sword?"

His mouth twisted in regret. "No, but we could go back to look in the kitchen. As I recall, you did quite well with a kitchen knife against that Alp."

He was referring to the time they'd used Miles' magic to free Esme from an Alp that was feeding on her. Abby had finished the creature off by stabbing it multiple times with a kitchen knife, and though it hadn't been pretty, it had been necessary. Malevolents deserved no quarter.

By the end of his statement, Gwyn was back to grinning again. Every time she got violent, he would give her this approving, dreamy look. She wondered, half amused, if he had some sort of aggression kink.

"Okay, let's do this. I'll skip the knives." They couldn't allow multiple redcaps to remain loose in the city. "What kind of magic do they have? The stories don't go into much detail."

Gwyn's response came out in a rush as they ran back down the stairs. "Their magic isn't offensive. In my time, they beat their victims to death with whatever object was at hand. If they are armed, do not hold back on protecting yourself! Keep your aegis in place the entire time."

Abby disliked his uneasy tone. "Okay…"

"And watch your shins… Their talons," he continued as he bounded down the stairs. "They are very fast, Abigail, very. Let's hope they're weakened from their return. If anything happens to me, get inside, lock the door, and call Jacob or even Miles. Redcaps do not obey the sanctity of thresholds, but they also don't like being indoors."

Well, that wasn't an ominous suggestion coming from him or anything. Things were far better when he was his normal arrogant self.

"Got it." He wasn't going to like what she said next. "Fair warning, I'll be trying to take control of one if an opportunity presents itself."

He sucked in a sharp breath but didn't argue. From all of their scribing sessions for the Brotherhood, she'd begun to learn how Gwyn's mind worked. He was a tactician at heart. Though he clearly disliked her idea, he saw the benefits if she succeeded.

"I can do it from a distance, but it's harder. I'll try that first." She didn't add "to make you happy," but he seemed to relax a little at the news.

"Ready?" Gwyn halted with his hand on the garage door handle. "They may still be in your car. If they are close, I will hit them with fire immediately."

Abby nodded. "And I'll wipe any mundane minds that see us. But first…"

She stood on her toes and gave him a quick kiss. The malevolent magic emanating from behind the door was so strong that she could feel it through the metal and concrete. There had to be more than one out there.

"Exactly what I needed," he murmured. His words said one thing, but his tight features said another.

Gwyn spun and flung the stairwell door open. Abby followed, coming up on his left. Two scrawny, wool-clad rear ends stuck out of her trunk, wiggling as they soaked their caps in their fallen companion's pooled blood. When the sound of the door opening reached their sharp ears, both figures froze for a single moment.

Then both vanished, streaking toward them in a blur of motion. She trusted Gwyn's reflexes far more than her own. Ignoring her racing heart, Abby instantly threw up a shield around herself.

Her doubts about her ability to evade the redcap proved correct. It crashed into her shield, sending her sprawling.

The rules governing magic were not bound by logic. Abby's shield had protected her from the force of the redcap's supersonic charge, but it couldn't save her from the hard concrete. Only the ER's mandatory self-defense training saved her from a concussion. She tucked her head into her chest as she slammed into the wall, her body skidding sideways along its rough surface. Her left sleeve was nearly torn away in the violent movement.

Scrambling back to her feet, Abby pumped more power into her shield. Gwyn had already downed the redcap that had hit her. He stood next to the nearly shorn in half body of a wrinkled humanoid she'd rather never lay eyes upon again.

The stories were true. Dark rivulets of blood dripped from the redcap's unmoving face, its hat completely soaked. The cap itself appeared to be woolen in material but was so sodden and foul that she couldn't be certain. Its face was that of an underfed centenarian that had grown wickedly sharp fangs. One small hand draped over its neck. The malevolent Fae was no larger than a toddler, but the outsized talons looked like they would be more at home on the claws of a vulture.

Gwyn stood, fierce, vigilant. His eyes scanned the garage for signs of movement of the second malevolent.

She gritted out, "I'm dropping my shield."

"Why?" His voice was incredulous.

"Control."

Abby found that protective shields cut her off from the outside world and weakened her magical senses. With the shield gone, the world sharpened, and she could sense the malevolent presence of the remaining redcap.

Without a word, Gwyn moved behind her, and suddenly, she felt a surge of power flood into her. It was more power than she'd ever experienced at once before, like a blazing summer sun burning within her. Now she understood why Will was so keen for Gwyn to do this with him again—it was almost intoxicating. She wanted to close her eyes and bask in the warmth burning within her, but their reality was far too unpleasant for that.

Tapping into her sixth sense, she searched for the wrongness again. It didn't take long. The sickening, stomach-churning wrongness of the redcap emanated from behind a gray car that hadn't seen the inside of a car wash in months.

Equipped with her seemingly endless well of power, she whispered a silent word of thanks to Gwyn and struck. Whipping her magic forward like a lash, she grabbed the small mind and wrapped her own will around it like a noose.

Gwyn must've sensed her surge of power because he gave her even more. Abby fought to concentrate amidst the intoxicating flow of magic but forced herself to focus because she had a killer to subdue. The redcap's intelligence may not have been the match of a human's, but its mind fiercely resisted her intrusion all the same. She squeezed tighter, silencing its protests.

"Thanks," she murmured, her voice strained. The mental struggle consumed most of her concentration, but Gwyn seemed to understand.

The redcap froze, and its will crumbled beneath her mental grip. Rigid and motionless, it stood with arms straight, legs so tense its knees bent backward slightly. She advanced, Gwyn's magic moving with her. Contact with the creature instantly solidified her control, cutting her required effort in half.

Still, the moment she separated from Gwyn's magic, its absence felt like taking off a jacket in a snowstorm. With her attention less myopic, less focused on maintaining control, she watched as Gwyn moved with predatory grace, sword pointed downward to flank the captured Fae on the other side of the car. He was boxing it in.

The Fae's filthy, blood-soaked cap dripped onto the ground as she held it by its forearm—the cleanest part of its body. She recoiled from the grime caked on its talons and the stench of rot clinging to its compact frame.

It would have been smart of her to ask Gwyn earlier if redcaps could speak. Most humanoid Fae could, and she'd rather do a whole host of unpleasant things than dive into its horrid mind. She pulled tighter on the rope of magic she'd wound around its mind and pushed her will deeper.

When Abby was younger, she'd imagined using her powers would make her look like a superhero—hair blowing in a magical wind and eyes glowing with the unearthly presence of her power. The reality was far less glamorous. According to the few who'd seen her use this power, her only tells were the murderous expression on her face and the subtle change in her voice. Its pitch deepened, grew huskier, and sounded more aggressive.

"How many are here?" she demanded, twisting, pulling, pushing. Even though she asked in English, her subject understood. Her magic in its mind was the translation medium.

The redcap's response was slightly high-pitched and raspy in the way that disuse causes. Its words were unintelligible and yet grating on her ears. It wasn't speaking back in English. She should have seen this coming.

"Uh..." she muttered, confused.

"He said 'four.'" Gwyn supplied. Thank goodness he was here with her. She hadn't even considered that interrogating the creature would be stymied by her inability to understand it. *Not smart, Abby, not smart.*

This one was the third. *Where there's one, there's six.*

"Where is the other?" she pressed.

Gwyn frowned as he listened, then said, "Near."

"In the parking garage?"

"Yes."

If that was the case, she needed nothing more from this creature—other than its death. It would kill her the same as it would any innocent walking on the street. In the past, she'd been critical of her brother's cold-hearted killing of a fully restrained nøkk. Yet, now, she thought she understood him better, and maybe herself a bit more.

Her next order was cold. It was heartless. But it was necessary.

"Tear out your own throat." Her hand still gripped its forearm.

The redcap made no sounds as the blood poured down its shirt. She dropped the body as it collapsed to the ground, carefully avoiding the spreading pool of blood. The deed was done, and her hands remained clean—physically at least.

Surfacing from her intense concentration, she saw Gwyn scanning their surroundings like a wolf waiting for the next attack in the darkness. Her magic reserves had taken a hit from the mental struggle, but the fight wasn't over yet.

There was another redcap somewhere. It must have been hiding for them to have missed it.

A split second after she sensed the surge of malevolent magic behind her, blinding white-hot pain exploded from her left leg. Her mind barely registered the fact that she couldn't stand on two feet any longer as she crumpled to the ground. She cried out, unable to stop herself because of the agony. The creature must have been carrying a weapon of some sort.

She forced the necessary words out through gritted teeth. "I'm okay."

Hoping Gwyn would do the right thing and remain vigilant, she erected another shield around herself as she sprawled on the ground, clutching at the misshapen mess that had been her calf a few seconds before.

But Gwyn was distracted. With more force, taken from the blinding agony, Abby ordered, "Kill it."

When she glanced up from her spot on the asphalt again, Gwyn's back was moving away from her. He wore his new leather jacket and was holding his sword, looking for all the world like a modern-day Viking.

Abby was a nurse. She knew that attempting to stand with broken tibia and fibula was idiotic, so she stayed put, focusing on maintaining her protective magic. The redcaps had singled her out as their primary target. It made sense. She was the weaker opponent, physically and magically, compared to Gwyn. As he prowled around the parking garage, she lay on the ground, barely able to hide her agony.

Gwyn spun around, walking toward her with unconcealed worry etched on his face. It was a small thing, an intensity in his eyes that had nothing to do with his concern over her, that clued her in to his game. He was baiting the last redcap, trying to convince it he would soon be an easy target as he tended to his companion.

Gwyn leaned over to check in on her and to make a show of doing it. He gently guided her hand away from her mangled leg and placed the grip of his sword within it. Gwyn wanted her to... But no, she instead moved her hand to the metal cross-hilt. She had a better idea.

With a desperate surge of power, she rapidly warmed the metal using her hot hands spell. It heated so swiftly that Abby nearly dropped it before she magically buffered herself from further injury. She didn't have time to weigh the intelligence of this idea. Abby only had time to strike.

A blur of red and pale wrinkled skin appeared from their left. Abby raised the sword.

A blaze of fire burst out of Gwyn in the same direction she had her sword raised in. Her aim must have been good enough. The jolting impact of the fourth redcap shot up her arm. As Gwyn's jet of fire continued, she clumsily dropped the blade. The weapon clattered to the ground, its leather-wrapped handle charred and crumbling. She hadn't expected Gwyn to use fire magic. Rather, she'd expected him to mist walk behind the creature or something like that.

Abruptly, the burst of heat ceased. Gwyn turned back to her. Over his shoulder she saw the smoldering corpse of their victim lying mere feet from them. A small club-shaped piece of wood, now burned, lay discarded nearby.

A deep, nearly disemboweling gouge running along one flank marked where her blade had made contact. It had worked not because she was skilled, but because she'd been lucky and the redcap was small and had been going fast enough that her ineffective method had worked anyway. That alone would have been fatal had Gwyn not completely sealed its fate with his pyromancy.

"Abigail, Abby…" Gwyn was touching her face, brushing aside curls of hair. His eyes were filled with a wildness, seeing everything and nothing at once.

"I'm… okay." At least her calf bones hadn't pierced her skin, so she wasn't bleeding everywhere.

His hands gently touched her sides, his attention solely on her.

"Gwyn," she snapped. "I need to get to the hospital, but that can wait while you put those bodies in the same trash bag as their companion."

"But," he started.

"Gwyn, I am a fully oathed Corded Brother and member of the Assembly, first things first. Yes, my leg is broken. But I'm also too tapped out magically right now to erase mundane minds if someone walks down those stairs or pulls in with their car. Go!"

He tore his eyes away from her and swore in one of the many languages he knew. Whether he was cursing her oaths, the Assembly, or the Brotherhood, she didn't know.

"Go!" she repeated. "I could really use some distraction right now, so tell me what language the redcap spoke while you do it, please? It was almost Gaelic but... not."

He briefly lowered his head before rising to his feet. "I do not know the name. It is what the Picts spoke."

Abby's brain lit up like a Christmas tree. "Pictish? Gods above, Jacob needs to have you writing and translating stuff instead of constantly having me ask you about magic. You speak two dead languages that scholars would kill to learn."

Gwyn experimented with the word "Pictish," saying it a few times as he picked up the two halves of the first redcap he'd killed with his sword. He was too intent on his task to distract her from the pain enough for her liking, so she shifted slightly to pull her cell phone from her back pocket.

His gaze shot back to her as she yelped from the movement. She said, "I'm going to call Jacob to tell him we need a few cameras erased and then Miles to tell him we have bodies to dispose of."

"Miles!" Gwyn stood up abruptly, blood dripping onto the ground from his gruesome task. "We are taking you to him, not the hospital. He will heal you..."

He trailed off, speaking to himself in the language only he and Leon shared. It sounded like he was cursing again.

Abby had resigned herself to using her paid time off and being immobile for the next few months. But if Miles could heal her, those problems would go away. Chances were that Miles was staying with Esme again following the fight after the gala.

A flash of inspiration struck Abby. There was a way to use her crisis to benefit their team. That wasn't selfish, right? Esme would probably actually listen to Abby's explanation of the assassination because of her injury. In certain circumstances, resorting to guilt-tripping your best friend should absolutely be considered an acceptable choice—especially when they needed to be saved from their own self-destructive tendencies.

"I agree with going to Miles. Let's discuss how you're going to get me into the car, then. Because this is going to be the worst possible upsies scenario imaginable. I wonder if I can make myself pass out..."

"Abigail..." he warned.

Through her pain, Abby sent him a wicked smile.

CHAPTER FOUR

IN TIMES OF NEED

Miles

The tension from the events at the Solstice Gala spilled over into the next day. Miles had distracted himself by tackling his endless paperwork while Esme had been at work that morning. But after she'd returned home, she'd barely spoken to him. He'd expected her to be overwhelmed with emotions, but being greeted by her chilly avoidance was... unexpected.

Was it grief? Her eyes were distant, her back rigid as she sat at her little dining table by the window, hands wrapped around a mug she'd long finished drinking from. It was wiser to wait for her to come to him when she was ready to talk, but the desire to press her for answers ate away at him.

Clad in sweats and a workout shirt, he slid into a seat, joining her at the table. Maybe sharing a quiet minute together would break the ice. "Chamomile to calm down," she said, her violet eyes brimming with unshed tears and a simmering emotion too close to resentment, which made him flinch. Fuck.

They both jumped as Esme's front door was unlocked telekinetically. Miles instantly braced himself for a fight.

Lily's head jerked up, alarmed, but she refrained from barking. The door shuddered as a familiar boot slammed into it, sending a wave of vibration through the entire frame as the door bounced off the wall.

In stormed Gwyn, cradling Abby in his arms. How the hell had Gwyn gotten past Esme's wards like that? She must have asked Jacob to exempt Gwyn from the protection. He'd have to ask the Bastion to reverse it. The many fights they'd shared hadn't yet erased the knot of distrust he harbored toward Gwyn.

Esme shot up from her seat just as quickly as he did. "Abby! What happened?"

Abby's face was pale, a faint whimper escaping her lips.

Gwyn answered in a single word that held all the meaning Miles required for understanding. "Redcaps."

Bloody hell. Gwyn had brought Abby to Esme's house for one very obvious reason.

A ready and eager Lily pranced forward, prepared to assist with doggy enthusiasm. Miles warned her off sternly. If she manifested her healing power again, it could lead to a problem that they'd have to fix by breaking Abby's bones for a second time.

Miles effortlessly slipped into command as if it were a comfortable second skin. "I'm going to clear the coffee table. Gwyn, you're going to place her gently down onto it. Abby, this is going to hurt like hell, okay?"

"What's new?" she wheezed out, voice weak but defiant.

"Keep that attitude. Esme, grab the med kit. There should be scissors in there. If not, grab your best pair."

Esme's eyes, previously distant, sparked to life as she moved.

"Slowly," Miles cautioned Gwyn as they lowered Abby onto the coffee table.

"I know how to handle her," Gwyn snapped back. "Why didn't you pick up your phone?"

Abby groaned, cutting off Gwyn's tirade. "Gwyn..."

"My ringer was off. I'm sorry. I was trying to get some work done before Esme got home." To Miles' surprise, Gwyn didn't push the issue further. In the past, their arguments would drone on for hours. The change had to be Abby's influence.

The position of Abby's dangling leg demonstrated a fracture of both the tibia and fibula. The absence of blood indicated a lack of skin perfusion. That was a massive relief because the risk of infection would be far worse than the breaks themselves.

"How long ago did this happen?" Miles asked, his voice calm despite the urgency.

"An hour or so," Gwyn answered, his tone grim.

Esme returned with the med kit, handing him a pair of trauma shears.

In his surprise, Miles' voice was sharper than intended. "You've been like this for an hour?"

"She wouldn't let us leave until I cleaned up the bodies," Gwyn explained.

Abby grinned, though it was more of a pained grimace. "First things first."

Miles met her gaze and repeated, "First things first." It was an informally adopted Corded Brotherhood mantra. It meant that if someone wasn't dying, they had to secure the scene immediately to avoid creating more problems for themselves down the road.

"Alright, brave girl, time for cutting. You ready?"

"Yep." Abby nodded.

When he started cutting the side of her jeans on the uninjured leg first, Gwyn shot out a hand to stop him.

"What are you doing?" Gwyn's tone was hard, protective.

"Stop it," Abby snapped, giving him a death glare Miles was glad not to be the recipient of. "I can't get out of these jeans on my own. He needs space to work."

"To be fair, mate," Miles added dryly, "I've seen plenty of bare arses in my line of work. One more won't make a difference."

"Same." Abby managed a weak chuckle, a shaky sound that died in her throat as she winced.

He finished cutting along the outside of one leg of her trousers and moved to the injured side. "Alright, Abby, even this might hurt. How about you tell me a bit about what happened?"

"It hit me with a stick going two hundred miles per hour," she said between labored breaths. "Fast little bastards."

"I've heard they're fast. How many were there?"

"Four. Leon killed one before we met the other three in Gwyn's parking garage."

Miles' attention briefly snapped away from his task. "Leon?"

"He visited us for a quick chat this morning after dropping off his *present*." A grunt escaped Abby's lips as her face twisted in agony. "He left its body in my trunk, saying that he didn't know how to dispose of it. Said we could because of our 'connections.'"

"Was it a trap?" Miles asked, his temper rising.

"We didn't feel their magic until half an hour after Leon left." Gwyn shook his head. "But... perhaps."

Miles couldn't help but sense that there was more to Leon's "gift." The timing was too perfect, the way the redcaps had shown up only after Leon left... too convenient.

Esme, frowning, asked, "Why would Leon do that?"

The three of them exchanged puzzled glances, trying to understand what would prompt her to defend Leon.

"E, we're going to have a long talk about Leon, but not now, okay?" Abby pressed Esme, then added, "All four redcap bodies are in my trunk in a garbage bag,"

Fantastic, more clean-up duty. David would love to hear about one of the Corded Brothers under his watch being maimed during a fight.

"You all fought three redcaps off? Impressive." Miles was deliberately being complimentary. He had to ensure Abby stayed positive for what awaited her.

Doctor's voice time.

"Abby, I won't lie to you. First, I may not be able to get through healing more than your bones right now. I don't know where my magic is after last night. Second, the process of setting the bones as I heal them will cause extreme discomfort. My healing works too fast to have a splint be effective. I need to be able to adjust the pressure immediately. That means I must manually align the bones... Yes, with my hands. Gwyn's help may be necessary to keep them in position."

Gwyn nodded. If Miles' dreams were correct representations of his father's life, Gwyn had seen his father set bones many times before. This shouldn't be new to him.

"Abby, it's going to be so bad you may pass out from the pain or from the shock. Understood?"

She gritted her teeth and nodded. "I hope to pop out a baby in the next decade, so let's count this as training for that."

Miles commented, "Nice way of thinking about it," as Gwyn asked, "You do?"

Abby snapped, "I am thirty-one years old. Certain biological activities have expiration dates, even if I get extra time because I'm a mage."

Esme's gentle laughter at that gifted Miles with a glimmer of hope amidst the darkness of the day.

Miles continued, "Unlike Gwyn's injury, these are weight-bearing bones. So even after I heal the surrounding muscle and skin, you need to stay off of it as much as possible for a while."

Voice sullen, Abby replied, "I'm totally okay with passing out now!"

"I have to feel the injury first, okay? This will be uncomfortable, but I think you're familiar with that by now." Miles hovered his hands over her mangled calf, touching it gently. It was difficult to put into words how his magic seemed to interact with flesh. But Miles could sense the wrongness in injuries through it.

The repeated injuries he had healed under David's intense training had fueled a growing interest in medicine and biology. His magic offered him a glimpse into bodies that even the advancements of modern science couldn't recreate.

Miles sent a small wave of his healing magic through her as a way of testing the waters. It gave him a snapshot of what was going on inside. The feedback was immediate—a jagged image flashed in his mind of her tibia, broken in two places, the bone splintered in three. The fibula was even worse, shattered into four distinct pieces, one small shard barely hanging on. If he had seen this in the ER, he would be preparing her for surgery with plates, screws, and a long recovery.

Her breathing had picked up the pace slightly, but she gave no other signs of being in more distress than before. Damn all the hells, Abby did not deserve to suffer like this. He could do this—he had to.

"You're lucky. No problematic blood clots." Thank all the magic for that. Tracking one down and destroying it with his magic was something he'd only learned to do in the past year.

Abby looked up at him with eyes opened wide in shock. "You can sense blood clots?"

He nodded and explained what the breaks and the surrounding tissues looked like. "I need to set and heal the bones before I work on the damage to the blood vessels around the pieces of bone. There is a small shard of your fibula that I may not be able to get back into place this way. You may require surgery to remove it."

"Okay, we can schedule an impromptu 'slice me open and remove it' visit with my mom as mental anesthesiologist. As long as the shard isn't too large, right?"

"Gods below..." Esme murmured. "I knew you were a badass, Abby, but geez."

"Uhh... it's not large." He honestly wasn't certain how to answer that.

The impromptu surgery was a crazy idea, but one that would keep this injury off her medical records. Plus, he could do it easily. He was fairly certain that Christi still didn't know about his healing ability yet. Although, with David around, some of his secrets might be short-lived.

"He'll do whatever you need," Gwyn growled. There was an undeniable threat underlying his words.

Miles ignored the threat and pointed at a spot on Abby's leg. "When I say to hold, don't move a millimeter. Abby, are you ready for that pain training?"

Esme encouraged her, "Break my hand if you need to, bestie. You got this, girl."

Grunting, Abby reached out and firmly grasped Esme's hand.

Miles tried and failed to catch Esme's eyes. He wanted to prepare her for what was about to happen with her best friend, because it was not going to be pleasant to watch. For all the world, it would seem like he was torturing Abby while he held her bones in place.

Both men lined up their hands exactly where they needed to be, gently placing their palms on Abby's swollen, discolored calf. She flinched. She couldn't move like that if they were to be successful.

Miles asked, "Abby, before we begin, I need to know if Esme should restrain you."

The question finally made Esme look him in the eyes. He already wanted to be back within the warmth she radiated wherever she went. Her facial expression clearly conveyed her unwillingness to do what he proposed. With a tender touch, he reached out and stroked Esme's arm, silently conveying his conviction that this was what they needed to do for Abby.

"I'll do it," Gwyn volunteered.

"No, you've done this before, and I don't want to risk Abby's future ability to walk."

Miles instantly recognized his terrible blunder upon seeing Gwyn's expression. He'd accidentally revealed far, far too much to the man who thought he was his father in disguise. Their silent interaction went mostly unnoticed by both women, focused as they were on discussing Abby's wishes.

"Esme, please. I really don't want a cast." The silent standoff ended with another loud grunt and confession from Abby: "I'm afraid I'll flinch."

Miles instructed, "Esme, sit on her upper thighs and hold her torso down by pressing on her shoulders. Abby, that's going to hurt too. Everyone got it?"

"Yes," Esme and Abby said miserably.

Miles once again reached out with his magic, making doubly certain that he understood the shape of the injury and exactly what was needed. He poured a bit of magic into her, healing the capillary damage near the surface of the skin.

"This is the nice part." He tried for a small joke. This part of his magic felt pleasant, like walking into a warm shower after being outdoors too long in wintertime.

Admittedly, his mind wasn't entirely on his patient. He was selfishly torn between his duty and wanting to put a smile back on Esme's face, even if he couldn't see it from where he worked.

"Gwyn, Esme, now comes the hard part," he warned them. With a quick nod to Gwyn, Miles pressed his hands firmly around her tibia.

Abby screamed.

For one long dreadful moment, there was nothing in the room other than the sound of her anguish and the feeling of her bones moving beneath his hands. Out of the corner of his eye, he saw Esme brace herself, probably infusing her strength with a bit of magic to keep her friend under control. And for a moment, it was almost enough to obliterate his focus. His memory, and that of the king's, was so full of screams that it shouldn't matter, but he was personally invested in this patient.

The bones beneath shifted slightly, resisting at first, but he pushed harder, applying pressure to guide the broken pieces back into alignment. Miles' hands worked with mechanical precision, but part of his heart wasn't in it. All he wanted was to reach out, take Esme's hand, and tell her that everything was going to be okay. He was a lovesick fool.

Duty came first... always duty first.

A tremor ran through Abby's slight frame as he worked. Pitiful mewling in between rapid, panting breaths. Then she came to a complete halt. Abby had fought long and hard, but eventually her mind couldn't handle the torture anymore and she blacked out.

Miles called forth more magic, letting it flow from the center of his chest, down his arms, and into his hands, the air glowing faintly as the energy poured into her leg. His fingers pressed harder as he adjusted the tibia, feeling the jagged edges grind against each other before they snapped into place. His magic followed, sealing the break with tiny threads of light, weaving the bone back bit by bit.

The fibula was slow to come together because the damage was extensive. He focused on the blood vessels that fed the bone, seeing the angry red where the shards had sliced through tissue. His magic probed gently, knitting veins back together, coaxing blood to flow properly again.

But the final shard wouldn't lock into place and there was still extensive damage to the surrounding soft tissues.

Miles grunted in frustration, his hands trembling slightly with the effort. If he used up all his magic now, he wouldn't be able to help her or anyone else for hours, possibly longer. His hands dropped to his sides, his heart racing, and sweat beaded on his forehead.

"I... can't finish this now, even if I went until I passed out."

Gwyn looked at him with a question in his eyes while Esme moved off of her now comatose friend. With any luck, Abby would continue to be unconscious for a bit longer because waking up without some pain relief was going to be unpleasant.

"The bones are set, other than the shard I mentioned," Miles clarified, his voice low, filled with relief and some lingering guilt.

"Thank you both." Simple as they were, Gwyn's words conveyed his deepest sincerity as exhaustion set in. "Let's move her to the bed."

Esme

The groaning moan that erupted from Esme's bedroom meant that nurse Esme was back on the job. All the hours she'd put in recently made her question whether she should try out a few online classes. At a minimum, some basic nursing knowledge would be helpful.

After Miles had taken a brief nap, she'd sent him to take care of Lily and sent Gwyn to grab Cerys from his apartment. While her approach to removing them from the house wasn't ideal, in truth, she was only mildly remorseful. Esme was desperate for a few minutes alone to gather her thoughts. She was desperate for a brief escape from the two individuals who had contracted a freaking assassin to murder her Sylas.

Holding a glass of water, she greeted the too-pale blonde stirring next to her on the bed. "Hey, lady."

"Am... Am I a bit high?" Abby asked, looking slightly cross-eyed.

"Yeah... Miles gave you a mix of pills while you were half-conscious there for a few minutes. We knew you'd be in a lot of pain when you woke up. He couldn't finish the job—yet. I think he's getting an IV from his house now. Why the hell he has that... Gods, I wish I didn't know."

"It seems to have helped." Abby giggled, then pointed at the water.

Esme brought it over, sitting on the bed next to her. "He said he'll finish the healing tomorrow."

"Awesome. Miles is *awe*-some," Abby muttered.

Abby didn't miss Esme's tight smile.

"Ohhhhh," Abby said, the word lasting too long in her currently altered mental state. "I forgot that you're mad at him. We should totally talk about that."

"You sure you don't want to nap?" Esme offered.

Abby's "no" was dramatic and drawn out, accompanied by a pout. In her drugged state, she was acting a bit like a petulant child, and it was hilarious. "I have to... convince you that you're *stupid*."

A genuine smile touched Esme's lips at that. "But, Abby, you do that without trying so frequently."

Truthfully, sometimes Esme found it difficult to keep pace with Abby's exceptional intelligence.

"Stop pretending like you're dumb... drama queen," Abby grumbled, taking a sip of the offered water. She was waking up more little by little. "You're stupid because of Miles and Gwyn."

What in the world was Abby talking about?

Abby continued, "We fight monsters now. They aren't monsters. No matter how stupid macho-man they can be sometimes." Abby sat up under the sheets, bracing herself on her elbows.

An uneasiness settled in Esme's gut. "You're using the word 'stupid' a lot, chica."

"Yeah, well, I'm trying over here, okay? I feel like I've been beaten with a baseball bat... Oh wait, I was hit by a friggin' Fae murder tornado. So you *have* to listen to me, Morgana."

"Yes, ma'am." Esme straightened her posture and clasped her hands primly in her lap.

Abby settled back against the pillows, letting out a heavy sigh. "Miles, Gwyn, Jacob... Gwyn explained... I realized they did nothing wrong, Esme."

Esme tensed. There was only one thing Abby could be talking about, even if she was half out of it. "So Gwyn told you what they did?"

"Yes," the affirmative was more of a groan than a word. Abby waved a hand lazily. "Was no different from Juniper."

"Explain," Esme said softly. Abby had been with her every step on the way to trying to save Sylas, so Esme had to trust her now.

"They killed what was left of him. That wasn't Sylas anymore."

Esme swallowed hard, her throat tight. "He was still our friend."

Abby covered her face with both hands in frustration, her fingertips pressing into her flesh.

"Was he, though?" Though pain colored Abby's eyes and voice, she seemed more alert. "He tried to kill you multiple times! Do you want a less extreme example than that? He forgot your birthday. Sylas would never have done that, ever!"

"But that doesn't mean—" Esme's voice cracked at the end.

"What you saw... that wasn't him. Not anymore. Not for a long time." Abby's eyes were faraway, her voice regretful.

"Malevolent magic... it took Sylas from us a long time ago. Exactly like it took Juniper away. Not Miles, not Gwyn, not Jacob—they just took the problem the magic created away. We simply couldn't see it while we were trying to save Sylas."

Esme's chest constricted, and she started discretely doing what she now called her anti-demon breathing exercises. She couldn't really argue with Abby, not when she was in this state. "But what if—"

"There's no 'what if,'" Abby interrupted, her tone uncharacteristically sharp, though it softened as quickly as it came. "You're mad because you loved him. We all did. But Sylas was gone long before they... handled it."

Esme's vision blurred. "We should've done more. We should've—"

"More? We tried Esme. He sent malevolents after you and Katia, after us, at the seated members' meeting. He came to the gala to *kill* us. Not once did he stop to talk or, hells, even negotiate."

That was... true.

"No more silent treatment," Abby mumbled, then, more clearly, "They had no choice, Esme. Miles, Gwyn, Jacob. They didn't kill him—they saved us. Saved everyone else from what Sylas became. Grace and Sitkum could have died in the fight against the spiders. Unfortunately, Leon didn't get the message about that part..."

"So what do I do, Abby? I feel... betrayed."

"After Gwyn told me this morning all about the deal they struck with Leon, he said something that stuck with me. I tried pressuring him into a promise to never lie to me again. He wouldn't make that promise. He said, 'if it protects you, I will do whatever it takes.' And, gods below, Esme, isn't that what we did to each other for a decade? We hid our roles with the Corded Brotherhood and the Assembly from each other to protect a person we loved."

Once again, the all-too-familiar mirror appeared in front of Esme's face, showing her the hypocrisy of her beliefs.

"And before you start arguing again, yes, this is different. But their reason was even better than ours. They wanted to keep us and everyone else alive."

"Okay, okay." Esme sniffled. "You win. Can we somehow manage a hug?"

Abby turned her head slightly and scratched at her neck. "Got any more of those drugs?"

The healing Esme was searching for started with their shared laughter.

Abby finished with, "Esme, I know you. I know you're going to need more time to sit with this before you're actually okay. I'm here if you need to talk more. Love you, girlie."

Chapter Five

The Plot Thickens

Leon

The streets of the Queen Anne neighborhood were quiet, still covered with autumn's decaying leaves. Leon's current path afforded stunning views of Elliott Bay through the bordering trees. He walked, his steps echoing his frustration born of a hunger he couldn't define, each a rhythmic release against the hard pavement.

He was far from his short-term South Lake Union apartment, which was in a vibrant neighborhood that was always busy. It was full of young and middle-aged single people come to work in the city's booming technology economy—a crowd he could blend into with his glamour seamlessly. Its location was ideal for easy travel, allowing him to hunker down or escape quickly if necessary.

The redcap he'd encountered after his rendezvous with Esme was no longer his problem, at least. The disgusting things worked in packs more often than not, so several being released from their imprisonment simultaneously was likely. Since the others had probably been scattered around hunting, it undoubtedly had taken them some time to regroup—precisely the amount of time needed to sow the seeds of doubt about his motives.

The ambiguity benefited Leon in more ways than one. Repeatedly offering straightforward favors would have made them suspect his motives even more than they already did. Having it appear as though he'd made a mistake, that he wasn't planning everything, was another benefit. On the other hand, it looked like a gesture of goodwill, peace even. He genuinely wanted to keep Gwyn as an ally until he became inconvenient.

To advance his scheme, Leon's next act had to be equally grand but less ambiguous. That was what his walk was about, thinking and hunting.

The thought had barely crossed his mind when Fortune smiled, sending a crying child his way. Having spent over four years in the twenty-first century, Leon instantly realized he was being played. The creature, feigning a helpless toddler, clearly hadn't been back in the real world long enough to understand that mothers in this rich society no longer abandoned babies they couldn't feed.

He felt the creature's wicked magic growing stronger with each of his steps down to the playground area within the greenbelt along the street. The telltale stench of sweetly pungent rot, faint but noticeable if you were familiar with its meaning, hit his nose as he reached the bottom. The monster's last meal, the remains of a corpse, must be rotting somewhere nearby.

When Leon had emerged from his imprisonment four years before, the world had been utterly unrecognizable to him. His new life had begun in Hong Kong, a place far removed from the Europe of his past. Dazed and disoriented from the magic's release, he'd been confronted by towering buildings, automobiles, and massive crowds in numbers that dwarfed the greatest armies of his time.

The Extinction event that had purged all malevolent beings from the world had been a revelation. It explained why the world was so prosperous, so easy, why everyone was so weak. But it also meant that every returned being—himself included—was drawn to those with powerful magic. This attraction was a constant nuisance, forcing him into fights when he would have preferred to avoid them. Several had even begged to serve him, most likely in a bid for their survival.

He stood out as a European in Hong Kong, so he'd adopted a constant glamour. Over time, it had become a second skin—one Leon often preferred. Looking into the mirror at his true face only reminded him of the past, of the man who had taken so much from him.

At first, ignorance of this new world had forced him into rash, violent decisions. The rules of concealment had changed. The sheer scale of surveillance and tracking methods mundane law enforcement had at their disposal made covering his crimes far more difficult than before. Killing was no longer as simple as silencing a witness—mundanes had ways of tracking even the dead. After many missteps, he'd learned that it was easier to wait for chance encounters like this one, where the body wasn't a name in a database somewhere.

Leon hadn't expected a second hunt in one day, but he didn't begrudge the opportunity. The madness his imprisonment had left him with hadn't fully consumed him, but for a time after his arrival into this world, he had teetered on the edge. Things were better now. His frequent hunts—sometimes by necessity, sometimes for sport—kept him balanced. They were a temporary cure, a way to reclaim a bit of the power he had lost—but *never* enough.

He scanned the playground, finding no obvious sign of a hidden body. The creature might have stashed it in the nearby ravine or bushes. There were a few types of malevolent beings that could appear as children, the tiyanak and the changeling being two prominent examples. Having encountered countless changelings in his life, coming across another one wouldn't be nearly as interesting as experiencing a tiyanak's magic for the very first time. New meant the potential for new powers to try out—exciting.

The toddler's cries fell silent as Leon reached the bottom of the stairs, but then started again as he glanced around for the source of the sound. It was hiding in the bushes along the second set of steps down the hill. Perfect. They'd be out of sight of the street when he silenced it permanently.

At first sight, he identified it as a tiyanak, not a changeling. A changeling would usually show itself as a helpless human infant. This one resembled a sobbing, hairless, chubby toddler, barely able to take a few wobbly steps. The tiyanak's pudgy cheeks were tear-soaked and red from exertion. Its act was impeccable, except for one glaring flaw: it was completely naked in the near-freezing weather yet energetic enough to wail and flail its arms.

The sight of the creature reminded Leon of his own age. Gray streaks had crept into his hair, and new lines framed his eyes. Time stopped for no mortal man... He hoped to finish his primary task in six months. But then what? Hopefully whatever he wanted, because he'd have eternity to figure it out.

He, Nudd, even Gwyn, had achieved ascendance before his incarceration. He wanted it back more than he wanted any-thing.

Taking it from Nudd was the only way he could devise to achieve it. Leon, as he'd taken to calling himself, simply needed to get Nudd to the moment before death when his power was unbinding itself from his body... then snatch it away.

"Oh, hey, little guy!" Leon couldn't resist playing along, knowing how the creature thrived on deceit. He could play the victim while turning the creature into one—fun.

"I'm going to take you somewhere safe." He reached down and lifted the grubby man-eater to his chest. The cherubic tiyanak let out another whimper, seeking comfort like a real child.

This type of vampiric creature was patient. The creature would only reveal its true nature when away from prying eyes, its fangs flashing like silver daggers as it ripped out the throat of its meal.

Leon didn't want to wait for the fangs to pop out. It was cold, and he'd already settled on his next move. Balancing the toddler-mimic on one hip, he removed his gloves one at a time. With what it thought was a heartbreaking mewl, the tiyanak nestled closer to him as he held it tight. With one hand, he reached into his pocket, while the other supported the malevolent.

Leon couldn't help but smirk at the creature's pitiful attempts to play the victim. "You should've studied your role better," he muttered, knowing the only audience was the creature that would soon be dead.

He slammed a blade between the tiyanak's frail ribs.

It let out a high-pitched, bat-like screech, and with a flick of borrowed magic, Leon cast a silencing ward around them, cutting off the sound.

The scent of rotting seaweed filled the air as the trickle of black blood ran from his blade. In the fleeting moment before its death, he siphoned every trace of magic he could steal from it. It wasn't much, but it would be enough to sustain and even enhance his abilities for a while.

He released the silencing ward and dropped the creature's body unceremoniously onto the ground, wiping his hands off on a few leaves. Now he had to get to delivering it. He could use an illusion to cover the fact that he was carrying a small corpse by one dangling leg, but that would cost him some of the magic he had stolen.

With a tiny burst of telekinesis, Leon overturned a nearby trash bin, scattering refuse everywhere. Sighting exactly what he needed, he left the rest for the crows to pick through. He stuffed the vampire's tiny body into a discarded takeout bag.

Before leaving, he followed the scent of decay to a pile of leaves about twenty feet away. A hand, then a face emerged—a victim still bearing the marks of magic. A mage. Only the layer of lingering snow had kept children from jumping in the pile over the past day—tiyanak were nocturnal.

He took a quick picture of the face, then covered the body again. Knowing the creature had a mage victim would make his intended gift even more valuable to his intended recipient. Bag in hand, he headed back up toward the street. A trophy and a message, all in one. He had long since learned that power wasn't only about strength. It was about who recognized it.

As he climbed back to street level, his thoughts drifted to the bigger picture. Influence still meant everything, and Leon had learned where to apply it while waiting for the leshy to make his move at the gala. Leon had used magic to eavesdrop on the crowd.

David Abington's presence had piqued his interest the moment he'd boarded the ferry. Everyone had wanted to talk to him or shake his hand. He also radiated a unique type of magic. Leon's interest in this new man had only intensified when Leon had seen Nudd's reaction to spotting him. Nudd—Miles—had gone rigid at the sight of David. Was it from dread or fury? Leon wasn't sure, but the depth of his reaction spoke volumes.

Leon had continued to watch as they'd fought the newborn jorōgumo. At the end of the battle, he'd left the leshy's head as a silent receipt of his requested services. Afterward, David had reappeared. From this, Leon realized Miles' earlier response to David Abington had been a mixture of both emotions. He hated and feared the man, whose every utterance was obeyed immediately by everyone around him.

David's power was political and personal; he was assuming Jacob's role. That made him the key to everything. If Leon wanted control, David was the man to charm, manipulate, or break if need be. Aligning with David was essential for advancing his own agenda, at least outwardly.

As he walked, bloody takeout bag in hand, he was glad he'd followed David home after visiting Esmeralda the night before, because he knew exactly where to go.

Fortune had led him here, but fate had given him direction. His travels from Hong Kong across Europe were a learning experience, teaching him the ways of the new world. Everything had changed the day he'd crossed paths with a Corded Brother in the United Kingdom. Before he died, he'd divulged a bit more than he'd intended and set Leon on his current path.

He had come to the U.S. hunting one ghost from his past—Nudd. Instead, he'd found two. Gwyn. The change brought about by Gwyn's incarceration was more profound than his own. Leon suspected that the magical transference had affected Gwyn's memory in ways his own had not.

Gwyn also seemed far less arrogant than before, and his control over magic seemed inconsistent. His weakened state could be advantageous if he allied with their jailer in the end. Every encounter with Gwyn was a careful game. Leon kept his magic masked, knowing that even a flicker of familiarity could stir old memories. And there were some truths he wasn't ready to reveal.

Gwyn had also achieved something that Leon would never have guessed was possible. He'd somehow taken two souls from Annwn and delivered them into the correct moment of time for his own return to the world. That was nothing short of extraordinary. For now, Gwyn was safe. Not from mercy or their connections—but from curiosity. Until Leon uncovered how he had bent time, fate, and the rules separating life from death, Leon's hunger would have to wait.

David Abington's suite was very near the mage's bar, a popular gathering spot for magic users in the area. Leon couldn't fault his taste. Every inch of his hotel was covered in glass that reflected the sky. The interior was inviting, warm, and had a refreshing sense of cleanliness—a jarring contrast to the dark abandoned playground where he'd just executed a vampire.

Previously, Leon hadn't followed David into the building, so locating his room would require some effort. Approaching the check-in desk, Leon smiled cordially and began chatting with the receptionist. A bit of flirting, a request for a pen, and a fleeting brush of hands later, the receptionist was calling David's room, urging him to come down.

When David appeared, he was still dressed in business attire—dress slacks, a perfectly pressed button-up, leather shoes and accessories. The absence of a smile made it clear that Leon's reception wasn't what he'd hoped. It was time to change that.

"Mr. Abington, pleased to meet you finally," Leon said, releasing the barrier he kept on at all times that contained the full force of his magic, borrowed and innate, from the senses of other prying mages.

David paused for a split second, measuring, and Leon had him baited. The man who David presented himself to be was the type who loved power, and Leon had an abundance of it.

"Hello, yes, I am David Abington. And you are?" David responded, clearly believing his name carried significant weight. It didn't to Leon, but he could easily feign sycophancy. His strategy of showing off his power had worked, as David's initial guardedness toward Leon had diminished slightly.

"Leon." Leon held up the shopping bag he was carrying, hoping that the rotting brine smell wasn't spreading too far. "I have a present for you, but I think you'd prefer not to receive it in your hotel room."

As Leon extended the shopping bag, his heart pounded, not from fear, but from the thrill of the game. When his attention was finally brought to the bag, David must have sensed exactly what was within because he asked aggressively, "Who are you?"

"A friend, Leon Chan."

David seemed momentarily surprised, giving Leon a second, scrutinizing once-over. Without missing a beat, Leon pulled out his phone and opened the picture application.

"So, I've dealt with a few of these problems around the city over the past few days and haven't quite known what to do with them. I also found this." He turned the phone to display the tiyanak's victim's face.

David recoiled slightly. The dead mage lay on her stomach, blood pooling with gravity. Livor mortis had set in, giving her face a ghastly, half-bloated, half-anemic appearance.

"A mage," Leon said quietly, gesturing at the bag with a slight tilt of his head.

David lowered his voice. "The bag did that?"

The unexpected bewilderment on David's face caught Leon off guard. Expecting anger or displeasure, Leon quickly changed his opinion about the man. Though arrogant, David was actually a cowardly man who'd achieved success by falling upward. Whether it was because of birth or charm, it truly didn't matter.

"Mage is still there, park in the greenbelt off Olympic under some leaves. I took care of a redcap this morning as well."

"A redcap? Just one?"

"I only encountered the one." The truth was only part of the story.

"Are you a visiting Brother?" David's interested eyes turned suspicious.

From listening in the previous night, Leon had learned Jacob was still controlling the Corded Brotherhood. Considering everything he'd overheard between Miles and David, Leon was willing to bet David was in Seattle hoping to take over all of Jacob's power base.

Leon's body language was purposefully open and upbeat. He held David's eye contact steadily. His honesty, freely given, was meant to project an image of trustworthiness. "I'm not a Brother. Although I have encountered a few when dealing with problems like this one. I think you're exactly the man I've been hoping to find."

Leon chuckled, feigning indifference toward the malevolent threat. "I think I'll be sticking around the area for some time. These problems find me regularly, so I'd love to make a friend with all the answers. That's *you*, I hope. Especially when it comes to disposal and not breaking certain... edicts."

By implying that David, not Jacob, was the go-to for malevolent issues, Leon suggested David's influence might be expanding in that direction. A bit of flattery and subtle suggestion could steer any conversation with an arrogant man in the direction one desired.

David scrutinized him once more. "Young man, I do think we should have that talk."

"That'd be great. Two problems in one day? I can't help but wonder if the local Brothers are lazy or ineffective."

Though David appeared calm, he took in a carefully measured breath. Following David to his suite, Leon silently savored two successes: he'd gained influence over a powerful puppet and had created a problem for Miles.

CHAPTER SIX

CONFESSION NIGHT

Miles

The black electric car with its cargo of two silent men and two innocent hounds pulled up to Esme's bungalow, now transformed with glowing reindeer and a family of elves since they'd left hours ago. The transition from fraught irritation in the car to a scene of holiday cheer was almost jarring enough to make both Miles and Gwyn forget their interpersonal problems.

After depositing the redcap bodies at the Brotherhood's least preferred crematorium and dropping off Abby's car for detailing, they'd spent hours in tense silence. Miles' disastrous slip of the tongue had made sure of that.

Miles could still hear the echo of his own words. "...You've done this before." A careless comment, but one that Gwyn had latched onto like a man seizing a weapon. Gwyn had probed the wound once and only once. Rebuffed, he seethed silently, the pressure cooker of his anger building, threatening to erupt. It was difficult for Miles to understand why it even mattered now. They were past that... At least they should be.

The two of them had already fought, and in their strange way, come to terms. Gwyn's capture and questioning by him had ended with Gwyn turning the tables, holding a dagger to Miles' throat. Forced together by circumstance, not trust, their collaboration had continued. Their shared purpose, ridding the world of malevolents and protecting the women who bound them together, had united them. Peace should be possible, yet each look, each silent accusation, destroyed their fragile truce anew.

Now, instead of sheathing their weapons, Miles worried that the two of them would go back to hiding daggers in the dark. Only those two women, and/or a healthy dose of honesty, could possibly save them from their self-destructive behavior. Either way, one of the two was certain to break them both.

They stepped onto Esme's porch, and her familiar ice elemental opened the door. Snowbert had abandoned his columnar form for a traditional snowman shape, complete with a too-small Santa hat. An unnamed elfin conjuration danced a merry jig in garish holiday colors as music played from somewhere inside.

The air smelled like baking cookies and hot chocolate, like a home filled with warmth and happiness, to him like Esme. A magical fire alit the fireplace on one side of the room, and floating magical candles adorned the tree. Explosions of garland, ornaments, and cheery decorations had been blasted onto virtually every surface. It hadn't been decorated this way when he'd left a few hours before—Esme must have been busy decorating to keep herself distracted from Abby's injury and her grief over Sylas.

They found Abby smiling on the lounge chair, injured leg propped up exactly as he'd advised her to do, but Esme was nowhere to be seen. Just as he had that thought, he felt a burst of magic enter the room. Esme and Finn materialized in a swirl of sparkling illusory snowflakes, the air around them shimmering and smelling faintly of peppermint.

Finn wore an outfit strikingly similar to the conjured elfin creature, but Miles would bet that the adornments covering his clothing were of genuine gold. Esme wore an "ugly" Christmas sweater and a smile—something he'd been missing. She looked different, lighter, than she had that morning.

"Merry almost Christmas!" she said with that signature warmth, and it hit him hard. Her heartfelt smile melted away his defenses, momentarily thawing the icy layers around his heart. Maybe, just maybe, things would be okay.

Finn added, "The night the fat man arrives isn't for two days, but we thought this would be fun while Abby's recuperatin'. Esme decided Gwyn's first Christmas movie marathon called for somethin' special."

The illusory snowstorm ceased as quickly as it had started, and the elfin creature stopped dancing. It and the ice elemental disappeared, ordered back to the place whence they came. Miles had to admit that it was an impressive display of sustained magic from both Esme and Finn—especially after using so much firepower only the night before. It was hard to believe that it had been less than a full day since they'd fought the jorōgumo spiders at the Solstice Gala.

Miles stole a glance at Gwyn, who was trying to read him for the fiftieth time that day, no doubt. Miles' smirk was a mask; inside, he was anything but calm.

Gwyn frowned and shot his gaze to the floor briefly. Was he embarrassed?

"It was quite the reception. Thank you." Gwyn shifted his weight on his feet and continued, "Surely, Finnegan, this is also your first Christmas movie marathon?"

"I will confess to bein' up to high doh," Finn admitted.

Since nobody understood what the hell that meant, Finn explained, "By all the... I'm feckin' excited!"

Esme squealed in delight. A bit of sunshine had reentered her eyes. "Don't worry; the movies I have planned are short since they're meant for children, but they're classics every-one should see at least once."

Lily curled up between Miles and Esme on the couch. Cerys kept Abby company by lying against her recliner, while Finn and Gwyn shared the loveseat. Finn's commen-tary, filled with gasps and colorful insults, made watching the same movies for the umpteenth time entertaining. "That shitehawk would rob the milk from yer tea, then come back for the sugar!"

The leprechaun made loud groaning noises throughout. "Those poor weans are going to wake up in shambles on Christmas mornin'!"

Gwyn's commentary was less colorful, darker. "Despica-ble villainy. Before the Extinction, the story might've ended with the family's slaughter, including the dogs."

"Aye, small mercies." Finn giggled, then suggested, "But a wee bit dark for a Christmas party, eh, Gwyn?"

"Apologies. I should have known better." At least Gwyn had the decency to be contrite.

After the last movie, Abby turned to Gwyn and asked expectantly, "So, what did you think?"

"These differed from the last movies we watched togeth-er," Gwyn replied.

Abby chuckled. "Yeah, I forget that you don't know what cartoons or clay animation are. The last movies we watched used human actors. These were done with paper and ink or moldable clay."

Miles shot Gwyn a sour, suspicious face, then quickly erased the expression before it started another fight—no one needed that.

Gwyn said, "It's intriguing how, even after the Extinction, humanity continues to incorporate malevolents into their modern stories."

"Aye, mayhaps given what we know about them returning occasionally, keepin' the precautionary tales around was intentional," Finn suggested.

Esme popped up from her seat next to him. Her tone light, she said, "I'm going to get everyone a hot chocolate nightcap. Miles said he was going to heal Abby a bit more before Gwyn takes her home, right?"

Miles nodded. "To help reduce the swelling so she can sleep, at least," he said, trying to match her casualness. What had changed so dramatically in the past several hours? Had she found peace, or at least understanding? He was a lost man adrift at sea with no wind in his sails and full clouds obscuring the sun.

Finn hopped up to follow Esme. On the way, he bent over to pester Abby some more. "Need anything, dovey? Ice, cookies, wine, anything?" He'd been excessively attentive to their injured friend invalid throughout the evening. Miles could sense that it stemmed from genuine empathy, but it was clearly starting to grate on Gwyn.

"I can only do a bit, mind," Miles warned Abby. He ordered Lily back as a precaution.

"Miles, the fact that your ability exists at all is a damn miracle. One that I'm grateful for. Thank you," she said warmly.

Gwyn joined him at the foot of her recliner. At this point Miles knew better than to poke the bear, so he gestured with his hands at Gwyn to lift the leg of the pajama bottoms Abby had borrowed from Esme for the day. When Miles glanced up at Abby, she rolled her eyes and smirked in understanding.

He was only doing a small amount of healing, but he'd run his tank at nearly empty for the past day and night, so using his magic took a bit more concentration than usual.

When he was midway through repairing some of the damage to the fascia of her muscles closest to the break sites, Gwyn asked, "Care to explain what you said earlier about my prior experience with setting bones?"

"No."

Miles' seemingly casual dismissal clearly exacerbated Gwyn's tension, which had been building all day. He leaned forward slightly, his voice low. "Stop the games, Miles."

"What are you talking about, Gwyn?" Abby asked. Pain must have clouded her memory of all that had been said during her first healing.

"It's nothing, Abby; he heard me wrong." Miles tried to diffuse the situation.

"Incorrect," Gwyn snapped with a small snarl.

Miles finally met Gwyn's gaze, irritated that the man was using Abby's confusion to further his aims. "We have a funeral tomorrow, and I need a good night of sleep after last night and healing Abby twice. Can this wait?"

"That's not an answer," Gwyn retorted, his tone rising despite his obvious efforts to control it.

A muscle in Miles' jaw twitched. His voice rose in response to Gwyn's. "That's all the answer you're getting tonight."

Their words echoed in the suddenly too-quiet room. Miles immediately regretted engaging in an argument with Gwyn right in front of Abby. "Sorry, Abby," he muttered.

Esme and Finn arrived in time for the mood to change. It was clear from Esme's stormy expression that she had noticed the shift.

"Enough," Esme snapped, her voice cutting through the tension like a blade. "Sit down. Talk. I'm done waiting."

A heavy silence settled between them, stretching out for what felt like an uncomfortably long time.

Finally, Esme offered a chilling smile and began, "All right, I'll confess." She crossed her arms over her chest. "Leon told me last night what you two arranged. Watching you bicker again after that—I'm over it."

Miles' heart plummeted. Three simple words, "Leon told me," and the world collapsed beneath him. *She knew.*

She knew exactly what they'd done. *Fuck.*

Gwyn

Gwyn eyed the leprechaun as Finn drew one bejeweled finger over his throat in a slicing motion while tilting his head toward him and Miles. While Gwyn had known that some sort of response like this was sure to come from Esmeralda, Miles had clearly been blindsided, and she was calling Miles out on something specific—something that had to do with him.

Gwyn sat back down and hung his head for a single moment, then said, "I apologize, Abigail, Esmeralda."

Esme continued, "Thanks to Abby, despite everything, I'm almost ready to accept the utter fucking bullshit thing you all did. Abby's very persuasive, even while half out of it on painkillers. Finnegan"—Esmeralda's finger shot out like an angry mother's—"do not ask her for any. This isn't your opportunity to experiment."

Guilt briefly flitted over Finn's face. Then the leprechaun grinned and casually shrugged it off. "Ya know me too well." He settled back onto the couch, making himself comfortable, ready to enjoy the spectacle that was unfolding around him.

"Esme, I..." Miles started, but Esme interrupted him.

"I know, you're sorry. We can talk about it later. But, right now, what I can't accept is that we're trying to have a pleasant night in together and you two just ruined the end of it because you still haven't talked about your bullshit. I haven't pushed, but I'm asking now. Can we please be honest and put some of this behind us?"

Esme, in her wildly patterned sweater, stared Miles down. As Miles looked back at her, the same torn facial expression that his father had often worn when conversing with Elena appeared on his face. It was an uncomfortable reminder of too many memories.

Gwyn realized that being snappish twice over would cost him this opportunity. So he cleared his throat and said, "I am content to have a polite conversation without threats or arguments."

Esme prompted, "Miles, will there ever be a better time?"

"... No."

Esme handed out the hot chocolates as they sat in the cozy living room, a blanket of snow and twinkling lights visible through the window. Inside, the festiveness had faded.

Gwyn sat stiffly across from Miles, Abby off to the side, seeming more confused than anything, and Finn far too self-satisfied for Gwyn's liking—Finn knew far, far too much. Esme stood between both men, her gaze flicking restlessly from one to the other. Miles was quiet, nothing abnormal for him, but the silence between them stretched long once again.

Gwyn broke it first, his voice low and tense. "You said... you've done this before when healing Abigail. What did you mean by that?"

Miles shifted, his hand brushing against Esme when she moved to join him on the couch. Miles didn't meet any of their gazes, staring instead into the fire. "It's not easy to explain."

"Then make it easy," Gwyn pressed, impatience creeping into his voice. "You're an educated man. We've fought beside each other and have had each other an inch from death."

Abigail and Esmeralda both visibly reacted to this last. Each was ignorant of how close Gwyn and Miles had come to killing the other already.

Instead of addressing Gwyn immediately, Miles gave Finn a cold, intense stare. "Finn, you have two choices. Go out and charge Jacob's wards of silence on the house *then* hold your tongue about what I have to say to any other living soul, or leave. Now."

Finn took a sip of his hot chocolate and smacked his lips. "Aye, I'll get to the wardin'."

"Say you'll do both steps, leprechaun. *Thrice.*"

Finn rolled his eyes and even stomped once like a petulant child but did as Miles bid.

Esme squinted in confused frustration. "So when Jacob was here after the Alp thing, he also put wards of silence on my house? What the hell did he think was going to happen in here? Gods below..."

Miles ran his prosthetic hand through his unruly hair. The device had obviously stopped responding to his commands. He rested the motionless prosthesis in his lap.

"I'll plug it in while you think about your speech, Shakespeare," Esme quipped, noticing the same thing. She kissed him on the cheek and whispered a "thank you" before leaving the room.

An undeniable truth lay before Gwyn: if Miles was his father, this version of Nudd had found happiness the one Gwyn had grown up with had never known. In truth, Esme/Elena had as well. Now that he thought of it, he couldn't say that he wasn't far happier than he'd ever been in his past life. Assuming Gwyn had violated a cosmic law, was this outcome worth the price he might have to pay for his transgression? He could only hope...

By the time Esme returned, Finn was back from his work as well.

Taking a deep breath, Miles began, "I've been having dreams." His quiet, hesitant tone was unusual for him. "Not just dreams, more like... memories. They started when I was young, when my healing magic manifested. At first, I thought they were nightmares, but over time, I realized they were too vivid, too real."

Gwyn frowned, not at all liking where this conversation was headed. The thought of Miles admitting to being Nudd after all they'd been through sent a surge of fury through Gwyn; a fight in Esme's house seemed inevitable.

He was already preparing himself to stand and walk out the front door to prevent that eventuality when Miles sighed heavily. It wasn't angry; it wasn't frustrated; it was the sound of a man resigned to doing something he was not going to enjoy, and Mileshe feared the repercussions. "Because I've been reliving your father's life almost every time I've closed my eyes for the past twenty-five years."

Gwyn's mind went blank; only his eyelids moved in a slow blink. The revelation left him dizzy, his grasp on reality crushed by its impossible ramifications. Was this proof that he had also retrieved his father's soul from Annwn? What impossible price could he have to pay for freeing a demigod from death?

The only person not flattened to their seat by his admission was Esme. She took up Miles' left hand in hers and squeezed.

Only Finn knew that Gwyn might have been responsible for Creiddylad's and Elena's souls being reincarnated. Now Miles was heaping a possible third onto his list of sins. But since neither of them had told Miles, Abby, and Esme about that, Gwyn needed to be very clear on what exactly Miles was admitting to.

Gwyn somehow found the words to ask, "My father, Nudd Llaw Eraint... son of Beli Mawr?"

Miles shrugged, but guilt flickered across his expression. "I wasn't certain until a few weeks ago when I saw you in a dream for the first time after I healed you."

The second revelation hit harder than the first. "You recognized me?" Betrayal resonated in Gwyn's hollow voice, seeping into every syllable. "For weeks, you knew and chose silence?"

"No. I didn't want to believe it," Miles interrupted, his face a mask of stoicism.

Esme leaned forward. "Miles didn't understand it himself, Gwyn," she breathed. "He's been trying to figure it out, just like you."

Gwyn didn't know what else to say, so he challenged, "Prove it."

Miles matter-of-factly recounted, "Last night I watched you walk into the great hall with a broken clavicle, complaining about some twat named Velly."

"He... Llefelys." Gwyn was having a difficult time stringing together English words that would make him sound intelligible.

"Your uncle broke your collarbone?" Abby sounded incredulous when she spoke for the first time since the initial blowup between him and Miles. They'd talked extensively about his family during their Jacob-mandated scribing sessions, so she was well aware of the dynamics of his household while he was growing up. But Esme looked at him with a question, so he tried to answer both ladies.

"Yes..." was all that he could muster at first. "He was my father's half-brother, not much older than me."

Miles added, "Nudd hated him."

"They were like oil and water," Gwyn remarked, his mind reeling from what he'd heard from the man he'd thought was his father, lasting in his immortality through the centuries, not ten minutes before. Now he had to accept that he might be something else—his fault, a reincarnated version of Nudd instead.

Miles swallowed forcefully, meeting Gwyn's questioning gaze with a defiant expression. "For years, I thought the dreams were nothing but a quirk of my subconscious mind. That, maybe, I was a genetic freak cursed to dream wrong. Bloody hell, I still don't fully understand it. I hate it more than you can possibly understand." He raised the stump at the end of his right arm in the air as proof.

"Try."

"I'm not your father—he's gone. Somehow I know that. And yet... I feel like he's traveled through time and made most of the choices in my life for me."

Gwyn was no stranger to that feeling. By all the magic... could this ridiculous tale be true? Before him stood the truth in the form of the man he'd nearly killed, a chilling embodiment of his suspicions concerning Creiddylad and Elena.

Esme interrupted his musings with a soft clearing of her throat. "I, uh, actually have a new theory about all this insanity that only has one hole in it so far."

"Lovely," Miles said, shaking his head and breathing out a frustrated sigh. "I want nothing more than to have a theory that explains the insanity of my dreams."

At first, her voice was hesitant. "Stories, especially when they've been around for hundreds, if not thousands, of years, have a way of snowballing out of control, right?"

Seeing Esme's emotional distress, Abby offered enthusiastic verbal support to her friend.

Bolstered, Esme continued, "Well, what if all of this is just history repeating itself in a magical woo-woo way?"

"Woman, use your vocabulary." Abby playfully nudged her. "What do you mean, repeating?"

Esme stuck her tongue out at her. "What if this isn't the first time Miles' unique healing power has jumped between people? First there was Nodens, the Celtic god of healing, hunting, and dogs—silver hand and all. Then there was Nudd—same place, only later. What if Nodens was the original god who transferred his blessing to Nudd somehow? Then it happened again? What if Miles is just lucky number three or four? With how secretive people have been about magic for the past few hundred years, who knows how many could have had this power? Maybe somehow these dreams are a part of the magic transfer?"

"But does he dream of Nodens?" Gwyn couldn't believe that he was considering the idea, but nothing else made sense of what Miles had told him other than reincarnation—yet.

"No. Only Nudd." Miles' answer was simple, finite.

It sounded more and more like he'd created this disaster for himself. If only he could remember...

"Uh, Esmeralda." Finn's thready voice, a sudden reminder that the Fae pest had been sitting right beside him the entire time, startled Gwyn. "Ya mentioned a hole in yer theory."

Esme made a disgusted face. "I did... And I can see that I can't get out of talking about it now."

"Well, grace our ears with yer voice, lassie."

Esme admitted, "The only thing that doesn't make sense about the whole power-skipping-a-few-generations thing is that Miles' voice, his accent, changes when he's worked up—it's a bit like my eyes, I think."

Miles' eyes widened in shocked disbelief. "I... what?"

"You sound a bit more like Gwyn when it happens," she clarified.

The leprechaun rubbed his hands together in unrestrained glee, a mischievous smile spreading across his face. "I'm so glad I stuck around. I'm havin' the time of my life, and I've even got a date next week!"

Gwyn wrenched his head to the side, momentarily distracted. All the other eyes in the room did likewise.

When leprechauns felt like it, they loved being in the spotlight—such an unpredictable bunch. Finn feigned surprise at the focus on him. "Y'all look at me like I'm the main course, but my date said I could be the 'snack.' I'm very much lookin' forward to findin' out exactly what that means."

"Finn." Esme's voice took on a stern, disapproving tone. "Do you have a 'rendezvous' with *Katia*?"

With a comical flair, Finn waggled his eyebrows at her. "Can ya blame a man? The succubus is an eleven outta ten. She enjoyed my fireworks display at the Gala."

Esme buried her face in her hands and groaned. "I'm going to pretend that I never, ever, *ever* heard any of what you just said."

While Gwyn laughed along, he contemplated how Miles' revelation changed things. Miles hadn't appeared to be lying when he'd said that he hated seeing Nudd's life play out nightly. But Esmeralda's comment that his voice occasionally changed sucked every ounce of relief out of hearing his honesty.

What was he dealing with? His father, reincarnated? Nudd sharing a body with Miles? Perhaps a middle ground between those two possibilities? Or Fate playing another trick on them all?

They'd circled back to their beginning. Except now Gwyn faced an impossible moral quandary—how to question the ghost without destroying the (mostly) innocent vessel. The blade he'd held at Miles' throat now felt like it was pointed at his own conscience. And still, even knowing better, he couldn't entirely dismiss going with the brutal option.

Did that make him a bad man? Maybe. Either way, Gwyn needed to discover what information Leon possessed before drawing blood and risking everything he'd built.

Chapter Seven

PLEADING

Esme

After everyone else left, Miles and Esme lingered on the couch, with a massive wolfhound and the raw pain of Sylas' absence between them. A third presence, the raw pain of Sylas' absence, filled the room. Esme shifted slightly, her fingers fidgeting with the hem of her ugly sweater. "We need to talk about you hiring Leon."

His shoulders tensed, and for a terrible moment, she thought he wouldn't want to talk about it. Their hardships were supposed to be a burden they bore together. But unspoken worries still weighed heavily on him. Every fiber of his being screamed tension; his jaw was clenched, his shoulders hunched.

Not meeting her eyes, his voice a deep murmur, he said, "I'm sorry. I didn't see another way."

A gusty breath left his lips, his expression as serious as a doctor delivering a cancer diagnosis. "He was going to kill you, lovely. I won't risk losing you. *Ever.*"

Esme pulled her knees to her chest, cocooning herself in the throw blanket, arms crossed protectively over them like a shield. She realized she was intentionally building an emotional and physical barrier between them, but she couldn't help it. "That's it, though, Miles. You take control, deciding what's best and safest, unilaterally."

"But you would've tried to save him," he said, voice rising with urgency as he sat up from where he'd slumped, guilt clinging to every word. "And there was no saving him. That magic—"

"Maybe you're right," she interrupted, her voice low but firm. "But you didn't give us a chance to make that choice together. You did it all on your own. And that's the part I can't get past. The last time we talked about this, you said you weren't used to working with others. Miles, I want to be your partner. But you have to let me in."

She was nearly breathless, struck by the earnestness of his expression as he confessed, "Esme, you're in here so deep already... I don't think I would survive you being taken away."

She knew the feeling.

Her phone buzzed with a meaningless notification, a tiny burst of sound that broke the stillness that had enveloped them. She tossed the phone onto the floor without a second glance. The outside world had no place in this conversation.

Finally, he reached for her hands with his one, his touch tentative. "I'm sorry. For all of it. I will do better. But you're right." His laugh was humorless. "I struggle with infrequent bouts of being a bit too domineering, and I'm not as good at working with a team as I would like."

His self-deprecating smile, which failed to reach his eyes, faded as his gaze fell to their joined hands. For a long moment, he didn't speak. The Christmas tree lights cast shadows over his face, accentuating the weight of whatever war he was fighting internally.

"I don't know if I know how," he admitted, his voice barely above a whisper. "You're right—I take control because... it's what I was taught. No, more like... what I was beaten into."

The frown that had grown on Esme's face deepened, but she didn't interrupt, sensing this wasn't easy for him to share.

"You know that David Abington was my mentor growing up. He called it mentorship, anyway, but really... he owned me. Every decision—what I fought, when I rested, how far I pushed myself—was his to make. It was simple for him, since my parents handed me off to the Assembly like I was a problem to be solved when I was twelve. To a boy that young, David inspired nothing less than hero worship. He was a powerful mage. Everyone respected him, hung on his every word. He was, and still is, also a fantastically wealthy man with a fancy title—that's a big deal to us Brits."

Pausing briefly, he asked, "I can talk about this, right? You're okay with me tossing some of my baggage your way after everything we've been through lately?"

Esme cherished his regular check-ins. She'd never been with a man who understood that she might not always be able to cope with something. He realized that even if they were together, they still had their separate worlds to attend to and the best way to do that was to figure out what your partner could reasonably take on in that moment. She said, "I want to know everything—every scar, every story—that made you the person you are."

Leaning down, his eyes searching, he gently brushed his nose against hers.

And just like that, the worries that had weighed her down seemed to melt away. The soft bunny kiss that asked for nothing from her other than affection had made truly forgiving him that much easier.

Before he could pull away to explain further, she stretched up and gave him a quick reassuring kiss on the lips. "Please, continue."

"Alright, lovely." A charming, slightly lopsided smile curved his lips, marred only by the thin scar along his cheek. "I hung on David's every word until, like all young men, I started to rebel a bit in my teens. By sixteen, I was accompanying Brothers on hunts to gain experience. The Assembly and the Corded Brotherhood aren't as separate in the UK as they are here, so David had a say in what I did.

"The trouble started when I first told David about my trainer's off-the-books dealings. He wasn't doing anything wrong. In fact, everything he did was for a good reason—Corded Brotherhood moral ambiguity and all that... I didn't think anything of my comments at the time—it was trivial, unimportant. I thought I was providing my mentor with a good report. The next week, my trainer was sent to hunt a few kobolds solo. Turns out it was a nest and David knew it. David dragged me in to heal my trainer because he was... he was dying.

"I healed him every day for a week straight. Every time I entered that room, David reminded me that the bloody mess I sat in front of was the result of going off script."

Still holding her hands, Miles moved his stump to wipe something from his eye. Esme's breath stuck in her chest. She'd been told bits about David, but Miles rarely spoke of him.

Her fingers tightened around his, reminding him of her presence and silently urging him to continue.

"It only got worse as I got older. If I tried to say no or even questioned him, there were consequences. From all of that, I learned to handle everything myself. No teams, no discussion, just get it done before anyone else could get hurt. Involving others meant putting them at risk. The more people who knew about a situation, the more leverage he had. David equated control with safety and independent decisions with protection. That rubbed off on me."

"But you're not him," she said softly. "And I'm not someone who needs to be protected like that."

"I know," he whispered. "Old habits from survival die hard. But you deserve better than choices I made from fear."

Esme reached up to brush her fingertips against his jawline and cupped his face in her hands. Maintaining eye contact, she assured him, "I'm not someone David can use against you. I can't just be someone you protect. I need to stand beside you, not behind you."

He nodded, wiping away something from his eye once again. "Esme... David is in Seattle. He's taking over Jacob's Assembly position. He's going to create problems for me—for us."

A wave of protective anger, as hot as molten gold, welled up within her. The anger allowed infernal magic to sneak its way past her defenses. It was a pulsing, living thing desperate to strike out at the potential danger. She stifled her emotions with a reinforcing breath, saving all the nasty things it whispered she could do for when such actions would be useful. The rage and hatred that simmered beneath her surface had no place in their calm discussion. Her recent dream and her nightmares induced by the Alp attack had violently shown her as much.

"Not all of David is bad, though."

Esme could tell that he actually believed what he was saying, even after describing the abuse David had put him through.

Miles continued, "He helps people. I still wrestle with the bittersweet truth that he was as much a father to me as my own."

Esme considered how volatile her emotional connection to her parents' memory had become recently with all the information coming out about how much they'd hidden from her. She said, "I get it. Maybe almost as much as you do. I'll keep an open mind when I meet him."

"Thank you, love." He switched focus, pleading softly, "Don't give up on me. Please?"

She glanced down at his hand, then back at his face. In his eyes, there was a deep and unwavering sincerity, a stripped-away type of honesty that shone brightly and was impossible to ignore.

Esme leaned forward, pressing her forehead against his. "We'll work on it together."

"I don't deserve you," he murmured.

Her response was a closing of the distance, her kiss meant to silence his doubts. The warmth of her breath mingled with his, and the earlier tension melted away bit by bit with every touch.

"I really don't deserve you," he whispered, his breath warm against her skin between kisses. "Every time you invite me in, it feels like a gift. When I can touch you, I'm just so... grateful that you gave me the chance to choose love. And I'm so glad I was smart enough to accept it."

The rush of warm fuzzies caused Esme's brain to short-circuit. The unbelievable romanticism of the moment and Miles' hand gently caressing her back beneath her shirt inevitably caused her to let out a gasp of pleasure. Waves of longing pulsed, and she couldn't help it, she "pulled an Esme."

"Okay..." she gasped again, "that is definitely pants-off talk. Get up! *Go*. The bedroom—now please."

Miles started toward the spot where his prosthesis was charging. Not keeping the bossiness from her voice, she said, "What I'm dealing with right now does not have time for that thing to reboot."

He looked a touch shell-shocked for a moment, then a roguish grin blossomed on his face. "Yes, ma'am."

Physical intimacy couldn't fully ease the burden in her heart, but it was one further step in healing things between them. Laying Sylas to rest the next day would be another step toward healing.

Chapter Eight

GOODBYES

Esme

In the mountains, the clouds were fluffier and less oppressive than the heavy gray ones hanging over the city. But it was bitterly cold and damp, the crisp breeze stinging Esme's skin through her snowboarding jacket until she warmed up from hiking. Even the sky couldn't decide how to feel—shifting between tears of rain, long exhalations of sleet, and the silent grief of snow.

Fitting for a day when nothing felt right.

Abby managed to get off work to come, trading shifts to cover holidays, but Miles couldn't. He'd already had to reschedule so many patients over the past month that he couldn't continue making exceptions without their suffering. Esme understood—she really did. His work changed lives for the better and even saved them occasionally, but his absence on such a day stung.

Miles wasn't the only one missing. Finn had declined to attend the funeral, claiming that leprechauns weren't creatures you wanted at them. There was also the fact that Sylas really hadn't liked him while he was alive. So Esme understood his absence, but it hurt, too.

Although Maureen was still out of town, she pleasantly surprised Esme by sending a bouquet of fragrant lilies and a set of snowdrop flower bulbs to be planted at the gravesite. The small white flowers would bloom just before spring broke out in the mountains. Sylas would have loved them. It was a small act of kindness that Esme hadn't expected, but one that made her hopeful for their relationship's direction.

Getting to the burial spot Esme had decided was best took a bit of doing for all parties involved. Esme was used to hiking with ice spikes in the winter, but the others weren't. Cerys proved to be the MVP (most valuable pup) of "Operation Get Abby Up the Mountain." Gwyn tied a rope to Cerys' harness, and the dog single-handedly (four-pawedly?) pulled Abby in a sled along the snowy trail.

When it came to the bushwhacking sections, the humans took turns carrying Abby piggyback. Naturally, her brother, Colin, turned it into a competition with Gwyn, both of them eager to prove their strength. Even Will, to everyone's surprise, including his own, it seemed, didn't complain when it was his turn to carry her.

Jacob's easy ascent of the mountain stunned everyone. Esme was shocked to see him in winter sports clothing—a far cry from his typical button-down shirts, blazers, and dress pants. Jacob started out the hike like everyone else, trekking normally—behind, but normal. No one expected anything more out of a one-hundred-six-year-old man.

But then he'd disappeared without the telltale sound of mist walking to accompany his departure. No one had panicked at his disappearance, but they hadn't expected to find him sitting calmly at the burial site, sipping tea from a thermos when they finally arrived, hot and tired, while he was untouched by the climb. Knowing he wouldn't tell them how, no one asked.

A leshy's funeral was simple. He was to be returned to his forest, buried with a bushel of pine cones or acorns, depending on location, so that his body could nourish new growth in the place he'd spent his life protecting. This was a private burial for those who knew the truth about his death.

The announcement of the public funeral would come after Christmas—a calculated move, weighing a respect for the dead against political necessity, the holiday season providing a temporary buffer. The holidays meant fewer witnesses, fewer questions, fewer rumors.

Chance provided Jacob with a lie to spread about Sylas' death. During a family's cross-state RV trip, a three-year-old girl had wandered away while the family was spending what was supposed to be a magical night in the snowy mountains. Luckily, she'd been wearing her snowsuit. She was found the next morning, without a bit of frostbite on her fingers or toes. Everyone called it a miracle, but the magical community of Seattle called it Sylas' work. It was rumored that, after keeping her warm all night, he died while protecting her once again from a falling boulder—so fast that his magic couldn't even save him.

Sylas would leave behind a positive memory. His story would end as a hero's—even if it was a lie.

Jacob offered to use magic to blast a hole in the clearing she'd chosen for the burial spot, but Esme thought Sylas wouldn't have wanted that much destruction because of him. So they all took turns fighting the frozen ground with a shovel. Although Miles had finished Abby's healing that morning, he strictly advised her to stay off her feet. She stubbornly insisted on digging one shovelful. In the end, no one begrudged her that.

Just as no one asked Jacob how he'd made it up the mountain so quickly, no one asked how Sylas' remains were there waiting for them. After returning Sylas to the earth, Jacob spoke first.

"He was my friend, my right hand for forty years. There is too much that I could say and yet not enough words. Thank you, Sylas. Your legacy will live on in all of your students."

"Students"—the word alone made Abby burst into tears. Abby had told Esme that years of Sylas' tutelage had helped her control her powerful, and technically illegal, neuromancy.

Jacob's speech was much briefer, his tone much more informal than she had expected. His clothes, the casual way he was acting—she realized Jacob was simply being himself. He wasn't performing as the leader of the Assembly or the Bastion of the Corded Brotherhood. He didn't have to put on airs or impress anyone there. He only had to say goodbye to an old friend.

Colin and Abby told stories of their unique experience in growing up knowing a leshy. The fairy tales had always been true for them, and Esme couldn't help but feel a little jealous of their long history with Sylas and the magical community. Will shared a story about a toddler chewing on one of Sylas' horns for almost an hour while Sylas sat at the bar, placidly talking to the child's parents. Will admitted that he'd finally found the courage to speak with Sylas after seeing that.

Esme drew in the frigid mountain air, hoping it would numb the twin pains of grief and guilt twisting in her chest—one for losing Sylas, one for failing to save him. Esme's gaze fell to the freshly turned soil. She wasn't sure what she could say that would feel adequate. Maybe that was why Jacob had left his speech so short. There truly weren't enough words.

"I think we all knew Sylas in different ways, but to me... he was my protector," Esme began. "After my parents died, I was lost. I couldn't even stand to be alone, terrified of the empty house, the silence. Without a word, Sylas left his beloved forest to stay with me. He wasn't comforting in the usual way. He was always grumpy, but he was *there*."

The memory brought a small smile to her lips. "He complained every day about the noise and the city, but he stayed. He gave up his peace to give me mine. That... isn't a small thing."

Her voice softened, and her eyes were misty as she glanced around. To better reflect the man who was so important to her, she adopted a slightly more formal tone. "In all the ways that mattered, Sylas showed how much he cared. Sylas was a guardian, a protector—not only of the land, but of the people in it. And for that, I'll always be grateful. The hundreds of people whose lives he impacted would agree."

Silent nods surrounded her as Esme dropped to her knees, pressing her palm against the frozen earth. "He'll watch over this place, as he always has. You're back home now, Sylas... And we're all going to be okay."

Abby limped over to hug her, and Esme didn't fight the tears that came. Colin joined in, and it only got worse. When they finished, they were all sporting puffy faces and wiping away snot with gloved hands.

As they prepared to leave, Jacob stopped Esme with a gentle touch on her arm.

"Darling, I'm so sorry." His tone carried a layered meaning. He must have realized she was aware of his role in Sylas's murder.

Esme accepted that this was how things would always be with him. What other choice did she have? It was Jacob's job to protect the people under his care from threats. If that meant killing someone they both cared about, he'd do it. All she could offer in response was a nod. Her heart was still broken over their choices, but she understood why they'd made them, and now wasn't the right time to broach the subject.

He cleared his throat and said, "You should know that I won't be around for a while. I'm heading back to England to deal with some... business. I'm leaving immediately after this, in fact. So we'll need to say our goodbyes. I realize this is horrible timing, but you'll all be in expert hands. Miles will lead the local Brotherhood operations in my absence, and his old mentor will handle the leadership of the Assembly. Keep an eye on my house and the bar, yes?"

"Okay." Esme sniffled. The unwelcome reminder of David's presence in Seattle annoyed her anew. She didn't look forward to plastering a cheerful mask over her true feelings and pretending to be happy to meet him.

Jacob warned, "Please start wearing your dagger. I'm worried about everything that has been happening lately. I need you safe. We can't lose more... Have you tried the magic on it yet?" He was keenly interested.

For her birthday, Jacob had given her a very expensive magic-siphoning dagger to help her fight the malevolents. She rarely wore it; the magic irritated her skin. "No, Finn said it might store magic for later use, but I didn't feel any extra magic in it this morning when I fiddled with it."

"Really now?" Jacob's bushy eyebrows showed his surprise. "I tested it myself, Esmeralda. It works. Give it another try for me, yes? You should be able to release the magic the dagger has stored up as either physical force or heat."

Esme shrugged and nodded. Maybe she'd accidentally drained it somehow. "Will you disappear down the mountain in the same way you got up it?"

"Can you really blame an old man?" Jacob chuckled. "Now, Esmeralda, darling, keep everyone in line for me. That's an order."

Jacob winked and shooed them all away, saying he'd see them later. She was curious about how he'd descend but wisely refrained from asking.

When she turned around, Abby was already climbing onto Gwyn's back for the descent. Cerys, now weighing in at two hundred fifty pounds, was making Gwyn's task twice as difficult by leaning into his legs and demanding equal attention to what Abby was receiving.

"Cerys!" Esme called out to the gwyllgi. "Come here, girl. Let's walk together and leave Daddy and Mommy alone."

Abby shot her the stink eye, but Esme just smirked back. The huge hellhound trotted over, and Esme gave her new hiking buddy ample attention. Eventually Colin forced Gwyn to give him a turn at carrying his sister—more macho bravado. So Cerys rejoined her master, and Will wandered over to Esme's side.

"Hey, chica," Will greeted her. Considering his usual outspoken and animated nature, it was rare to see him as restrained as he'd been that day.

With a curious tilt of her head, Esme prompted, "You finally gonna tell me what's going on with you? Because your whole vibe right now is about more than this funeral. I know you were terrified of Sylas. I don't expect you to grieve like I do."

He smiled weakly—another thing he rarely did. If he had an expression on his face, it was always out in full force. "Yeah... I kinda didn't want to say anything today, but with the holidays coming up and my family being how they are…"

Will's family was a lively group, just like him. She'd attended several family gatherings to see for herself what the chaos he described was really like. The Cruz family was the kind of group that laughed hard, cooked more food to share than anyone could eat in a week, and ribbed on each other relentlessly. Esme loved them.

Will sighed. "I'm leaving… I'm leaving Seattle after the New Year."

Esme stopped dead in her tracks. "You're what?"

"Woman, this is hard enough." Will grabbed her hand and tugged, urging her to keep walking. "I'm moving to Los Angeles."

Esme's voice fell to a conspiratorial murmur as the surprising news sank in. "You're shacking up with Colin already? The sex is that good?"

Will scoffed. "I mean, yes, but think about it. Why not? I can do the same thing there that I do here and probably make more money. They even have more than one mage's bar. Colin said they're hiring."

The deflection worked like a charm. Offer a quick pivot, a well-timed joke, and no one looked too closely at the cracks forming beneath.

"I mean, you'll obviously be successful wherever you go, but what's the push now?" Esme could sense her anxiety rising as she faced the reality of multiple people departing from her life, one gone forever, one temporarily, and the last returning only rarely.

It was a day for goodbyes. The universe was delivering a harsh lesson on love and loss, first with her parents, then Sylas, Jacob, and now Will—and how to let them go.

Will continued, "I have a lot to figure out about myself, ya know? Now I feel like I've got someone who has my back. My lease is up and Len can afford that apartment on their own. They're practically forcing me to leave, saying I should take my 'creativity-stifling happiness elsewhere.' But... Chica, I'll miss you and the harpy." With that last moniker, he was referring to Abby.

"Gods below, you're leaving too," Esme said, blinking back tears. "Well... need help packing?"

Being supportive was the only action a true friend could take. If Will thought his future might be somewhere else, she was happy to support him in any way possible. With a flight to Los Angeles taking less than three hours, she and Abby could enjoy long weekends with him every few months. In the meantime, she'd have to work hard not to be extra clingy with Miles and Abby—even Finn and Gwyn were in danger of a lonely Esme.

Miles

"I'm not doing this right now, David. I'm at work. Shouldn't you be, too? You look like you've been under a lot of stress lately." Miles closed the examination room door behind him, trapping himself in with the one person he wished to avoid above all others.

A small, smug grin played on Miles' lips, a fleeting moment of petty satisfaction that brought him no real joy. David's hair had gone completely white, his face etched with deep lines. The short year since Miles had left London had taken a heavy toll.

"This *is* work, Miles," David replied, his tone cold and insistent. "Unless you would prefer I discuss the Brotherhood's shortcomings at your house."

Miles wished he were a million kilometers away. "Then show up at the house. I have patients to see." He reopened the door and emphasized with finality, "Goodbye."

David Abington was not the sort of man who took well to being dismissed. If this conversation followed the usual pattern, there would be some kind of consequence for Miles' "insolence." It wouldn't be overt. Miles was no longer a boy, after all. But David would find a way to exact some sort of quiet retribution.

There would be a calculated inconvenience here, a roadblock there, something like that. Miles had learned that the hard way after years of being naively blind to the man's true nature. His youthful trust had lingered well past its expiration date, all because David had kept him so carefully sheltered.

The familiar darkness David had cultivated around Miles for decades, comforting in its certainty, beckoned, but Miles, scarred from his hard-won climb into the light, wouldn't retreat. He wouldn't be isolated any longer.

Miles' dismissal made a crack form in David's typical iron-clad composure. His usual calm slipped as shock flickered briefly in his eyes. Rarely had Miles seen him so unguarded, his controlled demeanor breaking down even for an instant.

But that didn't change what had to be done.

Miles repeated, with a firmer edge, "Goodbye." And silently hoped he and everyone around him wouldn't come to regret it.

CHAPTER NINE

A MASSIVE PROBLEM

Esme

Esme, emotionally spent from the funeral, couldn't bear the thought of returning to the suffocating emptiness that awaited her at home. The second she crossed the threshold, her house would conjure the memories of solitude that death inevitably brings. So Esme went to Miles' house instead. The only memories his house held were good ones, and it came with the bonus of Lily to cuddle with.

After a shower to wash off the hike, she changed into a spare pair of clothes she dug out of her side of the dresser and snuggled up with Lily in the bed. She figured she could use the time until Miles got home to catch up on the mundane tasks she'd been putting off. Convincing the Irish Wolfhound to keep her massive head off Esme's chest so she could see her phone screen took some effort, but eventually, she managed to check her bank account to pay a few bills.

The week after the Solstice Gala was the only time she was ever excited to check her bank balance. It was the one time every year she could reliably look forward to a big fat bonus on her paycheck. But excitement quickly gave way to disappointment when she saw that the bonus was missing... and there were no pending credits. Maybe they weren't getting one this year? Perhaps the jorōgumo cleanup had strained the budget too much. Damn.

Lying on Miles' bed with her furry cuddle buddy meant sleep came easily—especially after the past few grueling days. A knock startled Esme awake; her mouth felt thick with cobwebs. She checked her phone—Miles was probably already heading to the bar, and he definitely wouldn't be knocking at his own door. She pulled on one of Miles' hoodies and took Lily with her to see who it was.

As she entered the living room, it was obvious Lily disliked whoever was behind the door. The dog's tail was rigid, her eyes locked forward, ears flattened against her head. The gentle giant looked like she was ready for anything, including a fight. Esme hesitated for a moment, considering summoning one of her conjurations, but quickly dismissed the thought as paranoid and opened the door.

An older man, not as ancient as Jacob yet equally refined, stood there, holding an umbrella against the light drizzle. That single accessory meant he definitely wasn't a local.

Before Esme could get a single word out, the man's gaze swept over her, nose wrinkling slightly. In his posh accent, also matching David's, he remarked, "I understand now why he's been so lax in his duties."

Was he...? Had he just...? His words, masked by a slight smile, struck with the precision of a calculated insult.

Her temper flared. She imagined a few satisfying scenarios that would wipe the smirk off his face before managing to reply, "Uh, I'm sorry, who are you?"

The man didn't sneer, but there was a coolness in his tone as he answered, "David Abington. I'm here to assist in completing Mr. Spencer's duties while he recovers."

Esme got the distinct impression that 'assisting' meant something different when it came to David Abington. She might have been overanalyzing, so she pushed the thought away. She offered her hand, trying to return to politeness despite her irritation. "Esme Turner."

She could be nice for Miles, even if David was a dickhead.

David glanced briefly at her outstretched hand before dismissing it, a flicker of disdain crossing his face before disappearing. Esme let her hand drop, feeling the sting of rejection. How had he made the slight so subtle that it almost made her doubt she'd experienced it?

David forced a thin smile. "Ah, yes. I saw your name on the Assembly's payroll. Interesting... I'm doubly glad I'm here. Is Miles in?"

Just like she had when Leon had knocked on her door after the Solstice Gala, she sensed that David already knew the answer to that question. "No, he's still at the office—probably."

"So, he's falling behind there, too? Well, this is quite the disappointment." David's frown was real at least.

His expression held layers of meaning, each one more condescending than the last. Esme could only guess which failure he sought to highlight. *This is Miles' Jacob*, Esme reminded herself. She knew better than to snap back, but gods above and below, she wanted to.

She tried for diplomacy. "Well, I'm sure Miles will make it to the Sanctuary of Spirits outing we have planned. Maybe you can meet him there." She left it as an invitation, but with an edge of uncertainty.

"Ah, yes, your primary place of employment." His tone carried a sneer that didn't quite make it all the way to his expression. *Fantastic.* She'd barely met the man, and he already seemed to look down on her.

Esme swallowed the retort she wanted to blast him with and said instead, "Alright, see you then?" It was a struggle, but she resisted the temptation to throw his condescension right back in his face.

His smile reached the corners of his sharp blue eyes. "Oh, I'll be around for a while, Esmeralda. If that's where I need to speak with him, so be it."

She couldn't help but feel disappointment about that. This man was more consequential than an arrogant stranger. Miles' future could be negatively impacted by David's influence. Her concern was that David might try to exclude her from that future.

This was far from the ideal first meeting. As David's poor judgment of her wriggled its way into her brain, she couldn't help but think about how Sylas would have handled this—calm, sharp-tongued, and unbothered. His memory felt like a bruise she kept poking, the loss raw and tender beneath the surface. She needed to feel less negativity. She needed sanctuary. She needed to share food and drinks with her friends while listening to more stories about Sylas' life.

Miles

The Sanctuary of Spirits was silent when Miles slipped through the entrance. Against all odds, he'd somehow beaten everyone else there. It was unusual for him to wear scrubs to the office, but it was one last procedure day before Christmas and he didn't have time to change before everyone met at the bar. Luckily, he hadn't gotten messy at work, so it shouldn't be a big deal.

The bar was closed until New Year's Eve, so they would have the space to themselves for the funeral repast. Miles dropped his coat on an empty table and then went to the bar to begin pouring drinks. The liquor organization was logical until he reached the liqueurs. Then he lost all hope of quickly finding the chartreuse and settled on simply searching for a green bottle. To cheer Esme up, he had memorized her and Abby's favorite cocktail recipes during his downtime between patients.

An unexpected sound broke the silence he'd grown comfortable in.

At first, he dismissed it as something coming from the convenience store that hid the concealed entrance to the bar. But then a low, throaty grunt erupted from behind him and was followed by the unmistakable sound of metal kitchen equipment clattering down on the tile of the kitchen floor. With a bottle of bourbon in one hand, he froze, realizing he had no weapon to protect himself if it wasn't a friendly.

Then he felt the magic, subtle yet clammy and foul. Malevolent magic, barely noticeable above the background noise of all the other magic present in the bar.

Miles frantically searched the bar, rummaging as quietly as possible through every drawer and shelf for something, anything, that could be of use. There was naught there but a few small knives for fruit, ice mallets, and a couple of muddlers.

Another crash. Bloody hell, things were seriously getting problematic if they had another malevolent in the city less than a day after the redcaps. There was a gun in his car, but what if the creature left the bar before he returned? Losing a malevolent in the heart of downtown was unacceptable. He had to handle this here and now.

Miles was wearing his trainers with his scrubs, so it was diffi-cult, but not impossible, to creep on the bar's wooden floor-boards silently. He'd grabbed the ice mallet and two paring knives to act as distractions until he could come up with a better plan when he got into the kitchen. Wexley, the bar's púca chef, had at least one full set of knives back there.

Pushing open the swinging door, he found the source of the sounds: a hulking shape large enough to obscure the oversized door that led to the kitchen's walk-in refrigerator.

It was possible the creature was either deaf or too distracted to notice him immediately, as it didn't turn around. On swift feet, he lunged for Wexley's precious knife block, grabbing a wickedly sharp example of a large chef's knife. The sound of the steel scraping out of the wooden block finally caught the malevolent's attention as it spun around to face him. Though smaller than depicted in stories, the creature was undeniably an ogre—far too large for a one-on-one duel in the tight confines of the kitchen or bar.

The ogre had yellowish-brown skin that was mottled in places, making it look like its body was covered in bruised leather. His eyes, a muddy yellow, blazed with furious, unthink-ing rage. Initially, his face seemed almost human, unsettlingly so, but as his mouth opened, a horrifying glimpse of huge, jagged teeth proved otherwise. Bits and pieces of vegetables and egg shells covered the front of his shirtless torso. The ogre had obviously been eating straight from the refrigerator, and Miles had interrupted his fridge raid.

The ratty loincloth he wore barely concealed the ogre's manhood, leaving little doubt as to his sex. Every kid who grew up in the United Kingdom heard about giants and ogres in fairy tales. Miles had fought countless malevolents. Miles had never encountered an ogre before, so while he wanted to be thrilled, he realized he might have gotten in over his head.

His pulse quickened, ready for the fight. The ogre snarled wordlessly and charged at him. With two paring knives held in one hand, a kitchen knife in the other hand, and an ice mallet in his pocket, Miles darted quickly out of the way. Instead of connecting with him, the ogre slammed his fist into a stack of stainless steel pots and pans, sending them flying across the room with a horrible raucous sound.

With a swift motion, Miles hurled both paring knives, leaving shallow gashes on the ogre's shoulder. Miles gained a precious second as the ogre gawked at his minor wounds. Frantically, Miles searched his surroundings for something—anything—to slow the hulking behemoth down, but he came up short.

Fear crept in. The setting provided him with nothing but disadvantages. With no real weapon and no help, he was nearly defenseless. This matchup was a bad one for him; he was too vulnerable and easily overpowered. Coming up with nothing better, Miles threw the ice mallet at the ogre. The impact landed directly in the center of his forehead. Bullseye.

The ogre raised one meaty, food-covered hand to his forehead and rubbed, temporarily stunned. Then, recovering far too quickly for Miles' liking, the ogre sent another fist flying at him.

This time, Miles ducked the blow and rolled out of the way while casting a shield around himself. At the end of his roll, he stumbled into a huge soup pot. Its lid was a few feet away, so he grabbed it and held on to it like it was a shield. He wasn't a trained shield fighter, but it might absorb some of the blow if the ogre managed to get past his aegis.

Jumping to his feet in one swift motion, he wielded the chef's knife like a sword and the pot lid like a shield. He probably looked like a bloody fool.

In the cramped space, the ogre's size made it difficult for Miles to maneuver except in small bursts. The creature's broad shoulders seemed to scrape against the ceiling and his limbs to fill the entire room. Miles swung the knife, aiming for the ogre's thick arm, but the ogre batted him away with a heavy fist, sending him painfully stumbling back into the stainless steel prep table behind.

The ogre charged again, and Miles barely managed to parry with the lid, the force of the blow reverberating up his prosthesis and through the stump of his arm. The force pushed him back, causing him to slip on the dirty, food-covered floor.

The possibility that his life might end at that very moment flashed through his mind. An accidental slip when your opponent was as fast and large as the ogre could be deadly. As he tried to correct his fall, he waited for the final blow to land, pumping as much magic into his aegis as he dared.

He hoped only happy memories would surface as his life flashed before his eyes—the newest ones being some of the best.

Miles failed to save himself. His vision blurred in the fraction of a heartbeat between accepting death and slamming onto the tile below. A golden light flickered at the edge of his sight, and his grip on the knife adjusted without his conscious choice. He rolled again, avoiding a heel strike from the ogre. Feeling like he was being guided by an unseen hand, he shot upward and spun, driving the blade into his adversary's side.

The strike was nothing like the knife style of fighting he'd learned. What he had done was undeniably swordcraft.

Pulling the blade out of the creature's side, he twisted his body and pivoted on his heels to increase the space between them. Feeling like he had little choice but to heed the power guiding his movements, Miles crouched low, then surged up with strength increased by a swell of magic. He jabbed once more at the ogre's unprotected flank while the creature swung at him again. The pot lid absorbed the ogre's glancing blow as Miles' knife landed home.

Blood sprayed across his scrubs and onto the floor tiles. He was glad he'd chosen the black scrubs that morning and doubly thankful he hadn't yet changed into the spare clothes he kept in his car.

As his whole body burned with magical warmth, Miles could feel the soothing energy of his healing magic radiating outward from his chest. Guided by the magic, he moved forward, the pot lid held high like a knight's shield, his stance defensive yet firm.

Then he heard the kitchen door fling open.

Gwyn

For a moment, Gwyn and Esme froze at the sight before them. The sound of a struggle in the kitchen had sent them running.

Neither had anticipated finding Miles in combat with a bleeding ogre. The kitchen was in shambles around the fighting pair.

Nudd's power poured out of Miles, flowing out through his eyes, burning brightly golden on his skin. With the skill of a seasoned pugilist, Miles dodged the ogre's lunge. Despite lacking a sword, despite being surprised out of his wits at the magic Miles was exhibiting, Gwyn searched for an opportunity to join in the attack.

As Gwyn gawked, calculating, Miles used the pot lid he was holding to thrust the ogre's massive arm back. With an opening made, he plunged the blade deep into its chest. Gwyn's breath caught as he recognized the ancient combat style—the sharp, precise strikes and fluid movements that reminded him of the countless practice bouts he'd shared with his own father.

The creature's roar died in its throat, and it crumpled to the floor. It twitched and bled from the from the hole in its chest. Esme rushed over, unsheathed her dagger, and grabbed the closest thing she could, a large cooking pot of some sort. The dagger she rammed into its neck. The pot she slammed into the ogre's skull—again and again without ceasing.

The man who had been Gwyn's host, his healer, was not completely himself as he stood watching Esme savage the fallen ogre. The small smile on Miles' face was one only few ever saw on Nudd's. Gwyn watched, speechless, as his father's power ebbed from Miles' eyes, and his slight smile vanished.

Miles blinked, then crouched over to forestall Esme's attempts to cave in the creature's skull. The ogre's purplish blood now pooled on the tile floor around its body and was already dripping down the floor drain.

But Gwyn still couldn't move.

He'd become trapped by his memories. Of his father. Of Elena. How different would Elena have been if circumstances had been more favorable in their era? How much more like Esme? And Creiddylad, she...

Abigail hobbled through the swinging door behind them in time to see Miles comforting Esme as she fussed over him.

Completely ignoring the dead ogre taking up most of the floor space, Abby said, "Gods below... Gwyn, you're pale. You look like you've just seen a ghost. Everyone is okay, right?"

Reaching his side, she cupped his face and tried to get Gwyn to meet her gaze. The problem was, she was right—he *had* just seen a ghost.

Chapter Ten

Sanctuary No More

Esme

Abby shook Gwyn hard enough that he eventually stopped staring and, on orders, went out to Miles' car to fetch him a change of clothes. While Miles took a sink bath, Finn, then Will and Colin, showed up.

Back and forth to the bar Finn went, tirelessly supplying the table with more alcohol than they could possibly drink in a single evening. He also ate enough of the takeout they'd brought to feed two full-grown adults. The ogre in the kitchen? Nobody brought it up, even though everyone could feel the malevolent magic emanating from the corpse hidden in the back room.

Instead, they rapidly filled Miles in on the funeral and the news about Will and Colin moving. Though Miles was exhausted, he offered his heartiest congratulations to the new couple. Business-minded as ever, Miles also highlighted an issue with their joint departure from the rainy city.

"With you lot gone, we're out anyone who can see." He was referring to seeing magic, specifically Will's special trick. Colin had somehow learned it faster than anyone else, despite the group's many attempts.

Colin tipped his chin in Abby's direction and suggested, "She could always try taking a peek inside"—he tapped at his forehead—"to see if it speeds things up."

Abby's jaw dropped in amazement. "Colin Henry, are you asking me to break into your brain? I'm flattered by the trust you're showing."

He sheepishly admitted, "I may have forgotten to get you a Christmas present this year, so that'll have to do."

"Cheapskate," Abby grumbled, smiling through the sibling banter. Then, more seriously, Abby addressed Miles. "Whatcha think, boss?"

He shrugged. "I'm not getting between a pair of siblings, but it would be useful."

They shared their favorite stories about Sylas and toasted to his memory. The only tears that were shed were happy ones. It was a great send-off for one of Esme's oldest friends.

It was all in her head, but Esme could almost feel the temperature of the room drop as David Abington walked through the magically concealed threshold to the bar.

He hadn't said a word yet, but she already regretted inviting him.

Gwyn

As Gwyn heard footsteps approaching, all of Miles' attention focused on the door to the bar. Gwyn watched as Miles started drumming his prosthetic fingers on the table, the rhythm echoing the one Nudd had used when concealing agitation. Miles' shoulders tightened involuntarily before relaxing again as he wrestled them into submission.

An older man, whom Gwyn had only briefly glimpsed at the Solstice Gala, approached their table. Dressed for business even at this late hour, he exuded authority. Gwyn's first impression was of someone unaccustomed to spaces like this bar but who nevertheless expected command wherever he went.

The man tipped his gray hair first in Esme's direction, greeting her by name, then Miles, Abigail, and Colin, and finally introduced himself to the others at the table. "Good evening. I'm David Abington, recently arrived from London to assist Mr. Spencer with his duties while he recovers. A pleasure to meet you all."

David's attention zeroed in on Miles immediately. "I hoped to find you here. I stopped by your house earlier, as instructed, but only found... her." He pointed a thin finger at Esmeralda.

Gwyn's attention sharpened. The unspoken challenge in David's words was clear: he thought he could provoke Miles by insulting Esmeralda, and do it without consequence. He reminded Gwyn of some of the more underhanded nobles from his youth.

As Miles held David's gaze with clear challenge, Esme rose to grab the newcomer a chair. Tension hung heavy in the air.

One dismissive look from David while Esme did him a favor was all it took to reignite Gwyn's frustration with the men like David who had treated Elena badly. Though he tried to reject the notion of a connection between Esme's and Elena's souls, his thoughts always returned to it. His distrust for David was sudden and intense.

Once David was seated, Miles was the only person at the table who held even an ounce of David's complete attention. "The recent deaths among seated members are deeply concerning, Mr. Goodwin. Leadership must step up in times like these." His words carried the weight of judgment.

The comment was a clear jab at Sylas' demise, a bold move, considering this was the man's celebration of life. Miles' expression remained neutral, but a flicker of discomfort didn't escape Gwyn's notice.

"There have been complications, yes," Miles replied, his drumming fingers stilling. Surprisingly, he wasn't giving David the icy stare Gwyn had expected.

"It's unfortunate what's happened lately. The Brotherhood needs stronger leadership—someone willing to make tough decisions. Don't you agree, Miles?"

Each barb and sidelong glance was another move in a subtle but vicious game David was trying, and succeeding, at instigating with Miles.

Abigail had told him that Jacob had left the Corded Brotherhood in Miles' hands while he remained abroad. This David Abington was directly insulting Jacob's and Miles' leadership to his face. Bold indeed.

Miles replied evenly, "It's been a difficult time for everyone. We're doing what we can to keep things steady."

David's smile appeared strained, not fully reaching his eyes. "I'm sure you are. Though some might say a firmer grip is needed. Fortunately, others have stepped up in unexpected ways."

David nodded toward the door, and Gwyn's heart sank as Leon walked in, radiating his usual self-assured arrogance. By all the magic... He was the last person Gwyn wanted to see again in company and especially not on that night.

Showing up at the most inopportune time was the man who'd professed he desired an alliance. Gwyn wanted to solve the mystery of who he was above all else, but not right then. Leon strolled in with a confident swagger, as though he owned everyone's attention. Coincidentally, that was exactly what was happening.

Pulling up a chair farthest from Miles, Gwyn noted, Leon greeted David with a surprising level of familiarity. "David, good to see you again. Looks like I'm just in time."

"I didn't think you were invited," Miles said, instantly adopting a more aggressive tone.

Rapid movement caught Gwyn's eye. The leprechaun seemed not to know what to do with himself, eyes darting around, fingers twitching. Eventually, he settled on grabbing Leon a drink. When he passed it to Leon, Finn abruptly recoiled, as if he feared getting too close.

Esme stared at the intruding mage with a blank expression, devoid of either disdain or admiration. It was hard to tell what she thought about him at that moment. Colin, Will, and Abby had the look of people who knew that the best course of action was to keep their mouth shut until they found out what the next big play was going to be.

Leon took a sip of the offered drink, which appeared to be whiskey on ice. "Thank you."

Everyone, including David and the leprechaun himself, looked a bit shocked at this. Either Leon was so arrogant that he didn't think twice about flouting custom around the Fae or he was completely naïve, which Gwyn highly doubted.

Finn's only response was a simple "Aye," but Gwyn swore he saw his left eyelid twitch. If nothing came of that exchange at a later date, Gwyn would suggest that it be written in a history book for posterity. But he doubted it.

Paying no mind to the shocked reactions around him, Leon directed his attention to Miles, a sly smirk spreading across his face. His magic was again conspicuously closed off from Gwyn's seeking awareness.

Leon said, "I've been keeping tabs on things, lending a hand here and there. You know, filling in where others might be falling short."

David nodded approvingly. "Leon's been quite proactive lately. A shame not everyone in Seattle is as eager to protect our interests."

The statement landed like a punch, meant to challenge Miles publicly. Miles' grip on his glass tightened. Gwyn now understood David's play. He was using Leon as a tool to provoke Miles. But to what end?

Gwyn was conflicted between testing if pushing Miles would bring Nudd to the surface and refusing to let an interloper gloat over the man who had saved the lives of multiple people sitting at that table. Maybe it was the tempering effect of Abigail, or the sad expression on Esme's face, or the leprechaun's fidgeting, but Gwyn's decency eventually won out. "Mr. Abington, Miles has done a lot more for the Brotherhood than some outsider passing through. Maybe you should ask him what he's been handling before you start handing out condemnations."

David's amusement barely masked his displeasure at the idea. "Oh, I have no doubt Miles is... diligent. But sometimes diligence needs a bit of direction, don't you think? Or was it not outside help that resolved his last few malevolent issues? Including yourself, Mr. O'Malley, Mr. Cruz, and Ms. Turner?"

Gwyn suddenly understood the motivation behind David's aggressive behavior toward Miles. David wasn't here to support Miles. He was here to undermine him because Miles was in the way. David had come to seize Jacob's power for himself—and Leon had signed on to help.

The game Leon and David were playing made Leon's information far less attractive—the cost seemed suddenly too high. Regardless, Gwyn intended to keep his promise to listen to whatever Leon had to say. But Leon would have to present something truly life-altering to have Gwyn sign on for any more than that. Particularly given Miles' recent candor. After seeing Miles fight with Nudd's martial prowess, Gwyn was more committed than ever to unraveling the secrets behind it, but in a way that wouldn't hurt the innocent, if infuriating, man whose mind they were locked away in.

David landed one calculated strike after another at Miles' leadership. And every time, Miles' grip on his glass tightened. He had a tell. The mounting pressure was affecting him. Gwyn could see it in the way Miles' shoulders hunched, the slight pause before each measured response, like he was fighting to keep control. Gwyn's offer of verbal support hadn't made him happy, but he also didn't show direct disapproval. The more Gwyn learned about Miles, the more their relationship grew even more complicated.

Leon leaned in, addressing the group but directing his smirk at David. "Seattle's been unpredictable lately. It's good to know someone's got their eye on things, isn't it?"

David chuckled, but it was a humorless sound. "Yes, I've found it necessary to make a few adjustments." His gaze flicked briefly to Esmeralda.

She did a fine job of controlling her famous temper, because Gwyn watched an array of emotions skitter across her face. A few strong ones translated easily enough—dawning understanding, followed by despair, and ending with anger. What had David done to her?

Gwyn gripped Abigail's hand. If David had already sunk his claws into one friend, Gwyn wouldn't allow him to try it on another.

Leon's presence only made things worse. They needed to talk, and soon, because it was time that Gwyn decided what was he going to do about Nudd.

Miles

The only way out of this sticky situation was by maintaining a productive atmosphere. But Esme's frown tempted Miles to respond aggressively. He only restrained himself from lashing out by taking one of Esme's hands in his.

David's eyes flicked to the gesture, his expression betraying a brief, knowing satisfaction. The triumphant glint in his eyes betrayed that David had already made his opening move. There was more to the story of what had transpired between David and Esme than she had let on.

Taking a long sip from her drink, Esme stared David down over the rim of her glass. *Good girl*. Miles would rather see her ready to fight than ready to cry.

Leon's smirk deepened as he watched the conversation play out. His continued shielding of his magic from the room was suspicious. And he looked far too eager to see how Miles handled the pressure. He said, "Yeah, Miles, tell us what you think. Do you still have a handle on things, or do you think it's time to step back?"

It had only been a day since Miles had taken charge of the Brotherhood, so asking that question seemed *a bit* premature. He wouldn't validate Leon's question with a direct answer.

Instead, Miles met Leon's fixed gaze with metaphorical daggers hidden behind his back. "The safety of our community isn't a prize to be fought over. I'll keep doing what needs to be done, with or without outside help. To clarify, David, Gwyn is no longer outside help. He's moved to the city permanently. Esme and Will are also on the Corded Brotherhood books."

Out of the corner of his eye, he saw Gwyn shift uncomfortably in his seat. He'd hoped that confessing his dreams to Gwyn would improve their relationship, but it appeared to have worsened his distrust. Add to that what Esme had said about his accent changing and how his magic had almost taken over him in the battle with the ogre... Well, Miles couldn't completely blame him.

But that was a problem for later, because he currently had two other assholes breathing down his neck.

David said casually, "Glad to see you have competent help. It's always best to have a firm grasp on things. Wouldn't you agree, Miles?"

Firm grasp? He was a millimeter away from breaking the glass he was holding. *Steady,* he reminded himself.

Miles responded, "We have seen an unprecedented rise in sightings lately. I'm certain you've seen the report we submitted to the closed meeting."

David's face turned sour. "Yes, I have. I may have a few thoughts to share about that and our staffing at the next closed meeting."

Esme spoke for the first time since Leon had entered. "Do you think Jacob will be gone that long?"

A brief, genuine smile flickered across David's face, disappearing almost as quickly as it appeared. "I intend to prepare for all eventualities, Ms. Turner. It is a tried-and-true life strategy that has never let me down." He looked at her directly and added, "Prepare for everything, and you can be surprised by nothing. Speaking of which, why has no one mentioned the malevolent magic emanating from the back room, over there?" David pointed at the swinging door that led to the bar's kitchen.

"'Tis a dead ogre, who was slain single-handedly by the man whose balls you've been bustin' all night." The bold response came from Finn. If David wanted to tussle with Finn over this slight, he'd learn a thing or two about trading barbs with a leprechaun. Miles hoped David would make a mistake in his attempt to save face.

Esme covered up a single victorious snort of laughter by turning it into a cough. Will struck her back multiple times to further solidify the deception. Esme and Abby were going to find it very challenging to lose Will to Los Angeles. Even Miles would feel his loss.

Clearly frustrated that his constant criticisms hadn't landed a killing blow yet, David stood abruptly and adjusted his jacket, readying himself to leave. "I see you've made up your mind, Miles. We can't afford to be complacent, especially not now. I'll be watching closely. I have my responsibility to lead as well. And get rid of that body. Disgusting..."

He nodded once toward Leon, as if reminding Miles that Leon was a viable replacement for himself. David turned with a self-satisfied sneer on his face and left.

Behind his back, Abigail raised a one-finger salute.

Leon lingered a moment longer, grinned like a madman, and gave Miles a mock salute. "See you around, Doc."

He then winked at Gwyn, probably to further unsettle him, and turned to follow David out of the bar. There was a brief silence as everyone digested all that had transpired. Miles squeezed Esme's hand for support. That hadn't been a comfortable encounter for either of them.

Mile truly didn't know how he was going to manage it. The list was too long. He was behind with his patients. Lately, Seattle had attracted record numbers of malevolents. From across the table, Gwyn stared at him like he was a puzzle he could solve with a blade. Leon was now in the mix and seemed to be on a crusade against him. Esme had lost Sylas thanks to Leon's handiwork. And dealing with David was going to become a full-time job in its own right.

Miles was well and truly screwed.

Finn, in a departure from his usual banter, gritted out through clenched jaws, "I have some serious work ta do on those two." No one seemed to know what he meant by that, but no one seemed to be against it either.

"So, yeah," Esme said next. "I'm pretty sure David fired me from the Assembly payroll."

Fuck. Miles had been wrong. David had already made at least a few moves in the petty game of revenge he always played.

Finn slowly raised his glass to toast: "To new beginnings for our friends"—gesturing at Will and Colin—"to final goodbyes for an old one, and to telling those wankers to sod off!"

Miles gladly raised his glass to toast to that.

After everyone drank, Esme commented, "So, I noticed that the back exit door in the kitchen was still deadbolted. The kitchen wasn't frozen, or even wet from the melting ice, as it would be if a malevolent prison had failed in there. So how the hell did the ogre get in without anyone noticing?"

Now—*now* the list of bullshit Miles had to deal with was far too long.

CHAPTER ELEVEN

GETTING SCREWED

Abby

The timing wasn't ideal for this thought, but it wasn't like Abby had been given a choice when they were handing out brains before she was born. She lightly tapped Gwyn, and he pulled away.

"Is everything okay?" His voice betrayed his worry.

The chill air against her naked skin heightened her feeling of vulnerability. Her thoughts, as she prepared to lay them bare, felt far more exposed than her body. "I get stuck in my head sometimes, and the only way to get it to stop is to talk about it."

Gwyn scooted over a foot and made room for her beside him, lifting the duvet to invite her in. "How about we talk where it's warm?"

Abby agreed, and two big hands pulled her under the sheets. A small squeak escaped her lips as Gwyn roughly pulled her to cradle her next to his warm body.

Playfully kissing the tip of her nose, Gwyn urged her to speak. "So?"

True to form, Abby had once again waited until the pressure of uncertainty had become unbearable, leading to a poorly executed delivery of her question. "What are we doing?"

There was a laugh in Gwyn's voice when he responded, "While technology has certainly changed some practices, the fundamentals of what we've been doing remain unchanged. If that's what you mean, I'm open to trying new things."

His room was dark, so it was difficult to make out his expression, but she had the feeling that he was making a joke—sometimes it was hard to tell with Gwyn. She let out a sigh, feeling some of her earlier bravado slowly fading away. "Well, we've obviously been doing a lot of... *this*, but what else are we?"

"I thought how I feel about you is obvious." His tone was very serious. He actually thought that was a good enough answer. Poor, silly ancient man.

Knowing there was no other way forward for her, she spoke without hesitation. "Sometimes I feel like you don't see me. Like maybe you're lost in her memory or something."

"Abigail..." Gwyn took in a measured breath as his body tensed. "Are we speaking of Creiddylad?"

Like an invisible wall, Creiddylad's ghost separated them. Abby collided with it daily, while Gwyn passed right through it, oblivious to its presence. Gwyn must have felt her nod, because he pulled her in close again.

Speaking into her hair, Gwyn asked, "Are you worried about where you fit in my heart?"

Gods above and below, he was going to kill her with the way he spoke sometimes. Like arrows finding their mark, his words pierced her defenses. Something about his past life had given him a vocabulary of heartbreak and hope that made her modern cynicism crumble to dust.

She didn't move. He took this as a sign to continue.

"I will always love her memory. I retain a few memories of her passing before my imprisonment. So I've already mourned her, cariad." Gwyn kissed Abby's forehead for a long moment while sucking in an unsteady breath.

"But you... Abigail, there's enough room for both of you in my heart. You've brought back feelings I thought were lost to time. I can't explain it, but you've always seemed... inevitable to me."

Did Abby really need to take him to task on this, or was it her own self-esteem issues popping up? Comparing herself to Creiddylad, Abby couldn't help but feel a bit of doubt about her own worth. Abby was flawed—not a magical princess preserved perfectly in his memories.

"Well..." It was Abby's turn to blow out an unsteady breath, not knowing exactly what to say in response to that on-the-spot poetry. "There's no doubt that you really know how to make a point when you try."

Shaking slightly, Gwyn pulled her in for another kiss.

Gwyn

A man of his word, Gwyn walked into the same coffee shop where he had first encountered Abigail and Esmeralda. Leon's eagerness for the meeting was obvious; though Gwyn was early, Leon beat Gwyn there. It had been busy the last time he'd been there, but that day it was utterly empty except for the barista. Privacy would be a simple matter.

Gwyn thought that Leon's clothes were designed for anonymity. It was an obvious conclusion, as Gwyn had dressed likewise. Leon wore a fitted tan sweater with dark jeans, but he had notably lost his thick-rimmed glasses.

Gwyn took his time ordering a latte and sat across from him. "Fixed your vision?" he asked, pointing at Leon's eyes.

"Well, merry Christmas Eve to you too, Gwyn. The glasses are all a part of my look, but I decided I could be a bit more of myself with you today."

"Doubtful." Gwyn didn't hold back the scoff. Considering that Leon had continued to shield his magic from him, Gwyn suspected that Leon would ever be truly honest.

"Gwyn"—Leon smiled with mock reproach—"you're supposed to wish me merry Christmas back. Christmas is kind of a big deal nowadays. Just remember that."

Gwyn hadn't truly grasped the holiday's importance, but apparently it explained the café's lack of customers. There was always something new to learn about this world he found himself in. "I don't have all day, Leon. Let's get straight to the point."

Ignoring Gwyn's insistence, Leon cracked the knuckles on both of his hands. "So, what did you get Abby for Christmas?"

Gwyn's response was a blank stare.

With dramatic flair, Leon rolled his eyes and tutted. "Dude, you're supposed to buy your girlfriend a Christmas present. Even if she says she understands why you didn't, she'll definitely be super sad if you come empty-handed."

Gwyn knew without a doubt that he'd buy Abigail something as soon as the meeting ended. Something small, like a new pair of earrings she could wear with her ridiculously patterned scrubs, came to mind. But Gwyn didn't need to let Leon know he'd saved him from a romantic disaster.

"I think she'll understand," Gwyn asserted. "She knows exactly who I am. The question is, how do you know so much about this time?"

"So you didn't get her anything. You're *screwed*." Leon shook his head sadly, as if he were looking at a dead man walking. "To answer your question, I like television. Do they all know the truth about who you are?"

"Yes," Gwyn said flatly. "I came here to listen, not answer all of your questions. Start talking. You could begin with your real name."

In a telling display of his calculating nature, Leon strategically switched to their shared mother tongue. The inherent formality of the now dead language added a sense of gravitas to his words. "We both know I will not be honest about that. My purpose is to reveal the truth about others, not myself. Are you really surprised?"

Gwyn remained silent, a deliberate gesture to convey his intention of avoiding conversation.

"Be that way," Leon began, showing a hint of frustration. "I have missed talking so easily."

Gwyn could understand the sentiment. He had grown quite comfortable conversing in English, but he still had to think about most of the words he wanted to say before speaking.

Leon asked, "Do you remember that I said we could be allies? I believe it should be clear to you by now that I am from your time. You are not the only one your father condemned to one of those prisons."

Leon had dropped subtle hints in the past, but now he was finally stating it explicitly. Gwyn asked, "What did you do to incur Nudd's wrath?"

"That's not what I came to talk about." Leon shrugged and leaned in closer. "The reason I'm here is to discuss the potential for an alliance between us. Now, I must know. From my perspective, you have changed significantly from the demigod I remember. Do you have missing memories like I seem to? My recollection of the time right before my confinement is hazy and distant."

Now *that* was something that demanded Gwyn's attention. So he offered the truth. "Yes."

Leon's eyes gave nothing away, hinting he had already suspected this. He said, "Your vigorous defense of Nudd last night suggested a serious lapse in your memory. Your friendliness is misplaced. If you remembered his betrayal, you'd act differently."

Gwyn pressed, "I said that I would listen, but not that I would believe. If you can prove to me that your words are truth, we shall see about that alliance."

Leon folded his arms and sat back in his chair. "Not long after your ascension, a plague swept across the island. It claimed your beloved to Annwn."

The sudden sting of his words landed on Gwyn like an unexpected slap. "This I remember... Are your words meant to wound or give truths?" Gwyn took a long sip of his drink to cover his frown.

"Patience. My words are on the journey to the whole truth." Leon truly was a different person when speaking in Brythonic—far more serious, far more politic. "Your father's inaction sealed Creiddylad's fate. Did you know that?"

A second sting, but Gwyn doubted the validity of this statement. Nudd had loved Creiddylad almost like a daughter. Her demise could not have happened by his father's inaction. Nudd would not have...

Heedless of Gwyn's apparent reservations about what he'd said, Leon continued, "You had her cloistered in your country house. The miller's daughter paid her a visit, bringing along a sack of freshly milled flour she'd ordered. That simple, innocent act irrevocably spelled Creiddylad's death. She caught sick the next day. Naturally, you were unaware. You were understandably busy."

Gwyn absentmindedly twisted the insulating paper ring on his latte, his memory running to keep up with the torrent of words coming from Leon.

"Do you remember those times? I'm certain the Wild Hunt was running itself ragged with the wars that ravaged the population during the plague. The fever burned through her body so fast that she was gone within two days. You returned on the third. By then, your servants had already placed her death shroud."

A tidal wave of memory crashed over him, bringing with it the sickening taste of a grief so old it felt brand new, a grief as cutting and fresh as the day he'd discovered she was gone.

At first, all Gwyn remembered was the inhuman sound that had ripped from his lungs when he'd realized Creiddylad's magic was gone from their home. All the pottery inside had shattered. Gwyn's mind conjured the vision of a shroud, its wool as white and bright as a summer foxglove, draped over the loveliest face.

Leon continued, oblivious to Gwyn's internal unraveling—it wouldn't take much more and Gwyn would come apart. "Your father was, what, a single day's ride from the house you kept for her? Nudd could have gotten there in time, but he never left his keep."

"Explain." The blunt ridges of Gwyn's fingernails cut painfully into his palms. It was all that he could do to keep from shaking. His father had been able to remove impurities from wounds, but curing fevers? He was not as confident about that. Even so, that vision of the shroud forced his attention back to Leon.

"It was within your father's power to leave his keep. He could have forced some of the contamination out of her body. He could have given her a fighting chance, but instead, he turned a blind eye. Nudd didn't stir himself to do it. If you want me to add weight to the truth of my words, consider this. Would he sacrifice her to save just two peasants? We both know the answer to that question is *yes*. Because that's what he did."

"Who are you?" Such intense agitation seized Gwyn that a tremor ran through him, making it a physical struggle to remain seated.

"I think it is obvious by now that I lived within the keep, but as to who I am, now is not the right time. Understand that I want the truth out of Nudd as much as you do. He took as much from me as he did from you. If I can't have my life before back, I at least want revenge. The people of this time are soft. They have forgotten the value of honor. I have not. For Creiddylad, for myself, even for you, I will gain recompense."

"Do you aim to slay Miles, then?"

Leon's expression turned markedly cold. Gwyn suspected it was his most honest one yet. "And why not?"

Gwyn saw a chilling echo of his own vengeful past intentions in Leon's casual cruelty. The realization left a bitter taste in his mouth. Had he really been so belligerent?

Against his better judgment and with some reluctance, Gwyn interrupted Leon's trajectory. Damn his decency. "That would be murder, not revenge. He is not my father pretending to be someone else. Though Miles resembles my father in appearance, actions, and even magical abilities, he is not Nudd."

A genuine laugh escaped Leon. "I find that very difficult to believe."

"I have seen Nudd's magic take over Miles, control him with my own eyes." Had Gwyn said too much?

"And yet I saw you flinch just now. You don't fully believe what you're saying, either," Leon accused.

"I will admit that Miles knows far, far too much not to have some of my father in there somewhere."

"So let's rip Nudd out and take him to task," Leon said, the casualness of his tone belying the merciless violence in his words. If nothing else proved to Gwyn that Leon was of his age, his ruthlessness did.

Gwyn was shocked by what he was about to say, but it seemed the prudent thing. "Miles is a far more cunning opponent than he appears to be."

"So... you will live out your days, happy in the bosom of your lover, but never seek the power you've lost? She is worthy. But you, you wore the mantle of the Wild Hunt and now you live in a peasant's apartment filled with borrowed furniture."

That stung. "What do you want from me?"

"Help me get the same thing you want—the truth. Why? Why did he do it?"

Gwyn was tempted. It had been two months since the Dullahan attack. The intensity of his rage had diminished with all that he had gained in that time, yet his anger still smoldered.

Each route to the answers he wanted led to an alternate reality, a different future where a precious thing—truth, love, or his hard-won peace—was lost. He could join up with Leon. They could join forces to plunder whatever essence of Nudd remained within Miles. Or Gwyn could even try to persuade Abigail to see what she might take from Miles' head. But neither option would enable Gwyn to claim he maintained any righteousness. And Gwyn could only allow his sins to tarnish his own soul.

Gwyn could ignore everything Leon said and go on with his life, exactly as it was. He could continue to hunt for the Assembly, pretending to be a Corded Brother, sharing words and drinks with friends, and cherishing every stolen moment with Abigail.

He was making progress on regaining his magical prowess. He could mist walk again, and he could summon lightning. Instead of relying on raw power, he was improving his magical precision. He had made great strides since aligning himself with this Corded Brotherhood. Joining with Leon would put it all at risk.

But ignoring Leon meant a continuance of his ignorance. His long search for the truth would be fruitless. Gwyn, the hunter, didn't fail in his pursuits.

The temptation of answers, justice, and renewed power was almost too strong for Gwyn to resist, each whisper more captivating than the next, exposing parts of his former self he had tried to leave in the past. Instead of agreeing outright, he said, "I acknowledge your words and even find some of them believable.

But you have not yet truly proven yourself to be a friend. How am I to know that this alliance you propose will not end in my own death?"

Leon scratched at the table with one perfectly polished fingernail. "Taking the malevolent magic from your leader's mind was not enough? Killing the feral leshy for you? Delivering the redca—"

Gwyn interrupted. "To answer your first point, your convenient arrival, armed with *precisely* the right skills, at exactly the right moment, reeks of calculation, not coincidence. I've hunted too long not to recognize when I'm being maneuvered by someone else. For the second point, you received a handsome payment. For the third, your actions brought more trouble than they solved!"

Leon grimaced, his face displaying either regret or shame. With slow, deliberate words, Leon said, "Then I shall have to prove myself your friend when you ask it of me."

That offer, Gwyn would use. He only hoped it wouldn't come back to haunt him like so many of his other choices had.

Chapter Twelve

Seeing Things Differently

Abby

Abby's fingers drummed an erratic rhythm on Colin's desk, the sound sharper than she intended. "This feels wrong," she muttered. "Like I'm about to pick through parts of you I shouldn't touch."

"Oh, yeah, like you haven't done that before," Colin retorted with a smirk that suggested he was trying to rile her up.

Abby couldn't keep the snark from her voice. "Yeah, and you're taking away one of my best friends."

Her brother grinned. "Sorry, not sorry."

Old sibling habits died hard, even when you were in your thirties. There was an undercurrent of familiarity—the banter they'd perfected as kids, back when their arguments were more about toys and curfews than life decisions, was still there. Abby rolled her eyes at Colin's teasing. She couldn't be mad at her brother for finding happiness, even if it did come at the expense of losing Will. Since Colin was home for the holidays, he was staying with their mom in his childhood bedroom. He took a seat on his childhood bed, still wearing his pajamas, as Abby occupied his desk.

"After you extract the magic from my head, could you put me to sleep for an hour or two? I could use a good nap."

"Gods, I do not want to know why you're so tired. But, speaking of Will, seriously, don't hurt him too badly, okay? He was my friend first."

A flicker of understanding crossed Colin's face, making him seem older, more knowing, to Abby. "That's not my plan, but if things did change, I would make certain the breakup was gentle. I get it. Will is special. Abby, he's the first person, man or woman, who doesn't question my ability to be monogamous simply because I'm bisexual. Everyone else has been afraid that I'm going to waltz off to the next available warm body. It's a huge relief at the end of the day. You have no idea."

Abby didn't, but she could understand the sentiment. She wanted to get out of there before their mom started pressuring her to help cook more of the holiday meal, which would make her late to pick up Gwyn for said gathering. "Alright, let's do this. I'll mind my business in there, promise. Next time you see me it will be dinnertime?"

Colin nodded his assent.

Abby's hands settled on either side of Colin's head, her fingers pressing his blond hair down around his temples. The familiar hum of magic crept down her arms, spreading through her fingers and sliding into him. She'd been in Colin's brain many, many times before, but it was the first time she'd done it in several years. From her first glance, she found confirmation that he was far more mature than he'd been before he'd moved to Los Angeles.

As she snaked her magic through his memories, her magic snagged on pockets of tension, places where memories stuck like half-chewed gum, sticky with anxiety. From long experience, she knew this was anxiety wrapped around the memory. She could pluck them away, relieve him of his worries, whatever they were, but she left those alone. Along the way, she came across a few memories that radiated warmth like a welcoming campfire on a cold night—happy memories.

A jarring, metallic chill seeped into her awareness as she brushed against a section of memories, so cold it stung just from its proximity. No one was immune from forming these. Each mind she had entered had at least one. Despite being terrible, these frozen, uncomfortable memories were still a part of a person's identity. Colin hadn't asked, so she left them be, departing the area untouched—even if she wanted to tear them away for the wrongness she sensed emanating from them.

There was something special about the memories made by and about magic. A small spark of magic infused the memories, producing an unmistakable tingling sensation when her own magic neared them.

How Abby sorted through Colin's magical memories was more an art than a science. She shuffled and shuffled until she found a few that felt like "Will" to her buried in Colin's larger trove of those tinged with magic.

Among the three, one emanated a type of warmth that reminded her of friction. That was a... private memory. Gross. Fiery anger emanated from the second. That must be from fighting the nøkk or the jorōgumo with him. Ignoring the first and second options, she enveloped the third in her magic, drawn to its warm and sunny essence that resembled the elation of learning a new skill. Like picking a ripe apple from a tree, Abby forcefully plucked it from his mind and pulled it into her own.

Her own mindscape was far less real than when she entered others. To her, her brain just *was*—probably a lot like everyone else experienced their own minds. Abby didn't feel the memory lock into place like a puzzle piece finding its home. The moment it touched her mind, it seamlessly became hers.

Now to do what she'd promised. All it took was a whisper of power. Nothing so complicated as what she'd just done, sorting through his memories like that. But before she left his mind with the order to sleep for a few hours, she left behind something small, an earworm of a song he'd hated when they were growing up that would last for a few hours.

"That's what you get for forgetting my Christmas present," she whispered with a sly grin as she stood to leave Colin's room.

Quietly closing his bedroom door behind her, Abby decided there was no better time than the present to try out this new skill. She had the memory. Practicing shouldn't be necessary. She should immediately know how to make it work. She turned on her vision for magic and had to brace herself on one wall as she nearly fell down from the shock of it.

Swirling, twirling wisps of gunmetal gray mist were concentrated at the edges of the doors. It took her a moment, but she eventually realized that she was looking at her mother's wards. She walked into the living room to see the same, but far more concentrated on the windows and doors that led outside. Wow...

Abby's mother, fully aware of what her daughter was supposed to take from Colin, met her in the living room for a farewell. Abby gaped to see her mother glowing with a purplish-pink glow—her magic, her aura.

Her mother cracked a wry smile. "You're using it now?"

Abby nodded. "You're purplish-pink!"

The doorbell rang, cutting off her mom's reply. To Abby's surprise, when she opened the door, David Abington was standing there, the last person she'd expected to see at her parents' house on Christmas Eve.

Except David was... wrong. His magic had a pinkish-yellow hue, but flecks of other colors contaminated the surface like hundreds of corrupted dust bunnies hiding in plain sight. Some flecks were black, some were blue, green, yellow, and orange. And then, beneath it all, tucked deep near his heart, a golden glow pulsed.

The only other time she'd seen that color was when Miles healed. Except Miles' magic had flowed freely, finding damage and repairing it, or it had repelled malevolent magic. This golden magic was just circling there, constrained as if held in reserve. Seeing magic was still a novel experience to Abby, but the hidden golden magic felt wrong... discordant.

It gave her the impression that he was keeping it a secret. But, then again, maybe her impression was skewed by the fact that David was a total jerk.

Abby rubbed at her eyes, willing the magic sight to stop. Will was right; she needed eye drops badly after that. She also wanted to put as much distance between herself and David as she could after seeing the magical detritus covering his aura.

Abby shivered at the thought of the wrongness. Why did it shake her so deeply? Maybe she was overreacting to something that was completely normal to see. She'd have to ask Will when she got a chance.

Abby tried to soothe herself, to force a calm farewell, but she couldn't stop her pulse from overreacting. She hurried to her car, nearly running, calling over her shoulder to let her mother know she'd be back for dinner with Gwyn.

***

As Abby arrived back at her family home earlier than planned that day, the Dullahan battle flashed back vividly in her mind. The tightness in her chest, a familiar echo of the anxious drive over, made the past and the present situations feel unnervingly alike.

So much had changed since then. The person who had arrived that day holding a bowl of cookie dough and a risky plan to prevent her Corded Brother and one-date fling from killing each other seemed like a fading memory.

The woman who had existed before the first crack of the Dullahan's whip was gone. Her secret was out—her friends knew of her true magical abilities. She'd even used her illegal magic right in front of their faces. Only a few months had passed since Gwyn had joined their lives, and he was already something special to her.

Colin had downplayed the urgency, yet Abby's hasty steps to the door betrayed her anxiety. This was her mother—the fiery, unstoppable woman who had been a seated member of the Assembly for years, who'd held the Bastion in mental handcuffs for nearly an hour, all while keeping her day job and being a great mom to her and Colin.

Even though her father had moved out, the familiar warmth of her family home felt as reassuring as ever. Colin met her in the hall, looking drawn, and led her into the living room. There, she spotted her mom, the pint-sized matriarch with her signature crown of red hair, fussing over a tray of snacks with Will as he tried to take it from her.

"Mrs. O'Malley, please let me help!" Will was half a second from turning his highly effective puppy dog eyes on her.

Abby's mom narrowed her eyes. "Will, I love you like my own son, but step away from the snack tray."

Uh-oh, Christi O'Malley was pushing back against all the worrying over her. The puppy dog-eyes wouldn't work this time. Abby caught Will's eyes and shook her head subtly. He took the hint and grabbed a seat on the couch instead—smart man.

"Mom, I just walked in on you passed out cold on the couch. I don't know if you fainted or what. I thought you'd had a heart attack or something! Let us handle things for once?" Colin shot their mother a look, jaw tight, brows raised, his exasperation clear.

"Colin Henry, I had a screening last month. Fit as a fiddle," their mother retorted, crossing her arms with a "say one more word and violence will happen" expression. Their mother was in her mid-sixties but looked at least a decade younger, since mages tended to live longer than mundane humans.

"Fine, you gave me a heart attack!" he shot back. He stood rigidly, his fists clenched tightly on his hips, his jaw set. Though Abby saw him trying to hide his worry and frustration, his voice trembled.

"Oh, don't mind me," Abby said, throwing her hands up in mock surrender. "I'll just stand here while you two process your feelings. You need a separate therapy session, I swear."

She took a seat next to Will, placing her bag of personal medical supplies off to the side. "Mom, I'm here to check you out. Are you going to fight me on that, too?"

Her mother finally placed the tray down and her shoulders slumped. "No. Do your thing. Look inside while you're at it."

Will took this as an opportunity to make a small plate of food stacked so high that it looked like a gentle breeze would make the entire assemblage fall over.

Abby said, "While I do this, tell me again what happened, Colin."

Still standing, Colin ran a faintly shaking hand through his blond hair and nodded. "I was in my room shooting off emails for work, hoping to minimize the backlog of stuff I need to do when we return to Los Angeles. I came out to find her unconscious, slumped on the couch in an awkward position. One leg was practically dangling off the edge, and her arms were spread wide, as if she'd fallen asleep mid-movement. I shook her, and she woke up immediately, thank the gods."

"And I ran straight to the powder room because it felt like I had a bad case of magical exhaustion." Their mother chuckled, miming gagging.

Their mother was always unflappable, even when she had good reason to be rattled. Abby regretted not inheriting more of that.

Colin finally made his way to the couch and sat down, his leg jittery from the pent-up nerves. "I couldn't feel her magic. So I called Will, and I called you."

Abby was almost finished with her examination. "Your blood pressure is a bit low, but everything else seems fine. O$_2$ saturation, respiration, heart rate, temperature, all good. Now follow my finger." Her mother's extraocular muscle function test revealed no concerning communication issues between her muscles and nerves either.

When Abby opened up her ability to see magic, a flood of information immediately overwhelmed her. Colin sported a strange yellow-pink hue, while Will radiated a purplish-yellow combination, which unexpectedly harmonized given their opposite positions on the color wheel. And their mother... her magic was a mere shadow of the brilliance compared to what she'd seen after Colin had shared his magical insight that same morning. Her mother's magic was so weak it barely left a trace of an aura around her.

Following her mother's instructions, Abby pressed into her mother's mind to see what she could remember about the few hours between Abby leaving and Colin finding her on the couch. Her mom's memories flashed before her eyes like a movie playing at 32 times speed. Except that this movie had a noticeable skip—like the DVD was scratched—until Colin woke her up.

Gods below. Abby sat back and indicated that she was done.

"I couldn't feel my magic either." Her mom came out of her stupor, sounding both indignant and, for once, a little defeated. She tried to brush off everyone's worry, yet she couldn't quite hide her unease. "But I woke up, and I was fine—mostly."

Their mother sighed. "You know what, actually, I am going to disappear to lie down for a bit and see if my stomach will settle. I'm still alive, so don't start planning on how you'll spend your inheritance yet. Obviously Christmas Eve dinner didn't get fixed."

"Don't worry, Mom; we can handle making dinner," Colin assured. "It won't be as good as yours, but we can handle it—promise."

With enthusiastic nods, Abby and Will readily agreed—anything to ensure she rested.

"Gwyn can take a taxi," Abby added. "You're excited about us being together, which is great, but please take a break. It will seriously be okay, Mom."

Once their mother was out of earshot, Abby turned to Will. "What did you see when you looked at her magic?"

"Something was wrong when I checked," Will responded, his expression far more serious than she was accustomed to.

"I never really checked out your mom before." Will chuckled at his own lame joke. "So for me, it's hard to tell exactly how bad it is. But that firecracker is definitely not acting like herself."

Abby swallowed, processing everything she'd seen and learned. Their mother was a formidable figure. Her fierce protectiveness and tough attitude made her someone few mages underestimated. But now, she seemed so small, so vulnerable, even if she was showing them a composed facade.

Why did her magic weaken so drastically if she had no memory of using it? It made no sense.

"Do you think it's possible that Mom accidentally used her mental abilities on herself? I've joked about doing it in the past, but I've never tried it."

"Harpy, if you think it's possible, try it," Will encouraged her.

Drawing on her abilities, Abby attempted to command herself to stand. Colin and Will traded glances between her and their plates as they nibbled on their snacks. Her repeated attempts yielded no results. Eventually, she gave up and announced, "It doesn't work."

"Damn," Colin muttered. "That would've been a great way to wrap this whole mess up."

Will nodded with a slice of cheese sticking halfway out of his mouth. "Right?" The cheese fell to the table. "Oh, sorry."

Colin picked it up and popped it into his own mouth with a mocking smirk directed at Will.

"Hey!" Will tried to feign offense, but the grin tugging on the corners of his lips exposed his enjoyment of the flirtation.

"Gross, just don't start making out on our parents' couch. Back to the topic of our ailing mother." With a downturned mouth, she shot a reproachful look at Colin. "Did anything else happen while I was gone?"

Unfazed, Colin reclined, his hand absently rubbing the stubble on his chin as he pondered. "Uh, I napped. Thanks for that, by the way. Then I worked for a bit in my room. A few hours later, I came out and made lunch for Mom and me. Then I did more work. The doorbell rang. I heard her talking to someone. An hour later, I was ready to do a quick workout and found her on the couch."

Abby picked up a decorative pillow and tossed it at Colin's unsuspecting face. "You idiot! Who was at the door? That might be important. I was surprised to see David this morning; I didn't realize she had another visitor."

Colin's earnest answer, after setting the pillow aside, proved the maturity she had sensed in him. "I honestly don't know," he admitted. "A mage. I sensed another magic user at the door. Voice was male... probably."

"Fae? Other non-human? What? Dare I ask if you noticed any traces of malevolent magic?" She knew it was probably unfair, but she couldn't help feeling annoyed that her brother hadn't paid more attention.

"Not Fae. Not malevolent. Probably human. I'm not an expert on feeling auras from like, thirty feet away through walls, Abby. I'm sorry."

The harrumph she made unconsciously made Abby realize she was slowly turning into her mother. "I'm sorry for being so pushy. Just worried about Mom. We can ask her when she wakes up." Abby hesitated. "There's one more thing. I took a look inside like she asked and, Colin, there was nothing there… for hours. Her memory was either erased or she didn't make any memories."

"I… I don't even know what to do with that information, Abby." Colin stood up and started clearing away the snack tray. "What are our next steps? Watch and see? Should we contact Jacob?" Will and Colin looked at her expectantly.

Jacob was busy abroad. He wouldn't be able to examine her from all the way over there. Abby had a different idea. "Maureen is out of town, too. I'm contacting Josiah. He plays the lax Native Hippie, but he's a genius and he and Mom are besties."

Colin ran a hand through his hair, nodding. "Good idea. I'll ask around the Corded Brotherhood to see if something like this has ever happened before. Whatever we need."

Chapter Thirteen

A Holiday

Esme

Miles always ran warmer than her, and after showering, he was even hotter. So it was impossible for Esme's frozen toes not to find their way up his pant leg as they lay down that night.

"Oi, ya tryin' to freeze a man out of his own bed?" His protest was perfunctory at best. He guessed what was on her mind, because he reached out his arm, beckoning her to cuddle close.

With her all snuggled in, Miles spoke softly with his chin resting on her head. "So, I have some good news and I have some bad news. Knowing you, I'm going to start with the good and see if that sells you on the bad."

Esme wiggled her bottom to ensure that she had one hundred percent of his attention. "Better make it a good sell then, mister."

"The good news is that I've rented a gorgeous A-frame cabin on Lake Wenatchee for Christmas *and* I already bought both of us snowshoes. It has a hot tub and heated walkways, so no slipping on icy concrete, and we won't have to dig ourselves out if it snows. We can leave after I finish a couple hours of work tomorrow morning. What do you think?"

She was already getting excited. Skiing and snowboarding had never been her thing, but she loved snowshoeing. "The village on the way will have a big lights display."

The mountain town they'd drive through to get to the lake was famous for its Bavarian-themed architecture, restaurants, and shops. Throughout the winter, a blanket of snow covered the area tucked away in the Cascades, transforming it into a winter wonderland—a stark contrast to Seattle's chilly, damp weather.

Esme was thrilled at the prospect of a mini-vacation. But the set of Miles' jaw was a bit too rigid for the bad news not to be a big letdown. "Gods, please just tell me the bad news."

Esme's frozen toes crept up his leg. He'd spent the last few months exercising constantly, lately mostly to escape Gwyn, and it showed. His legs were solid blocks of muscle.

Miles sucked in a sharp breath, enduring her icy digits, and then spilled the truth. "The cabin will be all ours, but... We'll have a certain leprechaun in the back of the rented SUV."

"Please tell me he invited himself." Her frozen fingers were going under his pajama top next if she didn't like his answer. Miles couldn't see her roll her eyes in the dark room, but he probably guessed she was doing it, anyway.

There was the slightest hint of a whine in Miles' voice. "I legitimately thought he might cry if I refused."

Esme lightly tapped his chest. "Wow, Finn really got one over on you, didn't he?"

Miles rested his chin on her head, defeated. "Yeah... he did."

***

"I can't wait to bring out the whiskey to celebrate Christmas with my besties. I've been smellin' the food in the trunk for over an hour now and I'm fit to dyin'."

"Of course you brought whiskey." Esme tried to smile. Anticipating Finn's voracious appetite, she had gone a bit overboard cooking an extravagant Christmas feast for the three of them to reheat and share at the cabin.

"And I knitted matchin' ugly sweaters for us."

Out of his, well, wherever Finn pulled anything he carried with him out of, he retrieved three sweaters. He held each up so that Miles could take a peek at them in the rearview mirror. Lily's face, stitched to perfection, smiled from the front of the largest red and white sweater.

Next to the leprechaun, the muse dog herself leaned over and sniffed at it while her tail loudly thumped the seat. She seemed to approve. Next, Finn displayed the smallest. The front of the garment sported a vibrant green four-leaf clover that was peeking out from a glass of whiskey on the rocks.

Ever dramatic, Finn saved Esme's for last. Four conjured ferrets, each with bright, curious eyes, circled Mr. Snuffles, her neighbor's tabby cat—whom she considered hers more often than not.

"Oh, Finn, I love it!" She reached back to take the offered garment.

"Impressive, mate," Miles agreed.

They wanted to make it to the cabin before dark, so they skipped visiting the town until nightfall, when the lights would look most impressive. Snow was piled up high on both sides of the narrow two-lane road around the lake.

The tiny cabin was barely visible amidst the massive pines. A towering pile of firewood, seasoned and ready to burn, stretched the length of the driveway. Only the steeply pitched roof resisted the glistening snow that was piled high on the sides of the cabin's dark, weathered wood walls. Thick icicles, clinging to the eaves, sparkled from the lights that had been strung across the roof. To Esme, it looked like a slice of heaven.

A tiny replica of the main house sat on the other side of the driveway. "Is that where is Finn staying?"

"Aye, it's perfect," Finn conceded.

Esme grinned. "Perfectly *away* from us, interloper!"

*****

The next morning, Esme pulled her scarf higher, her breath forming wispy clouds in the frigid air. Though she was warming up from the activity, the subzero temperatures that day were unexpected. Careful of every step, she smiled, the crisp, clean air filling her lungs as she looked out over the snow-covered expanse. Lily found the snow too deep to move around in, so they'd left her to relax in the cabin while they snowshoed last night's dinner off.

Heavy snowfall characterized this area of the Cascades, with monthly totals often exceeding fifty inches. Each step through the deep snow was a bit of a struggle—for the humans, at least.

"Wish I had Finn's tricks right about now," Esme teased, nudging the leprechaun. He practically floated above the snow like it was solid ground, leaving barely a footprint in his wake.

Finn flashed her a wicked grin. "Just a wee bit of an advantage. Seriously, though, do ya think these little stilts could manage a pair of snowshoes properly?"

Miles, trudging ahead, threw Esme a sidelong glance. "Bet you're glad now for all those hours in the gym, huh?"

"Yes…" Her eyes narrowed playfully at his teasing, but the corners of her mouth betrayed a smile. "This feels like the old days when it was just the three of us hunting down malevolents. I wonder when I'm finally going to go on a malevolent hunt in a place that has sidewalks."

"Dove, it's not advisable to use a batterin' ram to knock on a front door." Finn snorted. "If my metaphor wasn't clear, you're the magical batterin' ram here."

She threw a snowball at Finn's head and, for once, he didn't reciprocate. He simply laughed it off.

For the next half hour, comfortable silence accompanied their stroll, the crunch of snow beneath their feet filling the icy air. Finn scuttled here and there, checking out random things along that trail that caught his attention, and Miles kept reaching to hold her hand. It was a wonderful day, even if it didn't turn out to be a strictly romantic vacation.

A sudden sharp crack to her left stopped them in their tracks; hesitation seized Esme as a primal sense of danger flooded her senses.

"Did you hear that?" she whispered. Esme scanned the dense tree line. They were avoiding such areas because those places likely concealed treacherous tree wells—areas where the snow hadn't filled in around the base of the trees, creating pits that could be twenty feet deep and swallow a person whole.

Miles was also on high alert. "Yeah. Could just be some animal. I didn't feel malevolent magic."

"It was close," Finn murmured, eyeing the surrounding area suspiciously.

Another rustle, closer this time, and the three of them froze. Esme's breath fogged in front of her as she waited. She'd gotten so used to tapping infernal power that she did it then, unconsciously. She didn't even stop to pause to ask herself if she was overreacting.

Her senses heightened, while the infernal's emotion-numbing influence sharpened her concentration to focus solely on the threat. Bracing for whatever lurked beyond the trees, she conjured a short sword made of shadows and brimstone.

All this only for a familiar, and most welcome, towering figure to step into view. Relief washed over Esme as the adrenaline faded. She fought free of the infernal magic's numbing grip, blowing out a held breath with a shudder.

"Gods below, Sitkum!" she gasped, recognizing her sasquatch friend. "You scared me half to death."

A wide, toothy grin and a surprised expression accompanied the creature's friendly grunt. Standing at just under seven feet tall, Sitkum was shorter than most of his species—that plus his friendly face made him instantly recognizable.

"Didn't mean to spook you," he rumbled, his voice like gravel underfoot as he pointed at Esme's sword. "Checking up on you folk. I heard you were headed our way and wanted to say hello before I return to the mine."

Even though Sitkum had fought with them at the Solstice Gala, he had never witnessed her summoning a weapon. She dismissed it with a grimace. Miles was also sheathing his weapons. The relief of realizing she wasn't the only one to react defensively was short-lived. Judging by the grin Finn was wearing, the sasquatch's arrival had not actually been a surprise to the trickster—he'd been playing them.

Mindful of his strength, Sitkum patted Esme's shoulder gently after receiving a warm hug from her.

"It's been too long. How are things with Matika?" she asked.

His face split into a proud grin. "She said yes! We'll be married in March or April at the latest. We want to have the wedding while the hiking trails are still quiet and when we can count on a few days of decent weather."

"Who could deny that handsome face?" Esme beamed. "You'd better invite me!"

Finn and Miles spoke over each other. "Congratulations, mate!"

Sitkum chuckled, scratching the back of his shaggy head. "Couldn't keep you away if I tried, Esme. Or that one." He gestured toward Finn, who was bouncing happily on top of the snow.

"We'll be there," Esme reassured him.

He turned serious. "You ought to be careful out here," Sitkum warned, eyeing Miles. "I felt traces of malevolent magic yesterday near my camp. While not strong, it was enough to get me considering moving mining spots."

For generations, his towering vegetarian ancestors had evolved to use their size as a defense, not for hunting. Their senses, designed to detect danger rather than track prey, lacked a predator's sharpness. As far as Esme knew, the People also didn't use offensive magic. They were obligate pacifists unless attacked.

Saying goodbye, Sitkum gave Miles his characteristic old-fashioned advice to provide for Esme and promised Finn a celebratory drink at the wedding. "I need to finish mining the gold for Matika's bridal circlet. I've only found a pound so far, and I think the vein I'm working on is drying up."

The sasquatch wandered off, disappearing into the trees, while all three of their mouths hung open. Finn's eyes bulged and his face turned white as he stammered to Sitkum's retreating form, "Only a pound... Pure... gold..."

Esme feared the leprechaun might never recover from the gold lust that had taken over his body. Surprisingly, it was Miles who broke him out of his stupor by throwing a snowball at him. "Oi, snap out of it, mate."

Shaking himself like a dog trying to rid himself of water, Finn mumbled a meek apology. "Sorry, sorry. I can't help it."

Esme's face broke into a grin that she shared with Miles. "Yeah... Sitkum was definitely trying to get a reaction from you with that last line, but I also think he meant it. If sasquatch valued material possessions, they'd all be incredibly wealthy from their mining and lumber operations. My hands are starting to get cold from this inactivity. Let's head back."

Seeing Finn's slumped shoulders and the way his head hung low as they trudged along, Miles tried to reassure him. "Maybe if you get married, Sitkum will tell you where to find a vein."

Finn waggled his eyebrows. "There's too much love in this body for me to settle down with one lassie."

"Just..." Esme shuddered. "No. Gods, no more, *please*."

They were all surprised to find what looked like bear tracks. That shouldn't be possible; bears should have been hibernating for weeks. It had snowed last night, so the tracks had to be fresh.

For better or worse, they were spared from any prolonged anxiety about the fate of what they thought must be a sleep-deprived bear because the twisted face that was a blend of bear and hyena erupted from the tree line, plowing through the deep snow like a living bulldozer.

CHAPTER FOURTEEN

OLD WOUNDS

Esme

Muscles rolled beneath the malevolent's matted, spotted fur. Its hunched shoulders swayed as it blasted forward. Fangs jutted from its elongated muzzle. Its ears were jagged and uneven, and its nose was similarly ruined. Frostbite—it had to be.

It was Esme's nightmare in the flesh—a nandibear. One had killed her parents.

The eyes, piercing, intelligent, and calculating, stopped her dead in her tracks. They were closing in, moving far too fast, and straight at her. Pure terror ignited her magic. The sword that materialized in her hands was a replica of the one she'd summoned earlier.

Body paralyzed, her mind whirled. Was this the way her parents had felt before the end? Was this creature the last thing they'd seen? The malevolent was almost too close for her to get out of the way in time, but her feet wouldn't move, even to save herself. Panic seized her, body and mind. Her breaths came in short, shallow gasps.

A popping sound of magic splitting through space burst near her ear, making her cringe involuntarily as she was grabbed. But it wasn't Finn who moved her.

Miles carried her through the mists of his magic, dropping them both twenty feet from where they'd started, their snow-shoes landing half-buried in the powder. His entire body radiated a warm golden light, shimmering with magical energy.

An unearthly crack raced across the clearing, the sound echoing like an avalanche in the quiet, distracting all beings present. A malevolent prison split open less than twenty feet away. The frigid energy of the magic poured out into the winter air, releasing the prisoners held within.

Chaos unleashed as a swarm of hairy black bat-like creatures streamed out of the fissure torn in reality by the failing prison. Their flight was haphazard at first, a few dropping to the snow immediately. But it didn't take long for the creatures to right themselves. There had to be twenty, thirty of them. And each and every single one went straight for Finn on the other side of the clearing.

With a frustrated snarl, the nandibear circled back, its massive paws crashing through the snow. The muscles of its hulking forequarters rippled with lethal power as it turned its focus to pursuing the blazing beacon of magic that Miles had become.

Without a word of warning, Miles scooped her up again. Esme watched as the world flew past her in dizzying streaks of color. He'd moved them to the other side of the clearing, creating a triangle of space between the scrambling nandibear, the leprechaun furiously fighting off a pack of bats, and them.

Feet back on solid ground, Esme began to berate herself. She needed to be more like Miles—tougher, always professional, less *broken*.

But when her eyes met his, she saw a terrible rage simmering on his face that was like a wildfire ready to engulf everything in its path. Miles was practically trembling with it as he unholstered his Glock, took aim at the swirling malevolent bats, and fired off five rapid shots.

Almost immediately, a second malevolent prison failed. The sound, more distant this time, was less jarring to the nandibear. It wavered only momentarily to look in that direction. A swarm of the same bat-like creatures erupted into the frigid air farther down the trail. Once again, their dark wings aimed straight for Finn.

"Blasted things don't care for the Fae!" Finn's muffled shout carried across the snow, barely audible over the flurry of wings and the hissing sound of the leprechaun's fire.

Glow beginning to fade, Miles emptied his clip toward the now charging nandibear. It barely staggered from the impact as dark rivulets of blood ran down one flank.

Whether it was his anger, the gunshots, Finn's scream, or the splintering of the second prison, something snapped in Esme. The shadows of her demonic blood came flooding back, pooling all the way up to her eyes. Somewhere in the frenzy of being saved, she'd either lost or dismissed her weapon—she didn't know.

Fuck the sword. Maybe if Esme had been a few years into her training with Gwyn, instead of a few months, she would have had a chance at using a sword against the enormous monster. What they needed was an ally. Now practiced at changing her conjurations on the fly, it was Esme's turn to create her own rip in the fabric of reality.

Oatmeal burst forth. Her shadowcat, a creature made of darkness, pulsed with infernal power. A lambent red replaced the swirling mercury of her eyes. The embodiment of Esme's fear, rage, and, at the forefront of it all, grief, crouched, the size of a hulking grizzly.

She wanted to rip this malevolent to pieces.

Starving and enraged, the nandibear reacted to the newcomer. Though built for a warmer climate, the malevolent moved with surprising speed as it lurched toward them. Esme shifted Oatmeal to take the hit.

Her shadowcat was only partially successful.

Pouring her emotion into casting Oatmeal had freed Esme's legs to move again. She lunged.

Miles moved with her, creating an aegis around them both. The nandibear collided with it sidelong as Oatmeal forced its trajectory to the side. The impact was a bone-jarring, earth-shattering crash, a sound more akin to smashing through a brick wall than impacting a flimsy magical membrane. The strength of Miles' magic pulsed around them—the amount he'd put into that shield was nothing short of extraordinary.

The nandibear staggered to its feet after its brutal collision with Miles' shield.

Oatmeal charged.

Inspired by videos of grizzly bears fighting in Alaska, Esme moved Oatmeal like one. The two giants reared up in the air, claws outstretched, fangs bared, seeking the vulnerable area at the front of the neck, eyes, or really anywhere either could dig into. The ruthlessness, the savagery of Esme's thoughts didn't matter to her when her demon side was seeking vengeance.

Off to the side, Finn screamed, letting loose a torrent of flames. The leprechaun was barely visible beneath the swarm of winged creatures, their black bodies forming a cloak of death around him. Fear intensified the already potent cocktail of emotions churning inside Esme.

Unbidden infernal power snuck through the cracks of her defenses and flowed through her into her conjuration, feeding Oatmeal with a surge of pure dark energy. If she didn't pull it back, she'd lose control...

Enveloped in golden light, Miles created a shield to repel the bats encircling Finn.

"No more!" Esme cried through the blood and magic pounding in her ears. Something told her Miles' unprecedented display of power when he'd mist walked had caused both malevolent incidents, even if she couldn't explain why. To her relief, no new prison failed this time.

Her momentary distraction allowed a bit of that unbidden infernal influence to sneak its way through Esme's connection to her conjuration. Whip-like tentacles emerged from Oatmeal's back. The demonic tendrils ensnared the malevolent.

The temptation to surrender fully to the power coursing through her conjuration was almost overwhelming. The force wanted her to sink down into Oatmeal—to lose herself. It wanted to take control. Esme fought it tooth and nail, wrestling control of her magic and her sanity even as her fury pulsed with the desire to rip and tear.

Her sword.

Holding it had helped her maintain her sanity at the Solstice Gala fight. Esme summoned it once more as Miles sprinted across the snow, daggers in hand, to reach Finn. He made it barely ten feet in that direction before a geyser of fire burst from the tangle of bats. The shield he'd put on Finn must have failed. The heat singed the air, brushing Esme's cheeks from where she stood twenty feet away, fighting against her inner demon while maintaining control of her conjuration.

The explosion distracted the nandibear long enough for Oatmeal to sink her fangs deep into the malevolent's neck. Miles had fallen in the snow due to his proximity to the explosion, and now he was slowly rising, beginning his recovery. He was unhurt, and the radiance that had surrounded him had fizzled out completely.

The bats surrounding Finn plummeted from the sky, consumed by the flames of Finn's detonation. With the nandibear now quieted from its continued struggle with Oatmeal, the plop plop plop sound of their little bodies hitting the snow sounded like a cloudburst splattering upon the snow.

Oatmeal held the malevolent pinned to the snow, but the nandibear's scratching claws were damaging the shadowcat to the point that Oatmeal was nearing collapse. Feeling she had no other option, Esme turned her back on Finn, now lying motionless in the snow.

She needed to finish this.

The nandibear thrashed, heedless of the fangs ripping its neck with every movement, as Esme drew closer to the battling creatures. Perhaps it sensed the greater threat posed by another living, breathing predator, unlike the conjuration it had been fighting before.

Like the snow crunching under her boots, Esme's sympathy had hardened from being trampled on. After hearing Jacob's tale of her parents' last night alive, she'd researched this type of malevolent extensively. So much so that their snarling faces invaded her dreams.

Her sword shimmered, then solidified into an axe, its surprisingly light weight a welcome feeling. She spread her legs wide for balance and repeated a move she'd seen Miles do once before—not that she was actually doing much thinking just then.

As Oatmeal struggled to hold the malevolent in place, Esme arched up. The conjured ax fell onto the bear's neck in a merciless strike, imbued with magical strength, that landed a split second after her shadowcat disappeared.

A dark red gush of blood pulsed weakly around her weapon, splattering onto the ground and her boots. And just like that, Esme was clearheaded again.

Gods below, she had almost lost her mind—and she'd known *all along* that her sanity was trying to slip away.

When she looked back up, Miles was bent over where Finn had been when he'd gone nuclear. She dismissed her axe and ran as fast as her snowshoes would allow to reach his side.

Finn's explosion had burned a depression in the snow all around him. Miles pulled him out of it and laid him out on a foil emergency blanket. Nearby, open chemical heat packs hissed faintly as they oxidized, preparing to warm the leprechaun's body.

Half of the tattered remnants of Finn's clothes were lying in the snow depression; the other half barely clung to his skin in places. The leprechaun was practically naked.

Yet he looked entirely unharmed, not burned at all.

Esme asked, "Magic exhaustion?"

"Yep," Miles replied. "He's going to be fine."

"Then brag about this incessantly," Esme added, trying to smile. Not wanting to look at his... *parts* anymore, she ripped the scarf off from around her neck and handed it to Miles. "I'm not touching him while he's naked. Please cover... all of... *that.*"

A sound close to laughter escaped the man who'd saved her life—twice in a span of less than ten minutes. "Thank you. This imp seems to have nine lives."

"The People will help the bodies return to nature if I send them a message," he mumbled as he worked.

The way Miles moved, heavy and slow, made her worry.

Wanting to help ease his burden, she offered, "I can have a troll carry Finn back to the cabin. Just keep him wrapped up in the scarf. He should be fine with how hot he runs."

The cabin wasn't far, only two miles away. Bert, her head troll, trudged ahead of them, heedless of the cold and snow that he sank into with each step. As usual after a fight, Miles retreated into a brooding silence.

The image of the dead bear and sixty oversized bats, their wings spread across the pristine white snow, was so vivid in the silence it triggered a wave of nausea. Both Esme and Bert momentarily paused, waiting for the feeling to pass.

While she struggled, bent over, stomach heaving, a firm hand caressed her back. Miles never pushed, but he said her favorite line: "I'm here, lovely."

That creature, or at least one like it, had been responsible for the death of her parents. Haunting memories of their demise kept a firm grip on her thoughts, refusing to release her from their torment.

"Gods, *fuck*, Miles, please talk to me about something." She spit out the taste of bile from her mouth onto the fresh snow.

"Well." He scratched at his beard with his gloved prosthetic hand. In single-digit temperatures, it was important that he prevent it from freezing. "I think the things that attacked Finn were Minyadian bats because they were too small for Camazotz."

"Cam-what?"

"South American death bats—very nasty. Minyadian bats are smaller, less vicious. The Corded Brotherhood has multiple records of them spawning in groups."

Knowing her passion for malevolent lore, he used it as the perfect lure to get her moving again. "So you're saying we were lucky?"

Beside her, Miles shrugged his big shoulders. "In that respect, yes. But two prisons failing right on top of us? Not so lucky."

"Yeah... about that. Babe, I think *you* caused that."

Miles paused mid-step, placing his snowshoe down as gently as his shock would allow it. The hair peeking out from underneath his beanie was as unruly as usual, even while he fought to keep his expression in check.

He mumbled, "Fuck," his lip caught between his teeth and his eyes averted.

"Babe, you mist walked—twice. Once carrying me. When did you learn how to do that? Miles, that's like... a lost art, according to Jacob. He can't even do it reliably. That's when both the prisons failed."

Frozen in place, Miles gave the slightest nod.

The impossibilities of what had happened tumbled from her lips, each word a fresh wave of disbelief. "And the magic you poured into maintaining that aegis... That was also insane."

Their eyes locked for a second, and she read the fear reflected in his pupils.

"Miles, you were also glowing again. Just like at the Gala and when you fought the ogre. You are consistently a marvel to me, but, babe, what is going on?"

He murmured his favorite curse word again, this time on an exhale. As if that last expletive had unlocked something within him, his feet started moving. "I don't know."

Finn woke up not long after they arrived back at the cabin. He didn't seem the least bit concerned about his nakedness. So she and Miles reheated their leftovers while he got dressed. They settled in for an early, unusually quiet meal. The car ride home was just as silent, but Esme couldn't shake the feeling that both men were hiding something from her—again.

To be fair, she hadn't mentioned her realization either. The uncanny parallel between her conjuration magic, which itself tore through reality, and the malevolent prisons freeing their captives was impossible to overlook. The obviousness of the connection was deeply troubling and worth thinking on...

Chapter Fifteen

SCHEMING

"*Come on*," Leon said, voice low and coaxing. "You know our kind should be together. We're reckless and troublesome when we get too lonely."

He let the words settle, calm and easy, like bait in a placid lake. He hadn't expected this game to be so satisfying, not after everything, but it was turning out better than he could've hoped. Toying with Nudd had been amusing. This, though. This was purpose. A millennia-old goal finally within reach, all because David Abington thought himself clever.

David almost failed at controlling the corner of his lip from sneering upward in disgust. That disgust wasn't for Leon. It was for the demon blood they shared. It was the truth David buried beneath tailored suits and eloquent politics. A truth he hated most when it stared back at him with eyes just like his own.

Unlike David, Leon had never been ashamed of who he was. He was power. He took power. That was what their kind did best.

Leon felt a surge of triumphant glee at David's invitation into his warded private space, though he masked his excitement with an air of casual disinterest—a predator patient at the threshold. It was almost too easy, watching the mage lower his guard, unaware that the tables had already turned. Leon waited as David released the ward of protection guarding his threshold. Recognized, memorized, and mapped in his mind so the next time Leon encountered the ward, he could snap its bindings without relying on his store of borrowed power.

They were finally at the point that David was desperate enough to trust Leon this far. David thought he was being clever, thought he was using Leon to solve his Esmeralda problem without getting his own hands dirty. But the truth? The arrogant mage, for all his money and power, was utterly blind to the fact that the power dynamic had never actually been in his favor.

Leon offered him a slow smile, not too wide. "I could tell from our conversation at the bar that you didn't like your golden boy being with her. So give her a valid alternative." He gestured to himself, as if that was explanation enough. "She and I already have a rapport. She's powerful. Don't let that go to waste."

David's gaze sharpened, but there was a hesitation, an uncertainty behind it. Leon could almost hear him calculating, grasping at angles he didn't fully understand. It must've been maddening for a man like that, to realize something was slipping out of his control and not know how or when it had started.

David probably thought he was being intimidating, but Leon had stared down far more dangerous men. David was no predator. He was a well-dressed opportunist, grasping at power he barely understood. Weak.

Leon supplemented his words with a suggestive gaze. "I am more than willing to have her as my partner," he said, his voice velvet-smooth.

David's nose scrunched up fractionally once again. Leon had the power to make this man reveal the reason for his hatred, but he didn't care to explore his thoughts again—especially when a few persuasive words could achieve their shared goal.

David was the first siphon that Leon had met in his long life. He was not as powerful as Leon had initially thought, weak-blooded, but still fascinating. While they shared a common desire to take from Miles, they had contrasting strategies and end dates.

David studied Leon for a long moment. "We do have a pressing concern that could use the proper type of pressure applied..."

Leon clapped his hands, grinning widely for the show. "Perfect! No time like the present, right?"

If he played his cards right, Leon could set up this job to force Esme to try harnessing malevolent magic through an infernal conduit. That untapped magic called to him like a siren song. Esme was simply a means to an end. Her trust, her safety, her very soul if it came down to it were all acceptable collateral damage in his pursuit. She was a vessel. An offering. A weapon. He'd use her the same way he'd used Nudd.

In Leon's world, it all boiled down to two kinds of people: him and the exploited.

Chapter Sixteen

MEETING THE PARENTS

Esme

"Miles Rhun Goodwin, you are doing nothing today, nothing!" Esme pointed her finger at him as he rose.

He moaned loudly, acting like the giant baby he truly was, and sat back down on her couch.

"Well, nothing besides that video call we have with your parents in like five minutes. Gods, do I look alright?"

"Yes, lovely, I already told you that five times." He mumbled, "Which might have something to do with the reason I was getting up to help you," probably thinking that she couldn't hear him over the sound of the exhaust fan running in the kitchen.

She could. But she had to admit to herself that she was quite enjoying this snarky side he was revealing for the first time. "Surely there's some British Christmas special to keep you still for five minutes. No magic. Rest!"

Esme's worry about his excessive use of magic and how battered his body had become over the past week made her act a bit like a mother hen. He'd gone from battling jorōgumo and using magic to repel their venom from his body, to healing Abby's fractured leg, to defeating an ogre all on his own, to tapping into abilities he didn't even know he had with minimal rest in between. In her mind, instead of grumbling about being bored, he needed to transform into a complete couch potato immediately.

Anticipating Finn's arrival for dinner later, she had gone above and beyond, cooking an extravagant feast for the three of them. It would be a day of firsts. Despite being thirty-two years old, Esme had never had the opportunity to enjoy a holiday dinner with a boyfriend or meet her significant other's parents. Her clandestine work for the Assembly for the past decade had made getting too close to anyone far too difficult.

Relenting the slightest bit, she shouted back across the house, "Fine! You can get the laptop ready. I need to pull a few things off of the burners."

"Already did!" He sounded positively gleeful at ignoring her protestations at him moving whatsoever.

She looked at the clock on her stovetop and cursed under her breath. At this point, she'd have to dip out of the video call for a few minutes to check on her cooking. Being careful not to muss her hair, she stripped off her apron and joined Miles on the couch.

"You ready?" he asked.

Esme took a deep breath and nodded. "Let's do this."

"Dad will love you immediately. Mam will be reserved but not judgmental."

"So you say," Esme grumbled.

Miles reached out, his fingers brushing against hers as he searched for her hand. Finally finding it, he gave it a gentle squeeze before planting a soft kiss on her cheek. "It's going to be okay, lovely," he whispered. As he leaned back, he clicked the call accept button.

Two faces she'd only seen on his phone screen smiled and greeted her. She searched for resemblances between them and their son, but they were scarce. His hair color mirrored that of his mother, and his eyes were an exact match to his father's, but the rest... he could be adopted. Was this the working of the magic that he'd been blessed with? Had it gone to the extent of completely overriding his DNA?

They made polite small talk, the kind that was rehearsed but necessary. His parents informed him about recent developments at home, the weather, neighbors, work. He reciprocated by sharing details about his office and his fondness for his new house. They asked about her work and hobbies. Everything went smoothly until Esme had to pull a few things out of the oven.

When the timer went off, she excused herself, grateful for the brief escape. That was when the covert exchange began.

James, his father, whispered first, "Good job, lad; she's a looker!"

That brought a smile to her face as she moved one dish from the top rack of the oven to the bottom. However, that smile began to fade when Ann, his mother, spoke. "David called us, Miles. We're concerned."

Esme froze, one hand holding a popover pan while the other moved the roast aside. She strained her hearing.

"Oh, c'mon, Ann, this isn't our business!" James' attempt at deflection didn't seem strong enough.

Ann pressed on, her tone sharper. "But he hasn't called us in years. So I'm taking what he said seriously. He says you're missing work for this girl. I'm sure she's lovely but... darling, really?"

The silence that followed was louder than anything before it. Esme waited for Miles to respond, to set things right.

After what seemed like an eternity, he sighed. "Mam, I've missed work because I've caught cold and because I've helped out a bit with the Assembly. I don't know what David is on about."

Miles' parents were ignorant of his Corded Brotherhood involvement. They didn't know that their son was on the front lines in the fight against the returning malevolents. His only option was to skirt around the truth.

"Well, he said Esme..." Ann started again.

"Ann, let it go," James interjected, his voice strained.

His mother soldiered on. "He said that girl isn't good for you. That she has a questionable past and is only interested in money."

Was that really how they saw her? Just a gold digger? The words burned more than she wanted to admit.

By mutual agreement, mainly on Esme's insistence, she and Miles weren't going to exchange presents for Christmas. It wasn't that she didn't enjoy the tradition; it was that she was flat-out broke. Which was only the case because David had fired her. Trying to turn his parents against her was another level of whatever game he was playing.

She listened, her cambion hearing suddenly a curse. The sound of Miles shifting on the couch was unmistakable. He cleared his throat, but still, the words she needed from him didn't come.

"Mam, he doesn't know her like I do. She's…" He trailed off. Another long pause.

Defend me. Say something.

But there was only silence. He was usually so eloquent. Why not for her?

Ann's voice cut through it, though softer now. "I'm just looking out for you, love. We worry."

Esme stood frozen, unable to return to the screen. Should she pretend like she hadn't heard a thing? Should she re-enter the room, smiling as if nothing had changed in the last five minutes?

She closed the oven and set it to keep the food warm, her hands shaking slightly. She plastered on a fake smile and headed back to the living room in time for the conversation to fall back into awkward pleasantries.

She slid beside him, her gaze meeting his briefly, searching for reassurance, for something more than that weak defense he'd given. But all she got was his forced smile and a quick squeeze of her hand.

It wasn't enough. If he couldn't stand up for her now, what did that mean for them in the long term?

CHAPTER SEVENTEEN

DANGER AT THE DOOR

Esme

Esme didn't want their first holiday break together marred by an argument, so she ignored her hurt feelings over Ann's comments and continued on that afternoon as if nothing had happened. She knew bottling up her emotions would come to bite her in the ass at some point, but she didn't expect it to be already in the making.

Their fight against the malevolents over the past few months had been so time-consuming that everyone had a to-do list a mile long.

With Jacob still abroad, Miles was spending a couple of hours at Assembly headquarters completing paperwork for the Corded Brotherhood. Abby was working that day so she and Gwyn could go off on their own little adventure on the coast the next morning. And Esme had her own work to catch up on. Since the bar was closed and she was religiously avoiding doing inventory there, Esme was catching up on the housecleaning she'd neglected for far too long.

Just as she began scrubbing the soap ring on her tub, the doorbell rang.

Esme opened the door expecting a package or her neighbor asking about Mr. Snuffles again, only to find David and Leon, framed by the cold gray winter and a waiting taxi outside. She tried to play it cool. She really did. Except the words that escaped her lips were, "What in the nine hells are you two doing at my house on Boxing Day?"

"Well, hello to you too, Ms. Turner. Manners." David was as haughty as ever. "I didn't think you Americans celebrated the holiday." He wasn't wearing a formal suit jacket for once. But she could see that he still had a vest on under his woolen peacoat.

Esme felt her eyes narrow, considered stopping herself, but really, what did she have to lose at this point? Face? The thought made her want to laugh. "Oh, right, *manners,* like notifying your employee that they've been terminated. Unless that's what this is. In which case, why do you need the punk standing next to you?"

Leon's restless fidgeting betrayed his struggle to contain his laughter, like he was barely keeping it together. He recognized she was calling him out with that last line, but he found it amusing rather than insulting. Leon wore comfortable tennis shoes, black jeans, and a navy-blue jacket, but oddly enough, the glasses she'd come to associate with him were gone.

David answered, "I'm actually here to offer your job back, Ms. Turner. The Assembly has encountered an issue where your particular skill set could be of use," completely ignoring her question.

"That answers why you're here. But him?"

Leon grinned. It was brilliant enough to make the corners of her mouth drift upward.

"Your partner. There is also a sizeable bonus included with the task."

The word "bonus" jolted Esme, the meager sum in her bank account flashing before her eyes. Being principled was a luxury she simply couldn't afford. It wasn't like she had to let down her guard around him...

"I'm kind of in the middle of something here." She was still wearing the rubber gloves she used for cleaning. She certainly did not plan on inviting them in for a chat—especially not David.

David's response to this escaped on a sigh. "Well, Mr. Chan can explain the particulars, Ms. Turner. Your stipend should already be in your account. Merry Christmas."

Leon, equally surprised by David's sudden exit, remained after his departure.

Once David was back in his taxi, Esme asked, "Why are you so buddy-buddy with him now?"

Leon shrugged. "We want similar things."

Her arms crossed, Esme prepared herself for another round of diversion or smooth-talking. "Oh, yeah, and what is that?"

"An end to the malevolent problems."

More magic words. Esme could feel herself caving already. She really needed the money. It also didn't help that Leon's smile was genuine, for once.

It didn't hurt to find out what this was all about. "So, what's the job?"

"There's a nisse clan war going on south of downtown. Knowing nisse, it is probably over something silly, but it is causing enough problems that they want to bring in an impartial mediator."

Everything was coming together in her mind now. "And that would be me?"

"You are correct." Leon's grin morphed into a smirk. "Plus, they all know you or of you. I'm the one who's supposed to be the bad cop."

Esme snorted. "Is David aware that I can handle this job on my own?"

Leon shrugged, not denying her assertion. "I think he's trying me out for a more permanent role."

A grim expression settled on her face, making any attempt to hide her emotions useless. "I thought you only did contract killings."

Her feelings for Leon were a chaotic mess, making any conversation with him incredibly confusing. There was something about him that both repelled and attracted her. When she least expected it, her hatred for him would unexpectedly give way to a compelling curiosity about his seemingly endless trove of knowledge. What kind of person did that make her? Too forgiving or gullible?

Leon's expression turned serious. "Look... I know you're still upset. I'm sorry for the hurt my actions caused you. I thought I was doing the right thing. Maybe I wasn't."

They looked at each other for a long moment, appraising, wondering.

"So, what do you say, partner?" Leon's cheer was infectious.

Esme narrowed her eyes. "Just how big is this bonus?"

The light teasing she'd done unconsciously bothered her. Was her behavior crossing the line from friendly banter into flirting? That wasn't what she wanted at all.

Leon chuckled, rocking back on his heels. "Bigger than usual, I suspect. David wants to have nothing to do with this one. I don't know why. But it will probably be a nice cushion to pad the wallet after all that Christmas shopping."

Yeah, because she'd been able to do a ton of that. She rolled her eyes, but she couldn't deny her interest. "Fine. But while you're here..." Esme glanced away, hesitating. "Can I ask you something about the whole cambion thing?"

Leon shrugged. "Happy to help."

With so many questions buzzing in her head, she couldn't decide which to ask first. The last thing she wanted was him in her house, but Esme figured she could chat with him on the porch. "Want to sit down?" she asked, pointing to the swing that her father had made for her mother, its worn paint chipped and faded from years of sitting outside. "While I grab a jacket?"

She ripped off her cleaning gloves and snatched her jacket from the coatrack in a flash. Though she was inclined to befriend everyone, she had to remind herself that he was not and should not be her friend. Her years working at the bar gave her the skills to turn this fact-finding mission into a casual conversation.

Esme sat down next to him on the swing. "Thanks for agreeing to chat."

Her voice was cautious, almost tentative, as she explained, "Miles and I fought a malevolent yesterday. It, uh... brought up a lot of memories. And I really don't have anyone to talk to about this stuff."

"You've got me," Leon said as he turned to face her, his arm stretching across the back of the bench.

"You're really going all out with this performance, aren't you? What's the point of this flirting act? Seriously, cut the crap." Her glare could have frozen hell itself. She deliberately moved farther away on the bench, creating a physical barrier to reinforce her verbal boundary.

"Sorry," he said, not looking the least bit shamefaced. "Oh, I'm genuinely flirting. Not sure why you'd doubt that."

"I'm involved with someone. *Stop it*. We don't have to do this nisse job together, and we don't have to have this conversation, either. You can either take me as a friend or walk away," she said firmly. She added a shooing gesture to emphasize her demand.

Leon's brilliant smile faded, giving way to a softer one. He leaned forward, resting his elbows on his knees. "I'll take you any way I can get you."

With a dramatic roll of her eyes and a heavy sigh, Esme resigned herself to ignoring his behavior as long as it remained innocent.

"So, what about this malevolent hunt makes you want to talk to me?"

"My parents both died fighting the same type of malevolent we killed."

Leon raised his eyebrows at that. "Did you go into a Nergalian berserker rage again, like at the Gala?"

Her anger flared. "So you watched us and you did nothing?"

"I was kind of busy with my own malevolent at the time..."

Esme forced herself to step back from yet another conversation about Sylas. Sitting up straighter, she concentrated instead on what he might have hinted at. "Wait, are you Nergalian too?"

A sharp intake of breath, punctuated by the hiss of air through his teeth, reached her ears. "Nope," he said, offering no additional information.

"My friend is a succubus. She says she can't tap into the infernal realm for power like I can. Can you? Can other cambion?"

"I think the type of cambion you are and how much demon ancestry you have will influence that. If she's a succubus, she doesn't have to tap into the infernal because it's always open to her... just differently. Chances are you're less human than she is, anyway." He was tense as he answered her other question. "And, yes, I can open a conduit to the infernal."

So that was what her connection to the infernal was called—a *conduit*. Esme added cheekily, "Before you ask, I am not introducing you to her."

With a gesture of refusal, he replied, "Not my type."

"She's literally everyone's type," Esme said, disbelieving, "Anyway..."

She took a deep breath, glancing past him at the bare trees lining her street, their branches stark against the gray December sky. She was reluctant to share her next thought for fear it would sound insane. But, then again, Leon was exceptionally abnormal. "Sometimes, when I'm angry, it feels like the infernal pushes at me, like it wants to call the shots. Have you ever experienced that?"

Raising his eyebrows slightly, Leon offered a tight, almost strained smile. "It used to be hard to control, but it's easier now. These days, I rely on general magic more frequently than infernal. Mages who rely too much or too often on the infernal often lose the fight against it. But I've seen you pull back from a rage. I'd say you're doing alright, lovely."

"That's the second time you've called me that. Stop," Esme snapped back. She *almost* felt sorry seeing his face fall, especially since he was being so honest. "What are the risks of relying on it too much?"

Leon shrugged. "You lose all sense of who is friend and who is foe, killing anyone in your path. Maybe rip a few limbs off."

"That was... very specific."

"Yep." The sharp edge in his voice, something she hadn't heard from him before, and the single chilling glance from him effectively silenced any further questions she might have had on the topic. She quickly steered the conversation in a different direction.

"Thanks for being so forthright. I realize talking to me is optional for you. Sorry about being snappish."

She crossed her arms, leaned back, and attempted to recapture her earlier comfort. "Back to my parents. They were experimenting with infernal magic to see if they could control malevolents. You and Gwyn clearly understand magic better than us modern folks. Do you have any thoughts on what they might have been working on?"

"No—" Leon shook his head slowly, a thoughtful frown furrowing his brow. "Not yet, but I think I can see where they were going with the idea..."

Esme said, "Something about how malevolent magic is an offshoot of infernal magic. Like because Fae magic stems from general magic, the rules of general magic take precedence over it."

"Right..." Leon rapped a familiar tune on the bench, but she couldn't quite remember where she'd heard it before. "Controlling malevolent magic would be extremely useful. I'd be happy to help you explore the power in whatever way I can."

Shifting, he crossed his arms. A feather-light touch, barely a graze on her neck, left a lingering warmth in its wake—so subtle it might have been a figment of her imagination.

"Oops, sorry," he murmured, eyes betraying nothing.

She nodded, biting her lip. It wasn't the answer she'd wanted, but talking about it with someone who seemed to understand was suddenly a monumental relief. An unusual warmth bloomed in her chest as he spoke, melting her defenses in a way that ought to have concerned her yet didn't.

"Look, Esme." Leon exhaled and waited until he was certain that he had her full attention. "Being what we are can be hard. It means always being different. It means being judged and sometimes shunned."

He scooted fractionally closer to her, and for some reason, she let him. "They think that they're better than us, but the exact opposite is true. You. Me. We, *we* make them nervous."

A spark of something more pleasant than fear curled inside her—understanding, perhaps even an odd sense of camaraderie with him. Leon's every word seemed to sharpen her frustration with Miles, turning her general unease into something akin to resentment.

She asked, "So how do you reconcile... everything?"

Leon tilted his head, seeming to weigh his answer carefully. "The modern equivalent of what I do is raising my middle finger in the air."

She cleared her throat and said, "I think I get that."

Back when she had been feeling unjustly blamed for the fate of Philip Luis and Maureen after the pishacha, she'd wanted to give all of her critics the finger.

A playful smile curved her lips. "Just so you know, though, if this whole 'working together' thing doesn't work out, I'm fully prepared to blame you for everything."

Leon's laugh, a warm, genuine sound, seemed to chase away the winter chill. "Duly noted. But you know, I think we could really work well together."

"Maybe," she conceded, though her grin widened. "Now get off my porch."

Chapter Eighteen

History Repeats Itself

Esme

When Miles got home, he was overjoyed to hear David had been by and offered her position again. The only hitch was that she neglected to mention Leon's involvement.

It wasn't that she was listening to the little demon on her shoulder, precisely. It was that she'd spent the rest of the day doing a desperate calculation. Either Esme did the job for David or she put her homeowner's insurance bill that month on her credit card. _No way_; that simply would not happen.

Plus, she was determined to buy Miles a late Christmas gift as a surprise. Because even though they'd talked about it, Miles beat her to it. To "save him from freezing in his own bed," he gifted her fuzzy socks and a matching robe to keep at his house, a set of fleece pajamas, and a new forearm holster for her dagger that matched his own since she'd complained about hers itching.

The gifts sounded small, but they weren't inexpensive. Which reminded her of Ann's private comments during their video chat, the ones she thought Esme hadn't overheard. Esme supported herself well enough, but she'd been unexpectedly let go from her job without pay. Her credit score was perfect, damn it! She'd mostly gotten over how Miles hadn't defended her enough to his parents, putting it down to nerves.

Unfortunately for Esme, "mostly" wasn't nearly enough. The hurt was still there, dulled but not gone. She wasn't sure it ever would be unless something changed.

True to form, this led Esme to being on the verge of ruining another perfect evening. Except this time, she was determined to handle it properly. They'd built this relationship brick by brick, and even if the foundation sometimes showed strain, Esme wasn't ready to abandon it over a few cracks.

The warmth of the dinner they'd shared earlier lingered, but her mind was a jumble of unsettled thoughts. The fire he'd set for them crackled softly, casting flickering shadows across her living room walls. On the couch, Esme leaned into Miles' chest, her head resting just under his chin.

Esme tilted her head, looking up at him with a faint smile. "It's been a day. We should talk about the video call with your parents. How do you think I did?"

"You were great," Miles said, pressing a kiss to her temple.

She gave a small, humorless laugh. "Oh, I don't know. Something about your mom basically calling me a gold digger gave me a completely different impression."

Miles tensed beneath her, his arms tightening slightly. He held her one-handed as his prosthesis charged. Was he trying to keep her from running again? He sighed, heavy and slow. "I didn't know what to say, lovely."

Esme traced her finger along the seam of the blanket draped over them, her voice light but unmistakably laced with hurt. "But you're always so good with words. Always."

Esme knew what others thought of her—a demon-blooded bitch when angry. But in moments like these, when she was hurt and not looking for a fight, she became a sullen, mopey creature.

Anxious, he held her too tightly; his arms were like bands of steel.

She tapped out. "Careful, babe, you're gonna suffocate me with all this affection. Then who's gonna put up with your overprotective streak? Maybe we should hit the gym if you're looking to practice grappling."

"Sorry..." He loosened his grip immediately. "It's just... I honestly don't let them in on much in my day-to-day life. They barely know what I do professionally. And they act like David makes the sun rise every morning. Esme, I'm sorry. I didn't want to make things worse."

"Worse for who?" A single ember of her fighting spirit flared to life. She moved to sit across from him now, needing to see his face clearly. "Me? Because, Miles, I can promise you, nothing feels worse than sitting there while someone insults you and your boyfriend says nothing."

Miles nodded, his expression pained. "You're right," he admitted, his voice gravelly and low for how close they were. "I should've said more. I screwed up—again. I guess I was also afraid of making things with David worse. I just... David complicates things."

In any other relationship, she would relish the feeling of triumph of being told she was right. But in this one, she was learning that wouldn't help. Though it was the right thing to do, she despised the bitter taste of self-advocacy, the way it left a burning residue in her throat every time.

"David complicates everything, apparently." She met his eyes, searching. "Is there something else going on?"

Miles' jaw tightened. "This job offer of his—I don't trust it. Be careful. It could be completely innocent, or it could be his way of creating trouble between us."

Esme gently withdrew her hand from his, the gesture as significant as any words. "You see? That's exactly what I mean. You're consumed with David's potential schemes, but when your mother practically called me a gold digger thanks to his meddling, you sat there silent."

Her impromptu speech, for better or worse, had gained momentum. "I get that David holds power over you, and I get that you don't want to start a mess with your family, but you didn't just let them insult me—you let them insult us. And if you don't draw a line somewhere, it won't stop.

"You know," Esme added, voice steadier now, "whenever Jacob oversteps or I find out that he's lied to me, I confront him. Directly. I call him on his bullshit."

Miles blinked, surprised by the shift.

"And you never do that with David. You maneuver around him, but you never actually confront him about his behavior. You can face down a damned *ogre* while you're armed with a chef's knife and a pot lid but can't confront your old mentor." Esme's voice gained conviction. "Maybe before we talk about us again, you should talk to him about interfering in your personal life. About using me to get to you."

Esme scooted over, increasing the distance between them. "You need to establish boundaries with him the same way I do with Jacob. Otherwise, we'll see this pattern repeat itself."

Miles ran a hand through his hair, considering her words. "I don't know if that would work with David—"

"Maybe not. But at least you'd be addressing the actual problem instead of dancing around it." Esme's eyes softened. "So here's the deal, babe. I need you to figure this out. Not for me, but for you. And until you do... I think we, I, need some space."

Miles flinched, but he didn't argue. "For what it's worth, I do see your point," he murmured, standing. "I'll handle it. Please don't give up on me, Esme."

As Miles stepped outside, he turned back. "Esme? Just... be careful with Leon. There's something not right about him. I can't explain it, but—"

"I'll be fine." Her half-smile held a gentle finality. "I've been taking care of myself for a long time."

After he left, Esme closed the door and pressed her forehead against the cool wood. Without him, this house was overwhelmingly spacious and lonely. She hated the distance between them already, but she knew this was the right call. If Miles wanted to be with her, really be with her, he needed to end his power struggle with David.

Miles

Fuck.

Chapter Nineteen

West Coast, Be(a)st Coast

Gwyn

"The weather is seriously foul on the coast this time of year, but I hope that the two things I'm surprising you with will make up for it." There was a distinct mismatch between Abigail's cheerfulness and her words. Despite his complete trust in Abby, Gwyn experienced a rare moment of hesitation.

"I had to threaten Finn so he wouldn't try hiding in the trunk." Abigail laughed as she steered off the highway. "I'll admit their trip inspired me for this one. Also, I wanted to talk with Josiah in person about what happened to my mom. So this is a Christmas present for you with a side mission for me."

"For Christi, anything," Gwyn replied, the truth of it settling in his chest like an oath. Witnessing her fierce, protective maternal love had rekindled something long asleep inside him.

"And only you, Cariad," he murmured, "could convince me that happiness exists while I drown in misery. So, what are we doing?"

The monotony of the road had lulled Cerys to sleep hours ago, sprawled out to cover the entire back seat. The endless trees, reaching up to the sky like green skyscrapers, had been their constant companion as they drove westward.

Even though she'd done all the packing for the trip, he'd still peeked into the boot of the car to see that his crossbow and sword were within. He didn't usually carry them around, so it was clear she had a plan that involved hunting. Miles' borrowed waterproof clothes also filled his bag in the car's trunk. Abby must have asked him for the favor without Gwyn hearing about it. Gwyn, she knew, would rather use all his Corded Brotherhood earnings before borrowing another scrap of clothing from Miles.

If that came to pass, Gwyn had at least become used to living in poverty in the months before he'd moved to Seattle. He was glad that Abby hadn't witnessed how clumsy his initial fall from grace had been. His princely pride and arrogance had withered away over the past year. He found a surprising sense of freedom in a world that placed little value on one's prowess in battle or honor. It didn't matter that he wasn't Gwyn ap Nudd anymore. Being Gwyn Newman was enough.

She grinned. "I have two questions. I think I know the answer, but just in case. Can you ride a horse?"

His eyebrows shot up in surprise. "Of course."

"Good. Josiah says he has a single Icelandic pony he adopted a few years ago for when they need to move around in the winter. They're a bit smaller than modern horses, still really strong, but maybe more the size you're used to?"

Gwyn had only seen a few horses since his reemergence into modern times, and even then, they were always in the distance. "Horses are larger now? I noticed the sheep are larger..."

"Oh, yes. Search for Shire horses on your phone to see what I'm talking about. They're the biggest, but pretty much all breeds are larger than they used to be, thanks to selective breeding."

"The humans are larger, too. Is that also selective breeding?"

Despite his seriousness, Abigail let out a gentle laugh. "If that was true, I was definitely left out of the scheme. No, that's because of better nutrition."

The images of a thousand starved faces, cheeks sunken in and eyes barely animate, flashed before Gwyn's mind's eye. He refused to allow the barely remembered pain of his past to overshadow their present joy. His depression and trauma wouldn't hold sway over his life if he could help it. Abigail had said that his mood disorder could be alleviated with medication, but the idea was so utterly foreign to him that he had trouble accepting it. With him being fifteen, maybe sixteen centuries out of sync, his core identity and understanding of mental health was behind the times.

Gwyn eventually managed, "Yes... nutrition. The second question?"

The wind and rain combined forces outside the windshield, creating a sideways downpour as Abby concentrated solely on the road. For the next minute, the only sounds were the GPS directions from her phone and the rhythmic clicking of the turn signal. Turning the car onto an overgrown dirt and gravel driveway, she finally responded to his earlier question. "Are you up for a malevolent hunt in this glorious weather?"

"What are we hunting?" The familiar thrill of the chase stirred in his blood, gratification warming him at having correctly guessed her intentions.

"We?" The sound of Abigail's laughter filled the car as the driveway's sudden right turn brought a quaint cabin into view through the dense trees. "Oh, no, this is a 'Gwyn does the whole manly thing and hunts the big bad all alone' trip. I'm meeting with Josiah while you're out. Plus, Miles says I should still limit how much I walk. Don't fret; you won't starve, because I have a trunk full of groceries to make meals while you're out."

As she put the car in park, her eyes searched his. "Did I seriously screw this up? You've told me so many stories about hunting and the things you used to do that I thought this would be a fitting Christmas present."

Clearly overcome by uncertainty, she started chattering. "This seemed like the perfect moment to let you experience that feeling again. Especially because it comes with a Corded Brotherhood bonus check at the end. Plus, you can use magic freely because basically no one is around."

A hunt and money? He couldn't think of a better Christmas present. Worry creased lines into Abby's forehead as her eyes scanned his face. Gwyn reached out a hand and tenderly stroked her cheek, and, blessedly, she leaned into the contact.

Gwyn took that as permission to lean in, whispering, "It's excellent," before kissing the most perfect woman. The woman he'd been lucky enough to get to meet for the first time twice.

Before they could finish unloading their bags, a tall Native American man, perhaps in his early fifties, emerged from the trees, leading a horse by the reins. Josiah walked sedately, seemingly unfazed by the rain falling around him wildly and the freezing mud squelching into his sandals as he approached.

With two overflowing packs already straining his grip, Gwyn had to brace himself as Abigail thrust her third bag into his hands.

Gwyn nodded a greeting. They had met earlier when he'd presented Cerys to the seated Assembly members during their last meeting. Josiah's face, deeply etched with the lines of a life well-lived, held a gentle kindness, a faint smirk playing on his lips that spoke of a man who knew his appearance was out of place but had stopped caring a long time ago.

In contrast to Abigail's description of a small Icelandic pony, the horse Josiah led was a giant. The massive black stallion stood at least a foot taller than any horse Gwyn had ever ridden. Its powerful muscles rippled with each step. Captivated, Gwyn hardly felt the weight of the bags as he stared.

"Abby-girl! Nice to see you." They hugged like old friends. Gwyn finally realized why Josiah seemed so unperturbed by the weather—it touched neither man nor horse. He was powerful.

Gwyn rushed to put the bags on the cabin's front porch as Abby and Josiah followed.

"Unfortunately, the pony I promised is down with something," Josiah explained, patting the stallion's neck. "So I've brought the big oaf instead. Meet Agent Shadow." He chuckled at the name. "Daughter named him when she was ten. It stuck, so don't think too hard on it."

"Agent Shadow," Gwyn echoed, stroking the stallion's powerful neck. All the humans had gathered on the porch, Agent's enormous head poking in.

Josiah's expression was a blend of exasperation and amusement as he looked at the horse. "I've burned through ridiculous amounts of magic to keep him from complaining about the rain. Upside is, you'll stay dry while riding. Keep him tethered away from cliffs—this big baby spooks at heights." He patted the horse affectionately.

"I can do that." In truth, Gwyn was as excited as a child about the chance to ride again, especially on a steed as magnificent as this one. Through their bond, he urged Cerys to join them so she could get acquainted with the horse. "And you'll be here with Abigail?"

After what Leon had said about Creiddylad's end, he was worried about leaving Abby alone with malevolents lurking about.

"I'd like to get him out of here by dark. Otherwise, the small covered area on the other side of the cabin can hold him overnight. I'll send my son to get him tomorrow." He eyed Cerys sidelong. "He'll be fine with the hellhound if he can see her, so keep the dog out front when you're on the move."

"Agent Shadow looks like a strong, capable horse. I appreciate the chance to ride one so fine," Gwyn remarked, tipping his head in gratitude. "But allow me to ask, why are you, as a master of magic, not handling the malevolent problem yourself?"

A hint of humor flickered in Josiah's sharp gaze. "You're foreign, so I'll cut you some slack and not give you the whole 'just because we're brown doesn't mean we're the same' talk. This isn't my tribe's land. We coordinate on magical threats, but otherwise? I mind my business. No sense stepping on toes."

Gwyn respected that. It reminded him of the old alliances and feuds he'd once navigated. "Thank you for your honesty. Politics never changes."

Pleased by his understanding, Josiah chuckled. "You got that right. Anyone object to heading inside to finish this discussion? Agent will be fine out here with his magical umbrella."

Abigail said they would stay overnight, giving Gwyn a chance to rest before returning home early the next morning. Though small, the sparsely furnished cabin was comfortable.

But the view... The view out the windows took Gwyn's breath away. From faraway clouds, rain cascaded down onto the restless ocean surface that spread out before him in a vast expanse. Waves crashed on the beach below, a rocky stretch strewn with pieces of driftwood and kelp. Towering stacks of rock, some adorned with miniature self-contained forests, rose in defiance from the turbulent waves. A sense of peace and wonder transported him back to memories of watching storms roll in on the coast of his homeland.

He could hear Abigail and Josiah speaking behind him, but the sheer marvel of the scene before him muffled their words until he heard his name.

"The local tribe did a bit of reconnaissance after they found cougar and bear skeletons, picked clean. Judging by their description, it sounds like a pair of ponaturi to me. They were last seen on the beach not far from here."

They talked a bit about ponaturi, and Gwyn excused himself to change into his borrowed clothing. Daylight was wasting. They had left before dawn to arrive before lunchtime, but he wanted to make the journey back home swift for Josiah to repay the loan of his horse. Grabbing the sandwiches Abby had thoughtfully prepared for him, he, Cerys, and Agent Shadow set off.

The path along the cliff's edge was uneven, with thick roots jutting out of the ground, slick from mud. The stallion's power was evident in every steady step as Gwyn rode across the difficult terrain. He thought about Abby's thoughtful planning for the hunt, knowing he'd enjoy the challenge and reward. Abby had planned this hunt with the precision of someone intimately familiar with his very soul. It was as if she could see every hidden part of him. And not for the first time, he felt something close to gratitude for his imprisonment.

With every stop along the cliff, Gwyn scouted the coastline below, the chill seeping through his coat as he secured Agent to a sturdy tree. He searched for signs of magic and rustic dwellings along the beach. Ponaturi were a breed of goblins from New Zealand, capable of living in both water and on land. They were as smart as humans, and therefore quite dangerous.

While Cerys appeared completely unconcerned about the weather, every time he left the horse's back to scout, it was as if he had been thrown into a freezing bath. Agent's steady pace tore through the distance until Gwyn found signs of habitation about an hour into their ride. Retrieving his crossbow, he prepared for the descent toward the beach.

He and Cerys prowled the edge, searching for a path down the cliff that wouldn't end with broken necks. Precious daylight was vanishing with each passing minute. Gwyn would have preferred funneling the goblins through the narrow track he found to shoot them with his crossbow. But it wasn't to be. Unfortunately, the track's distance from the ponaturi encampment prevented him from attracting their attention.

Abigail had mentioned that the sea-faring goblins were nocturnal, but the report Josiah received said that they were active during the day. Gwyn privately thought their magical imprisonment had instigated this change and hoped any other changes they'd suffered would make them easier targets.

Freed from their magical prisons, malevolents emerged weakened and mortal, regardless of their former strength. It was as if the rules magic had imposed on them when they were strong were loosened when the returned malevolent became more vulnerable. If that was the case, their weakening was not unlike the way magic restored balance after a broken vow, transferring energy from the breaker to the harmed. It was becoming clearer to Gwyn as time went on that magic was so much more than the chaotic force that had its own set of rules. Magic acted as a great balancing agent for the entire world.

From his hiding spot, he spied three, not two, pale, red-haired creatures with gills step from the waves one after the other. They were much larger than he'd expected for something called a goblin. Almost as tall as him, they had long claws that looked as sharp as knives. They made soft slapping sounds as they walked on webbed feet up the rocky beach.

Having just exited the water, the three were undeniably male, their bodies covered only by loincloths. Each gathered and donned roughly worked pelts they'd stored above the waterline. Each carried their catch, the fish still wriggling, toward the small shelter woven from branches and driftwood that sat on the edge of a small tide pool...

Cerys' excited panting quickened, growing more rapid with each careful step as they made their way down to the encampment. The ponaturi had sought shelter inside the tent, likely to prepare an early dinner out of the wind.

For his plan to work, the goblins needed to leave their tent and cross the tide pool. He could easily shout to lure them out, but that approach lacked finesse. No—a more fitting prelude was needed for this hunt.

The sound started low, almost a guttural rumble. Then it climbed. The unearthly, high-pitched howl stretched into a keening pitch. It was the blend of a wolf's cry with the scream of something far older, far more malicious, less of this world.

The cliffs amplified Cerys' voice, reflecting it back on itself in a chilling, endless cycle that would invoke primal fear in any who heard it—except Gwyn. He was grinning.

The first ginger head barely peeked out of the tent before Gwyn had his crossbow trained on it. He added a small punch of telekinetic power to the arrow before it exploded through the back of the ponaturi's skull.

One down.

The dead goblin's friends weren't far behind. Gwyn managed to squeeze in another shot, striking the next ponaturi on its flank and sending it stumbling into the tide pool. Despite being only steps behind in the tide pool himself, the third goblin didn't pause to assist his fallen comrade.

Gwyn unleashed a bolt of unrestrained fulminomancy at the leading ponaturi's feet. The electricity ripped through the saltwater, transforming the tide pool into a cauldron of bubbling, exploding fury. The blast of water and rocks sent the lead ponaturi flying backward. Behind him, the fallen goblin stopped its crawl, its body stiffening and disappearing beneath the roiling surface.

Although he was improving at managing his expenditure of magic, he worried over the amount he had unleashed. If the pair were still alive, it would be prudent for him to dispatch them with his sword, as the electrical hazard had likely subsided.

With an ease born of practice, he re-slung his crossbow over one shoulder and unsheathed his sword. He had taken two steps when a rumble in Cerys' throat brought him to a sudden stop.

Though shorter than the others he'd seen by at least a hand span, the previously unseen fourth ponaturi crackled with the promise of magic. A cold dread gripped him. He couldn't believe he'd missed sensing her power.

The realization that he might be in real trouble struck Gwyn with the force of a sudden gust of wind—both literal and figurative.

The ponaturi shaman's wind magic was enough to send Gwyn skidding across the gravelly shore. He almost lost his footing on a patch of washed-up kelp but righted himself just in time to receive a second blast of icy, cutting wind that hit him with a glancing blow.

The goblin shaman stood fifty feet away, preparing another volley of magic. Thick furs, of far higher quality than those worn by the males, concealed her smaller frame. But there was no mistaking the quality of her magic. Gwyn would bet almost anything that the males had been her bodyguards and servants before their imprisonment during the Extinction.

Unease settled in his gut; this situation had become far more dangerous than he liked. She raised her bony arms and summoned the wind. It whipped out of her, her wild red hair snapping with the movement of her arms like a banner in a storm.

Gwyn braced himself, gritting his teeth to meet the oncoming barrage. The gust of wind hit him like a battering ram, throwing him back. He staggered and was fighting for balance for a third time when a follow-up assault came. A flash of lightning arched toward him from her fingertips.

By all the magic... He was holding a steel sword.

Infusing his legs with magic, he sprinted in the opposite direction Cerys headed. He made it just far enough for the electrical discharge to dissipate harmlessly into the rain-soaked air. That had been far too close.

Luckily, the shaman seemed to be focused on him. A distance of twenty feet now separated him from Cerys. He was exposed, forced to rely on his agility and luck. Since he wasn't particularly skilled at creating an aegis, he didn't attempt it.

The goblin was probably eager to use as much of her magic as necessary to kill him quickly, but Gwyn wasn't taking any chances with his own. He had a few choices. He could step through the mists of magic to surprise her with a sword in her gut. Yet, given what she'd shown him so far, and with no signs of slowing down, she might be skilled enough to exploit his vulnerability during the transportation.

He could create illusory copies of himself, diverting her aggression away from his true form, but he wasn't great at that either, so she might see right through the deception. He could direct a second surge of fulminomancy in her direction. Or he could do exactly what he did—make a decision that was probably the most foolish of all, though he thought it clever right then.

He recalled something else he'd read about these ponaturi on the drive over. They hated fire. He willed a blaze into existence, flames licking up the side of his sword. With a battle cry tearing from his throat, Gwyn charged directly at her, sword arm raised, brimming with fire.

Instead of moving out of the way, as she should have when an armed man was barreling toward her at high speed, the goblin's eyes fixed on the fire. She stood in place and, with a flick of her wrist, sent a wall of wind to snuff out the offending flames.

The new leather grip he'd wrapped around the hilt nearly caught fire before the flames went out from the sheer strength of her directed gust. He still charged, closing the gap between them with his short sword at the ready. Right before he reached her, she raised her arms in another attempt to summon either more wind or lightning.

Her threat became irrelevant because Cerys was precisely where he required her to be. She leaped onto the shaman's back from behind, teeth outstretched to savage the back of her neck.

Cerys outweighed the ponaturi shaman significantly. The hellhound fell on her with crushing force, but the ponaturi fought back, moving only enough to prevent the teeth wrapped around the back of her neck from slicing deeper. Gwyn arrived at the heart of the battle as the shaman, consumed by rage, spat her last curse at the heavens, a defiant yet hypnotically melodic jumble of words.

Then the gravel, water, and air around them crackled with electricity as she sent a final shock raging in a sphere outward. Gwyn's whole body stiffened as he fell to the rocky beach. The last thing he saw was Cerys' smoking, still form. The last thing he felt before darkness consumed him was a strangely familiar energy surging through his veins.

CHAPTER TWENTY

FOSSILIZED FEMALE RAGE

Abby

In the cabin, Abby looked to her mentor for any insight that might clear up what had happened to her mom. Hoping, but knowing she might not find any, she asked, "So, have you ever heard of anything like it?"

Josiah's face scrunched up in thought. "You said her memory was blank for hours?"

"Yeah, and that's part of the problem. There was nothing there. Not even blips. Nothing, Josiah, nothing until Colin woke her up."

"That sounds suspiciously like one of your type got to her." He leaned forward, resting his elbows on his knees. "But I don't know of any in the area powerful enough to have done it as cleanly as you described."

Josiah likely knew more about everything than he let on, but then again, maybe not—he enjoyed being mysterious like that.

Abby added, "There's one person I know of who might be able to do it, but I can account for his whereabouts during that time."

Josiah's paternal gaze drilled through her.

"Ugh, fine," she yielded. "Leon. He was with Gwyn, having coffee. Happy now?"

"As a clam." Josiah smirked. "And you said it was impossible to do to yourself, even unintentionally..."

Abby worried her lower lip. "Hence the mystery. Thanks for talking through it with me." Rain drummed against the cabin's windows, muffling the sound of the storm outside. Her mind wandered to Gwyn with only Cerys and Agent for company in this horrible weather. He'd been out there for hours while she and Josiah caught up. She hoped he was enjoying the hunt—she hoped he was safe.

A loud thud broke the comfortable silence that had settled over her and Josiah. A figure slammed the front door open, followed by a gust of wind. Gwyn staggered in, drenched and trembling, bringing the scent of dirt and the tang of seawater and blood with him.

He stumbled under the weight of something very large in his arms. "Can you," he choked out, voice barely a whisper, "help her?"

The strain of carrying the hellhound finally proved too much. Man and dog plummeted to the ground together. In the last second, Gwyn caught himself and Cerys with one knee, slowly lowering her to the cabin's floor.

Gwyn's injuries were unmistakable—pallid face, singed clothes, bruises forming beneath his skin. Abby reacted instantly, lunging forward as Josiah moved toward Cerys, his tone becoming a gentle murmur.

"*No*, help Cerys," Gwyn pleaded with her, feebly attempting to remove himself from her attentions.

She tried to calm him, her voice soft as she urged him to remain still, hoping to avoid worsening his condition. "Josiah is far more knowledgeable about promoting healing with magic than I could ever hope to be. Trust him. Tell me everything that happened out there."

As he spoke, Gwyn never took his eyes off Josiah, bent over Cerys on the floor. "I thought there were only three, but there were four. One had magic." Then he said something in Brythonic or Pictish or some other language. She didn't think he even realized the lapse, because he seemed to be talking to her.

Four? They'd thought there were only two. Gods below, ponaturi were as intelligent as humans. Since he was here, he must have killed all four, all alone, and one had had magic.

"Gwyn, look at me. English only. What happened?" They needed specifics for proper treatment.

Eyes straining to see Cerys, he whispered, "I can barely feel her, Abigail."

Josiah stood from the gwyllgi, still motionless, only a few feet away. His expression darkened. "Fulminomancy—lightning magic. Dangerous stuff. I have a salve and tonic in Agent's packs. He's outside?"

As always, nothing seemed to bother Josiah. The only tip-off that he was worried was that he was moving slightly faster than normal. While he was composed and collected, Abby was sweating and practically ripping off Gwyn's clothing in her haste to check him for injuries.

Gwyn croaked out his answer as Abby lifted his shirt to listen to his heart. "Tied outside."

Mild palpitations. "Gwyn, focus. You got hit with lightning?"

He nodded, his gaze fixed on the quietly panting Cerys. "My body stiffened. I fell. She was... Cerys was on her when it happened."

Abby touched his face gently, trying to move his eyes from the hellhound. "Gwyn, she's breathing. With electrocutions, that is an incredibly good sign."

As Abby checked his burns, his eyes met hers with a haunted look—like he was seeing through her, past her, to something or someone else entirely. It wasn't the first time she'd caught that expression, but before she could dwell on it, he relapsed into speaking in one of the other languages he knew.

She nodded, playing along like she understood. If it kept him alert and focused on her instead of panicking over Cerys, it was worth it.

Gwyn's frantic, worried words were a senseless blur, the sounds a confusing mix of fear and distress, until one name sliced through, bringing sudden, sharp clarity—Creiddylad. He looked directly at her but spoke to her as if she were another.

Her hands froze in the midst of treating his burns with supplies from the cabin's first-aid kit. For a moment, the cabin seemed to tilt sideways. Her shock quickly gave way to anger, which she shoved down so forcefully that in a million years an archaeologist would be able to chip it out of rock and declare they'd found the first fossilized evidence of female rage from the twenty-first century. That single word confirmed all the secret fears she'd harbored since they'd restarted their relationship.

Now wasn't the time. She shut out the memory, the emotions, everything tied to the implications of what he'd just said as he looked her dead in the eyes. *Focus on the medicine.* His hands were burned. His palms bore burn marks that resembled fire damage, but the faint branching patterns leading up his wrists suggested an electricity. When she lifted the hems of his torn trousers, she saw the same dendritic burn patterns there as well. Gods, those probably hurt like hell.

The first-degree burns on his hands were probably self-inflicted, given his history. His heart showed that he was likely suffering from the electrocution as well. Opening her ability to see magic, she discovered his aura was weaker than before. That morning, he'd shone with a brilliant wine-colored hue. Seeing it at full power, there was no doubting how much magic he could call upon when required.

He wasn't in imminent danger. The best thing for him would be a good night of sleep.

With a jar of sloshing liquid in one hand and a battered tin in the other, Josiah returned, slipping off his sandals on the mud mat. He kicked the door closed with his bare foot and walked sedately back to Cerys. Mumbling a simple, "Thanks for keeping Agent safe," he went straight back to work on the gwyllgi.

Gwyn struggled to sit up, to watch over the proceedings as Josiah rubbed a thick green paste from the tin over Cerys' horribly burned paws. He was so distracted that he barely noticed Abby wedge her arm and shoulder under his back. Ready to brace for the dead weight of his upper torso, Abby heard him plead, "We have to get her to Miles."

Abby whispered, "We will," as she pressed magic into him through their contact, sending him into a deep sleep.

Gwyn's weight hit her faster and with more force than she was expecting. To break his fall, she fell with him, absorbing the impact. It was her fault, after all. She tried to make her voice playful. "What you saw didn't happen, Josiah." But it came out sounding angrier than she'd intended.

"Ms. O'Malley"—Josiah's voice dropped to a conspiratorial whisper—"I have absolutely no recollection of whatever you think you just did."

Josiah winked. Then his expression sobered. "Everything's going to be okay. You hear me?"

Gods, she hoped he was right.

Abby left Gwyn sleeping on the floor and moved to Cerys. The hellhound was barely recognizable— whimpering weakly, eyes dull. From the burn patterns and Gwyn's fragmented account, she pieced together what had happened: Cerys had both pounced on and bitten the ponaturi shaman at the exact moment the creature had unleashed its magic. Her snout and paws were bloodied and cracked. Abby thought the hellhound might be deaf because her ears, normally very sensitive, weren't twitching to take in every sound as usual.

Josiah unscrewed the top from the bottle that contained a liquid and eyed Abby. "I need to put a bit of this in her mouth, but I don't feel like getting my arm chewed off as thanks. Can you make her comply?"

Cerys had teeth the size of a black bear's, so it was understandable why Josiah didn't want to put his hand in there. "I can try."

From a few feet away, Abby could feel Josiah's magic soothing Cerys. Though he excelled at his craft, she grasped his reason for overdoing it. Cerys was a magical beast, but technically, she was also sort of a malevolent. For those reasons, magic simply didn't stick to her as easily as it would to a normal dog, or even a magical being like Finn.

His calming presence was so great she started to feel herself relax, wanting to lie down boneless on the floor next to the hound. Josiah wasn't affecting their emotions directly like an empath would. What he was doing was more like coaxing their bodies back into their natural equilibrium—with great force. Abby tilted her head, the crack of her neck echoing in the silence as she fought to shake off the effects of Josiah's magic.

Snaking her fingers into Cerys' warm fur, she sent a tendril of her magic into the dog. It collided with a wall—the hellhound's natural defenses. Abby patiently probed for a weakness, a crack in the defenses, until the barrier suddenly yielded, as if Cerys finally recognized her presence.

Abby signaled Josiah, who lifted Cerys' massive head and administered the tonic. The hellhound's ragged breaths evened out almost immediately. Trading the bottle for the battered tin, Josiah gently applied the same green paste to her burned mouth.

"Hands off," he warned.

He closed his eyes and placed his hands on Cerys' side. An odd warmth rippled over Abby's own skin, as if the surrounding air had thickened. The scent of the herbs in the salve seemed to deepen, rich and almost alive—like moss, rosemary, and rain all at once. The dog's wounds were raw, but the salve seemed to be working, the angry redness of the skin giving way to a softer, calmer hue.

"Now, if only I could actually heal with magic, this would be quicker," Josiah said, with a sideways glance and a smirk. "But this should help. She needs to sleep as much as possible."

Was that his cheeky way of hinting that he knew of Miles' ability? You never knew with Josiah. She didn't elaborate on that remark, leaving it hanging in the air.

"Thank you, Josiah." She had the irresistible urge to hug him, but first things first. "Before you leave, will you help me strip Gwyn and get him into the bed? He's a bit heavy for me to handle alone."

Josiah shook his head, stifling a laugh. "Your mother can never know about any of this."

Abby rolled her eyes and quipped, "Please, I know you used to smoke up with her all the way back in high school and through college. You two have gotten up to enough mischief together, so you really shouldn't be judging my shenanigans."

Josiah sighed. "True, Abby-girl, too true."

***

The next morning, bellies full of the remainder of the groceries she'd packed, they drove home. Gwyn slept through most of it—the entire Olympic Highway and most of the ferry ride. Wanting to see the awe on his face as the city skyline grew on the horizon, she woke him a few minutes before they docked.

What she took for granted, the everyday sights and sounds of her life, filled him with a rare type of fascination. His "the fact that this can float with so many cars, a marvel" statement combined with the childlike astonishment on his face as he stared at the skyscrapers and mountains beyond felt like a gift. Being with Gwyn was like seeing a discovery at every turn.

"Gwyn," she began once they were closer to home, her voice hesitant but steady. "Can we talk about Creiddylad again?" Cerys was asleep in the back seat, car harness and seatbelt keeping her stationary as Abby drove.

He shifted in his seat, glancing over, expression cautious. "Of course, but... I thought we already did."

"Yes. I mean, we talked, but the discussion isn't finished." Her fingers ached from gripping the steering wheel too tight as she tried to piece her thoughts together. She swore she could hear the slight catch in Gwyn's breathing every time she said Creiddylad's name. "You said there's room in your heart for both of us, and that should make me feel better. But..."

He was still drowsy, but she could see the moment when his eyes became wary. "Abigail, you know how I feel. What is it that bothers you?"

"Maybe," she said, fighting against the words catching in her throat, "it was the moment you looked directly into my eyes and called me by her name instead."

His silence stretched long enough that she wondered if he was trying to pretend he hadn't heard her. But he cleared his throat, his voice carefully controlled. "That was a mistake. I didn't mean for it to happen."

She swallowed, a dull ache growing in her chest. "It's not only that you called me her name, Gwyn. It's that... sometimes, I don't feel like you're really seeing me. Like maybe, somehow, you're seeing her instead."

He exhaled, his shoulders sagging. "I see you. You've brought things back to me that I thought were lost forever. And memories linger."

"But memories don't call out names on their own," she replied, her voice tighter, more brittle than she'd intended. "And now I can't help but wonder if I'm always going to be in her shadow. Don't know if you've caught on, but coming in second place isn't exactly my style."

Gwyn flinched slightly, as though the words stung. "I'm sorry for hurting you, Abigail."

"And I'm sorry for putting you to sleep without asking."

"Don't be. I would have hindered Josiah's work." He gave Cerys an appreciative look.

Abby bit the inside of her cheek as she took the exit toward Miles' house. "Look, Gwyn, when you look at me, I don't want to be a replacement. I want to be... me. I understand if it was a mistake, Gwyn. But I am upset. I know you promised you would only keep things from me when it was necessary, but I cannot, for the life of me, think of a single scenario in which addressing your past romance is necessarily a secret."

A quick look at his face revealed his confusion; his eyebrows were raised, and his mouth was slightly open.

He said, "You mean everything to me. I can't... I don't want you to feel this way."

The worst part for Abby was that he looked utterly terrified, face pale, at what might happen next.

A heavy silence, full of unspoken words, settled in for the next few minutes as Abby waded through city traffic. At last, she took a deep breath, and the words poured out. "We've been inseparable since this started, and it's been... Honestly, it's been amazing. But now I need space, Gwyn." Abby controlled her voice, which was on the verge of breaking. "Space... until I can stop wondering if I'll ever be enough on my own."

His hand twitched toward her, then fell away—the first of many small distances that would grow between them if they didn't truly talk. His baggage and her ego had joined forces to steal the comfortable warmth that had been growing between them, becoming... something.

"Okay." He hung his head for a moment and looked at her one last time. "I'm sorry, Abigail."

Was this a breakup? To Abby, no, not really. It was more like a falling out... as her heart fell into a bottomless pit. Her fingers itched to reach for him, to take it all back, but the echo of that other woman's name as he looked at her held her still.

Gwyn

Gwyn was a drauger once again, a shell of a man, as he strained to carry Cerys to Miles' front door. With a sense of desperation, he prepared to beg the man he usually considered something close to an adversary on bended knee.

The urge to tell Abby everything fought against every reason he had to keep her in the dark. If she knew, maybe she'd understand why he was terrified of losing her. But right now, all he could do was wait for Miles to answer the door, gripped by a fear that the truth might drive her away for good.

Chapter Twenty-One

Turf War

The feuding nisse factions had chosen a "neutral" warehouse in the Sodo district. Esme burst through the shimmering magic barrier to find a naked nisse toddler darting past, giggling uncontrollably while his wild-haired mother chased after him, muttering furious curses. The scene was chaotic, comical, and unexpectedly damned cute.

Esme couldn't turn a blind eye to a struggling mother with a clear conscience, even during official business. The nisse woman was about two feet tall. She wore an empire-waist dress that looked like a relic from the 1800s, her nearly white hair adding to the effect. The nisse toddler was small enough that Esme's idea might work. In a flash, she conjured a slightly larger than normal Irritella and had her pixie give the mischievous little one a ride.

"Wheee! Mommy!" The nisse toddler screamed in delight as Irritella lifted him a bare two inches off the ground, flapping her wings wildly to keep his body aloft. The purple conjuration made a hard bank left and circled back toward the nisse mother, who had her hands on her knees, gasping for breath. Irritella deposited the elated toddler back into her arms, waved at the little one, and disappeared with an order from Esme.

"That was well done, lady mage!" The nisse mother held the squirming toddler to her chest, undoubtedly fearing that he would run again if she let go. "Ms. Esmeralda, I presume?"

"That's me. It's freezing in here! I'm surprised the little guy wasn't covered in goosebumps. I don't think we've met. Nice to meet you...?"

"You can call me Agnes. Our kind is cold hardy, thankfully. It's the summer we have trouble with. Your partner is already inside."

Esme thanked Agnes and followed the path she'd pointed her in. The warehouse was almost as cold inside as out. Agnes seriously wasn't kidding about their cold-hardiness. Esme wished she had worn a sweater under her coat. Now eager to return to her warm house, she determined to finish as quickly as possible.

Expecting blinding brightness from the harsh chemical lights typical to warehouses, she blinked into the near darkness of the virtually empty warehouse. Only a single corner of the vast space was illuminated from above. Leon stood in the center of the spotlight with at least two dozen nisse surrounding him.

The fleeting warmth Leon's smile evoked in her chest was surprising, considering her usual low level of mistrust for him. The sensation vanished instantly, causing a fleeting moment of disorientation. Strange. *Get it together, Turner.* She'd had a sleepless night after turning Miles away, nothing more.

From a distance, it looked like he was also doing a great job of playing the bad cop. He'd changed his look since the last time they'd talked. Tattoos snaked up his neck, across his knuckles, and up his wrists. He was wearing a leather jacket with a wide collar, and both ears were pierced. He fit the image of a bad boy perfectly.

He was putting on a show of fitting into his role as well. Leon scowled down at one red-faced nisse man. The object of his ire was pointing a crooked finger at an equally red-faced nisse woman standing on the other side of the crowd.

With Leon and David suspiciously tight-lipped about what she was walking into, Esme fell back on her greatest strength—improvisation. She had two choices. She could be the kind and compassionate friend or the hard-ass who cracked jokes occasionally. Given the nisse were already at each other's throats, she opted for the latter.

Pausing before reaching the spotlight, she listened for a few moments, then summoned Bert. Standing at over nine feet tall and nearly as wide, Bert was a behemoth compared to the squabbling nisse surrounding Leon. His appearance in the middle of the mass made Leon and the nisse take two steps back.

With their attention redirected from one another, there was a chance they could achieve something with this talk. Stepping out of the shadows, she brought up the nugget of information she'd learned while listening in. "I've been your bartender for over ten years, and I just found out that more than half of you live in the underground! Now it makes total sense why the Sanctuary of Spirits was set up in Pioneer Square and why so few of you need help to get home at the end of the night. The bar is on top of your houses!"

The Seattle underground was a relic of bygone times. Before the streets were raised in the early 1900s to prevent flooding and redirect sewer flow, the now buried passageways and rooms had once been at ground level. A few sections of the underground were safe to visit. Esme had even been on a tour of them, but most areas were closed off. Although she knew most areas were genuinely dangerous, she now suspected some "unsafe" zones actually concealed hidden non-human settlements.

Leon smirked at her. She did her best to ignore the twinkle in his eye. Speaking to the red-faced man and woman, she said, "I know you both care deeply about your homes, but we won't make progress without taking turns."

Esme gestured to the woman first. "You claim the room originally belonged to your family?"

The nisse woman huffed, crossing her arms. "My father placed the structure-strengthening spells before the first Krum set foot in Seattle. That marks it as Torp ground."

"We only need one small room!" Mr. Krum shot back, his face darkening further. "With the baby coming—"

"Maybe if yours didn't breed like rabbits!" Ms. Torp snapped.

"It's your boy who's the father, Synne Torp! Rabbits indeed!"

Esme noticed Leon slipping into the shadows as she signaled Bert to separate the feuding nisse with his massive hand. "Enough," she ordered. "Are you both the grandparents of the baby?"

They nodded grudgingly, and suddenly the simple solution was clear. Esme wondered why David hadn't resolved this himself—laziness or zero patience for family drama?

This was a family struggling to accept that real-life Romeo and Juliet scenarios existed. "I have a tidy solution to your problem, but it comes at a price."

"Anything to make them stop hounding us!" Mr. Krum offered.

Esme waited for Ms. Torp's agreement, which came after a prolonged staring contest between her and Mr. Krum. She put on her enforcer mask and declared, "Both sides of this argument have wasted the Assembly's time. That is inexcusable. This baby makes the Krums and the Torps family! Are the parents here?"

A tiny nisse woman with a belly nearly as rounded as she was tall stepped forward, holding the hand of a young nisse man. Amidst the arguing, it seemed like they leaned on one another for support. That looked a lot like love to Esme.

Esme nodded at them with a small smile on her face. "As recompense for wasting the Assembly's time, both parties will work together to host a baby shower. The second price both sides will pay is peace. If they are amenable to living together, the Torp father and the Krum mother will settle in the disputed area as a neutral zone. They are the bridge—the connection between your clans now." She looked at the expecting parents and asked, "Agreed?"

Both eagerly nodded.

But Ms. Torp's face turned red with indignation. "And what if we don't agree to your terms, lady mage?"

Esme's small smile turned into a smirk. This was a rare treat. She pointed at Leon, who was hiding in the shadows, and bluffed wildly. "He's quite good at unraveling magic. I'll have him take down the structure reinforcing magic." Then she pointed at Bert. "Then my friends will make the space truly unlivable. Don't waste the Assembly's time any further."

With an indignant huff, Ms. Torp reluctantly nodded in agreement. Esme dismissed her conjured troll. After that, it only took a few minutes for the remaining nisse to file out of the room, leaving Esme and Leon behind.

"Well, that was incredibly simple. Why didn't David handle it?" she asked. "Like the new look, by the way, fits you perfectly."

Leon shrugged as he tried to hide a smile. "I guess he didn't want to get too entangled in local politics."

Esme rather got the impression that David wanted to be fully entangled in local politics, but only of the sort he thought worthy of his illustrious concern.

She thought Leon was about to say something, but he tilted his head back and let out a comical groan that echoed through the empty warehouse. What the...? Esme snickered at this strange behavior from him until she felt it too. Her eyes widened involuntarily—malevolent magic.

He shook his head, as if he hated what he was about to say. "I'm sorry, lovely; they follow me. Lock yourself in the office over there?"

Was he seriously asking her to lock herself up in the equivalent of a broom closet while he faced a malevolent monster alone—all after calling her lovely again? In one sentence, Leon had pushed one too many of her buttons for her to consider doing anything he suggested. She just hoped all the nisse had vacated the premises in time.

A door squeaked open in the darkness. Then came the sound that sent her heart plummeting through the concrete floor—a tiny, tearful voice saying, "Mama, find my toy!"

The nisse toddler. His mother. Gods below, they were still in the warehouse, searching for a lost toy. She risked bringing more attention to them if she ran toward them. But if she didn't, she might be too late to save them from whatever emitted that dark magic.

When she turned in Leon's direction to ask what the plan was, he had vanished. By the time the distinctive popping sound of mist walking echoed from across the room, Esme was already summoning Bert back. The gut-churning sensation of the malevolent magic intensified suddenly, as if drawing nearer. Was it following Leon as he'd suggested, or was it attracted to the privacy spell placed around the building?

Esme's eyes adjusted as she stepped cautiously out of the circle of light to see Leon holding both nisse. The mother was objecting, though not too strongly. Her major concern seemed to be the fact that she was being held by a human rather than how Leon managed them both.

Esme heard him whispering to the mother, nondescript words without meaning. As she got closer, the malevolent magic continued to build nearby. Bert materialized in front of Leon. Her troll held his arms out, urging the other mage to hand over his burden.

Esme directed Bert and his two unusually silent charges to the office Leon had tried to relegate her to. She was certain Leon had magically pacified the nisse. Despite the undeniable moral wrong of manipulating them, she wouldn't criticize him. This was a life-or-death situation.

Then she witnessed Leon perform an action she had only seen one other person do in her life. One moment, he was standing there like any other guy, alert but not wary. The next he was unsheathing a short sword that looked a lot like Gwyn's, ready for a fight. He must have had it glamoured to disguise it. She hadn't noticed it because he always walked around with a glamour so thick it was like trying to peer through concrete in her magical senses.

"Since you're not hiding, you ready, beautiful?" he whispered.

"What is it?" she hissed back.

"I think it's one of my failures come full circle." With that last cryptic message, he stepped to place his back to hers, just like Miles would.

She could sense that Bert had successfully hidden both nisse in the nearby closet. All were inside with the door closed behind them. She had Bert lay them out on the desk inside the room. Then positioned her troll to block the door. He would be their shield against danger. He'd also helpfully stop them from walking into danger should they wake. They were safe, so she pushed thoughts of Bert and the nisse to the back of her mind.

Esme instead focused her magical efforts on summoning a blade to match Leon's. He sniffed the air, likely detecting the familiar scent of sulfur from her infernal summoning. "Very freaking cool," he murmured.

She hated how Leon's praise warmed her from the inside even as it made her skin crawl. Her feelings whiplashed between distrust and a desperate craving for his approval. The contradiction should have alarmed her more than it did. She dismissed it as some sort of sibling dynamic she'd never experienced as an only child—but deep down, Esme knew better. Still, something made her ignore that nagging feeling.

Esme heard the door creak again but saw nothing.

Without warning, Leon shoved her forcefully to the side, sending her careening through the air. Her first logical thought was to dismiss her sword.

Then—she didn't know what made her do it—with tendrils of her magic, Esme struck out and tried to grab a hold of the malevolent streaking past. It was the only method that made sense. If her ties to the infernal could control malevolent magic, she had to be a puppeteer. It wasn't all that different from her connection with her conjurations.

Time seemed to slow as a string caught.

With a tug, she tried to draw it in. All this happened in the split second before she hit the floor. She saw the creature hesitate briefly. Had that been her order? Regardless, it was enough time for Leon to react.

He pivoted. His blade arced up. As she hit the floor and rolled, his sword made contact. Her fragile connection to the creature vanished as quickly as it had come.

When she recovered enough to look back up at him, Leon stood over the fallen body of a grotesque-looking Fae creature—a redcap judging from Abby's description. It wasn't neatly sliced in half like Gwyn had done, but it was lying in a pool of its own blood, gasping pitifully for breath, a piece of rebar it had been carrying discarded nearby.

Gods below. Leon had saved her from Abby's fate.

The redcap's labored breaths were unbearable to her ears. But Leon didn't seem to notice it—his eyes had eclipsed. Two black orbs studied her as she unsheathed the dagger Jacob had given her. She heeded his warning about demonic rage, terrified of becoming the next victim. "I'm ending it," she whispered in a gentling tone.

Uncertain she could locate the heart, a silent prayer for the creature left her lips. A pang of guilt, as sharp and sudden as the blade itself, struck her just as the blade met the creature's throat.

Leon watched her, the rage draining from his eyes. Was that how she looked when she was enraged? That... intense? In-trigued by the similarities between them, she found herself increasingly eager to learn as much as she could about being a cambion and, admittedly, more about him.

He reached down and touched her shoulder. A foreign sensation crept through her mind like honey, sweet and thick, making her wariness of him seem less important. "Thank you, Esme," he said, and his voice seemed to echo in her thoughts.

She didn't know what came over her—literally didn't know. A tiny, easy-to-ignore voice in the back of her mind screamed wrong wrong wrong as her body moved of its own accord. Maybe it was the brush with danger, she thought hazily, as her arms opened wide for an embrace. The gratitude flooding her was overwhelming, like someone else's emotions had been poured into her skin.

And, just like that, the memory of the manipulative magic faded from Esme's awareness and the poisoned emotions within her crystallized into her truth.

A moment later, Miles walked through the door and flicked on the lights. Standing next to him, Finn had a rare frown on his face.

Miles

Miles had tried to stay away. He'd really, really tried. But his vivid dreams of Nudd's mysterious brother, coupled with his anxiety, compelled Miles to check on her while she was on a job for David. The David part of this situation he trusted the least.

Finn poked his head into his business like usual and volunteered to "stretch his magical legs" as he called it. Being nosy was more like it. In the end, the leprechaun had been helpful by scouting the area where Esme was supposed to be while Miles finished out his mundane work day.

Finn's cryptic text—*Something's off*—had Miles abandoning his paperwork the instant his last patient left. Charting be damned.

Parking his car, he noticed a group of angry-looking nisse leaving a warehouse Finn had marked as where they were meeting. Another text message rolled in: *Malevolent action somewhere nearby.*

His anxiety immediately spiked. His job was to eliminate the malevolent threat, even if it meant risking being seen as overprotective—again. Noticing the nisse weren't running, just angry, he relaxed slightly. Finn couldn't mean from there. Right? It didn't take long for the stream of nisse exiting the building to dwindle down to none.

Like calling the devil himself with the thought, Finn materialized next to his driver's side door as Miles prepared his weapons. The leprechaun pointed toward the warehouse where the nisse had all come out from with a grim look on his face. Through the glass, Miles saw Finn mouth, "Everyone is okay." Small mercies.

Miles felt lingering malevolent magic the moment he left his car. Strangely, once inside, the malevolent magic weakened significantly. Never one to take chances, and hoping to blind the malevolent if it was in the warehouse with Esme, he turned on the lights—only to come face-to-face with something much more terrifying than a charging monster.

Esme was body to body with Leon, holding him tightly over the corpse of a bisected redcap. Leon's arms circled her waist; his face was pressed into her hair like he was seeking comfort... or something else. As their eyes met, Leon's victorious grin told

Miles that the rogue thought he'd achieved victory on multiple fronts. Why was he there?

Miles' prosthetic hand betrayed him, twitching toward his holstered gun in perfect sync with the rage thundering in his chest. He strained against his own limb, clenching his forearm muscles to force the hand away. What the hell was happening to him? Around Leon, his self-control evaporated like mist. Was this another symptom of his magic going haywire or something more sinister?

The redcap's blood spread slowly across the concrete floor between them, like a line being drawn in the sand. Miles silenced the insistent alarm bells in his mind, only for Esme to scowl when she looked up at him.

"Maybe David was right," she said, her finger pointing at the bisected redcap. "Maybe we do need Leon around."

He'd never tell her, but the impact those words had on Miles was greater than the pain of losing his hand and having a chunk taken out of his side. Physical wounds healed. This might not.

CHAPTER TWENTY-TWO

SUSPICIOUS SHENANIGANS

Esme

Anger flared at Miles's sudden appearance when Esme had specifically asked for space. She swallowed it back with a deep breath. With the redcap showing up, he had every right to be there. Taking care of malevolents was his responsibility.

She must have dropped her dagger during that bizarre hug with Leon—it now lay on the floor. As he gave it back, their fingers brushed. A blush crept up her neck as she mumbled her thanks, avoiding his gaze.

With the adrenaline surge fading, the penetrating cold of the warehouse crept back in. Pulling her coat up to her chin and stuffing her hands in her pockets, she nervously glanced back and forth between Miles and Leon. Miles' expression remained untroubled. Relief washed over her; he had nothing to be jealous of. She'd simply been grateful Leon had saved her life. Nothing more.

(Right?)

Her eyes dropped back down to the body lying next to them. "Is this going to mean another trip to that skeezy mortician?"

"Unfortunately," Miles replied. Though spoken coolly, the single word, along with his steady gaze at Leon, held the same intensity she'd witnessed from him when they'd met before.

Finn leaned in close, whispering something to Miles that even Esme's sharp cambion hearing couldn't catch. Whatever Finn had said, Miles nodded, then turned to her. "Finn will help me with it."

"Oh, okay..." she said, feeling awkward as hell. "Oh, gods, I totally forgot about Agnes and her son!"

Mind split, she moved Bert, still holding the nisse mother and son, out of the office. Having calmed down after Leon's whisper, they were both now asleep. It was probably for the best.

Leon's eyes were locked on the troll transporting the nisse. He snapped out of it when she asked, "Did you wipe their memories too?"

A small frown appeared on his face. "Was I not supposed to?"

Miles piped up. "No."

"He's right, but practically speaking, I'm glad you did." Esme added, "I'll carry them outside myself. Don't want any mundanes seeing a massive troll walking around. I'm assuming you can also implant a small false memory of some sort?"

Leon nodded and walked over to the troll. She assumed his magic worked like Abby's, which was easier when done by touch. So she had Bert lower them so he could make contact. After she felt two small surges of magic come from him, he stepped back and started fiddling with his watch. "I'll set a five-minute wake-up timer if you can have them set up in the back seat of your car. As far as they know, you invited them to use it for Junior's naptime and Mommy fell asleep too."

"Perfect." She looked to Miles for confirmation. He watched them intently, his shoulders giving a barely perceptible shrug in response.

While she and Leon walked out together, Miles and Finn started planning how they'd move the two parts of the redcap's body without getting covered in blood.

Leon was proving to be far easier to work with than she'd expected. He volunteered to open the car door for her while she placed her charges, snoring soundly, in the back seat. She closed the car door and Leon shifted, casually running a hand through his hair. "Hey, uh, Esme, would you mind calling me a taxi? I left my cell at home."

"At home? You moved here?" She turned, a little surprised.

"Nah, just an expression," he replied with a slight grin. "I'm at a hotel in South Lake Union. I go where the wind takes me."

She raised an eyebrow, glancing at her small hatchback parked by the warehouse's now cracked bay doors. She could hear Miles and Finn continuing their argument inside about how the body should be handled. "That's not far from where I'm going. I could give you a lift."

Leon's eyes lit up. "Really? That'd be amazing! I'll owe you one. Thanks."

When Leon's five-minute timer was up, Esme pretended to wake up Agnes and her son. Then things only got more awkward in the minutes that followed. All Esme wanted to do was nuzzle into Miles' neck and hug him goodbye, but she had established boundaries and was determined to uphold them. With nothing more than a small wave to Miles and Finn, she departed silently. She felt Finn's intense stare on her all the way to her car.

Leon trailed behind Esme as they exited the warehouse, the deafening silence from Miles and Finn fading with every step. Not a moment after their seatbelts were on, Esme asked something that had been nagging her since she'd met Leon. "Are you ridiculously hideous under all that magic or what? The constant glamour makes us trust you less—you know that, right?"

Leon smirked, that Cheshire grin stretching his lips. It looked a bit more sinister now with all the changes he'd made to his image. "Maybe I'm on the run."

"Oh, that's it?" She rolled her eyes, feigning disbelief. Hell, for all she knew, it was true. Miles and Gwyn had hired him to... Nope, she wouldn't think about that. She could repress all those messy emotions by asking the other question that was on her mind.

"And the tattoos? You also lost the glasses. We like ugly people too, you know. Just look at Finn!"

She could see out of the corner of her eye that he was grinning. "Finn is quite handsome for a leprechaun. How is he so tall?"

Esme pursed her lips and activated her turn signal. "Not my story to tell." She still wanted to know the full story behind that herself.

"Ah, Esmeralda, I assure you, it's not my looks that I'm hiding." He leaned his head back on the headrest. "But you'd already guessed that."

"Oh, come on, you have to give me something," she insisted, pushing for more. "At least a hint?"

"For you?" Amusement flashed in his eyes. "Anything. I know someone here who doesn't exactly have my, uh, health and safety on their list of interests."

She tilted her head, curious. "So that's why you're here? Are you... spying on them? Or planning some spooky magical revenge?"

"Let's say it's complicated."

The lighthearted banter faltered as she considered the implications of his words. Her stomach dropped at the realization he might have someone in his sights.

"Do I know them?"

"If you do, not well." He let the words settle between them without inflection. Damn, he was hiding something.

"Good," she said softly, brushing it off as best she could.

He pointed down a side street. "My hotel's right there."

Their shoulders bumped as the car hit a pothole she hadn't seen. His fingers brushed against hers on the wheel, and warmth radiated up her arm. She wanted to find out more about being a cambion and more about his potential connections to Gwyn. She found herself about to speak without thinking.

"Would you like t—"

Her phone erupted in a frenzy of beeps and buzzes, slicing through that silly idea.

"What in the..." She glanced at it, confused. She could've sworn it was on silent.

After she pulled into the hotel's porte-cochère, a series of images pinged through from Finn. Picture after picture showed him in a ridiculous pose while Miles gave him a face of aggravation, both inside and outside the car. She laughed. Any thoughts of inviting Leon over slipped away in the wave of fondness for her friends.

It was a ridiculous idea, anyway. She couldn't understand why she had thought it was a good idea to invite Leon, a near stranger, into her house for tea and conversation in the first place.

Leon hesitated for an awkward long moment before finally stepping out of the car. Worried that he was going to give her gas money or that he was waiting for something else, she was relieved when he merely expressed gratitude with a simple, "Thanks for the lift."

After her spontaneous decision to hug him and then invite him in, she was thankful he was gone. Before she pulled away, she drafted a quick text to Abby, needing to talk to her best friend. What Esme received back proved that boy troubles weren't unique to her.

Forgoing the drive home, Esme went straight to Abby's place.

Jacob

The landline's shrill ring roused Jacob from his recliner. He pushed himself up, his fingers bracing against the worn fabric. After several failed attempts by his London house manager to dispose of it, he'd realized he needed to protect his favorite sleeping chair, like he did its Seattle twin. He'd enchanted it specially—the moment his weight left the cushion, it vanished from sight.

Jacob picked up the old model phone that still had a twirly cord attached to the end. "Hello. Jacob Spencer speaking."

Only a few knew his direct number to this room, so there was little point to playing at being someone else. A voice he hadn't expected to hear so soon came from the other end of the line.

"Heyo. It's time we start talkin' about that plannin' you hinted at."

"Well, hello to you too, Finnegan. How are you today? Other than completely lacking in manners like normal."

Jacob's failing ears barely picked up on the leprechaun's grumblings about "not buyin' into yer English ways," but Jacob chose to ignore that.

Finally, Finn answered in a clear voice, "Oh, you know, as well as I can be at my age. I probably should have called ya earlier, but I've been a wee bit busy dealing with all the shenanigans happening in the rainy city."

"I'm surprised you didn't immediately launch into a tale. Care to catch me up?" Standing while the leprechaun gabbed his ears off sounded like a horrible plan, so he used a bit of magic to drag the recliner over and made himself comfortable.

"Well, where to start? Redcaps infestin' the place like cockroaches. Then our hired killer—don't get me started—took out some baby vampire and another redcap. That's a tale for another day. But yer golden boy? Slayed a feckin' ogre single-handed—in your bar, Jacob. Not outside, not in the alley. In. Your. Bar. Ogre didn't emerge there either, which means someone let the bastard in. And that was just the beginnin' of it."

The leprechaun kept talking, barely taking a breath. He usually crafted a more colorful tale than the simple reporting he was doing—strange. "Then David fired Esmeralda. I hope you heard me correctly, you old bat. He fired her. I was fit to burstin', but I kept my cool and didn't meddle... much."

Jacob hadn't expected that David would go to such lengths, but he also couldn't deny feeling unsurprised at the move. The man plainly did not like cambion. Plus, Jacob sensed that the other leader had a hidden agenda involving Miles. Unraveling

David's motives was the greater part of the reason he had returned to London after all these years.

"What did you do, Finnegan?"

"Nothin' much, so far... Just meddled with a bit of the uppity wretch's clothing while he wasn't home. Anyway, that shitehawk turned back around and hired 'er back. Only to force her to work with our hired killer to solve a problem he could have handled easily himself. As a master meddler myself, I can see that he's meddlin' with our girl. I think he's tryin' to keep your golden boy away from her."

"And that would not play into your plans, would it?" Jacob was aware that the leprechaun had mysterious motives for staying and interfering with Esme, Miles, Gwyn, and especially Abigail, but he sensed no malice behind it. He couldn't tell if he was meddling for the sake of it or if there was a larger, more important reason behind his actions.

Finn was unexpectedly quiet for a long moment. "No, it wouldn't."

"Have I been bestowed with the highest privilege of your candor? I'm shocked and humbled."

"No, yer not."

"You are correct." Jacob stopped himself from snorting out a laugh.

"Look, Jacob, we want the same thing. That's all I'm sayin'. Can you please get on board with what I'm tryin' to tell you? We have a problem, Mr. Spencer." The imp pronounced his family name like it was a taunt.

"As far as I'm concerned, you have listed things that seem to have either fixed themselves or present problems that are not my own. What do you need me for, leprechaun?"

It may have been unwise for him to mention the last part over the phone, but the likelihood of someone eavesdropping was low. As far as most mages knew, he was convalescing in his family home.

"Jacob." Finn's voice dropped to a grave whisper. "I'm tellin' you straight—Leon isn't just trouble. He's a tragedy just waitin' to hatch."

"Finnegan, I need to take care of the... leadership problem we discussed. Maureen has been delayed in returning by some nonsense Eddie's family came up with. You're better suited to keep an eye on him than she is, anyway. What would it take to get you to monitor our rogue mage for the next few weeks?"

Finn's answer was immediate. "Send me a box of proper tea, the red box, not the green, and a few varieties of jam and marmalade. I can't find a good clotted cream here either."

Jacob should have suspected his answer would have something to do with his stomach. Had he not heard Finn shifting something, he might have wrongly assumed the call was over. The leprechaun's unusual silence for the second time in one conversation was concerning. "What are you doing? Is there anything else you want to add?"

"Aye, sorry, just workin' in my garden while I have you on speaker."

"I sense a 'but' coming from you."

"Uhh... no 'buts.' Everything here is just grand. Just grand. Nothing to worry about here at all."

Jacob didn't believe that for one second. "You pronounced the 'g' at the end of 'nothing.'"

While Finn couldn't lie to him, he could skirt the truth. As far as Jacob knew, the "here" part of his statement only applied to his garden.

"Fionn, grant me one yes or no answer, please. I'll owe you a favor in exchange."

"Usin' my proper name and all. Must mean you're serious. A favor... That's a lot to offer a Fae... Depends on the question."

"Is Esmeralda in danger from Leon?"

"No deal. Consider my 'yes' to that question freely given. I followed them earlier, and I felt strange magic comin' from the car. I thank the stars it wasn't the violent sort of magic. But, whatever it was, it was aimed at her. I used a bit of Fae trickery to get rid of it."

While the sensible, measured part of Jacob wanted to bring Leon in for using magic on another without their consent, the darker part of him wanted to end it more quickly than that. This rogue mage wasn't enough of an asset to take chances with. But he couldn't shield her or fix the issue from halfway around the world.

"Finn, your preemptive surveillance of Esmeralda is... worthy of my gratitude." That was as close as he'd skirt the line of outright thanking the insufferable Fae. "If she's a danger, then why the dissembling earlier? It was clear to me that you were holding something back."

"They need to come to understand a few things on their own first." Finn made a scoffing sound. "Mayhap it's time I kept my word to our fallen demigod. Just not in the order he expects it."

The sound of unrepentant laughter, brimming with gleeful mischief, echoed from the other end of the line. If there was anything that could convince Jacob it was time he got a move on and returned home, it was the combination of Finn's freely given "yes" and that disturbing laugh. He would have to throw some magic and money around to make that happen.

Chapter Twenty-Three

A Friend (?)

Gwyn

Gwyn stood in his barren apartment, the emptiness around him a perfect mirror of the void he'd hollowed out of his own existence. His fear of losing Abigail had inadvertently pushed her away. Even his hound was gone. Leaving Cerys with Miles had been a necessary choice. The growing complexity of their relationship was becoming a source of a different type of frustration with the man—vulnerability.

Gwyn couldn't shake the feeling that he had become too dependent on Miles. A million secrets lurked inside the mind of the man who wore his father's face. And yet Gwyn had made a quiet admission of profound significance in leaving Cerys with him. He trusted Miles. His growing trust almost felt like a betrayal of all that he had worked for since his reemergence.

As planned, Leon was sitting across from him, running his mouth like normal. Distracted, Gwyn barely registered the mage's words. His repeated urging of an alliance against the very man he'd just silently declared trustworthy was... unsettling.

"Your slang is quite good," Gwyn said, desperate to escape his own thoughts.

A well-placed compliment could loosen a man's tongue, revealing secrets he'd otherwise guard.

A grin spread across Leon's features. "Thanks. Your English is better than mine was less than a year after my return."

"A year? How long have you enjoyed the modern world?"

The clinking of ice in Leon's glass accompanied the satisfied sigh he let out as he drank his water. Not surprisingly, an answer was not forthcoming.

Well, Gwyn had tried. "Let's get started, then?"

Leon, desperate to prove his friendship, had enticed Gwyn to a meeting with the lure of forgotten magical secrets. His decision to (re)teach scrying to Gwyn either revealed a lot about his actions or was purely coincidental. Gwyn bet on the former. Leon's uncanny insight into their lives was explainable only through scrying.

Gwyn had grown too complacent, believing that modern magic practitioners used magic sparingly and were less skilled compared to mages in his era. He hadn't anticipated encountering someone with ancient knowledge who also recognized him, aside from his father. Gwyn wanted to slap himself for being so unguarded.

Gwyn forced a smile, trying to appear entirely at ease. Leon's face mirrored his own strained composure, showing a matching tightness around his mouth and eyes. When Leon reached for a curly blonde hair clinging to Gwyn's shirt, Gwyn's hand shot out like a viper, deflecting Leon's arm with enough force to make him drop it. The hair drifted to the floor—like Gwyn's pretense of civility.

Leon chuckled, a flicker of unease creeping into his tone as he picked up the stray hair. "Why not start with her? See what she's up to at work?"

Abigail had returned to work, using a sprained ankle as an excuse to have lighter tasks for a few days while her leg healed all the way. Even if he was giving her space, Gwyn had memorized her schedule like the lovesick fool he actually was.

Leon had either guessed correctly, or he was observing her far too closely for Gwyn's comfort. In a different time, Gwyn would have drawn his sword and already have it pressed against Leon's neck. But that wasn't the modern way. So Gwyn allowed his expression to convey a warning of immediate bloody redress in the place of action.

Leon's hands went up in surrender, marking what seemed to be the millionth time to Gwyn. *Perhaps if he wasn't so presumptuous,* Gwyn thought, *he wouldn't find himself having to repeat the gesture.*

Leon's decision to converse in Brythonic seemed strategic, a deliberate move to strengthen the illusion of their connection. "On my honor, I swear that I have no ill intentions toward your woman. I give you this truth freely, to assuage your concerns. I avoid her. An enchantress as powerful as her could easily leave my mind in ruins if I gave her a single opportunity."

If only she was still his woman. It had been nearly impossible for Gwyn to sleep the night before, thinking of ways he could mend what he had broken. Right then, all Gwyn could do was hope that Leon would maintain his prudent caution toward Abigail.

Resuming the discussion on the technique, Leon said, "I believe your talent is powerful enough for you to try incorporating both vision and sound on the first attempt. The strength of your connection to her should ease the linking process."

Out of curiosity, Gwyn asked, "Have you scried Nudd?"

Leon hesitated before responding. "No. I... can't."

"More honesty, and I didn't even have to bargain for it. Remarkable." He wanted to prod Leon on what prevented him, but Gwyn suspected he already knew—Miles' blessing.

That was probably the most he was going to get out of Leon, so he let the topic drop and focused on scrying. The control of magic like telekinesis, elemental evocation, and even nature magic relied heavily on the caster's willpower and proficiency in externally channeling the magic produced by their bodies.

In order to scry, Gwyn needed to connect his inner self by a thread of magic directly to his target. As he understood it, this mirrored Esmeralda's perception of how she managed her conjurations. Unlike conjuration, scrying did not involve control over the link, as the scrying target always retained their agency. The only exceptions to this rule were if a magically imbued object was spied upon or if a skilled enchanter, such as Abigail, channeled their power through the scrying connection.

Mages and other magical beings were highly vulnerable to scrying due to their distinct magical signatures. In Gwyn's time, strong mental defenses had been mandatory for all magic users. However, he suspected that very few contemporary mages maintained active mental defenses.

In the background, Leon droned on for far too long about how to make the connection. To block out his voice, Gwyn started the technique. Gwyn's hand automatically moved to his chest, and he searched for the familiar rush of his magic, his thoughts consumed by her—lately, not thinking of her had become the exception.

Dark thoughts of his failings clawed at his mind, distracting him. They never ceased their attempts to pull him back down into the shadows. Gwyn pushed them away with great effort, focusing instead on her unique pull, her light in the darkness. He hoped she wouldn't overreact if she discovered his spying.

At first Leon didn't seem to notice that Gwyn was kilometers away, but eventually he caught on and became silent.

Gwyn's first effort worked. In fact, it was far easier than he'd expected it to be. Why had he not dedicated more time to practicing the magic he had once mastered? As a human, he remembered his capabilities—it was the processes that eluded him. While his distraction was understandable, his poor performance remained inexcusable.

When he saw Abigail, she was taking a sip of something from a large thermos. Her hair was tied up, and a smile was on her face. Half of her attention was on a computer screen and the other half was on another female sitting beside her.

As if flipping on a TV with a remote, the sound in the world around Abigail suddenly turned on. The unfamiliar woman's voice reached his ears. She chuckled as she recounted, "And then the attending tapped the resident on the shoulder, saying, 'Good time to practice removing this manually. Glove up, and don't forget to lube up, kid,' and walked out of the room."

Abigail replied, "I wouldn't have been able to keep it together. It's amazing you made it through that without losing it."

Listening to her laughter pained his heart. He missed her so much. His stomach clenched, a sickening twist of fear at the thought of losing her permanently for a second time.

He had to find a way back to her.

Gwyn withdrew before Abigail could sense his presence, unwilling to violate the trust she'd placed in him any further. She deserved her private moment with a friend, and admittedly, he would prefer not to find out what being forcibly expelled by an enchantress felt like.

Back in his reality, Gwyn picked up Abigail's hair, held Leon's gaze, and set it aflame with a silent warning: Abigail was off-limits.

The question he'd neglected to ask when they'd first met weighed heavily on Gwyn's mind. "You've made it clear that you want me as an ally. But why do you need me?"

Leon's appearance took on a more menacing edge as he breathed in deeply, showcasing the changes he had made to his glamour.

"I don't think I need you to achieve my goals, Gwyn. I can do it on my own. But you have never been my rival, either. I mostly ignored you in our past life and was rarely around after your ascension. Maybe I'm hoping to make up for lost time."

"Who are you?" Gwyn would ask the same question again and again until he found the crack in how Leon was blocking him from sensing his magical signature.

Leon wagged his finger at him.

"Fine. I appreciate your help in jogging my memory. You must perceive me as naïve if you think this sufficed to demonstrate your genuine support as my ally. What more can you offer?"

"So greedy, princeling. Fine," Leon said as he reached over so fast that Gwyn couldn't deflect his arm.

Leon's touch tore through his mind like a blade through a thread, overwhelming his defenses. The present dissolved—wood smoke filled his lungs, rushes crunched beneath his boots, and the great hall's fire scorched his face with remembered heat. The weight of his courtly clothes and the sword at his hip pressed against him with devastating realism.

The firepit at the center of the great hall burned steadily, casting flickering shadows along the entire length of the room. His king, his father, sat at ease in the place of honor on the raised dais. Nudd looked to be a man in his late forties, his brown hair mixed liberally with gray.

All at once, the memory of why he was there hit him. He stood rigid beside Creiddylad, who bowed with practiced grace.

"Will you not protect her?" Gwyn demanded, each word tight with frustration. "The nobility challenge her to duels and humiliate her at the warriors' table."

Nudd retorted, "Am I to negotiate not only all the squabbles of my people but also those amongst my trusted household?"

To calm the rising tension, Creiddylad smoothly said, "Her bravery in rescuing the men from the gwyllgi is renowned. Her swordsmanship is unmatched. The ladies of the court would be honored to have her sword and shield as our protection."

Nudd gazed at her appraisingly, impressed at the political move that she'd just chosen. Having Elena guard the ladies would leave her reputation as a warrior intact while sheltering her from the scornful attentions of her detractors.

"It is an inspired idea." Nudd took on an assuaging tone. "Lady Elena is new to the household. She must stand on her own if she is to garner their respect."

"Father." Gwyn could almost feel the steam rise from his brow, he was so incensed. "One attempted to assault her in her bedroll. An assassin, probably hired by a wealthy nobleman, also tried to kill her."

Nudd shot upward from his chair like a hawk taking flight. His voice boomed to nearly shake the rafters. The rumors at the time were that he had become something more than a man. That he had escaped mortality. The rumors were correct.

"Attempted—" Nudd's words cut off, strangled by purest, fiery rage. "Murder—in my household? This, against one of my chosen, is treachery."

Creiddylad pointed to the central fire. The pit was now engulfed, and the flames from the wall torches threatened the thatched roof. Without a second of hesitation, Gwyn bellowed, "Control yourself or you will burn down the keep on our heads!"

A sudden gust of freezing air swept into the room. Creiddylad just barely held her skirts in place, fighting the force of the sudden breeze. Only Nudd's steady breaths seemed to control the magical turmoil inside him.

It was Gwyn's duty to speak when other men could not. "The whispers in the court say that it is improper for an unmarried king to have a female guard."

Fifteen years before this memory, his mother and infant sister had died during her birth. Nudd had never remarried. The faint memory of his mother flickered in Gwyn's mind, a woman as unreachable in life as she was in death.

"The men call her your whore," Gwyn said flatly. "Those who know her nature whisper 'succubus' or 'corrupt.' They claim she'll bring demons back into our realm."

A long silence fell upon the three after that. Gwyn sometimes wondered if time passed differently for Nudd after his ascension because his patience had grown along with his power. Having not been dismissed, they waited. And waited.

Then, finally, after so long that Gwyn's feet were aching, Nudd said, "The ignorance gaining a foothold in my court is sickening."

He seemed poised to continue, but the hall's front doors flew open. The demoness herself strode in, carrying a small shapeless bundle.

Elena's amethyst eyes sparked in the torchlight as she first bowed, then raised the bundle into the air. A little breathlessly, she said, "Sire, a messenger has come bearing urgent news."

Just as Gwyn was about to ask why the messenger had been left outside, Elena placed the bundle on the ground. Out climbed a tiny Fae boy with bright blond hair. The slight creature, just one foot tall, righted himself and bowed first to the king, then the prince, and finally the lady.

The leprechaun first attempted to speak in broken Brythonic, but his words were hardly intelligible. His high-pitched voice did not add to his comprehensibility in the slightest. Elena remained in the shadows, faithfully waiting for instructions or permission to leave.

With a single gesture, Nudd hushed him. He encouraged the boy to communicate in his native Celtic language.

Nudd asked, "You are a long way from home, lad. What may I call you?"

The leprechaun child was speechless for a moment, clearly overwhelmed by the momentous occasion of addressing the ascended king. He mustered his courage and squeaked, "You may call me... Fearghal."

Elena poked the child lightly on the side and added under her breath, "My King."

"Please tell me, Fearghal," Nudd asked, his eyes twinkling with amusement at how cleverly the child had skirted Fae law by using a false name. "Why has a Fae child been sent to my court with news?"

The boy puffed out his chest proudly and announced, "Because I could sneak out. I'm good at it, ya know. And my ma hates 'em. Says they'll come for our gold after they're done with yer kingdom." He swiped his tiny arm in the air, miming a thief's hasty pilfering.

Gwyn couldn't contain it. He felt a laugh build in his chest at the child's wholehearted earnestness. Luckily, all that came out was a small chuckle because Creiddylad stomped on his foot, hard.

Nudd asked the leprechaun, "Your people are not native to my kingdom. Why is your family in my land?"

The child's face went as pale as the petals of a daisy, but he quickly roused his courage and answered, "I can't say. Ma says we mustn't speak of it in proper company, and you are the top kind of proper, uh, my King."

At this, Nudd's face cracked into a small grin. Gwyn could feel his face doing the same.

Nudd urged the boy, "Please then, Fearghal, tell us your message."

The words he spoke bore so much weight that Gwyn could swear that he felt the earth quake beneath his feet at their unleashing. "The red and white dragons have awoken. They're in top shape to wreck the kingdom!"

Gwyn's mind snapped out of the past, but remnants of the memory lingered, haunting in the space between his past and present. When Gwyn fully regained his senses, Leon's voice broke the silence. "I activated your first memory of Finn plus three more people you might like to see again. Tell me what you saw?"

Leon made a gesture signaling caution. "Before you get greedy, princeling, know that I can't do that again." Leon reconsidered. "Maybe once more for an outrageous price."

Only one word escaped Gwyn's lips: "How?"

"Magic I've been saving for an opportunity exactly like this one."

The burning compulsion to know more was an inferno, scorching him from the inside out. And all this time, Leon had known that it would consume him. The thing Gwyn had desired most since his reemergence was his memories back. Gwyn's heart raced with the possibility, each beat a quick staccato in his chest.

Eventually, his parched lips formed the question, greed running away with his reason. "What exorbitant price could I pay for one more memory?"

The demonic nature within Leon seemed to bubble up to the surface—Gwyn could practically see the avarice in his eyes. The intensity of Leon's predatory gaze, like a hawk zeroing in on its prey, made Gwyn instantly more suspicious.

Leon had been a bit too keen to know what Gwyn had seen. The memory of Finn as a child seemed so inconsequential, so disconnected from what was important in the here and now, that it made little sense. Did Leon fear Finn? The thought almost made Gwyn laugh. Only time would reveal the cunning schemes of either man.

But then it hit him. The time since the Solstice Gala had been such a whirlwind of activity that he'd simply forgotten one detail about his conversation with the leprechaun. How was he still alive? Had Finn also been imprisoned during the Extinction? And why was he in Seattle at the same time as four souls he'd met a millennium ago?

It wasn't just Serendipity that was playing a game with Gwyn's life. It was Fate herself, and she was playing with all of them. The only question was whether the Fae knew he was a piece she was moving around the board.

Dark memories he wished he could erase, coupled with the frustrating blankness where other recollections should have been, tried to drag Gwyn back down into despair. But Leon's voice abruptly yanked him out of it.

"What would it cost, ap Nudd? Tell me how you got Elena and Creiddylad here, and so conveniently timed," Leon suggested, his voice casual but his eyes sharp.

Like stones tossed into a placid lake, each word rippled outward with expanding implications. All of Leon's careful moves, even his choice of that specific memory, weren't random. They were pieces of a puzzle Gwyn hadn't even known he needed to solve. It had taken Gwyn far too long to realize how truly dangerous Leon was. Gwyn kept his lips tightly sealed until Leon took the hint.

Leon affected nonchalance. "Well, it's not like I'm ascended and capable of doing whatever you did to get them back here, anyway."

For some reason, Gwyn couldn't help but think that Leon wanted to end that sentence with the word "yet."

CHAPTER TWENTY-FOUR

OOF, GOLDEN BOY

Miles

The roast chicken glistened, the scent of thyme and sweet onions blending with the cool Lake Union breeze through the cracked window. As Miles removed dinner from the oven, a soft knock sounded at the door.

The sound and aroma roused Lily and Cerys from their shared couch slumber. Both noses sniffed the air in interest. With the hounds' well-being in mind, he intended to save them a portion of the breast meat. Esme's habit of giving Lily as many treats as she wanted (which was infinite) necessitated dietary control for the large wolfhound. Cerys he could be more lenient with, but it was prudent to give them an equal share.

Gwyn had visited yesterday, begging him to heal Cerys. Miles had unquestioningly healed both of them. Even if Gwyn was a self-righteous pain in the ass, he'd gotten burned while hunting malevolents. His injuries weren't severe, so it wasn't a big deal to heal him before he left.

Cerys was another story altogether. He had to split her healing into two sessions. Whatever Josiah had done had greatly encouraged her own healing processes to accelerate, but her heart, nerves, muscles in her legs and neck, paws, and entire muzzle were in bad shape. The gwyllgi had remained overnight with him, and Gwyn had asked him to keep her the following day—an odd request, but he'd agreed nonetheless.

Both dogs leaped down from their nap spots to greet the guest. Miles opened the door and raised an eyebrow at Finn's attire. He'd changed in the two hours since they'd seen each other last. He now wore an all-black ensemble that was more suited for time in a graveyard than a dinner invitation. Normally, Finn's wardrobe was a boisterous mix of greens, blues, reds, and the occasional touch of golden thread—dressed like he wanted everyone to know he was, indeed, a leprechaun.

"Dressed for a funeral, mate?" Miles smirked.

Finn chuckled. "Perhaps for that fine bird I smell roastin'. Hopefully not my elegy too, but we'll see how the evening goes."

Finn inhaled deeply, a look of almost carnal pleasure crossing his face. "And with all the fixings. Be still my starvin' heart."

"Yes, yes, you're invited to share," Miles said, leading Finn into the kitchen.

The leprechaun practically skipped inside, tossing his hat and coat onto the coatrack. Miles served out the food, piling Finn's plate as high as his own, never mind the hundred-pound weight difference between them. He knew well the leprechaun's appetite by now. For a few minutes, the only noises were Finn's content hums as he ate and the occasional clinking of silverware on plates. While Finn always ate with gusto, he was usually talkative while he did it. But not that evening.

Finally, Miles set down his fork and stared squarely at the Fae.

"So?" he asked, his pulse quickening despite himself.

Finn leaned back, dabbing his mouth with a napkin. "Look, lad, it's time I start bein' honest with you. Well... more honest than I've been, anyway."

The leprechaun's flair for the dramatic was on full display—except this time, it felt more like they were waiting for the executioner's blade to fall. On both sides of the table, the hounds eagerly begged for scraps. Miles held himself steady, refusing to give Finn the satisfaction of witnessing the anxiety his uncharacteristic caginess was causing.

"That whole Leon and Esme mess, dead redcap and all, made me realize it was time we had a serious conversation."

Miles forced himself to breathe deeply. Showing impatience would only play into the little imp's games. The cheeky git thrived on making everyone around him squirm.

Could whatever Finn was building up to be about the faint traces of magic he'd felt in the warehouse? It had seemed out of place—those traces shouldn't have been there with only nisse, the redcap, Esme, and Leon present. It had felt like another magic user had passed through, but their magic had somehow become intertwined with Leon's.

With a satisfied smile, Finn pushed away his plate, leaned back in his chair, and massaged his full stomach. "The meal was delicious, lad. I'm lucky to have been your guest."

With crossed arms and slipping patience, Miles also leaned back.

Finn hesitated, sucking in air through his clenched teeth, and admitted, "Yer gonna think I'm daft."

"What's new?" Miles tried to make the question sound light, but Finn's hesitancy was starting to worry him.

"I see you're catchin' her sense of humor." Finn smiled until he caught sight of Miles' expression. "Never mind, not when your face does that whole 'might murder you, might just stuff you in the boot of a car' thing."

It was hard to tell if overeating or the anxiety of what he needed to say caused Finn's restlessness. His nimble fingers fidgeted at his collar, then his cuffs.

Miles set out two glasses of sloe gin for them at the dining table. "Just get on, Finn. There's no pudding coming for you to use as another delaying tactic."

Finn's face lit up. "I thought you said there wouldn't be dessert! This is a lovely indulgence."

Miles used a bit of telekinesis to shove one glass closer to Finn. Without hesitation, Finn seized the glass and lifted it up. "To the truth. Sláinte!"

When his mostly full glass hit the table, Finn squared his shoulders. "Like I said, you're gonna think me daft. The first truth you won't like, but it's a prerequisite to grasping the rest."

A heavy coldness settled in Miles' stomach. Finn was enunciating all of his consonants. He knew from experience that when long-lived beings spoke out of character for themselves, what they said next could be life-altering. Miles scratched at his eyebrow and sent Finn a flat smile. "I can take bad news gracefully."

Finn's eyes narrowed in skepticism. Then he raised his right hand as if swearing an oath in a court of law. "Gwyn is no liar, Miles. I know because I met him a very, very long time ago."

Miles almost laughed, thinking it was Finn's usual nonsense, but the leprechaun's tone stopped him.

If what he said was true, which Finn had to truly believe because he could not lie as Fae, Finn should be very dead. Leprechauns were long lived, but they were not immortal.

"How?" Miles would go along with it until he understood whatever game Finn was playing at.

"I was only a wee lad when I was tasked with delivering a message to his father. Yes, Nudd Llaw Eraint."

"No, sorry. How are you still alive?"

Finn's eyes lit up with that familiar but incredibly frustrating, mischievous spark. He winked. "That's not important for what we're tryin' to achieve here, lad. Care to stay with the class?"

Maybe Esme was rubbing off on him because Miles imagined wrapping one hand around the leprechaun's throat for a split second. He attempted to appear relaxed, but his sarcasm revealed his true feelings. "Great. You've established that Gwyn is the Gwyn ap Nudd. And you won't tell me how you're somehow fifteen hundred years old. Got it."

Finn lifted his half-empty glass in the air. "I always knew you were bright. Here's an easier truth for you to accept. I know you're not his father." He took a moment to clear his throat before continuing. "But that doesn't mean you're not *not* him either."

What the hell was that supposed to mean? "Why are you telling me this now?"

"I've got a grandly bad feelin' about that Leon. Unlike Gwyn, this 'man outta time' chills me right down to the marrow of my bones. I don't trust him, and I don't like one jot how interested in our girl he is. He eyes her like she's a prize he wants back. And there's something about his magic that ain't natural."

Before Miles said a word, Finn added, "And you're not the only one who is and isn't someone else."

Miles blinked quickly to dispel the confusion from his mind. "Did you find mushrooms in the forest and decide to give them a go? Drop by a pot shop before heading over? Or did Gwyn give you one of the muffins to experiment with?"

The mention of a sweet treat piqued Finn's interest. "Muffins?"

Miles brushed the comment away with a wave of his hands. "Nothing you should be interested in. What exactly are you saying, Finn?"

"Well..." He held the word for too long.

"Oi, get on with it," Miles snapped.

"Fine, if yer gonna be pushy. You're not Nudd, but he's still in there." He pointed one stubby finger at Miles' chest. "Esmeralda and Abigail are also not exactly themselves either. Gwyn knows it, and I'm bettin' that deep down you know it, too."

"Uhh..."

Finn's smirk was smugness personified. "Well, get on with it then, lad. Do you or don't you know what I'm talkin' about?"

How could Miles explain that being with Esme was the only thing that gave him peace from his dreams? How could he say that Abby had always felt like an old friend? How could he possibly confess to knowing Nudd's guilt-ridden emotions toward Gwyn? How could Miles possibly find the right words to express how someone else's memories constantly blended with his own reality?

Finn complained, his voice a low grumble of discontent. "Should've known Gwyn had somehow finagled you as part of the deal with her bein' involved... Just wish he'd told me."

No longer sipping his drink, Miles placed his glass down a bit too forcefully. "Finn..."

Redness crept onto the leprechaun's face. He refocused on Miles and said, "Esmeralda and Abigail are, uh, born again."

Finn's tone, uncertain yet adamant, left Miles stunned and more than a little confused. With a silent plea in his eyes, Miles begged once more for clarity.

"Alright, sorry. We Irish can talk around a thing for too long." Finn let out a long breath. "Gwyn somehow pulled off takin' Elena's and Creiddylad's souls from Annwn. How they got reborn into Esme and Abby, I dunno. Gwyn knows it, and I know it. Why do you think he's so head-over-heels for Abby? Neither of us knows how or when he did it, but we all know why. And you know why too if you give it an ounce of thought."

Love.

Miles shook his head and fought to remain in his seat. Inside him, a persistent, though painless, pressure steadily increased. It was almost electric but possessed momentum and strength, seeming to energize his whole body.

He tightened his grip on the chair, focusing on his breathing to maintain control. This wasn't like the adrenaline of battle or fear—this was something else entirely.

What was this? It felt similar to the force that had urged him to use his magic in ways he'd never thought of before during the fight with the ogre and nandibear. But where that force had seemed protective, a reflexive response to danger, this was different. The presence within him wasn't desperate to keep him alive. It was more like it was pushing him to live.

Miles hesitated, questioning the illogic of what he was about to say. "Let's be very clear. Are you saying that Esme is Elena from Gwyn's mad ravings, resurrected? And that Abby is Creiddylad?"

"Aye, and I'll say the whole thing thrice." The look on Finn's face was as serious as Miles had ever seen it. Finn appeared poised to either take a punch or deliver a smack, whichever would make Miles think straight.

The room tilted slightly as Miles' understanding of reality shifted beneath him. Then it gave way entirely, dragging Miles' reality into uncharted depths. His fingers gripped the table, the grain of the wood under his fingers a solitary anchor to something substantial.

"Bloody hell," Miles whispered, the words a prayer and a curse at once.

"I suspect you are, too."

"Me. Resurrected?" Miles could feel how wide his eyes were, but that thrice-given statement of truth from Finn had made him no longer care what emotions he was showing.

"Well, your... situation feels kinda special to me. There's somethin' different about you. Somethin' you're not spillin' the beans about. Or you don't know. That seems more likely at this point."

Finn lowered his head and nodded to himself, clutching the sloe gin tightly. "Ya don't need to tell me anything more than you already have, lad. But you need to know what you're protecting here because somethin' about that Leon has me feelin' all the wrong ways. He's too interested in our business. And before ya ask, I don't know his connection to Gwyn, or you, for that matter."

There was a lot to unpack there. But it was far easier to talk about Leon than face the reality that the woman he loved might be the same woman *he* loved. "Leon's magic feels... wrong to me."

"Aye. There's somethin' off about that one. But I can't scry him. Have ya tried it yet? Don't give me that face. I know what you're up to when you think you're bein' clever. Can ya do it or not?"

Intuition had stopped Miles from trying to scry Leon. His last attempt at ignoring his instincts had worsened his dreams, leaving him sleep-deprived and increasingly frustrated. He wasn't keen on repeating that cycle simply to get a peek into Leon's world.

"Finn," Miles said, reclaiming the glass to take a fortifying sip, "something in my gut tells me I shouldn't go anywhere near that mind with my own."

The leprechaun shook his head. "Oof, Golden Boy, I think I might not blame you for that one... Look, I'll be following him for a while, tryin' to figure out what he's up to. I've already spoken to Jacob about it. You know Gwyn is currently with him?"

"I had a suspicion."

"As far as I can tell, they're only talkin' and practicin' magic. But we both know talkin' can be dangerous. You didn't ask for it, but you're gettin' my advice, lad. Think about what I've said and keep Esme safe. Keep both ladies safe. The only problem is gonna be not pushin' Esme away while you do it."

"Okay." Like he would make any other choice.

"And talk to Gwyn about it. You've taken this better than I expected, but you're as pale as a ghost. I don't plan on talkin' to either of the ladies about this. Not yet at least—timing's not right. So, make your peace with it." Finn threw back the rest of his glass and disappeared.

Miles' naivete was a deep wound, each pulse of his heart a fresh loss of his certainty. He'd been a new level of foolish to think he could walk away from a clandestine meeting with a leprechaun unscathed.

The time between his visitors blurred into a chaotic jumble of pacing, racing thoughts, and the echoes of Finn's impossible truth. Miles couldn't stop thinking about Esme, trying to reconcile her face with the image of a woman he felt he knew despite never having met her. When Gwyn knocked, Miles was pacing, still no closer to understanding any of it.

He opened the door to find Gwyn looking for all the world like he wasn't a fallen demigod—just a regular guy with a chip on his shoulder. Miles tried to appear as though his entire universe hadn't been upended in the past hour. Every fiber of his being screamed for him to yank Gwyn inside by the collar, slam the door shut with a burst of magic, and throw him against the wall, demanding answers.

But Miles clenched his jaw, balled his fists, and resisted. While such actions might be justifiable under duress, they were beyond the moral code he'd set for himself when he'd decided to leave the military.

Miles closed the door quietly as Gwyn bent to gather Cerys, her food, and her bowl. The worst of the turmoil had subsided, leaving him with a decision: now wasn't the right time for another confrontation with Gwyn. But he needed to know.

"Hey, uh, Gwyn." Miles' voice was unnaturally tentative, every emotion stuffed down so forcefully it nearly choked him.

Gwyn turned, still hunched in a crouch over Cerys. His face was a mask, revealing nothing of his thoughts.

"Yes?" Gwyn's voice was sharper than it had been of late, every word laced with a tense undercurrent. Was it due to how close Cerys had come to death?

"Fuck." Everything Miles wanted to ask stuck in his throat.

"Right..." Gwyn appeared to be confused at Miles' uncharacteristic ineloquence. "Thank you for allowing Cerys to stay here for the day."

Miles felt the bead of sweat trickle down his spine, a testament to his nervous energy, but something about that "thank you" made the words spill out of him uncontrollably, like water from a broken faucet. "Is Abby really Creiddylad?" His voice cracked so subtly he hoped Gwyn missed it. "Esme... Elena?" The names were odd and unsettling when he said them together aloud.

Gwyn froze over Cerys. But then he rose with the fluidity of a predator, sporting a smile that was a bit too much like the one Leon frequently wore. He took in a deep breath, not abandoning the false smile.

Then, all at once, a change washed over him. It was as if he'd realized he couldn't outrun the truth anymore. His body stiffened, and the smile dropped. His lips tightened into a straight line. He said a single word. "Maybe."

Gwyn breathed in and out heavily one more time, gritting his teeth, before asking, "The leprechaun?"

Miles saw a mirror of the constraint he himself was barely holding on to in Gwyn. He nodded.

Instead of denying what Finn had told him, as Miles had expected he would, Gwyn asked, "Do either of them know?"

Miles shook his head. How could this possibly be real? Right then, he would have preferred that this be his first normal nightmare. Due to whatever influence Nudd had over him, he hadn't experienced one of those since childhood.

Gwyn's fists clenched, relaxed, and clenched again. "No, of course, the imp will wait until the worst possible moment to do that."

Miles' heart was beating so fast his breathing picked up to compensate. A subtle shift in Gwyn's posture revealed he'd noticed.

"What?" Gwyn moved his hands to his hips and squared his shoulders. "The sole memory I have on this topic is a single dream from the night after the Dullahan battle. I do not know if it is true." He glanced everywhere but at Miles directly.

Miles shifted and collapsed onto the dog-hair-covered couch. He didn't even believe in the afterlife, so why the hell was he entertaining the idea that this was even a possibility?

Gwyn's demeanor turned chilly. "Do you plan on telling either of them?"

Miles shook his head again. If he dared to speak a word about this madness to either of them, he couldn't fathom the consequences for either Esme or Abby. He was already reeling from being told he might or might not be a resurrected soul even after having a lifetime of memories flood his brain every night, preparing him for that very moment. It would be far harder for them to accept.

And, selfishly, Miles worried about how it would affect his relationship with Esme. She'd seemed so distant earlier that day. He wasn't usually prone to jealousy. But seeing her hug Leon had caused a sudden and unexpected fury to rise within him. Add to that her abrupt change in attitude, plus Finn's warnings, and he was troubled.

A barely perceptible softening took hold of both men's faces as their eyes met. Was it shared understanding? Was it respect? Miles didn't know. Yet Gwyn's sneering words that followed immediately contradicted the shared moment.

Gwyn said, "Well, deal with this news however you see fit. I will leave you to it."

Staring at the floor, Miles said, "He said I wasn't like them."

Gwyn turned back in surprise as he prepared to leave. "What?"

"Finn said I wasn't like Esme and Abby. He said I'm not Nudd but I'm also not *not* Nudd. What the hell does that mean?"

"I think we all want to know the answer to that." Gwyn's voice cracked with anger, then softened. "Thank you again for healing Cerys and me."

Then he, too, disappeared, leaving Miles reeling and covered in dog hair. He picked up his phone with trembling fingers and typed eight words that now carried the weight of centuries: "I miss you, lovely. I will fix everything."

CHAPTER TWENTY-FIVE

FILTHY HANDS TO MEND A HEART

Miles

Miles arrived at the Assembly's Seattle headquarters under a sheet of drizzle. The sleek, modern glass and steel building was a stark contrast to the London chapter's stone halls. Ignoring the elevator, he bounded up the stairs, his boots loud on the concrete. He barely registered the flexing of his prosthetic hand, his body instinctively preparing for a fight.

He found David in his office, standing by the window with his hands clasped behind his back—the same infuriatingly serene posture that had defined their relationship for years. Through the glass, the Seattle skyline stretched into the distance.

The man's arrogance was galling, yes, but what truly annoyed Miles was David's uncanny ability to predict this conversation. Was Miles truly so transparent?

For years, David had dictated the rules of Miles' relationships—who was worthy of his time, who was a liability, and who was merely using him. The warnings had sunk in, leaving Miles with a perpetual fear of manipulation and a tendency to mistake control for love. When real consequences for his actions had come into play, it had been easier to keep his distance, to deny himself anything real, rather than risk them or himself.

And now, just as he'd finally found something real with Esme, David threatened to rip it away.

That, more than anything, made Miles' blood burn.

"We need to talk." Miles closed the door with deliberate restraint, though every muscle in his body screamed to slam it. He wouldn't give David the satisfaction of seeing him lose control. Not again.

"I am listening." David remained facing the window, silent. A calculated insult.

Miles shook his head. David's method was to remain calm and aloof, orchestrating events from above while others played the parts he'd forced them into below. Domineering the conversation, as he did everything else, was David's goal.

Not today.

"Stay the hell out of my life," Miles said flatly. "All of it. We only interact at closed meetings. Otherwise, fuck off."

David turned, a flicker of amusement crossing his features. "You're being dramatic."

Miles arched a brow. With his voice carefully measured, he asked, "As dramatic as the man who went to *my mother* and told her I'm being used by a gold digger?"

David didn't answer immediately. He took a long, slow breath, dismissing Miles' words as a trivial annoyance rather than a serious accusation. "That woman is a distraction."

"*You* are going to leave Esme alone." Miles stepped closer, his finger jabbing toward David's chest. "No contact. No interference. You don't fucking touch anything about her. Nothing. Or I swear, we're done."

"Language! I didn't spend a fortune on your education to hear you speak this way." David's tone was icy, his disappointment palpable. "Is that what this is about? A woman?" He sank into his chair, his posture as immaculate as his suit, and shook his head.

"You fired her to get to me," Miles said, his voice low and dangerous. "Don't pretend otherwise."

David's eyes narrowed. "She wasn't suited to the position."

"Bullshit," Miles snapped, closing the distance between them. "You did it to teach me a lesson about staying in line."

David didn't answer, but something flickered across his face—annoyance? Amusement? It didn't matter.

Miles took a step closer to make an impression. He planted his hands on the desk. The wood creaked under the weight of his grip. "I'm not a boy anymore, David. That leash you had around my neck for years? It's gone. You don't get to dictate my life."

For a moment, David said nothing. He studied Miles with the same detached curiosity he might give a particularly stubborn puzzle. "You wouldn't be who you are today if I had coddled you, Miles. I trained you; I shaped you. And despite everything I've done for you, you're still ungrateful."

"Shaped me?" Miles scoffed, his voice trembling with suppressed rage. "You *broke* me. You did such a fine job that you created a man who barely trusts anyone. You turned me into someone who isolates himself to protect others from *you*. And now, because of you, I might lose the one good thing in my life."

David didn't react. He never did.

Miles continued, "That's your usual approach, isn't it? You manipulate people, break them down, until they perfectly fit your needs." He waited for his words to sink in before adding, "I built my own life here. And I won't let you tear down someone I love simply to prove you can."

David's eyes narrowed ever so slightly at that.

"Your attachment makes you weak," David said, his voice flat and devoid of feeling, each word measured and deliberate, like a surgeon's scalpel. "It always has."

Miles' laughter was a harsh, grating sound, barren of any genuine mirth. "No, David. My partners in the Brotherhood are not a weakness. Esme isn't a weakness. She showed me exactly how entrenched your influence still is," he seethed, the words thick with resentment.

David's expression turned cold and hard. "You think we're so different, but you're exactly like me. Ruthless when it matters. This moral act? It's a lie you tell yourself."

"I'm nothing like you," Miles retorted sharply, his voice rising for the first time. "I don't use people. I don't manipulate them. And I definitely wouldn't ruin their lives to make a point."

David stood, his movements slow and considered. Circling the desk, he stopped a short distance from Miles. "Survival in this world requires getting your hands dirty."

With a frustrated gesture, Miles rolled up his sleeves, displaying one hand pulsing with his heartbeat, the other with magic. "My hands are fucking filthy. The blood is so thick I can feel it caked under my nails no matter how many times I wash them. Sometimes I swear I can smell it—the copper, the iron. Sometimes I can barely look at the red staining them. Yet you see *nothing*."

David glanced at Miles' hands, unfazed.

"You are correct, Miles." David's jaw tightened, a rare crack in his composure. "You are not a boy anymore."

David's exhale this time was a carefully constructed performance of sadness. "I expected more from you. Your future was secure in London and you threw it away. I thought your move to Seattle was about you finding your path to greatness... Not to finding a willing bedwarmer."

Miles didn't stop to consider his actions. He grabbed David by the shirt, shaking him hard. "Too far, David. We're done."

The silence that settled was punctuated only by Miles' heavy breathing. Seething with barely suppressed rage, Miles watched as David slowly raised both hands to place them atop Miles'.

Miles realized he had overstepped and started to release his hold.

But David stopped him.

David's grip tightened on his hands. There was history in that touch—decades of joy, pain, abuse. Complicated, like everything between them.

Then something else flickered at the edges of Miles' awareness. He was breathing hard when a peculiar sensation washed over him. Black spots swam at the edges of his suddenly blurred vision.

The world dimmed briefly, and when it sharpened again. Miles found his anger had slightly subsided, making him suddenly more inclined to listen. Disoriented, he blinked away his confusion.

Something about David's touch seemed to leech the fight out of him, though he couldn't pinpoint why. He found himself loosening his grip on David, unable to shake the unsettling feeling that something important had just happened—something he'd completely missed.

Now David was speaking again, his voice smoother, lighter, steering them toward safer ground.

"You still think this is about control," David mused, almost to himself. "Son, if I wanted to cut her out of your life, I would have done far worse than firing her. I can be reasonable, you know. I've already given her back her job."

"I know," Miles said curtly, still feeling the heat, even if the storm had passed.

David took a slow step backward. "You've always been rebellious," David said, a bitter smile tugging at his lips. "But this is an oversight I can fix."

Miles stiffened. "So you don't understand. I need you to disengage."

"You've never understood, Miles. She's not an obstacle—she's an asset. Strength isn't in isolation. It's in *leverage*."

Miles' stomach turned.

David saw his reaction and smiled.

"You can't ignore what she is," David said smoothly. "What she's capable of. What she could be. She's more dangerous than she knows. That kind of power? Untapped, unrefined?" He shook his head. "Esmeralda likely has abilities she doesn't understand. Since she's now operating out in the open, all thanks to you, someone will take an interest in her, Miles."

"What?" Miles' mouth went dry.

"Mr. Spencer has kept her abilities off the records for years. Now that she's working with the Brotherhood, that's all out in the open. Someone *will* exploit her to advance their own machinations. Think hard on what kind of person you want that to be."

"Not you." Miles took a step back before he could stop himself. Old patterns died hard. Miles felt his pulse speed up. Damn it, David wasn't wrong.

Settling into his desk chair, David said, "But it could be you. Who better?"

"She's my partner, not my puppet." He wouldn't use Esme—ever. But he would protect her. He simply had to be a bit more prudent about how he did it going forward.

Esme was powerful. Too powerful to be left unprotected. And if someone else decided to take an interest in her—

"I won't let you use her," Miles said, but the words weren't as sharp as they should have been.

"I'll take a step back, lad." David shook his head sadly. "I can see how much she means to you."

This was a major step forward (he hoped); one Miles could finally share with Esme. Still, it lacked the feeling of true success, something that bothered him as he turned to leave.

David's voice stopped him. "One more thing. You should know—Esmeralda's file has already been forwarded to the International Board. They'll be... curious about her abilities."

Miles froze, a chill running through him. "What did you do?"

David's smile was thin. "What I always do, son. I plan ahead."

And there it was—the twist Miles had known was coming, the stark reminder that he hadn't won, not really. But it didn't matter because he'd die before he stopped fighting for her.

Chapter Twenty-Six

LONDON

Jacob

The muted colors everyone wore blended into the gray sky, reflecting even more gray from the scattered puddles on the ground. As Jacob traveled through London, the weather, the dampness in the air, and the pungent mix of city smells, from coffee shops to exhaust fumes, made him think of Seattle in the depths of winter. They triggered an unexpected pang of longing for the place that had become his home. He'd missed celebrating Christmas with Esme, and now one of his oldest friends was dead. But that was the past now. All he could do was hope that his efforts today would make up for it.

At his age, Jacob felt justified in taking his time leaving the black cab. The dampness in the cold air made his bones creak with each movement. The driver, though, clearly disagreed, rudely suggesting that he "get on with it already."

It was unfortunate for the cabbie that Jacob had long ago come to terms with his moral failings. The mage's smile was self-satisfied as he watched the taxicab speed away. A slight wave, as though bidding farewell, was all it took for him to make the car lurch into the curb with a jarring skid. With shredded hubcaps on the left side, the driver would face a hefty bill for the repairs.

Manners were free, but rudeness could be expensive, after all. That was a useful reminder, as he'd need to be charming and polite when he met with the Lady Abington.

The waif of a woman surprised Jacob by answering her own door. He was sure they employed a house manager, and David was the type of elitist who would stick to traditional practices that reinforced his superiority. But, then again, Irene wasn't the same sort. Jacob had known her for over fifty years, but in the past few decades, he'd only seen her out of the house on a handful of occasions.

Taking off his hat, he greeted her. "Lady Abington, good day."

"Oh, do come in, Jacob, and forget the titles. I have a tea service waiting for us in the parlor."

The expected house manager, an updated title for someone who was functionally a butler, was standing on the other side of the door, waiting to grab his coat and hat.

Jacob followed Irene into the parlor, where an elaborate tea set had been arranged on a low table between two velvet armchairs. The room was immaculate. While aesthetically pleasing, the room's functionality appeared to be tailored more toward creating an impact on guests rather than facilitating the comfort of its residents.

"You've kept this home beautiful, Irene," he said, lowering himself into one of the incredibly uncomfortable chairs.

Irene was at least a decade younger than her husband. Her movements still held an ethereal grace. Vivacious and highly intelligent, she had been the belle of the ball before marrying David. After their marriage, her bright light had dimmed, turning her into a bit of a hermit, yet she was radiant that day. Jacob entertained the thought, with a hint of irony, that she was thriving in her husband's absence.

Her delicate hands were steadier than the last time they'd met, almost five years ago now, as she poured his tea. "Oh, it's not me doing the work," she replied with a soft chuckle. "You know how it is."

Jacob replied, "Still, I know the effort it takes to manage multiple households when your partner is as busy as David is."

Her smile faltered briefly, the barest flicker of something darker crossing her features. "Yes, well, we do what we must."

Jacob sipped his tea, his eyes scrutinizing her over the rim of his teacup as he took a sip. "How do you feel about him being in Seattle to take over my duties? Could you see yourself moving there?"

She hesitated, her teacup halfway to her lips. "Looking at you now, I can't imagine why you needed the break! David has started to slow down recently. But I suppose we all do with age. You seem the same today as a decade ago." She was already shaking her head. "Seattle? No. Our boys are here. My life is here. I'm used to David's traveling, anyway."

Jacob gave her a knowing smile. "Well, age has barely touched you. You look as spry as ever, Irene. I can't recall the last time I saw you up and about like this. Have the doctors determined something to help with your condition?"

She had disclosed to him many years ago that she suffered from an unexplained ailment, which periodically resulted in her being bedridden.

Irene's dazzling smile revealed pearly-white teeth. "I haven't had such a good stretch for years. Lately, I've noticed an improvement in my memory as well. For a while, the thought of me developing dementia hung over us like a dark cloud. But it seemed to disappear. My doctor mentioned the possibility that my body might not have been processing vitamins correctly or that I could have developed an unexpected allergy. I had no idea that sort of thing could come and go!"

Jacob tilted his head slightly. "When did the clarity return?"

"A week or so ago. We missed David for Christmas, but I was able to really play with the grandchildren. That helped to soften the blow." She paused, a faint crease forming between her brows. "Strange, isn't it? My magic is stronger too."

With a graceful gesture, she levitated the teacup into the air and lowered it back to the table without a sound.

Jacob leaned forward, setting down his own mug with a soft clink. He kept his tone gentle but probing. "Irene, you've known me for decades. If there's something on your mind, something that doesn't sit right, you can tell me."

For a moment, she looked as though she might speak, but then she glanced toward the door, her expression relaxing with practiced ease. "No, Jacob. There's nothing at all."

The haunted look in her eyes told a different story. The timing of her sudden return to health and happiness was also suspect. Jacob disliked the unspoken tension and underlying narrative hinted at in the silences between her seemingly light teatime words.

What Irene didn't know was that a clever lad was sneaking into her husband's home office while she enjoyed the morning with Jacob. That same clever lad absconded with David's laptop, under cover of Jacob's magic.

Following thirty minutes of cordial conversation and shared recollections, Jacob bid Irene farewell. Meeting with her had accomplished some of his goals, but he had one more with multiple layers to complete before the day was over.

By the time Jacob returned home, his hired thief had broken through the encryptions on David's computer. Jacob had learned from Esmerelda that people who own multiple computers typically use accounts to link them together. The bright young man showed Jacob how to find David's Assembly files and email accounts.

Once he had access to these, with directions on how to move between programs, he excused the lad with heavily lined pockets but no memory of how he'd gotten them. He doubted the young man would mind the confusion.

Two simple documents on David's laptop had damned him, as far as Jacob was concerned, to oblivion.

The first document was the sort of file he expected to find. It was a letter urging the president of the hospital system Miles worked for to release him from his contract. In exchange, Lord Abington would contribute a large donation to the charitable arm of their organization. Jacob already knew David wanted something from Miles. This was simply more evidence that he was willing to spend money and ruin the poor lad's career to get it.

But David's Assembly folder was the final straw for Jacob. A *persona non grata* file, completely filled out and ready to be submitted, caught his eye. This type of declaration essentially branded any magic user as unwanted, forbidding them from leaving their current district. These were common for magical transgressions that couldn't be ignored and amounted to something like house arrest.

However, the way David had completed the form for Esmeralda would label her a serious criminal who required magical incarceration to be followed by "reeducation." These sentences were only for the worst offenders who couldn't be killed outright for political or practical reasons. Most of the people set up under these terms ended up dead anyway—by suicide.

This left Jacob with two choices: to burn each of David's family homes down with his wife, children, and grandchildren in them or to simply ruin them.

But Irene...

Her haunted look, the look that made it clear to Jacob that she, too, was a victim, was more than enough to convince Jacob to move forward with the less messy of the two options. He still had a heart—mostly.

If David refused to cooperate once Jacob sank his claws in, Jacob's actions that afternoon would instead destroy the Abington family's financial security for at least two generations and make David look like a bloody fool. If, however, he cooperated, his family's doomsday scenario would not unfold.

Jacob got comfortable and drafted the documents that would divest the entirety of his holdings in every company owned by the Abingtons—each transaction deliberately structured to ensure that the family's assets would lower in value. Next, he signed the paperwork that would trigger multiple lawsuits penned by different shell companies against David's properties.

He prayed silently for forgiveness from the wonderful woman David Abington had never deserved. Jacob then wrote a letter that would be delivered after David's death to his blameless sons, the words seeking forgiveness for the difficulties he'd caused them.

Jacob wasn't a complete monster. He had first checked that Irene's sons had trusts to rely on for their families' basic needs while they learned how to actually work for a living. Irene also had her private inheritance that would see her through to the end.

But that's what happens, Jacob thought rather sardonically, *when you cross someone who's been betting against you since day one.* The situation underscored the importance of his contingency plans. He was thankful now for the careful preparations he'd made years ago against several powerful families across the globe.

Jacob only had one last task to finish before he could return to Seattle. What he learned from his next meeting would sway his decision on whether to torture David slowly, literally and figuratively, with the downfall of his family or to remove him immediately from the living world.

***

"My doctor in the States advised me to get a checkup before flying back. I'm thrilled that you were available during the holidays."

It was a considerate thing to say, but it was money, not kindness, that made this visit happen. The hefty fee Jacob paid the concierge doctor ensured his availability at the place of his choosing and time—his city house, after dark. That way, he could handle his business from the comfort of his own lounge chair.

"Mr. Spencer, I must say that you are in fantastic health, mage status and age notwithstanding."

The physician was middle-aged, perhaps in his early fifties. He projected an air of respectability, not arrogant exactly, but mindful of proper decorum.

The smile Jacob sent David Abington's personal physician wasn't pleasant or appreciative. It was wolfish. "Thank you. I'm so glad you brought your laptop today for quick note-taking. I'm assuming that system is capable of storing all of your patients' sensitive medical information securely?"

"Oh, yes, I can access any of my patients' records from here. It is quite secure, I assure you."

"I do appreciate my privacy." Jacob's fingers barely twitched as he wove magic, ruthlessly sucking the air from the other man's lungs, leaving him gasping and struggling for breath. "You have, what, three, four minutes before permanent brain damage?"

Instead of answering him, the physician continued to pull at his throat and look around the room for something. Inconvenient.

"If you're searching for a blade to harm me or, for gods' sake, do something foolish like try to give yourself one of those tracheotomies I've seen on television, it won't work. I've removed the air from your lungs. Here." He waved one hand nonchalantly. "Take a breath. Get it together, man."

The doctor may have been a mage, but he wasn't a very powerful one. He collapsed to the floor, breathing in three heavy lungfuls of air before Jacob spoke. "You remain quiet, you can breathe. All I want is information. You seem like the type to know the movers and shakers. Are you aware of my reputation?"

The doctor nodded.

"Good. It's half true and half false. All I need from you is information. But I'm also not above splattering your intestines all over that gorgeous Turkish rug you're standing upon. Am I understood?"

The doctor nodded mutely once more.

Jacob had grown so comfortable in his life that he'd started forming dreams for the people in his charge. Wanting something so large, something so beautiful, was dangerous for a man like him. Sylas' death, David's actions, Jacob's people being thrust into battle after battle with malevolents—all of it combined to create an irresistible force that now drew him back into the shadows. The problem was that Jacob probably enjoyed the darkness too much.

"Wonderful, Doctor! I prefer when we can proceed without unproductive antagonism. So much easier. You've also greatly increased your chances of living after our conversation. Now sit down."

Jacob pointed to the chair he'd magically shifted to face his lounger, inviting the other man to sit. The doctor sat stiffly in the chair, legs squarely in front of him, with his hands resting on his knees.

"Wh— What do you want?" he asked.

"Information you're technically not allowed to give. On a patient of yours. David Abington. Oh, I see the look." Jacob smirked. "Yes, I do mean the leader of your Assembly here in London."

With another flick of his fingers, Jacob once again removed the air from the doctor's lungs. This time, the doctor made the intelligent choice and remained in his seat instead of fighting it, eyes staring at Jacob pleadingly.

But supplication didn't work with Jacob Spencer.

Jacob said, "If you know my reputation, you know I'm not above repeating what I've done to you with one of your children, or even that new grandbaby of yours, Benjamin."

The doctor's face drained of color.

Jacob continued, "Disregard your oath. Your participation will remain untraceable."

He allowed the doctor to suck in a breath.

"Anything," the man breathed, barely able to speak as he tried to fill his lungs.

"For that, I'll remove Benjamin from my list. I'll check off one child per piece of useful information you can verify with data. Then your wife, and then you. Am I understood?"

"Yes, yes, sir."

"First, I want to see a report of David's health before last spring and then from his latest visit. If I don't find what I want there, I want records from twenty-five years ago."

Chapter Twenty-Seven

Taking Inventory

Esme

The Sanctuary of Spirits was quiet, the air still carrying the faint scent of conifer needles and the remnants of Christmas decorations. Esme shook her head, marveling at how quickly the year had flown by. The dead ogre in the back room? Miles had "taken care of it," as usual. Someone else was supposed to set the kitchen back to rights.

It was unbelievable that only a few days had passed since then. She hadn't stepped foot in the bar since, so she peeked into the kitchen. The sight of it all made Esme shake her head in wonder. Before, the room had been in ruins. The ogre had even dented the metal prep tables. Now everything was... immaculate. The metal tables appeared untouched, and all of Wexley's cooking equipment was back in place.

With a sigh, Esme turned her attention to the immense task of inventorying the bar's towering shelves. The bar's quiet hum was her only companion. Normally, she'd drown out the silence with music or an audiobook, but today, even that felt like too much. Miles had promised to join her to talk about his meeting with David, but, as always, duty had called him away.

"Take Gwyn or Finn with you!" she'd practically begged him through text, worry bleeding through with every letter.

Miles' reply was typical—he didn't think he needed the help.

She wanted to go with him. They could talk about his conversation with David after the malevolent fight, but she'd delayed the inventory for far too long. With New Year's coming, it couldn't be helped. Jacob had entrusted her with the bar during his absence. She refused to disappoint him on such an important day for business.

Between her own rocky relationship, Miles running off to play the Golden Boy hero, and Abby's breakup news, the usual boost she got from being back in the bar was lacking. Esme, left only to her thoughts, scribbled the names and numbers of bottles in her ledger. She was halfway through the tequilas when the door creaked open behind her.

"Leprechaun on the premises," she muttered, not bothering to turn around as Finn sauntered in. He was wearing a bright winter-blue suit jacket with a white button-up and a forest-green cashmere scarf draped over both shoulders.

"Gods, what is this color scheme? Things you see when careening down a ski slope?"

"Y-es, lassie. I'm surprised ya got it so quickly!" He said it with a straight face, as if it were perfectly normal.

A smile spread across Finn's face as he took a seat at the bar, his gaze drifting unerringly to the whiskey. "Just checkin' in, lassie. Makin' sure yer not drownin' in bitters over that absent boyfriend of yours."

"Oh, yeah. I'm sure your presence has nothing to do with stealing my best whiskey," she said dryly, though she couldn't help smiling in return. She handed him a nearly empty bottle and two shot glasses. "There's barely anything left in this one. Knock yourself out."

As she sipped the half-shot Finn had poured for her, she thought of Abby's news again. Gwyn was clearly determined to make his new modern relationship work, but Abby had been right to take a step back. The only thing Gwyn could have done worse was say Creiddylad's name when they were in bed together—that idiot. She understood, though, relationships weren't exactly easy when their lives were constantly upended by monsters.

A familiar snort that shouldn't have been present snapped her out of her thoughts. Stefan stood in the doorway, a menu clutched in his tiny hand, his expression utterly peeved.

"What do you want, Stefan? We're closed."

Depending on the day, this brownie was either a delight or a pain in the ass. Standing at two feet, he was almost human at first glance, but his skin had a slight orange tinge that set him apart. His head was also disproportionately large for his body, his nose comically oversized. Stefan was mouthy and moody but had just enough goodness in him for Esme not to feel like strangling him—yet.

"That one's here," Stefan accused, pointing at Finn.

Esme put her hands on her hips. "He's helping me with the inventory."

The brownie snorted. "Drinkin' it, more like."

Stefan approached the bar and clambered onto a stool. Sneering at the array of bottles spread before him, he said, "When's the last time that bottle of vermouth even saw refrigeration?"

"*That* is for decoration." Esme bit back a groan and looked around for a distraction. Seeing his loneliness made it hard for her to be firm with him. "Stefan, we really are closed."

"Clearly, because this cocktail list—well, I'm dry-heaving just reading it."

Finn stifled a chuckle. The final straw was Stefan's insult. She'd made that cocktail list! It made kicking him out that much easier.

"He really is here to help with the inventory." A little guilt trip from Esme could transform that lie into the truth. "Stefan, if you want a drink, you stay and help for a few hours. Otherwise, out!" She pointed to the door, and Stefan slouched away, grumbling about the "wasted talents" of bartenders today.

As the concealment spell buzzed Stefan's exit, Esme muttered, "Why do I even bother?"

She and Finn barely had time to clink glasses and take a sip before the entrance magic buzzed again. This time a tall, narrow figure strode in—David Abington, with an air of formality that would put a banker to shame. Esme blinked, resisting the urge to say, "We're closed," for the third time.

In that briefest of moments, between feeling the door's magic and her silent grumbling, Finn vanished. She doubted David knew he had been there. The little traitor, leaving her alone to deal with the newest asshole in the room. His disappearances were so common that she had to accept it and move on.

David ignored her surprise, his smile as fake as his casual tone. "Esmeralda, I've come to deliver your bonus for the nisse job. Well earned."

She leaned forward, curious but cautious. "Thanks, but, uh, my checks are on auto-deposit."

"Oh, probably something to do with that little... misunderstanding a few days ago. We need you to do your paperwork again."

Yeah, because firing her was a "little misunderstanding."

"Call it a touch of personal goodwill," David added, his hand extending for a handshake.

She hoped this was proof that Miles had finally confronted David. A sense of relief, or at least what seemed like it, settled over her like a warm blanket, easing the dull, heavy ache in her heart caused by Miles' absence.

Esme dared to hope David's visit meant a ceasefire, a fragile peace tentatively offered. Maybe, just maybe, she could finally be with Miles again.

In a blink, Finn appeared on the barstool between them, his grin sharp and uncharacteristically menacing. David's hand froze midair as Finn intercepted the handshake meant for her.

"Fu—Finn!" Esme yelped, startled by his sudden appearance. She was proud to have changed that curse word into his name at the last moment in front of Miles' old mentor.

Finn's grip was rough as he shook David's hand, his knuckles white. Briefly, David's normally rock-solid composure faltered just a little. Something in his eyes, something Esme couldn't decipher, caused him to straighten quickly.

He reached into his breast pocket and handed her a check. "Here you are. Now, please accept my apologies, but I have other business to attend to. Good evening."

He strode out without another word, the door buzzing its magical goodbye in his wake.

Relieved and baffled, Esme turned back to Finn—just in time to watch him sway. His face was paler than she'd ever seen it. One moment, his grip on David's hand had been iron-tight; the next, he was slumping forward, nearly toppling off the stool. She practically leaped across the bar to catch him.

"Finn?" She shook him gently. "Gods below, did you sneak whiskey behind my back?"

A barely audible mumble escaped his lips before every single drop of whiskey they'd shared, and some of whatever he'd eaten earlier, spewed out of him and onto the floor. Thankfully, his mouth was at just the right angle that she had escaped being in the splash zone. His eyes fluttered closed and his body grew limp in her arms.

Gods above and below, what had happened? She unconsciously called on a bit of infernal power to give her the strength to lift him off the barstool and ease him onto the ground. She needed Miles.

Panic coiled in her gut. She scrambled for her phone, dialing his number.

Nothing. She tried again and again, but his line rang and rang until it hit his voicemail.

Her heart thumping in her ears, Esme decided she needed to get Finn back to her house or to Miles'. She couldn't think straight enough to decide which was best.

Confusion and speculation swirled in her head, leaving her with only fragments of explanations for what had happened. Finn's shallow breaths and ashen face were all she could truly focus on.

Thank all the gods she'd driven that day. It would be far too hard to explain why she was propping up a little person who looked like he was blackout drunk on the bus. Deadlifting his weight off the ground, she positioned Finn in a fireman's carry by hoisting him over her shoulder. She walked out of the bar, giving the convenience store attendants a "you saw nothing" scowl. All of them were vetted by the Assembly, so they knew to shut their mouths when they witnessed something strange—not that Pioneer Square didn't supply enough of that on its own.

Abby's apartment was less than fifteen minutes away, but every single minute of the drive felt like an eternity to her. Esme's mind buzzed as she waited for Abby to pick up her call. How many times was this silly leprechaun going to get himself hurt in her presence? Could this instead be some sort of Fae flu he'd caught? Did leprechauns even get sick? Was this something simple, like magical exhaustion?

Visions of Finn's face after she'd interrogated him, after Miles had drugged him, of his bloodied body after Juniper had attacked him, the soot and guts covering him after the jorōgumo and Minyadian bats flitted through her mind. It was almost too much. He'd endured so much pain just to be their friend.

When she finally got Abby on the phone, Esme explained the events with a shaky voice. "It's not like I can take him to an ER, right?"

Abby listened patiently and replied, "Right. His ears and resting body temperature would raise a ton of red flags there. I'm off work in less than an hour. It sounds a lot like advanced magical exhaustion to me. Get him comfortable, and I'll run home."

Abby was right. The potential hassles of taking him in for medical care outweighed the benefits. The sheer absurdity of explaining a seemingly "healthy" leprechaun's problems to a confused ER doctor was almost comical once she was clear-headed enough to truly consider it.

Esme had a key to Abby's apartment, so she carried Finn up three floors and deposited him on Abby's couch. She thanked the stars that she hadn't run into anyone in the building because her eyes were blazing with shadows the whole way. Finn had to weigh close to one hundred pounds, so it was no mean feat, and she needed the help her special brand of magic could give her.

With each anxious check on Finn and each unanswered call to Miles, the quiet moments while she waited for Abby to arrive allowed her mind to wander. In a mere instant, it felt as though every ounce of life, every spark of vitality, had vanished from Finn, leaving him utterly depleted and lifeless. And there was only one person she knew who could do something like that—Katia. Maybe it was time for a quick consultation with an expert.

CHAPTER TWENTY-EIGHT

STAY AND FIGHT OR FLEE

Miles

The rain pattered on the roof of Miles' car as he sat in the hospital parking lot, staring at his phone. He'd promised to meet Esme at the bar after work, but life had other plans. He wanted, he needed, to tell her in person that David wouldn't be a problem for them anymore. But all he could offer now was a texted apology and a raincheck.

I'll be done before you're finished, he'd typed, hoping to reassure her. *If I can, I'll meet you there. If not, I'll call. We'll figure it out. I need you to know that I'm handling things. David included.*

Her reply begging him to bring backup filled him with much-needed relief. If she was still worried about him, their relationship was salvageable. *If he stopped being a bloody fool.*

Miles shook his head, though she couldn't see him. *This one's low risk*, he replied. *I'll be fine, lovely. I've handled far worse on my own.*

Since the malevolents were supposed to be secret, she asked him who was reporting them. He'd been too happy to be having a conversation to worry about keeping his response off the record. *Mostly non-humans. The older ones, anyway. They know about the malevolents, but it's not exactly public knowledge. It's something handed down from elder to elder. Quietly.* He paused, then added, *This time it was a selkie—not Sorscha, thankfully.*

He could almost hear her smirk in her response: *Small mercies.*

Sorscha, a selkie and seated member of the Assembly, had hunted him like a prize since he'd moved to Seattle. Her relentless romantic pursuit was almost as exhausting as the malevolent hunts themselves.

While he'd never go back to operating solo, this particular malevolent type presented negligible risk. Years of hunting had taught him that paranoia was often a deceptive friend. Miles had to admit he was slightly uneasy about the call since he hadn't recognized the caller's name or voice, but he dismissed his own worries in favor of expedience.

The warmth of the last time he'd been with Esme felt distant, an ember against the cold reality of their lives. Miles trailed his fingers over the steering wheel, his mind drifting to the way her skin had felt under his touch, the faint scent of her shampoo, the lingering tingle on his lips from their last kiss. He wanted more of those moments—needed them—but the hunt came first.

Work, work, and more work—that was the reality of his existence. The sighting had been in the Ballard neighborhood, north of Esme's house. Unfortunately, with a malevolent in such a densely populated area, taking care of the problem couldn't wait. The danger they presented went beyond their teeth and claws. Each appearance could chip away at the delicate facade of normalcy that concealed magic from the mundane world. History had taught mages how dangerous that was, and swift action could prevent uncomfortable questions from arising.

Now that he thought of it, it was strange that they'd had only redcap and ogre sightings in the city since the Gala. Maybe the malevolents had their own holidays, Miles thought wryly. Or maybe Leon had actually been helping with the malevolents like he'd claimed at the bar.

The drive to the Ballard Locks was short, with rain streaking the windows of his car the entire way. Thankfully, a quick-moving storm had raised temperatures in the area, eliminating the threat of snow. Because of the hills, Seattle dealt with snow worse than Cardiff, and that was saying something.

The report had called in a kappa. Nasty little creatures, but they were one of the more common malevolents. These amphibious demons resembled large turtles with a penchant for mischief and violence. With their numbers being so high, it was a good thing they weren't particularly clever or difficult to dispatch. A single solid blow could take one out, provided you didn't allow them to drag you into the water first.

Miles pulled into a paid parking lot, pausing as he fished for his credit card. Esme would've told him not to bother paying. That holiday parking enforcement was a joke. The thought made him smile. He loved they were so different; she would always make his life interesting. Still, he'd accepted long ago that he would always be a bit of a stickler. He paid the nominal fee—no need to take unnecessary risks.

Miles checked his phone again—no new messages. It had been an hour since that last text exchange with Esme.

He should have left the kappa to fester for the night. But instead, he was here, zipping up his waterproof jacket, about to head out on another hunt before they'd had a real conversation.

He stared at the screen a moment longer, then typed, *Heading out now. I'll check in later.*

A reply came almost instantly: *Be careful.*

He could picture her saying it, the tightness in her voice, the worry she wouldn't admit outright. It wasn't the same as hearing her say it, though, as feeling her fingertips press into his arms like they had so many times before when she didn't want him to go.

Finn's revelation still loomed in his thoughts, a distraction he couldn't afford. Occasionally, when he let himself think of Esme too long, another face intruded—one that didn't belong to her. Maybe it was Nudd's lingering influence, or maybe it was his own mind pulling him toward something he wasn't ready to examine. Either way, it didn't change the fact that he missed her.

Miles exhaled, silenced his phone, and buried it in his pocket. The one thing he didn't need was a call spoiling his element of surprise.

Darkness came early after the winter solstice. The dim street lights cast pale halos on the pathways, illuminating the occasional puddle and highlighting the dark shapes of looming trees on the path to the water's edge. During the daytime, brigades of boats would make their way through each step of the Ballard locks until they reached Elliot Bay. But that evening, the entire area was desolate.

The hiss of rain hitting the surface of the water in the locks below and the steel walkways above drowned out smaller sounds, making it difficult for him to track anything moving nearby. Pulling his hood tighter over his head, he watched his footing as he navigated the labyrinth of concrete walkways slick with water.

His senses strained for any hint of movement or magic. As he splashed through the shallow puddles, he allowed the tension of the hunt to build as he mentally prepared himself.

Then he felt it.

A sudden prickle moved across his skin, like static electricity that itched. Goosebumps broke out as the hairs on his arms and neck rose. Magic was building—close and fast. That was not something a kappa would do.

He barely had time to react. Instinct took over as he detonated a magical shield, the invisible barrier flaring out around him with a soft whoosh.

The impact came a fraction of a second later. Something glanced off his aegis, coming at him from behind. The force was powerful enough to make him stagger. He spun, daggers already in hand, heart pounding, but saw... nothing.

The rain passed through his aegis like it wasn't there, freely pelting his head. Magic, with its peculiar set of rules, allowed weather-related phenomena to permeate protective shields. Only druidic magic or beings like dryads and svartálfar could counter rain and wind.

There were no audible signs of his attacker's presence for him to track—no heavy breathing or footsteps. The only sounds were the rain and his own breath.

A familiar magical tingle made his arms prickle a second time. But it was off, like a favorite song played out of tune. Recognizing the sensation, exactly like in the warehouse in the aftermath of the redcap fight, his stomach clenched. This magic wasn't strictly malevolent, but it was wrong—twisted, a jumble of different magics all wrapped up in one. Confusion and adrenaline combined in a dizzying rush as Miles took in his surroundings.

The realization struck him like a blow: This wasn't a simple monster. This was something much more dangerous. A person, perhaps non-human, but very intelligent and playing games. The quarry had become the hunter.

Miles shifted his grip on both push daggers. He'd brought his longest pair, thinking he might need to penetrate a kappa's shell with a burst of magic enhancing his strength, but now he wondered if he'd have to pierce human flesh instead. *Alright, Nudd*, he thought. *You've been pretty heavy-handed lately. Now's the time to give me a little help.*

Nothing. No surge of strength, no new special magical ability. Just the rain and the quiet thrum of his own shield's magic.

He'd sworn he wouldn't access whatever latent power he'd used during the nandibear fight again—at least, not for himself. The first time he'd mist walked, reaching for it had been almost instinctive. Yet when he'd walked through the mists of magic with Esme for a second time and imbued his shield with extra strength, he had made a choice to do so. Two of the three incidents had caused a nearby malevolent prison to rupture.

Yet nothing like that had happened the single time Nudd's magic had undeniably possessed him while he'd been fighting the ogre. From that, he deduced the significance of his choices.

From Miles' perspective, it all seemed like a load of bloody nonsense, magically speaking. He'd been healing people with his special power for decades. How did voluntarily tapping into the other magic he never requested to have in the first place destabilize malevolent prisons? The only conclusion he could come up with was that it was a bit like Esme tapping into the infernal. She'd told him about the darkness pulling at her when she used too much. Maybe magic had an unwritten rule that strength had to be balanced with risk.

He'd been attacked once. Now Miles had a decision to make: stay and fight or flee.

He decided to stay, cautiously, to see how this played out but on his terms. Whoever had attacked him wasn't getting away that easily. It was his turn to hunt.

Just as Miles had the thought, a gust of wind, unnaturally strong and fast, whipped at him from the west. His shield ignored it, inconveniently obeying the laws of magic and nature. It was nearly enough to knock him off his feet. Every single one of his instincts screamed danger.

Whoever threw that bit of evocation magic had either already known, or was catching onto, his shield's inherent weakness.

He quickened his pace, his boots thudding against the wet pavement as he sped through the small botanical garden that was attached to the tourist area at the locks. The landscaped area wasn't much more than a long strolling circular walk, but that was the direction he felt the magic coming most strongly from.

A flicker of movement caught his attention, a shadow darting between two trees. Heart pounding, he pursued, the world around him blurred.

The shadow darted left. Miles pivoted. Another flash of movement—this time to his right. He was being toyed with. This quarry was the worst kind—elusive, cunning, and potentially deadly.

A darker thought came as he ran. What if this scenario wasn't about him at all? What if someone was luring him away from Esme? He choked on his next breath.

Miles skidded to a stop, heart hammering. He'd lost track of the darting shadow. He tuned in to his surroundings, opening himself, using all his senses to listen.

Nothing. He heard, he felt, absolutely nothing...

The wind magic... could it be a malevolent Fae? Unseelie? His solitude made him incredibly vulnerable to most Unseelie Fae. Time to re-evaluate his pursuit.

The next attack left him no opportunity to reconsider. The jagged edge of an ice spike gleamed in the lamplight as it shot like an arrow straight at his chest.

Time stretched. Miles had just enough of it to realize how utterly screwed he was. Whether his shield could protect him from this type of magic was a gamble. Sometimes an aegis would "sense" ice as a threat, sometimes not.

His training took over, and his body reacted before his mind could catch up. In a desperate, clumsy scramble, he flung himself to the ground in a move that probably looked like a poorly executed burpee. A hair's breadth from injury, he slammed his daggers into their wrist holsters and bolted.

His attacker had used more elemental evocation magic. They'd deduced his shield's weakness. And they were exploiting it. If he could find whatever or whoever was throwing magic at him, maybe he could track it. But he couldn't lock onto the magic to scry his hunter because it was a chaotic mess of jumbled energy.

Whoever they were, they clearly wanted him to feel cornered, to second-guess his every step. Fuck that. He ran straight toward the direction the ice arrow had come from.

The tingle of the strange magic pulsed stronger. *Found you.*

Miles was probably being a fool, rushing straight into danger, but this was a calculated risk. He had to know who, or what, was after him.

The caller. He hadn't recognized the voice on the phone, but it wasn't like he knew everyone in Seattle. This job had to be a setup.

A rustle of leaves jerked his attention to the left. Without thinking, he hurled his right dagger at the sound.

A short, forceful intake of breath was the reward for his efforts. With the dagger gripped tightly in his left hand and his Glock poised for action, he sprinted toward the bushes. Adrenaline pumping, he hoped to capitalize on the advantage his strike might give him.

Before he could reach the spot, a wave of magical energy slammed into Miles, as bright and sudden as a firework exploding in his face.

The lights from the old-fashioned lampposts that lined the botanical garden's walkways barely reached his hunter's hiding spot, but Miles already knew. He already knew that his pursuer had escaped.

The explosion of magic he'd felt was most certainly panicked mist walking. This left him with a significant issue—he didn't know where they'd gone. In the dim light, he spotted his dagger lying on the disturbed soil. He picked it up. It was covered in blood. Human blood from the smell of it.

Miles had had enough of playing this game. He didn't linger. He refused to play cat and mouse with whoever this was any longer.

He didn't care how stupid he looked. He darted back and forth, his movements erratic, like a person trying to outrun an alligator in an effort to evade anything else they might throw at him.

Whether they were nearby and would chase him all the way to his car was another gamble. But it was one he couldn't help. He threw open the door using telekinesis and practically flung himself into the driver's seat.

He peeled out of the parking lot, unpursued. The magic he'd sensed was unlike that of Gwyn or Finn, the only two people he knew could mist walk, other than Jacob.

Once he got a few blocks away, he turned his phone back on. He had a dozen missed calls from Esme. Double fuck.

After reading his text messages, he broke the speed limit all the way to Abby's house. Maybe Esme was right—maybe holiday enforcement all around was a joke.

"Probably a kappa," the caller had said. *Right*. And he was the King of Wales.

He had a gut feeling that things were only going to get worse.

CHAPTER TWENTY-NINE

THE HEART OF THE PROBLEM

Abby

"Did you seriously call Katia asking if she fucked the life out of Finn? Esme, you idiot, she wasn't even around."

Katia had texted Abby a string of laughing emojis, relaying the story in her usual blunt fashion. Thankfully, Katia didn't feel targeted or offended by Esme's questions. In fact, the succubus found Esme's endless dancing around the subject of her dalliance with Finn so hilarious that she nearly wet herself from laughing.

"I did not accuse her of that!" Esme groaned, covering her face. "I just wanted to know if this was a side effect of their... whatever it was. A date? Ugh, I don't even know what to call it."

Pointing at Finn's prone form, Abby said, "Absolutely not in front of the imp. He might get ideas, and we cannot condone him having ideas."

"I can't just sit here while he looks like... like this." Esme's voice cracked. She pressed her palms to her temples, pacing in panic, as she stared at Finn's still form. "What if he doesn't wake up? Could this be my fault?"

"No," Abby said firmly. "This is something else."

Abby had rushed to Finn's side the moment she'd arrived. He seemed stable, his breathing and heart not showing anything too concerning. He mumbled something about "grandbabies" at one point, so he must have been going in and out of sleep and unconsciousness. Whatever he was suffering from resembled magical exhaustion, particularly after Esme recounted his pre-faint vomiting episode. Its rapid onset, lacking any discernible trigger, was the problem.

However, Esme correctly countered, "But, you saw him throw an insane amount of fire at the jorōgumo. He detonated like a bomb during the nandibear fight and only passed out from it. I didn't see or feel him use any magic, other than his little disappearing act, after David walked into the bar."

"Whoa, back up, Esme. David was there?" Abby tried not to overreact, but this bit of information seemed important. "Why?"

Still, she couldn't really blame Esme for being flustered. The exertion of carrying one hundred pounds up three flights of stairs was enough to leave anyone breathless and slightly confused.

"Finn snatched David's hand when David offered me a handshake. Finn grabbed it like he was trying to rip it off, then passed out. It makes no sense!" Esme shrugged, then reconsidered. "Wait, do you think David had something to do with what happened to Finn?"

Certainty hit Abby like a bucket of ice water, making it hard for her to breathe for a long moment. Abby recognized her own rising panic mirrored in her best friend, and Esme didn't yet know how deep this unsettling discovery might go. A dread-filled "yes" was all she could get out.

The sound of hurried knocks, hard enough to rattle the door, startled them. They both jumped. Abby instinctively covered her heart with one hand, her eyes wide.

"Sorry, sorry, too loud," Miles called, apologizing from behind the door, his voice tight with urgency.

Esme bolted from where she'd wandered to the couch, beating Abby, who had actually been closer to the door. Esme's voice was equal parts worried and bewildered. "Holy shit, Miles... What happened?"

Miles' face was flushed. He had dirt all over the front of his jacket and mud on his boots. Kicking them off, he closed the door behind him and pulled Esme into a firm hug.

The sight was a bitter reminder of what Abby had lost with Gwyn. But that was her fault, wasn't it? But she wasn't the type of person who would settle for less when a bit of work was all it would take to achieve genuine happiness. If he fully invested himself and was more transparent with her about Creiddylad, they could have that kind of intimacy again.

Miles' grip was tight on Esme's arms as he pulled her close, his forehead resting against hers. There was so much unresolved tension in the gesture Abby had to look away.

"We have a problem," he murmured, his voice rough, "but first, Finn."

Miles walked to Finn's side and did a quick check of his vitals, and Abby went into nurse mode, telling him everything she'd found before he'd arrived. "From what I know about him, I think he's going to be fine."

Once they were done, Esme again explained, for Miles' benefit, David's arrival. "I got my hopes up thinking David might ease up on his hostility toward me. Barely thirty seconds after he left, Finn vomited all over the floor and collapsed. Cleaning that up when I get back to the bar is gonna suck."

After taking it all in, Miles rose from his crouch beside Finn and mumbled something that sounded like, "Huh."

Abby nibbled on her bottom lip. That wasn't the straightforward answer from Dr. Smartypants they'd been hoping for. "This is going to sound crazy, but hear me out..." She explained how David's aura had looked tainted, almost dirty, when she'd accidentally left her new ability on after taking it from Colin.

An expression of mild confusion, rather than alarm, crossed Esme's face. Miles went from confusion, to questioning, and then straight to alarm. A shadow crossed his face—something between anger and disbelief. "Tell me more," he demanded.

After years in the Corded Brotherhood and the emergency room, Abby had developed a habit of obeying commands quickly. Miles was technically her superior. Plus, he always rationalized his choices, so she accepted the pressure and didn't fault him. He was performing his duties with the authority of someone who had earned it—Abby didn't think Esme yet knew how much he'd done for the Brotherhood in his tenure.

"David's aura is..." Abby paused, choosing her words carefully. "It's not one solid color or blend of colors like everyone else has. And there's one piece that stands out—right at his heart, there's magic that looks exactly like yours, Miles. *Exactly* like it. I've never seen magic like that anywhere else since I've had this ability."

Miles' brow furrowed, the lines of worry creasing his face becoming more pronounced with each passing second. He shook his head. The changing expressions on his face made her think he was piecing together the implications. Then settling on a dark possibility, the same possibility she'd come to.

"I'm new to the whole 'seeing magic' thing, but it stuck out—big time."

He mumbled something under his breath. It sounded Welsh, something she'd never heard him do before.

"Babe, you're freaking me out." Esme grabbed his hand.

"I think I walked into a trap tonight," Miles said, his voice low and grim. "Someone knew exactly how to get past my aegis."

While he told them what had happened during his hunt, he brushed a bit of dirt from his coat, his face showing increasing strain. "That's why I look like I just crawled out of a ditch."

His voice took on a sharper edge. "Then they mist walked out of there like it was all a game. That narrowed down the possibilities to Fae or a mage. The magic I felt was completely chaotic, exactly like you described, Abby."

He reached into his coat and pulled out a dagger he'd stuffed into a small plastic bag, with blood streaked along its edge. "I managed to hit whoever attacked me before they vanished." He held it up, his gaze hardening into a dark sort of bleakness. "If there's enough blood here, we can get it DNA-tested, but that will take weeks. I'm unsure if these two situations are related, but I'm also not a fan of coincidences."

Esme's eyes turned black; she clenched her hands at her sides. "I knew David was rotten," she spat. "With how much of a rush he was to get out of the bar after shaking Finn's hand, it has to be him."

Knowledge of her demonic heritage must have removed whatever obstacle had held the change back before. Now, Esme's eerie full-eye darkening was becoming more frequent. Looking back, Abby should have realized her best friend wasn't entirely human.

Already sorting through Abby's tiny coat closet, Esme suggested, "Maybe we should head to his place right now to see if he's injured. I'd be thrilled to play bad cop for this. Thrilled!"

Crazy wench. Abby loved how unhinged Esme could be when she was angry. It was like watching a wind storm with a vendetta. Regardless, her job as BFF was to stay composed when Esme couldn't and vice versa.

"Slow down!" Abby cautioned. "If David is responsible for both attacks, then he's hiding something. We don't know how he did this to Finn. If that handshake was intended for you, Esme, this night could have gone very differently. We need more information before doing anything. What motivated him to do this? And why is his magic so unusual?"

Abby took a steadying breath, glancing from Miles to Esme.

Miles shook his head, running a hand through his hair, clearly still processing everything they'd uncovered. "This all seems mad to me. I've known him for twenty-five years. He's little more than a magical scholar. I've never considered him personally dangerous. I doubt he is physically capable of evading me like that... But I guess with enough magic..."

"Miles, you expected him to retaliate when you didn't give in to all of his petty demands. If he's not dangerous, what qualifies him to be the top dog in London?" Esme asked, eyes back to their normal violet shade.

Miles smirked. "Money, bloodline, and a mental library of obscure magical theory. In London's magical circles, those matter more than actual ability. David's family has been pulling strings in the Assembly since before America was a country."

"It's easy to have a blind spot for your family," Esme grumbled, settling back onto the worn couch beside Finn.

Abby took a seat at one of the barstools at her kitchen counter and leaned back, mirroring Esme by folding her arms. "I don't know much about him—just that I don't like him. He's always a little too interested in my life, asking about my training, my family, trying to have these forced conversations. It's almost... invasive."

"That confirms what I already suspected. David's been angling to become Jacob's replacement as head of the Assembly, and he's not thrilled about my leadership of the Brotherhood." Frustration and sadness showed on Miles' face as he let out a sigh. "He'd need to consolidate a lot of influence—and fast—to make that happen. Your family would play into that with your mum a seated member and you and Colin Corded Brothers. I just... can't see him trying to kill me as the method he'd use to take over the Brotherhood. We were close for so many years."

"Perhaps he's not as clean-cut as he pretends to be." Abby's voice dropped to a whisper, the words heavy with dread. Her stomach churned as the pieces clicked into place. "What if he's been playing us all along? Look at Jacob as an example. Everyone who doesn't work for him only knows that he's a powerful mage. They don't know what he's capable of, what he's *done*. What happened to Finn is eerily similar to what happened to my mom a few days ago!"

Esme gasped. "You think he was your mom's mystery visitor? I wouldn't be surprised. He acts like he's better than everyone, but if it benefits him? I'd bet he'd cross any line he could justify."

As Miles sat in thoughtful silence with a troubled expression, Abby watched Esme watching Miles, her friend's protective instincts practically radiating off her. The room was like a powder keg—Miles' disbelief, Esme's temper, and Abby's own growing certainty creating an explosive mix.

The real question—*how did we miss this?*—was left hanging unspoken between them.

A series of sharp raps on the door echoed through the quiet room, making them jump for a second time. Abby's heart skipped as she recognized the familiar rhythm. There was no helping the conflicted feeling that crept into her chest.

"It's... it's Gwyn," she murmured, moving toward the door almost on instinct.

Miles shot her a questioning look, but Abby ignored it. Esme would explain everything to him as Abby went to greet her visitor.

She barely looked at Gwyn before saying, "Well, come in." The words came automatically, but inside, Abby felt like she was juggling lit matches—one wrong move and everything around them would burn. Having him here, in her space, while everything else was falling apart felt exactly right, but it was damned frustrating when she had to maintain boundaries.

The moment their eyes finally locked, a ridiculous pain bloomed in her chest. Her relief at his presence collided with the unresolved space between them. She wanted to close the distance, to throw herself into his arms, but... they weren't there yet.

Gwyn's face reflected her emotion, but with a more profound anguish. Rain dripped from his hair as he stepped inside.

He took in the scene behind Abby—Miles, filthy and soaked; Esme, body held tight, irritable; and a leprechaun sprawled out on her couch, unconscious. She almost laughed seeing his eyes darting around the room like he was planning three different battle (or exit) strategies depending upon what he discovered.

As Abby turned back to her friends, Miles' expression showed a depth of understanding that was a bit too profound, given Esme's brief explanation.

"Well, you're here. Might as well see what we're dealing with." Abby gave Gwyn a meaningful up-and-down once-over. "Unless you've turned evil, too?"

She expected him to recognize her playful tone by now, but Gwyn appeared to interpret her joke literally. His eyes grew wide, and he shook his head. "No... No."

They all sat around her dining table, filling him in on everything that had happened. After they were finished, Gwyn offered a very Gwyn suggestion.

"The solution is simple." His voice was cold, his eyes dark with intent. "We end his existence before he can do more harm."

Gwyn looked around at their appalled expressions. "Why do you judge me for this? The man is clearly a siphon. Who has been stealing from you"—he pointed at Miles—"and the mistress O'Malley. He also put Finn on that couch."

Esme's eyebrows reached into her hairline. She asked the question that was clearly on everyone else's mind. "Gwyn, what the hell is a siphon?"

For a moment, he hid his face behind his hand. "A siphon," Gwyn growled, "is a parasite amongst mages. They feed off others' magic to supplement and feed their needs, like succubi—only much worse."

His eyes fixed on Esme. "Your people know them well. You were their primary hunters in my past. They are a rare type of cambion."

Esme grumbled, "Seriously? David is cambion? That's some next level internalized speciesism bullshit."

Abby couldn't disagree with that. Looking to Miles, she asked, "Is David cambion?"

Miles shook his head, his shoulders slumping in resignation, and shrugged. "To the best of my knowledge, no..."

"So, again, why are we not killing this thief?" Gwyn pressed.

Esme's answer, a quiet whisper that came after her fiery anger and grumbling, surprised everyone. "He's Miles' Jacob."

Love, be it for better or worse, really was at the heart of all of their problems. Abby's tiny apartment had never been more crowded—not with bodies, but with revelations.

Gwyn, as subtle as a sledgehammer, wasted no time in shooing Miles and Esme out the door. "If we have no decision on what to do with this thief, I'd like to speak with Abigail—alone."

"Yo, jackass, did you ask her first?" Esme took a threatening step in his direction.

Abby stepped between them before Esme started an unnecessary spat. Though she clenched her jaw to keep the groan down, the exhaustion and resignation in her voice were unmistakable for all parties present. "It's fine. Let's take the night to think about this."

Esme's last words before she left were, "I will make my trolls beat the ever-loving shit out of you, Gwyn Newman. Do *not* test me."

Miles looked at Esme like he was tempted to throw her over his shoulder, caveman-style, and drag her back to his cave. Yet he turned to Gwyn and asked, "Mate, do I need a heads-up or not?"

Apparently Gwyn understood what that cryptic question was about because he shook his head. "No." What was going on between those two? Not once during that interaction had they argued or glared. And Miles had looked far too sympathetic when Esme had told him what was going on between them.

When it was only the two of them, Gwyn seemed to relax slightly. Even so, the strained atmosphere between them hadn't eased enough. He shifted uneasily, looking like he was preparing himself for a speech.

"So," Abby started, crossing her arms, a defensive wall going up. "We haven't talked in days and now you're here. Why?"

In lieu of answering, he fell to his knees. Their height difference made it to where his head aligned with her chest. Damn her simple brain. Seeing him like that made her want to rub her fingers through his dark hair. She resisted, but it was a tough battle.

Gwyn's gaze first settled on the spot where her heart thrummed a rapid, erratic beat against her ribs. Slowly, his eyes rose to meet hers.

"Cariad, my heart." Gwyn's voice broke, raw with emotion. "I've been a fool. Please, forgive me."

Then he prostrated himself fully on the carpet of her living room, hands outstretched in supplication and all. Gods above and below, he'd lost his damn mind.

"Gwyn, people do not do that." She stared at him, mouth agape. "You need therapy. You know that, right?"

Face still directed at the floor, Gwyn mumbled, "Cariad, *please*, I want to mend things between us. I just don't know how."

His eyes were pleading when they reached hers once again. Seeing the mixture of desperation and regret written on his face almost made her break. The moment stretched before she exhaled sharply and stepped back.

"Stand up! You're holding back, and I'm not here for it, Gwyn. I am thirty-one years old. I'm done with half-explanations and excuses. We either need to talk through your Creiddylad problems together, or you deal with it on your own."

Not looking at her, he took a deep breath, hesitating. Thinking he might say something, she waited, but the moment never came.

With a pointed look and a subtle shake of her head, she turned toward the door, signaling that their conversation was over. "There's no point in this going any further tonight. I appreciate everything you've said, and I can tell that you mean it. But I need a productive update to move forward with us as more than friends. Can you understand that, Gwyn?"

A silent nod, his eyes squeezed shut. Then he stood and dragged himself through the open doorway. She moved to close the door behind him, but he stopped her abruptly, the sound of his hand hitting the doorframe audible in the otherwise silent hallway. "Abigail, I will present Lord Abington's head on a silver platter to your mother if that would please you. Anything, cariad, *anything*."

She didn't have to think twice to realize that he factually meant every word. Abby shook her head again and closed her eyes for a long moment. "Goodbye, Gwyn." With a firm push, she shut the door, leaving her in silence except for the leprechaun's soft snoring.

CHAPTER THIRTY

A CREATIVE SOLUTION

Gwyn

The transition from overt displays of wealth to its concealment was a fascinating swing in social norms from his time. The hotel lobby exuded the kind of understated luxury Abigail would call "expensive." Gwyn smirked when he saw Leon casually lounging in a high-backed chair, looking almost like he belonged there. Leon's easygoing demeanor was a practiced mask, concealing calculating intelligence. Today, however, his infuriating charm would be their key to success, much to Gwyn's chagrin.

Leon stood, still sporting the tattoos and new piercings he'd added to his glamour. They spoke in their mother tongue, as usual, except for one glaring word. "Honestly, Junior, I had no idea David was capable of this. I regret not having informed you earlier. I knew he was a cambion, but I thought he was so weak blooded that it didn't matter."

"Junior?" Gwyn addressed this new epithet Leon had granted him. "You claim this is an act of friendship, yet you insist on provoking me with that title at the start. Why?"

"Yet it is an accurate term." Leon shrugged. "You are 'ap Nudd.'"

"Not here. I'm 'Newman.'" Gwyn bit back his frustration. He should thank Leon for arranging this meeting, but the man's constant needling made it difficult.

Leon winced subtly as he spoke. "Shall I do the talking when we get upstairs? You seem to be more in the mood for cutting off digits than talking. If you want to rough him up, let me join in before I leave. I've got two hours."

Gwyn dismissed Leon's flinch as a pulled muscle, but he knew Leon had a point. Gwyn had become a man stuck between an inevitable, disastrous truth coming out and protecting those he cared for. Reluctantly, he nodded. "You are certain that he is in his hotel room?"

"I scried him as soon as you called." Pausing briefly, Leon suggested, "We might not need to threaten him right away. David's clever. He'll see you as a valuable ally—he's been sizing you up since you met."

"Yes, so he can try to use me as a tool," Gwyn spat out. Given Leon's considerable prior interest, it was likely Leon also had similar intentions for Gwyn.

Leon shrugged again. "To get what you want, sometimes it's better to pretend to be a simple tool rather than to try to be the one in control."

Gwyn scoffed. "Even the idea wounds my pride."

"I would expect nothing less of you, Princeling. And yet... you work with the Corded Brotherhood here..." Leon said pointedly. "Don't worry. I have a way of dealing with David that won't require overt violence."

"Just in case." Gwyn revealed the hunting knife he'd bought after leaving Abigail's.

Leon did the same, pulling a dagger out from where it was concealed beneath his ever-present glamour.

The duo stood stiffly in the elevator, the silence between them awkward enough that Gwyn began to question the wisdom of their plan. Fury at David, the need to fix what had been broken with Abigail—it all drove him forward. Was he being reckless? Once, the answer had been simple: unequivocally yes. Justice was the right of the strong. Now, things were more complicated and the world demanded empathy.

When they got to the hotel room, Leon's judgment proved accurate. David welcomed them into his suite, his voice brimming with precisely calculated warmth the entire time. He offered drinks, and they settled into the sitting area, pretending to relax.

David's crisp shirt was missing a tie, the top button undone to feign relaxation. Despite a friendly demeanor, the calculating gleam in his eyes revealed his true nature.

"Mr. Newman," David began, slowly seating himself, "I was most pleased to learn from Leon of your interest in a professional meeting." His eyes flickered between Gwyn and Leon.

Gwyn suppressed any hint of aggression in his expression and played along.

Leon slid into his usual easy charm. "Gwyn here wants to get to know you. Officially, he's a Welsh newcomer, and that's correct, but I think we all know that the truth is more complex than that."

David examined Gwyn carefully, his gaze never wavering. "Yes, I am intrigued by your mastery over the hellhound I have read about. A pity you didn't bring it today. Are you an animal mage?"

Gwyn's forced smile faltered, his jaw locking as his fingers curled into fists. Every muscle in his body screamed for violence, but he forced the word past clenched teeth. "No."

The vile man had attacked the Mistress O'Malley and left Finn unconscious from the magical drain. He had also attacked Miles, repeatedly, a fact that frustrated Gwyn's reluctance to care to no end. On top of that, his second chance with the one woman he'd ever loved was in shambles.

Gwyn had many problems, but he could immediately improve only this one awful situation.

Leon had listened to Gwyn's explanation and request for help without objection, judgment, or hostility. Gwyn hadn't realized how much he needed the relief from the constant pressure to conform to modern ideals until he felt it. Talking with someone who understood the need for forceful justice brought back some feelings of home, of a different time when might was right and life was simpler.

The plan depended on Gwyn keeping his composure. With the shadows of melancholy constantly seeking him, his natural emotional reaction became one of aggression—he wasn't sure how much longer he could fight the shadows.

Leon must have read this emotion on his face because he stepped in, saying, "Gwyn and I thought it best to come to you directly. We are volunteering ourselves to get rid of an unpleasant element that seems to be new to the area."

David's eyebrows shot up. "Indeed? What kind of element are you referring to?"

"We believe a siphon has surfaced in the area," Leon said, with a grin that didn't reach his eyes. "This siphon has already targeted a few individuals in our circle. Given your role, we thought it was important to let you know."

Gwyn watched David closely as the words sank in. There was a pause—a split-second flicker of surprise that crossed David's face before he quickly masked it.

His voice bitter, Gwyn added, "This siphon injured the Mistress O'Malley. We suspect this siphon also targeted your protégé last night while he responded to a malevolent sighting."

David, leaning forward, tried to regain control of the conversation. "Do you have any leads on who this siphon might be?"

Leon smiled, rising from his seat with careful deliberation. He raised a single finger. "Only one."

Reaching out his hand for a polite shake, Leon continued, "We truly appreciate your allowing us to find the guilty party."

David's fingers barely clasped Leon's before David went utterly limp, slumping back in his seat. Leon stepped back, shuddering as if to shake off an unpleasant sensation. "By all the magic... that tingles!"

Gwyn blinked, aghast. "And how exactly do you propose we get him out of the hotel now?"

Leon shot him a wry smile. "Simple. I'll work an illusion. All you need to do is grab one of those bellhop carts and look inconspicuous."

Only Gwyn and Leon heard the soft, steady breathing concealed beneath the illusion as they strolled through the lobby. Nodding to the oblivious receptionist, they pushed what appeared to be a neatly stacked set of luggage out to the valet. Leather belts from David's closet secured him to the cart. Fine silk neckties bound his hands and feet.

Leon's rental car wasn't the one that showed up after his ticket was called. It was a large black sedan with blacked-out windows. The rear window rolled down to reveal a familiar face that was not supposed to be there.

Jacob's eyes glittered with a dangerous, predatory light. "I see that we have similar aims, Mr. Newman. Please place my... luggage in the boot and then come join me. Mr. Chan, it would be a wonderful favor to Mr. Newman if you could help him load it." Jacob's dismissal of Leon was executed with skillful subtlety. "I believe if you return your rental early you can get a refund..."

Leon shrugged. "Happy to help a friend." But Gwyn could sense the tension his body held.

Jacob harrumphed. "Indeed. Your work has not gone unnoticed. Thank you, Mr. Chan. Good day."

They loaded the "luggage" into the boot of Jacob's car, and Gwyn joined Jacob in the back seat. Leon left, whistling a merry tune with a self-satisfied grin.

Gwyn had barely fastened his seatbelt before Jacob asked, "Does Miles or Esmeralda know you are here?"

This was the kind of question Gwyn could not afford to dance around with a man like Jacob. He wasn't certain what ground they stood upon at the moment. "No, neither would approve of the necessary methods. Abigail is also unaware."

"Good. Miles has too much emotional entanglement, and Esmeralda doesn't need the stain on her conscience at the moment. Abigail... Well, her talents might have been useful. Too bad, she has the right kind of moral flexibility for undertakings such as these."

Jacob's perceptive insight into Abigail's true nature caused Gwyn to blink in surprised recognition. That was followed up by a wave of relief as he realized that this intervention wasn't about his misconduct being addressed. Gwyn had simply reached the brutal, violent part of his plan before Jacob had a chance to begin his.

Jacob said, "I know why I'm here, but I'm curious how you arrived at the same conclusion."

Gwyn told him everything about the impromptu meeting they'd had at Abigail's. From his reaction, Gwyn realized Jacob knew what had happened to Christi. However, Gwyn's narration of David's failed attack on Esmeralda and successful act of stealing from Finn surprised him. Gwyn's words, "Miles also questioned whether David planned a fake malevolent hunt that left him fending off elemental attacks from an unknown mage," caused his expression to darken.

For a long moment, as they drove through the city, Jacob's eyes remained fixed on a far horizon that only he could see. Gwyn understood that he was seeing nothing and everything all at once. Jacob was mentally elsewhere, in a dangerous realm of fantasy that could become reality if he wished it—where he was likely murdering the man stuffed into the boot of his chauffeured car.

"Jacob, we need to question David before you do all the things you've just imagined doing to him."

The switch to normalcy in the Archmage was instantaneous and so subtle that Gwyn nearly missed it. In a clear, strong voice, Jacob said, "Perhaps I have underestimated your value, Mr. Newman. As you are aware, Mr. Abington has been exploiting Miles for over two decades. It wasn't only greed that drove him—it was delaying the physiological effects of what could essentially be considered addiction."

Gwyn strained his seatbelt, leaning forward as he asked, "What was he addicted to?"

"Miles' magic." Jacob made a sound of annoyance deep in his throat.

As a siphon, it was necessary for David to absorb magic taken from others, similar to how succubi and incubi must absorb vitality through romantic contact. While agreeing to a romantic interlude that left you feeling exhausted but equally satisfied was a simple transaction for most people, almost no one would be willing to give up their magic regularly enough to meet the needs of a siphon.

"Do you know what a biological cell is, Mr. Newman?"

Gwyn shook his head, confused by the abrupt change of topic.

"They are the minuscule building blocks that make up every part of your body. Suffice to say that David was siphoning Miles so frequently that David's cells stopped repairing themselves properly. His body had a constant source of magic to rely on for that, so why would it need to repair itself? That left David degrading rapidly, aging rapidly, leaving him weak and desperate without Miles to feed upon."

A soft, regretful sigh escaped Jacob's lips. "And his audacious pursuit of Esmeralda is a direct consequence of my actions in London. Will you join me for a bit of interrogation, Mr. Newman?"

Gwyn smiled with pure, wicked delight. "Of course."

***

Exhausted, hours later, Gwyn dialed Leon's number with trembling hands.

Before Leon could utter a greeting, Gwyn said, "I gained some useful insights from talking with David today. You have shown yourself to be a true friend. I'm in. Let us see what Nudd has to say for himself."

"I knew you'd see it was the only way. Glad to have you as an ally, disposer of wrath, blameless and pure." Leon chose two of Gwyn's other epithets from books written about him to praise his good decision in joining forces.

Blameless? Never.

Pure? Not in this lifetime or the last.

But wrath—wrath, he could embrace.

CHAPTER THIRTY-ONE

BRITISH MATTERS

Miles

Miles' breath misted in the evening air as he stood by the edge of the dock. A cold dread clung to him, a bone-deep chill that mirrored the winter air seeping into his boots and coat. Sitting next to him, Lily offered her silent support. He had come here to clear his mind, but his thoughts were as restless as the ducks approaching him for food before tucking in for the night.

He and Esme had mutually agreed to postpone their discussion about David until they were both well-rested. He still found it nearly impossible to sleep well without her, but the sleepless night gave him time to plan what he would say.

Before dawn had fully broken that morning, the brownie Miles had posted the evening before to watch David Abington at his hotel reported he had never come back to his room that evening. That day, he didn't go to his hotel or the Assembly offices. No one in Miles' network had seen or heard from him whatsoever. David had simply vanished.

The man who had been like a father to him, molding him in ways Miles was just now beginning to understand, had disappeared without a trace. On the surface, it might have been a relief. Evidence pointed toward David being a predator.

But Miles couldn't dismiss the sense that things weren't finished. It was a pattern with David—either coming back or pulling Miles in. He was a master of manipulation. He could do it again. And now, unlike any other time in his life, Miles had significantly more to lose. He'd sworn off relationships before Esme, convinced they'd be weaponized against him. Miles had thought that moving across the world would free him from it, but Esme had already paid the price in so many ways for loving him...

As he sifted through years of recollections, the possibility of David siphoning him became undeniable, a recurring possibility that seemed to infect every shared moment of his growth from a teen into a man—and even recently. The memories of such moments were almost immediate upon his arrival in London as a boy. Understanding now how siphons worked, Miles realized he'd been barely twelve years old when David had started preying on him.

He had just settled into the boys' dormitory when David came round to check on him. Miles was brimming with energy and thrilled when his new roommate invited him to watch a football game with his friends. Except Miles hadn't gone because he'd fallen asleep in his room, a heavy, nightmare-wracked sleep that he'd later come to associate with exhaustion he'd thought was normal. Now he knew it was most decidedly not.

At fifteen, after his first kill, an adolescent bogle that had snuck into that same dorm room, David was the first person Miles had called for help. He had escaped major injury but was completely lost, lacking any idea how to proceed with a monster corpse out in the open. David had hugged him, seemingly for comfort, but Miles remembered sagging from utter exhaustion in his arms. At the time, Miles had put it down to a reaction to making his first kill, but now... now, he wasn't so sure.

The "training accidents" and "psychological exercises" that left him drained now seemed to make sense in a horrifying kind of way. David hadn't been mentoring him. He'd been grooming him, tending to him like a garden awaiting harvest. Just the idea of him doing that to a child was utterly repulsive.

Miles was normally logical and calculating in how he handled problems that needed violence. But in that moment, he wanted little more than to slam his prosthesis straight through David's skull. Maybe Gwyn was right in how David should be dealt with.

The anger, intense and fierce, concealed a deeper emotion: grief. Despite the manipulation, lies, and theft, there was still a part of him that loved David as a father. Still craved his approval. Still wanted to believe there was some explanation that would force it all to make sense.

But that was what abusive love was like, wasn't it?

Twenty-five years of manipulation, of carefully crafted dependence. Twenty-five years of being slowly drained, not only of magic, but of autonomy. David's disappearance wasn't a coincidence. It must be a confession. And now Miles had a choice to make: he could hunt David down and confront him, or he could finally, truly break free.

Knowing his magic-stealing secret was out provided him the best chance of keeping David away for good. But what kind of man would he be if he let such a monster continue unchecked?

Hearing footsteps from behind pulled Miles from his thoughts. Turning slightly, he saw Esme, her expression caught somewhere between concern and relief.

"I knew I'd find you here," she said softly.

"Sorry. Didn't mean to worry you," he replied, his voice gruff with repressed emotions.

"You didn't," she said, moving in close. "But something tells me you're not out here for the view." The fog was so thick the view was limited to gray, gray, and more gray.

Miles faltered, his eyes going back to the water. "David's gone."

Her eyebrows shot up. "Gone?"

"Missing. Vanished," he said, his tone bitter. "After all this... He's just... gone."

"You sound like you're not certain if that's a bad thing," she said carefully.

"I don't know what to think," he admitted. "I need to decide what I'm going to do about it—if anything."

"You will," she said firmly. "But you don't have to right now. You've been hit with a lot over the past few days. Let yourself feel it. All of it. Even if you didn't know it, you've been carrying this a long time."

He smiled, teasing her. "Who knew Ms. Turner was such an expert on this?"

Chuckling, she answered, "Just the therapy sessions Abby and Jacob insisted on dragging me to. Also, there's the whole ordeal of decades spent suppressing my own inner demon."

"Before all this, I talked to David." Miles began on the subject that had actually brought her there, his voice low but steady. He glanced at Esme, searching for her reaction. "It didn't go exactly as planned, but... I made it clear he needs to stay out of our lives."

Esme crossed her arms, her expression unreadable. "And how'd he take that?"

Miles sighed, running a hand through his hair. "About as well as you'd expect. He tried to play it off like I was being dramatic, but I didn't let him. I told him to back off—no contact, no interference, nothing."

Esme side-eyed him.

"It wasn't a clean win, lovely. He... mentioned your abilities. Said they're more dangerous than you realize. That someone will take an interest in you now that you're working with the Brotherhood."

Esme's eyes narrowed. "What does that mean?"

"It means he's trying to intimidate me," Miles said, his voice tight. "He wants me to think I need him to protect you. But I don't. *You* don't."

Esme turned to face him fully, her arms still crossed. "And what about you? Are you safe from him?"

Miles looked away, his gaze drifting back to the water. "I don't know," he admitted quietly. "He's always been good at getting under my skin. But I'm not the same person I was when I left London. I won't let him control me anymore."

Esme stepped closer, her voice softening. "I don't need you to protect me from everything, Miles. I need you to trust me."

He reached for her hand, his grip firm but gentle. "I do." He wanted to promise her that there would be no more secrets between them, but he couldn't—not yet. "But he was right about one thing. Someone will take an interest in you. We will have to wait and see if they are better or worse than David."

"Right, because I'm a 'batterin' ram.'" She mimicked Finn's accent.

"Yep." The small grin on his face was the first in days. "But the problem is out there now."

She was silent for a moment, staring at the water. Then she huffed. "That son of a bitch."

Miles gave a humorless chuckle. "That about sums it up."

Esme crossed her arms again. "So what now?"

"Now?" Miles looked at her, his gaze lingering on her face, drinking in the details of her eyes, the curve of her lips, the gentle dusting of freckles across her cheeks. "We go on with our life. On our terms. Not his."

She met his gaze, something sharp and unyielding in her eyes. "Damn right we do."

Then she slammed into him with nearly enough force to bowl him over. Battering ram indeed.

Esme's arms wrapped around him, warm, bare hands touching the skin on his neck to pull him into her. She devoured his mouth, leaving Miles feeling a rush of desire with barely any air left in his lungs. He didn't need to breathe. He only needed this.

He had a woman he loved, who loved him. A loyal dog, vying for his attention. Unique magic that could help people—truly save people. He had patients who needed him. He'd built a life for himself despite David's best efforts to keep him tethered. Maybe that was the best personal revenge: Thriving without him. Being free.

For the first time, Miles permitted himself to lament the younger version of himself, the trust that was shattered, and the potential man he could have been without David's influence. He was aware that some parts of him were irrevocably damaged.

But he was here, the happiest he had been in over twenty years, and everything seemed to have worked out for the best. Holding Esme's hand, he suddenly felt much lighter.

Jacob

Given Christi's meticulous work and his history of poor sleep, Jacob decided it was safe to sleep during the first half of the flight. The private jet was a luxury, but one this situation demanded. No security lines, no crowds. Few questions were asked when an old man spent a fortune to fly across the world with another old man—especially one as notable as David Abington.

His rest was fitful and full of scenes he'd rather forget. Even at his age, the brutal memories of bloodshed, the screams, how blood itched your skin when you soaked in it long enough—these clung to his mind more relentlessly than any happy memory, refusing to fade.

"Mr. Spencer, your requested alarm." The flight attendant shook his shoulder gently. "Mr. Spencer?"

He awoke to a pair of eyes, the blue glassy and sharp, fixed directly on him. Not the cloudy white, lifeless eyes of his nightmares. These were calculating—and very much alive.

David's awkward position made it obvious that he lacked complete control of his body. But Jacob wasn't fool enough to underestimate him.

"Yes. Thank you." Jacob smiled genially and hurriedly dismissed the flight attendant.

As soon as she was out of earshot, he flicked his hand, casting a soundproof barrier around them. Jacob's ears popped, and the hum of the engines faded, leaving only the rasp of David's breathing.

"Christi said you may have brief moments of clarity now and then on the trip. Feel free to express your outrage at the injustice," Jacob said, leaning back in his seat. "I'll enjoy it."

Drops of drool dripped down from David Abington's mouth onto his jacket, an outrageously priced product of Savile Row, now ruined. David's voice was a rasp, but the words cut deep. "You've only bought yourself time, Spencer. The viper is interested now. You can only blame yourself for that."

Jacob's stomach clenched, a cold knot forming in his gut. If she was involved, this was far from over.

"No," Jacob said, his voice steady. "I know you've leaked my private documents to the International Assembly. I can blame *you* for that."

Fear flickered across David's face, but it was gone as quickly as it had come. His lips twitched to form a retort, then failed, before his shoulders slumped. His head lolled back, and he was gone again, lost in the emptiness Christi had created for him.

Jacob exhaled slowly. So, he'd successfully removed a general from the board, only to find out that the warlord remained. And if David was to be believed the viper, Seren, was already setting up her first move.

Few knew Jacob had been in Seattle at all, let alone that he'd left with David in tow. He planned on staying in the United Kingdom for as short a duration as possible. Upon arrival, he would finally be rid of David Abington. Irene had arranged to collect him and transport him to a private hospital, which was anticipating their newest VIP patient.

The story was that David's health had taken a sudden and irreparable turn for the worse. True enough, though the causes were anything but natural. Jacob had come up with the plan, and Christi had executed it with ruthless zeal.

Christi had been eager to dig her mental claws into the man who'd attacked her in her own home. She'd poured her fury into his "pig roasting," as she called it, leaving him barely conscious for the flight. He'd wake in London, she said, but he wouldn't be the same. He'd emerge a mere shadow of his former self.

Christi had left him with the parting gift of memory loss. He would feel the urge to siphon power, but he wouldn't remember how to do it. Even if the ability returned, the facility was staffed exclusively by mundanes. There would be no one for him to feed on.

Whether that would kill him, no one knew. Frankly, no one cared. His wife certainly didn't.

Irene arrived at the airport with her hair neatly coiffed, wearing a posh woolen coat and reasonable boots for the wet weather. She was pushing a wheelchair with a broad smile on her face. "How is my dear husband, Jacob?"

The embrace she gave him lingered a beat too long for propriety, but Jacob wasn't one to complain.

"He drank plenty on the plane to keep himself hydrated. How are you feeling, Irene?"

The wattage of her smile amped up. "The best I've felt in ages. I have answers to all of my health issues, and I've arranged for David to get the discreet help he needs. Can't have any details of this getting out. Especially not with his violent episodes."

Of course, the press had already gotten wind of the story because Irene had crafted it all herself.

Jacob nodded, his "I understand" gruff but sincere. For anyone listening, it was just another performance.

After Jacob had revealed all of his findings to Irene, she'd gone into what Esme would probably coin "mama bear mode." She was desperate to keep her sons and grandchildren away from him at any cost, so she'd crafted a story of David's violent decline and leaked it to the press, ensuring no one would question his absence. His family would be safe in their homes for the first time and, especially in Irene's case, flourish.

The only piece of information Jacob kept to himself was about David's dependency on Miles' magic. David's body was already failing. Whether magic deprivation or age killed him first didn't matter. The outcome was the same.

Jacob walked alongside Irene as her driver took over pushing David in the wheelchair. With a hopeful glint in her expression, she asked, "Care to come for luncheon? I would appreciate it if you could share his state of mind before the flight was arranged. You know, so I can tell his doctors?"

Jacob thought it was likely that she rather wanted to indulge in a bit of schadenfreude. Half her life had been spent under his thumb, drained, diminished, used by him.

Today, she was reclaiming herself.

He nodded. "I have to meet with my property lawyer in Soho at two, but I would be delighted to be in your company in the meantime."

"Then it's a date, Jacob Spencer. I already ordered those sandwiches you like."

That inviting look in her eye promised it would be an enjoyable day in London before he needed to head back to Seattle. Dropping off David took no time at all. The facility was delighted to receive their high-paying guest. Over luncheon,

Irene's laughter was bright, but her eyes held a shadow Jacob recognized all too well. "Sometimes," she said, her voice soft, "I wonder if this makes me like him."

"My dear," Jacob said, setting down his fork, his gaze steady, "There's only one monster in this room. And you are nothing like me."

She reached across the table, her hand brushing his. "Then allow me to join you. We can be monsters together."

Time was short, his legal appointment loomed, and his flight back to Seattle waited. But for a while, they enjoyed what little time they had together.

CHAPTER THIRTY-TWO

NEW YEAR'S EVE

Esme

Despite the initial frustration of waiting to see if David would return, Esme now realized that the slower pace they had settled into over the past few days had its own merits. Finn's recovery was evidence they all needed a bit of leisure. As she looked around the bar at the familiar faces around her, Esme felt grateful for the time to rest and recover. It was New Year's Eve, and her batteries were fully recharged on all fronts.

The bar hummed with renewed energy, firework decorations replacing the holly and garland. Finn and Stefan debated beers while Carloff and Ivar bickered over who'd pay for the drinks. Colin tried to mediate, suggesting they rotate turns, but the svartálfar and gnome were too engrossed in the thrill of the fight to notice—a fact Colin hadn't yet grasped. Beatrice, her water nymph pearlescent-blue skin shimmering under the dim lighting, was in her element—on the hunt. She had her pick of interested young men and a few women, all vying for her attention.

Everything was as it should be. Esme hoped this was a sign of positive change for the coming year.

While she waited for Miles and Abby to show up, she got to enjoy the show her barback turned bartender was putting on. He was operating at peak "Will," radiating charisma and snark in equal measure. His sequined vest caught the light as he mixed drinks with unnecessary but impressive flourishes for his favorite customers.

Except not all were in that category.

"You're rude to my boy Miles, so you don't get service with a smile. Just the drink." Will slid the glass across the bar with a sharp movement. "You were really cute until you opened that mouth of yours. Bye-bye now, move along."

More polished than she'd ever seen him, Leon wore a neatly pressed shirt. His hair was expertly combed back in a style that emphasized his neck tattoos. A broad, happy grin stretched Leon's face as he accepted the cocktail from Will. He raised the glass and saluted. "I like the vest."

Good—a single impolite remark would have gotten him kicked out of the bar. Esme grabbed a shaker and began mixing a martini for a customer, keeping one ear on the conversation. A fight didn't seem imminent, since Leon was grinning so hard, but anything could happen on a holiday.

Before Leon could leave, Finn sidled up to the bar, taking the spot beside him.

It seemed the leprechaun wanted to join Will in dumping on Leon because his voice was pure sarcasm. "Ah, you're here. Jus' grand!"

Finn turned to Esme, ignoring Leon's glare. "Es, a shot of that spicy whiskey? Stefan bet it won't affect my flames—time to put on a show." He waggled his eyebrows at Leon.

"Don't burn anything down, Finn," Esme replied dryly, starting his drink. Leon started to move but Finn stopped him.

"Heya, before you go, lad." Finn grinned. "I have a favor to cash in. A small act marked by words of gratitude. One small favor for another small one: Leave early."

Leon's smirk deepened, but he said nothing, choosing instead to sip his cocktail with measured indifference. Unspoken tension hung between him and Finn, though Finn's usual mischievousness lightened the mood. Before she had to employ any other interventions, Gwyn smoothly claimed a spot next to Leon at the bar.

Awkward.

Mid-pour, she froze as she witnessed the two men exchanging nods and diving into what looked like a serious, yet cordial, discussion. But the distant, almost vacant look in Gwyn's eyes, unsettling in its stillness, was something new—something she didn't like. The fact that Leon had created a ward of silence around them made it even more suspect.

She experienced a strange unease. Something about the situation felt wrong. Esme couldn't pinpoint the source, but every instinct screamed at her that this wasn't simply an awkward conversation. This was danger in disguise. Her knuckles paled before she consciously released her grasp on the bottle she'd been clutching tightly.

It made sense, she supposed—two men out of time finding common ground. But Leon helping Gwyn adjust to the modern world? Esme doubted they'd be good for each other. She had hoped that Gwyn and Miles might eventually get along, become friends even. But if Gwyn and Leon became buddies, that hope would all but vanish.

The door buzzed, magically signaling the arrival of more guests to the already packed room. Abby entered, with Miles following closely behind. Their expressions turned sour upon seeing Gwyn and Leon together. Abby muttered something under her breath, pulling Miles toward the opposite end of the room. Esme waved, gesturing toward the two spaces she had saved for them with a small "reserved" sign.

Finn slunk away from the bar, saying, "I'm off to chat up my other besties. Sláinte, Esme!"

Time passed in a blur of laughter, clinking glasses, and one too many tipsily created illusions of premature fireworks. Gwyn left early at around ten, still carrying around the cloud of gloom that clung to him. Leon lingered just long enough to watch him go before melting into the shadows himself.

Finn buzzed around the room, his charm working overtime as he entertained everyone within reach. Several of the nymphs showed a great deal of interest in him, and he returned it. Esme shuddered, trying very hard not to think of the reputation he was building with the ladies.

The wards that muffled the sound inside were working overtime as midnight neared. The atmosphere in the bar became even livelier, filled with anticipation. As the countdown began, Miles found her behind the bar, pulling her close.

The crowd's voices blended into a chant that rattled the glasses. The crackle of magic in the air felt like static before a storm as those who could prepared their illusory fireworks. "Three! Two! One!"

Miles leaned in and whispered, "Happy New Year, lovely."

His lips met hers, and the world fell away. Esme melted into the kiss, her fingers curling around his shirt, trying to pull him as close as possible. She hadn't had any of this a year ago. Now she envisioned lazy Sunday mornings and shared coffee outings, dreaming of a future where magic wasn't the only extraordinary thing in her life.

She wanted a life where their biggest worry would be whose turn it was to vacuum, not whether they'd survive another malevolent attack. A life where magic enhanced their happiness rather than endangered it. There would always be a couple of troublemakers they could scare right when they craved a bit of excitement. Despite a small, persistent doubt nagging at the back of her mind, hope filled her heart.

"I love you, Miles Goodwin."

His lopsided smile was everything she needed. But of course he gave her more, making her heart feel like it was ready to burst.

"Good," he murmured, pressing his forehead to hers. "Because I need you, Esmeralda Turner."

***

Hours later, Esme's eyes snapped open in the dim pre-dawn light of Miles' bedroom. She lay on her side, staring at the wall, her breathing shallow, but something felt... wrong.

A quick-moving coldness started in her spine and radiated outward until it locked her entire body rigidly into place.

Panic clawed at her chest as her body moved on its own, swinging her legs over the edge of the bed. Esme stood, helpless, and caught her reflection in the mirror—inky black eyes stared back at her as goosebumps broke out over her skin in the chill air.

Her limbs moved as if submerged in tar, sluggish yet unstoppable. She was no longer in control of her own body as she pulled on her discarded clothes from the night before. Her mind screamed for her to stop, to wake Miles, to do anything but leave—but she couldn't. Invisible strings pulled her, a puppet, toward the door. As she thrashed against the bonds dragging her along, she prayed her captor wouldn't next arm her. She'd already seen that scenario in dozens of nightmares while the Alp had fed on her—she couldn't endure it in reality.

Miles lay motionless, breathing evenly, wholly unaware of the silent struggle mere feet away. Just hours ago, they'd talked about getting a bigger coffee maker for their mornings together. Such a simple, domestic dream. Now she couldn't even scream as that future slipped away with each forced step toward the door.

The compulsion held her tongue, but wrath welled in her eyes. A single frustrated tear slipped down her cheek as her hand shifted to the doorknob. She turned it quietly.

Miles stirred. For a moment, she thought he'd wake. She begged him silently to stop her.

He'd think she was running again, leaving him like before. That pain, knowing she'd hurt him again, was sharper than the struggle against her invisible restraints.

Once outside, her panic worsened. Where was Lily? If anything seemed out of place, Lily would wake Miles. Esme's feet carried her to a waiting car, lights on, idling behind Miles'.

The man sitting in the driver's seat had a face that nearly sparked a memory.

She sensed no glamour on him. His face... he could be Miles' brother. But his eyes were familiar. Now, though, they were devoid of warmth and soulless.

His voice confirmed her suspicion. She'd never been more wrong about a person in her entire life.

Too cheerily for someone stripping away another human being's will, Leon said, "Morning, beautiful. New year, new beginnings. Buckle up—we've got a little detour before we make ourselves at home."

Esme's hands moved mechanically to secure herself in the passenger's seat. She couldn't shift her head unless he allowed her to, but from the corner of her eye, she noticed the paw sticking out between the armrest.

This monster had taken Lily. If he'd... Her only hope was that Lily was unconscious, tied up, or anything other than what she feared most.

Leon reached over and stroked her cheek with one finger. She tried to flinch away, but she couldn't. She was forced to feel every second of his contact on her skin.

"Don't worry, lovely. That one thing you're worried about isn't what I want from you." Raising two eyebrows, he gave her a smile more genuine than any other she'd ever witnessed. "Well... unless you're interested?"

The only thing she wanted to do right then was drive her blade through his eye socket.

As he stole her magic, his triumphant smirk was the final image seared into her mind before she blacked out.

Miles

The sharp trill of Miles' phone broke through the sound of the white noise machine he'd bought to help Esme sleep. For a moment, he worried it might be Esme crying out from another nightmare. But no, he reached for it, hoping to silence the ringer before it roused Esme so much that she couldn't fall back asleep.

Miles' heart sank as he fumbled in the dark. The bed was cold beside him—too cold. She'd been gone for a while. He'd already promised to make them breakfast that morning, so he hoped she wasn't already up stealing his job.

Thinking it might be the on-call physician, he automatically picked up the call from the unknown number. Where was Lily? She should be jumping on the bed to wish him good morning by now.

Three long heartbeats of silence hung in the air before a familiar voice jolted him awake. "Happy New Year."

Before Miles could demand to know what he wanted, Leon said, "Say 'hello,' Esme."

Miles heard her swallow. In a mechanical tone, she said, "Hello."

Unbidden, Miles' eyes emitted a flash of golden light that was reflected on the phone screen. He almost crushed it in his grip.

He could hear the smug grin in Leon's voice when he popped back on the line. "We're at Esme's place if you want to have a little chat. Only you, though. We brought your dog along just in case."

Each word out of Leon's mouth brought the magic gathering under Miles' skin closer to the surface.

Leon's voice was too calm. "I wouldn't bring any… accessories you think might help. Because I can promise you, they'll hurt the girls more than they help."

The magic surged within him, threatening to take him over. Miles let it.

The voice that answered Leon wasn't Miles' usual warm baritone. It wasn't even in English or Welsh. It was altered, heavy with power that made the air vibrate like a plucked string. "I will come."

Fuck.

CHAPTER THIRTY-THREE

NEW YEAR, NEW BULL****

Abby

New Year's Eve wasn't just bad—it was its own special brand of torture. Abby's New Year's privilege? Watching her sort-of ex-boyfriend cozy up to an asshole for half the night. She briefly indulged in pettiness, something Miles, Colin, Will, Esme, and Finn were more than happy to encourage, thinking it would help her get over her heartbreak.

Spoiler alert: It didn't work.

At first, she thought Gwyn was suffering from terminal male stubbornness. But the more she watched him, the more she saw it—he wasn't just enduring; he was punishing himself. The realization that her relationship troubles weighed even more heavily on him made the evening that much more unpleasant.

To make things worse, the whole night, Colin divided his attention, preferring to make googly eyes at Will rather than fully engaging with his miserable sister. Miles was barely better and equally as guilty of watching Esme constantly. It was hard to blame him since they'd just gotten back together, but still. Abby couldn't even use delicious cocktails to drown her misery because she would regret it the next day. Terrible all around.

She lingered at the bar long enough to wish everyone a happy New Year before heading straight home. To make it through her twelve-hour shift starting at seven in the morning, she required at least five hours of sleep. Her work day would consist of dealing with the aftermath of holiday excess.

The first few hours at the hospital lulled her into a false sense of security. No drunk driving victims—just the usual aftermath of poor decisions: hangovers, twisted ankles from wearing unfamiliar heels while far too intoxicated, and split eyebrows from bar fights. Even the doctors were in a good mood, cracking jokes between patients. With her favorite team by her side, Abby almost forgot how miserable she'd been the night before.

Before her lunch break, she ducked into the break room to check her buzzing phone. Seeing Colin's name on the screen, she answered immediately.

"Hey, what's up? I only have a second between patients." She stuffed her favorite pen back in her pocket and waited.

"Abby—" His voice cracked, and it was like inherited panic spilled through the line. "It's bad. Abby. I stayed at Will's last night. When I got home, I found Mom collapsed again, and Dad..."

"Colin." Her voice dropped to a whisper as nausea climbed up her throat. "What happened to Dad?"

"Abs—" He choked back a sob. "He's in the ambulance in front of me. They were attacked. I wasn't there, Abby." The guilt in his voice was palpable as he struggled to speak. "Dad is—it's really bad. Mom is physically fine... Please, Abby, tell me what to do. Mom's at home resting, but... I can't feel her magic. It's like she's mundane. Cops said they'd come back for her statement in a few hours."

Abby steadied herself on the edge of the supply storage, then snapped her spine straight. Both her parents were alive. Her dad would arrive soon, and the doctors would treat him like a VIP. She could do this.

"Okay, Colin, listen." Her grip on the phone tightened. "Turn around. Stay with Mom. I'll handle Dad when he gets here. Divide and conquer."

"I should have been there." His voice was barely a whisper.

"Colin, stop it. Think for one second. At least they were together. What kind of miracle is that with how their divorce has been going? Focus on Mom, okay?" She hung up and rushed back into the ER.

It wasn't long before the ambulance arrived. The wheels of her father's stretcher rattled against the tile, each rotation dragging her deeper into a waking nightmare. Ignoring the curious glances from her colleagues, she moved to his side.

Sean O'Malley was unrecognizable underneath the swelling. His face was a patchwork of blood and bruises. Her stomach lurched as she examined his hands. They were a mess of bloody ruins. His gold wedding band was conspicuously absent—the EMTs must have cut it off hoping to save his finger.

"Daddy," she whispered, taking his hand in hers. His fingers twitched the barest movement, but his eyes remained closed.

"Abby," Dr. Novak said, his tone firm but understanding. "Let us handle this."

"A prayer," she pleaded, her voice breaking. The doctor hesitated, then stepped back.

Abby bowed her head, clutching her father's hand tighter as she reached out with her magic. Her father's mind flung the doors wide open for her, readily accepting her without hesitation.

Trust.

Inside, Abby ignored everything other than the newest memories that clung like tar but burned as cold as frost, an impossible combination that screamed disaster. They were fear. Anxiety. Pain. Trauma.

The ones she sought sat at the top of his mental heap, but they were interrupted, not complete. Something, or someone, had erased chunks of the memories, leaving the rest somewhat intact. The scene resembled work she had completed in her youth, patchy and unfinished.

This wasn't her mother's work—Christi O'Malley wasn't this sloppy. She thanked the gods that this wasn't a domestic dispute out of her worst nightmare. The attacker was either inexperienced or had been in a hurry.

Was this David's work?

Abby pushed past the pain caused by being so close to the memories. She reached for the nearest memory, ripped it open, and examined its contents. She then opened the others one by one. The images hit her in violent flashes:

Mom at the stove with "the morning after" hair, humming. Magic surged, shattering the scene of domestic peace as the door splintered inward.

The attacker. A face that could have been Miles'.

But wrong—so wrong. No familiar scars traced his skin. Black hair instead of brown. Cold violet eyes.

She heard no sound but saw him mouthing, "Stay down."

Dad standing. More magic.

Pain. The sickening sound of bones breaking. Knowing that they were his.

Mom's scream abruptly silenced.

Abby fought to maintain her composure as she withdrew from her father's mind, her breath coming in shallow gasps. He must have used his fists to defend his wife once the magic didn't work.

Dr. Novak's gentle hand on her shoulder reminded her of his duty and hers.

Bile again threatening to rise, she squeezed her father's hand once more before backing away. As the team moved her father into a trauma room, she removed her badge.

Walking down the hallway, she clenched her fists so tightly that she felt the moons of her fingernails leaving imprints on her skin.

That face, so much like Miles, yet utterly wrong, had to be a glamour. She needed to tell Colin, to tell Miles, Esme, Jacob. Then she needed to burn that piece of shit's face off.

As she walked out of the hospital, no one questioned her decision to leave. Not a single person moved to stop her. They recognized the look of someone whose world had shattered.

They just didn't know she was already planning her revenge.

CHAPTER THIRTY-FOUR

SHATTERED TRUST

Gwyn

The taxi slammed into a pothole, skidding on the rain-slick road. Gwyn's stomach churned with the remnants of last night's ale threatening to claw their way back up his throat. Cars still unsettled him, especially after last night's attempt to take the edge off his worries with an extra beer. He hadn't overly indulged, but the seductive pull of oblivion had whispered from the bottom of his first emptied cup, compelling him to order a second.

Gwyn's fingers fumbled with the bills as he paid the driver a generous tip for allowing Cerys along, the fog of depression clouding his thoughts. His boots crunched on Esme's rock-salted driveway. Leon's rental, last used in their botched attempt to abduct David Abington, sat behind Esme's battered hatchback.

These days, it was a monumental task for him to even step outside of his apartment. Depression had its claws in him, body and mind. Only Cerys' steady presence and the sliver of hope this job gave him kept the shackles of his self-imposed melancholy from clamping around his wrists, ankles, and throat.

He did his best to keep the struggles inside, but the pain of having his life upended, his power and memory yanked from his body to make him human again, to have happiness dangled in front of his face, only for his own actions in a past life to snatch it away again was sometimes too much.

Gwyn had failed last night at the Sanctuary of Spirits. He couldn't fail again—not today.

Leon had promised a quick check-in with Esme about the nisse job, then they'd be gone. Gwyn understood the necessity, but he still braced himself to bear Esme's scowl when she opened the door. Aside from the one incident at Abigail's, she hadn't been outright hostile. However, Esme had made it abundantly clear that she thought him as idiotic as he judged himself.

Instead of her scowl, Leon stood in the doorway, his habitual glamour in place, but lacking his customary smile. His neatly combed dark hair and perfectly cared for clothes didn't distract Gwyn's other senses from picking up on the waves of magic rolling off him. Gwyn's instincts prickled immediately. Leon appeared unnaturally rigid for someone who played at being the laid-back, carefree rogue.

Leon blocked the doorway with his body, eyes flicking warily to Cerys as she bared her fangs. Gwyn had to clamp down on their connection to keep her from attacking. "I couldn't leave her at home. I'll put her in Esme's backyard—she won't mind."

Gwyn didn't mention he'd already planned to ask Esme. Unable to refuse any animal she encountered, he knew she would say yes before he even asked. But something had told him he needed to bring her today.

Leon nodded, staring at the gwyllgi as Gwyn walked her to the side of the house. When Gwyn returned to the front door, Leon was there waiting for him, still blocking the view inside.

"Don't worry," Leon said in Brythonic. His voice was like a sheathed dagger, safe for now, but a hint of menace lurked beneath the surface. "It's all part of the plan."

"I thought you said we'd be leaving at once," Gwyn countered.

Gwyn stepped inside, and his heart froze. Esmeralda sat rigid on the couch, her hands clasped tightly in her lap. The only part of her that moved were her eyes. He was the target of their purest seething hatred.

Alarm sliced through his ribs where they'd been broken only two months before. His heart thudded against its cage, a desperate echo of Gwyn's hopeless urge to get Esme out of the room, away from Leon. Fear, only partially concealed at this most inconvenient time, sharpened his anger. The words tore from his throat as he instinctively moved to put himself between Leon and Esme. "What have you done to her?"

His body tensed, readying for a fight he would almost certainly lose. Magic rose in his chest, ready, willing to be unleashed. It became a physical manifestation of the hopeless terror that spiraled in his mind, each imagined scenario he suspected this monster was capable of more terrifying than the last.

"Calm yourself," Leon said, the unruffled man he was playing at firmly back in place. He settled onto the arm of Esme's oversized reading chair, at ease. "Magic, of course. She's only immobilized. She is unharmed."

Stick to the plan, Gwyn reminded himself. Though that felt hollow now. His life was no longer the only thing at stake with this scheme.

He glanced back at Esme, then at Leon, before biting out, "You will forgive me if I check her over for injuries." He switched to English deliberately, wanting Esme to understand. The familiarity of the place and the expression in her eyes as he approached her made his betrayal feel all the worse.

Leon shrugged. "I will not stop you."

Gwyn kneeled, his knees sinking into the rug like lead weights, as Esme's glare bored into him. He tried to catch her eyes, to convey a silent message with his that begged for patience, for understanding that he wasn't the monster she thought him. But her gaze remained locked on him, not black with a demonic fury, but blazing with all-too-human betrayal and disappointment.

He noticed there was something about the magic Leon had worked on Esme, something familiar...

"Doesn't seem too happy with you," Leon interrupted his inspection as Gwyn brushed Esme's hair aside, searching for any bruising. Up close, her pulse visibly raced, her body's stillness made all the more unnatural by the contrast.

Gwyn stiffened but didn't rise to the obvious bait. And like Esmeralda, he experienced his own wave of disappointment. He'd seen how perceptive she had been of subtle clues in the past. He had hoped she would see them now, but rage blinded her, and he couldn't blame her for it.

Leon switched back to Brythonic. "Shall we go over the plan again, princeling?" There was something in Leon's voice that set Gwyn on edge. "Because it seems like you're having second thoughts."

Leon was right, but he was wrong about the source. A special breed of doubt, with sharp teeth and claws, scraped its way through Gwyn's insides. Standing before Leon, Gwyn crossed his arms. "I agreed to getting answers. Not... this."

Leon's lips curled into a smirk. "Exactly. Answers. This task was never going to be simple." His voice dripped with mockery. With Gwyn committed to his scheme, Leon's true nature was already shining through. "This place is as warded as Nudd's keep was. Wards of silence, containment—nothing that happens in here will be obvious to the outside world. Even the wilderness wouldn't give us this much privacy. Elena is the bait."

"A name must mean little to you if you forget hers so easily," Gwyn ground out, barely stopping himself from reaching for the grip of his sword.

"Sure, it is now." Leon waved a dismissive hand. "But Nudd reacts to her the same way, so it doesn't matter."

Leon gestured toward Esme with a flick of his thumb, his nonchalance more threatening than any outburst. "All I want is Nudd. She can walk away after this. I'll erase her memory... and his, if he doesn't make us kill him."

Gwyn had expected manipulation, but this was cruelty. Honestly, it was something Gwyn should have expected of a man from his time. "No unnecessary violence," he repeated firmly. "I was very clear on that. All we need are answers."

"Oh, how the Bull of Battle has fallen." Leon sneered, laughing at him, intending to cut. "Doesn't want to get his hands dirty."

"Never with innocent blood," Gwyn shot back, his voice a low growl.

Miles

Terror had tried to seize Miles during the call with Leon. A vise had wound around his ribs, constricting his breathing and making each ragged gasp a painful struggle as his heart hammered against his sternum.

But then Nudd's power had once again exerted itself.

Now Miles' grip on the steering wheel was light, steady, as he drove through the unusually quiet streets of Queen Anne. He was the one driving, but he wasn't the only one in control. Nudd's presence, heavy and unyielding, anchored him. For once, the king's (demigod's?) intrusion felt like a lifeline, not a curse.

Miles didn't resist. As he drove, many houses still displayed holiday decorations, cheery mementos of bygone celebrations. A deflated Santa lay crumpled in a yard, its bright grin now a grimace—a hollow echo of the holidays, much like the hollow ache in his chest.

Everything Finn had told him put this sharing of autonomy into a new perspective. Twenty-five years of dreaming about Elena meant Miles understood the depth of Nudd's love for her, a depth equal to his own love for Esme. Though their objective was the same, protect Esme at all costs, understanding that he had an unreliable ally of sorts in this didn't quell the turmoil of emotions that brewed within him.

His hand itched to dial Colin, Jacob, Finn, Abby, anyone. But including them risked their lives. And there was a chance Leon could scry him or use some other ancient method of spying Miles didn't know about. It wasn't like Nudd actually talked to him, giving him nuggets of wisdom when he needed them.

He couldn't risk Esme.

Leon's handling of Sylas' assassination had revealed his true nature. Miles had learned long ago to believe people when they showed their true selves. But Esme—she was a woman who trusted too easily, who saw the best in everyone, even when it burned her. Miles regretted not keeping a closer watch on Leon after their deal had concluded, but everything had lined up to make him too busy to do a good job of it.

He parked behind a strange rental car at Esme's, and a fresh wave of fear hit him. Would the lingering vestiges of Nudd's power give him aid or false security? If he reached for the power his presence offered, would he weaken another malevolent prison like had happened before?

With Esme threatened by Leon, adding a monster into the mix would only put her in further danger. Miles would have to rely on luck or the power's unpredictable whims. The maddening uncertainty filled him with a frustrating helplessness.

He sat frozen in his car for a long moment, his mind scrambling as he desperately searched for a way out of this predicament.

There wasn't one.

Miles had no plan. He had no ideas on how to get Esme out of this situation—nothing. The full extent of Leon's powers was a mystery. He wouldn't be easily defeated; Nudd's response, the first active communication he'd ever made, while he was on the phone with Leon earlier had made that abundantly clear.

How could Miles prepare for something he'd been so blind to? His dreams had been warning him about Leon for weeks now. He'd been too preoccupied, too busy to notice.

Esme's captor's language, magical abilities, and swordsmanship all pointed to him being one of Nudd's contemporaries, like Gwyn. But Miles' dreams pointed to someone far closer to home. By now he'd pieced together that Leon was one of Nudd's brothers—the same one who'd been after Elena.

Miles understood, as Nudd seemed to, that Leon's chief aim was something to do with Miles' blessing. While his dreams never precisely detailed the method, he understood Nudd thought of his brother like one thought of a leech or vampire.

Like a freight train, the realization slammed into him, a crushing blow of understanding. Leon was like David—a siphon, only far more dangerous. It was Leon, not David, who had attacked him at the locks. David might have been behind the other attacks, but the last one was too sophisticated, too physical for him.

Now armed with little more than the knowledge of what type of mage he was up against, Miles left the car. In his rush to leave the house earlier, he'd felt a deep urge that had made his muscles tense to bring one weapon along—Nudd's doing. Miles had listened, but he didn't intend to use it.

Heeding Leon's warning about 'accessories,' he left Esme's dagger on the porch, trusting it wouldn't be seen as a threat from the other side of her wards. He was... simply returning it. If Nudd had a plan for it, he wasn't sharing.

He didn't bother knocking. Miles' key turned with a click that echoed like a gunshot. As he threw the door open, his heart pounded so loudly he barely heard the hinges creak. Inside, Leon waited on the couch, one arm draped possessively over Esme. She sat stiffly beside him, her eyes wide with fear.

Miles felt the anguish in her eyes like a physical blow twice over.

A form pulled free from shadows, and what remained of Miles' trust shattered completely. Gwyn stepped out of the kitchen, a grim expression on his face. They'd been working toward something, a fragile bridge of understanding—if not friendship, at least mutual respect—built on shared effort and begrudging appreciation. His presence here, his complicity in this nightmare, slid in deep, like a dagger twisted into his kidney.

"Kneel," Leon commanded, voice thick with hunger. A predator savoring the moment before he sank his teeth into flesh.

Miles' knees hit the floor without hesitation.

He would stay until his knees bled, until exhaustion overcame him—whatever it took. His eyes stayed on Esme's, conveying all his love and reassurance.

Chapter Thirty-Five

THE CALL

Gwyn

"She has not been harmed." It was meant to be reassuring. Yet the words tumbled out of Gwyn's mouth before he could even think of how guilty they might make him look.

Miles' eyes strayed from Esme's to his for a fleeting second. Gwyn read in his clenched teeth and lowered brows that his statement had been dismissed as false.

Gwyn's phone's vibration cut through the tense silence of Esme's living room. Leon, clearly irritated, raised one eyebrow. As soon as Gwyn saw the caller ID, he raised a hand in apology and stepped down the hallway to answer, ignoring Leon's simmering anger—Leon's silent fury following Gwyn like a blade pressed at his back. "I need to take this," Gwyn said apologetically, already halfway to Esme's room where the wards of silence were even stronger.

He wasn't exactly fleeing the debacle unfolding in the other room, but a brief respite to think, to plan, was needed.

Until he noticed who was lying on the bed.

Lily's breaths were shallow, yet even. Why had Leon abducted Miles' dog? Was he hoping her presence would help them get answers out of Miles? If anything, Gwyn estimated it would do the opposite. He was furious at how Leon had treated the animal and, even more so, Esmeralda.

"Abigail, hello," he began, attempting a smoothness his unsteady voice betrayed. The words barely scraped past his suddenly dry throat. He found himself straining to hear any movement from the hallway.

Her voice, sharp with panic, sliced through his immediate worries. "Gwyn, I've tried calling Miles a million times. Esme, too. No one's answering. Have you seen them?"

He faltered. Lying didn't come naturally to him, but the truth was too precarious to share. "Recently," he managed, his words careful. "Last night."

A puff of air, heavy with her displeasure, crackled over the speaker. "Colin went home this morning and found my parents had been attacked. My dad is in surgery now. Gwyn, my mom—" Her voice cracked, raw with emotion. "My mom feels mundane. I glimpsed Dad's memories before they pulled him into surgery. The person who attacked them had Miles' face, except it wasn't quite right. He had black hair and no scars. We haven't seen David since he attacked Finn. Do you think he used an illusion? I don't know what to do, and I can't reach anyone."

By all the magic... Stunned by her words and their implications, Gwyn could not formulate a reply.

How had he missed all the signs?

He collapsed onto Esme's bed next to Lily, feeling unsteady and disoriented. His problems seemed to be piling up, stacked like a house of cards, ready to collapse, each one adding to the precariousness. Leon. Esmeralda. Miles. Abigail. Each one a weight he had to bear, each one a failure he couldn't afford.

The air suddenly too thin, he rasped, "Tell me what their attacker looked like again?"

"Black hair, eyes the same color as Esme's. Miles' face without the scars and a tan. It was just a flash. It was like whoever did this to them tried to remove the memories of it from my dad, but they weren't very good at it because pieces were left behind."

It hit him like the Dullahan's whip to his ribs, shattering them for a second time. Leon was *Llefelys*.

The name carried the weight of ancient standing stones toppling—one after another, crushing him beneath their history. How had he not seen it sooner? The dismissive attitude, the ever-present smile, the charm. Leon embodied everything about his uncle that Gwyn had despised in his first human life.

Gwyn had faced challenges in the past, but his self-control was now being pushed to its absolute limit. Leon's question about how he'd managed to bring Creiddylad and Elena back from Anwnn... was unraveling that mystery the only reason Gwyn was being kept alive? Or perhaps he was merely being stored, a human power source for future consumption.

Llefelys had ascended like him, but they'd arrived there by traveling very different paths. It was easy to fall into the trap of thinking that the world, that magic, had this grand scheme to make things better over time. But there was no grand plan, and Llefelys was the perfect example of that.

Magic's only duty was to maintain balance. Llefelys was the opposite side of the coin for Nudd. Where Nudd healed and prolonged life for the greater good of all, even at significant cost to himself, his brother withered and injured for personal gain.

Llefelys had been kept on Nudd's lands by political necessity, a circumstance that had greatly displeased his father. A system had been developed to sustain the cambion's life, because Nudd, always just, too fair by far, had recognized that his brother wasn't responsible for his birth. Llefelys' duty had become to hunt malevolents, to take from them to sustain himself. He was supposed to drain only the wicked, the worst prisoners, the rapists. Not innocents and *never* for a reason as low as his greed.

Miles' dream about his broken collarbone? That had happened—when Gwyn was young, before everything had changed. As memory consumed him, Esme's room seemed smaller, his vision becoming more limited. Nudd's younger half-brother was only a few years Gwyn's senior, so they sometimes sparred when Llefelys was in the keep. The injury had happened before his uncle had relocated to France to take a wife there and assume the throne. It was before even Creiddylad had married that swine Gwynthr.

Even now, the memory of Llefelys' blade cracking his bones haunted him. The training yard, mud clinging to their shoes...

Llefelys despised losing and that day, he took it too far. Blades lost in the fight, they crashed together—grappling, twisting, fighting for control. While Gwyn had the upper hand, fist raised to punch, he felt himself suddenly weaken. Naturally, Nudd had cautioned his son regarding his brother's capabilities. Gwyn jumped to safety before his power could be further drained.

Llefelys, covered in mud, had gotten back up. He summoned his weapon with telekinesis, ready to strike again. Before Gwyn could find his own shield, his uncle had come at him with a downward chop using the hilt of his blade. The pommel cracked down on his shoulder with magic-enhanced strength. Gwyn heard the sickening pop before his body registered the pain. So incensed, he had fought back through the pain. House-hold guards pulled them off one another before more damage could be done.

His uncle hadn't simply broken the social contract to send a message that day. Llefelys' expression had made a silent promise of more to come, that harming his own family was of little consequence to him. That was merely one example among countless others of his uncle's illegal and unjust use of magic.

It was a lesson learned the hard way. His uncle was a monster hiding under a facade of charm and civility.

In the present, Abigail was still waiting on the line for his reply, but he needed to be clever about it. Gwyn wasn't certain that he could handle his uncle alone, not in his diminished state. He'd already proven to have regained more of his old powers than Gwyn could summon, and Llefelys had the benefit of stolen magic. His uncle might even now be cleverly circumventing Esme's wards to eavesdrop on his conversation.

Gwyn made a serious effort to keep his voice steady as he prepared himself to tell another lie. Only he knew Jacob had returned to the States for a short time and was already back in Great Britain again to deliver David. "Abigail, contact Jacob immediately."

"I have!" she snapped. "He's not answering. None of the numbers I have for him are working."

A trickle of sweat beaded down his chest. Llefelys' involvement demanded extreme caution. Every word to Abigail was like walking a tightrope over a pit of spears. "Then call your other Brotherhood contacts. Call Finn."

A heavy, tense silence stretched on the line. Then her voice dropped, laced with accusation. "Gwyn, that was not a real brush off. What is this? Why are you lying to me right now?"

This was his chance. "I promised you I would never lie to you, under any circumstances."

He switched on the white noise machine next to Esme's bed. "Sorry," he said quickly, feigning nonchalance. "Hit a button by mistake."

Abigail was clever. He only had to hope she'd figure it out in time.

"I have to go," he said, his voice pitched low. "I'll call you back in a few hours to check on your parents. Be well, cariad."

He ended the call, his hands trembling. Llefelys was a more serious danger than they'd planned for. Gwyn remembered too well how facing him alone had ended a hundred times before. Defending Esmeralda, even Miles, in this human body, was like he was walking into a roaring tempest, fully aware of how low his chances of survival were.

This wasn't a tale of a revenge-seeking, morally bankrupt lunatic targeting Nudd like they had thought. This was a maniac bent on reclaiming his former power through murder and theft.

And they had all lined up nicely to be his victims.

"Leon" clearly intended to betray their alliance, a mirror of Gwyn's own secret plans. To determine who would strike first, he needed to return to his uncle's twisted scheme unfolding in the other room. Trapped once again between loyalty, strategy, and the shackles of his own past, Gwyn steeled himself to make the first move.

Abby

The lingering antiseptic scent of the hospital clung to Abby's scrubs as she gripped the steering wheel. She'd left work only a few minutes earlier. Her car had not yet left the city limits.

Her father's broken form haunted her every thought, and she still hadn't seen her mother. And now Gwyn was lying. She could feel it.

It felt like a stab in the back. Although their relationship was complicated, rocky, if she was being honest, she still sought him out. She'd turned to Gwyn because she still trusted him, still believed in his fundamental goodness, trusted in his honest heart despite everything. She still cared for him—maybe too much.

But Gwyn had lied straight to her face when she needed him most. He'd said, "I promised you I would never lie to you." He hadn't even said that during the conversation he'd referenced.

When her whole world was falling apart, when her mother's magic was gone and her father was fighting for his life on an operating table, Gwyn, the one person who had answered the phone, had—

Wait.

She wanted to hate him, to scream at him for lying when she needed him most. But she couldn't shake a nagging feeling of doubt. Something didn't add up. Gwyn had said he couldn't guarantee he wouldn't lie to her. He'd said that he would leave out important details if it protected one of them.

Her foot eased off the gas as realization struck. That sound—that irritating burst of white noise, so rude...

Gwyn slept in silence. She'd learned the hard way that even the smallest sound woke him from slumber. Was he already with another woman?

No. Don't be stupid, Abby. Gwyn had looked at her like he was a kicked puppy all the night before.

The white noise machine... Abby had painstakingly explained to Gwyn how it worked when they were in Esme's room while they waited for backup to arrive during the Alp attack.

Gwyn was *there.* The pieces clicked into place, and her stomach dropped.

Tears of relief mixed with fear spilled over, hot and furious, while magic simmered under her skin, threatening a destructive burst.

"Oh, fuck," she whispered, pulling over to the side of the road.

These were the facts: someone had attacked her parents. Her mother had been drained of magic, possibly forever. Her father's life hung by a thread. Miles wasn't answering. Esme wasn't answering. Jacob wasn't answering. And Gwyn—the one person who should have been her rock—had lied to her while pretending everything was fine.

Except he'd done it to send her a clue. A warning. With the world feeling so bleak, how sure could she be that she wasn't seeing false hope? Despite her uncertainty, the coincidences seemed too perfect to ignore. She had to trust Gwyn. She had to trust her gut.

She love-hated him so much she wanted to scream.

Something so serious was happening at Esme's that Gwyn couldn't talk freely. It was bad enough that he'd risked their relationship entirely to warn her.

They needed help, and fast. Her gut told her that every second wasted was a second closer to losing them all.

Her fingers flew across her phone screen.

"Colin, have Will stay with Mom." She began barking out orders immediately. "You stay with Dad. They need protection. If anything happens, if you even suspect something's wrong, call me. I left work. I think someone attacked Esme and Miles too."

Colin didn't question her orders, only acquiesced. His voice had continued to exude guilt—at least this would give him purpose.

Finn answered on the first ring. "Dove?"

"We have a problem," she said, her voice unsteady. "Something is going down at Esme's house. I need your help. Now."

Katia picked up on the second ring.

"Please, please, tell me you haven't fed recently," Abby said.

The succubus' laugh was rich and unrestrained. "Abby, it's only been like a week since your breakup, right? You're already calling me for a favor?"

Reflecting on her question, Abby found the absurdity of it chipped away at the hard shell of anger that had formed around her. A hysterical laugh bubbled up in her throat. "Damnit, Katia, no."

Katia laughed again, then answered cautiously, "Okay... I wait until after New Year's to eat my fill. It's too risky for me to join in on the festivities when they're in full swing."

Abby laid it out. "I need you hungry because our people are in danger and I think you might be the perfect first distraction. It might be dangerous. Will you help your Brothers?"

"Tell me where to go."

Every traffic light seemed endless as scenarios played through Abby's mind—each worse than the last. Help was coming. She just hoped the B-team would be enough.

Abby's simmering anger had found a target. Whatever was happening, no one else she loved would end up like her parents. Not today.

Miles

Nudd's presence pressed against the inside of Miles' skull, a pressure that was both comforting and suffocating. Since the phone call with Leon, knowledge had seeped into Miles' consciousness from the demigod—not in the immersive way of his dreams, but in strained, deliberate droplets of memory. Each fragment seemed to arrive with effort, as though pushed through a narrow passage against resistance.

That was how Miles knew he was dealing with Llefelys. Leon was the same man who had used magic to put Nudd's court to sleep and enraged the king by showing far too much interest in the incapacitated Elena.

This wasn't like the dreams, where Miles was nothing more than a powerless passenger. In the waking world, Nudd's power had limits—but Miles was still the host, the body, the one in control. Mostly. When Nudd decided it was necessary, he could surge forth and take the steering wheel for a short time.

Just like whatever was left of Nudd had done during the jorōgumo fight, against the ogre, and the nandibear.

He felt a sudden internal wrench that felt like his consciousness was being pushed aside. It wasn't possession or even a splitting of cognizance exactly. It was more like the buried Nudd's identity was bleeding through. Nudd seized partial control of his speech. Somehow Miles' lips found a way to form the ancient words that Nudd placed in his mouth. "I am here. Take what you seek, brother."

Leon's grin slipped, replaced by a cold stare that promised violence. "Silence."

"Not as eager as I thought you were." Miles bit his lip, stifling another sharp retort Nudd wanted to send. Nudd may have been nearly immortal, but neither Miles nor Esme had that protection.

Esme stared at him, frozen on the couch, her wide eyes screaming disbelief. He couldn't blame her. He felt the same way.

"Quiet!" Beneath the glamour, Leon's eyes narrowed, a snarl barely held back. "I'm listening to your idiotic son in the other room."

Miles smirked and replied in English, "Not my son."

So Llefelys didn't trust Gwyn, either. Ignoring Nudd's urging to remain silent, Miles opted to provoke Leon. "Come on. Are you afraid? You called; I came. Take what you want and let Esme and Lily go."

Leon stubbornly clung to Brythonic as his composure faltered. His eyes shone with manic excitement while his hands twitched at his sides. "Bring Nudd back."

Miles laughed, his mockery on full display.

Leon lunged from the couch, sending Esme sprawling, and closed the distance between them in a heartbeat. He behaved exactly as Miles had expected. Miles braced himself, but the open-handed blow across his face still rattled his bones. Then came the insult—spit, hot and wet, searing against his cheek.

Esme's captor hadn't said he couldn't move his arms, only to kneel. So Miles wiped the spittle from his face and grinned. "Hope that blowup cost you something."

"We could have avoided all of this had that damned ogre simply done his job." Leon grinned back. "It's your turn to pay."

He placed one hand on Esme's exposed neck and closed his eyes in rapture. Her skin grew three shades paler, and her eyes closed. The sick fuck was siphoning her.

"Stop!" Nudd rasped, the words rough, ground out. "What you want is right here, brother."

Leon was practically feral now. "First, we get answers!"

The soft squeak of Esme's bedroom door cut through the tension like a knife. Leon—Llefelys froze, his attention snapping toward the sound. Miles sensed a slight, almost imperceptible, magical surge from that direction. And something else... He realized that he could feel Lily in the other room. Notably, Gwyn hadn't shut the door behind him, evidenced by the lack of a second telltale squeak.

Gwyn stepped back in, and Miles felt Nudd's presence surge with desperate hope. Miles, clinging to Nudd's guidance as his only chance of survival, nevertheless struggled to accept it. Here was the man who'd hunted answers about Nudd for months, who'd fought Miles with both blade and word—and who now might be their only chance.

Gwyn's blue eyes, sharp with assessment, took in the scene. They flitted over Miles' blossoming purple bruise, then froze on Esme slumped over, her head lolling to the side next to Leon.

Trust. Urgency. A lifetime of love, tangled with complications. Nudd's emotions flooded Miles, a silent command he couldn't ignore. "Gwyn," he rasped, their voices merging—plea and warning, rough and strained.

But they were too late. Leon moved with inhuman speed, launching for a second time from the couch. His fingers wrapped around the exposed skin of Gwyn's throat.

Time seemed to stretch as Leon's glamour fell away. Miles watched in horror as his own features emerged from the illusion, so similar and yet so distinctive. Llefelys' eyes glazed over with that same vacant expression he'd seen on Abby when she controlled Jacob, but this was worse—this was hunger given form. His hand was still on Gwyn's throat.

But Gwyn's eyes didn't widen in shock, as Miles had expected. Gwyn, at minimum, had suspicions about Leon's true identity, but the duration of those suspicions would remain unknown.

Because Gwyn's pale body slumped to the ground, still blessedly breathing.

Llefelys straightened. "Doesn't even know how close he is."

Miles' stomach dropped into freefall. He was weaponless, with Esme's too-still form on the couch and Gwyn sprawled at Llefelys' feet. He'd already failed them.

He'd hesitated, feeling helpless as he watched the tragedy unfold in mere seconds. Miles had hesitated and blown what might have been his one shot at killing the bastard.

CHAPTER THIRTY-SIX

THE B-TEAM

Abby

Abby drummed her fingers on the motionless steering wheel, her nerves fraying. She'd found street parking a block from Esme's where they could meet and plan their next steps. Beside her, Finn looked like a cartoon burglar come to life—striped shirt, dark pants, and a domino mask perched on his forehead. In broad daylight. Gods help her. The fact that he wasn't even five feet tall only made the ensemble more absurd.

"Don't be stupid, Finn," she argued, her voice strained with barely suppressed frustration over her powerlessness. "We aren't going in there with fire blazing. We don't even know what's happening yet."

Finn crossed his arms, his usual mischief replaced by a rare seriousness. "If you'd let me check it out, we'd know what's goin' on by now."

"We need to talk to Katia first! Why are you so impatient? You're never like this."

Finn's expression darkened. "It's easy to be this way when you've had a wicked bad feeling for months now that somethin' terrible was bound to happen. And of course, it happens while Jacob is out of town with David."

Abby's heart sank, dragging her insides with it. "So it's not David in there?"

"Obviously!" Finn's eyes widened in exasperation. "Jacob's in London, roastin' that swine. My gold's on 'Leon.'" He sneered the name.

She was gearing up for another retort when the gentle purr of an engine drew her attention. A very expensive luxury sports car pulled up behind them. Abby didn't think anything of it until her phone buzzed with a text from Katia: *I'm behind you in the black car. Let's talk about the plan over the phone. My aura is a bit charged right now, and I don't want to make the imp lose his mind. (Or you, sorry.)*

Abby rolled her eyes and shoved the phone at Finn.

He glanced at it, tittered, and shrugged. "Can't argue with that. So, fearless leader, what's the plan?"

"Now that she's here, go check on the house and report back. You can take a shortcut through the backyards over there." Kids had worn a shortcut between the neighborhood's 1950s ramblers that was perfect for a leprechaun to sneak through.

Grumbling, Finn obeyed, his boots crunching on the salted sidewalk as he disappeared toward the houses. While Abby watched, he faded from her vision mid-step, his Fae magic completely shrouding him from her perception. Weeks of training with him still didn't prepare her for his sudden vanishing act.

Abby pulled out her phone, typing quickly. *Your effect works on most "people" right?*

If they like to get down and dirty, they're fair game.

Abby couldn't help but smile. *How are you 88 and talk like this? Also, nice car.*

I look like this, I have to keep up with the lingo. I splurged on the self-gift for my double happiness birthday.

Katia's eighty-eighth birthday was significant, given her mixed Chinese heritage.

Gods, nursing pay is really falling behind if a librarian is raking in that much money.

The next text contained four laugh-crying emoji. *Oh Abby, I've had a while to invest and I'm a trust fund baby.*

Lost in her phone, Abby was startled by a sharp rap against her window. Finn stood there with a grim expression on his face. Except he wasn't alone. Glamourless and nearly as tall as he was, Cerys walked beside him on a leash. Finn looked more suited to being her mid-afternoon snack than someone capable of guiding her in any way whatsoever. If the gwyllgi hadn't wanted to come with him, she wouldn't have. This development was not a good sign.

With a curt wave and a brisk, "Get in the car. People are going to notice!" Abby ushered them inside.

Finn dismissed Abby's panic. "Eh, they'll just remember me lookin' smaller and brush it off as a little person walkin' his oversized service pup."

"Her eyes are glowing!" Abby pointed at the hellhound, who barely fit in the back seat.

Noticing Abby's attention, Cerys leaned forward and did her best to use her tongue to remove the scant makeup she'd put on that morning. Gasping for breath, Abby said, "Okay, okay, I missed you too, girl."

Finn petted Cerys' forehead and commented, "We leprechauns and hounds have a certain understandin'. We're always fast friends."

Abby went straight to business. "What is going on? Why is Cerys here?"

He grimaced and said, "Yer not gonna like it."

All day she'd held on, but Abby's patience finally snapped. "Spit it out, Finn. Gods below, I've been hanging on by a thread for hours now, and I'm going to fucking lose it if I don't do something soon!"

Finn winced. "Sorry, dove. I know... I know. I'm worried about your Ma and Pa too."

Already tapping on her phone, she said, "I'll call Katia so we can get this all planned at once."

As soon as Katia picked up, Finn started talking. "There's no other way to say this than straight. The man in there looks just like you described from your Pa's memories. Like the spittin' image of our boy Miles. It's hard to know from the outside, but I think he's done something to Esme and Gwyn."

"What do you—" Abby started to interrupt, but Finn held up a hand.

"Now, hold on, dove. I'm gettin' to it. I found this on Esme's front steps."

He handed Abby Esme's new dagger.

Abby was insistent. "Esme would not leave her new dagger outside. Katia, I'm assuming you know about the dagger Jacob had crafted for Esme?"

"Yes, he asked me which handle material she would like best."

"Right, Esme wouldn't leave it out willy-nilly." Finn nodded. "I think someone was sendin' us a message about what we're dealin' with."

"Are you saying we're dealing with another siphon?" Katia asked, a hint of fear coloring her tone.

"Exactly. We just didn't know it... I don't think either Esme or Gwyn is in danger at the moment. Miles... might be a different story. My guess is Miles has a brother, of some sort, who grandly doesn't like him."

As Abby's anxiety increased, her grip on the phone tightened. She shot out rapid-fire questions. "Katia, can you charm another cambion? Can you turn it up on demand? Is there a trick to avoid getting ensnared by it?"

Katia hummed, thinking. "Esme felt the pull, so it should work on another cambion. I can 'turn it up,' as you say, but not for long. To avoid it, keeping your distance is best, and I've heard breathing only through your mouth can help."

"We can do that," Abby said quickly.

Each piece of the plan was coming together in her mind. It was insane, but they were desperate.

Abby said, "Finn, I'm thinking of trying a few things remotely, exactly like we practiced in training. We haven't tried it before, but do you know if you can supplement my power? I know that general magic can charge Fae, but I'm not certain if it can flow the other way."

Finn went completely still, his usually animated face frozen in some mixed emotion Abby couldn't quite place. Eventually, he answered, nodding slowly. "Normally, I'd be worried, but I think you'll take to my magic just fine, dove."

Katia broke in, sounding like she doubted it. "Are you sure, Finn?"

"Quite, Mistress."

Abby groaned. "Eww. Gods, you two are worse than teenagers."

The tension eased slightly as Finn's contagious giggle filled the air, causing Abby's lips to quirk up despite all the anxiety she was feeling.

He was encouraging. "Lighten up, dove. We may not be the A-team, but we can do this."

"Yes," she said, snapping back into focus. "So here's the plan…"

CHAPTER THIRTY-SEVEN

THE HALOED TRUTH

Gwyn

Gwyn felt the rough-hewn wooden floorboards beneath his leather soles, each footfall accompanied by a soft, familiar creak. His mind, or magic, had transported him to the home he shared with Creiddylad. He sat and she smiled at him across the table, a goblet of celebratory mead in her hand, her eyes alight with joy.

The truth crashed through Gwyn's mind like a surging river during a flood. Where he was, why he was there, and the memories his imprisonment had stolen, all at once. He knew with absolute certainty that this memory, this dream, was the celebration of Creiddylad's halo appearing—that supernatural sign that marked her as one touched by the old powers, as worthy of them.

The memory was vivid, almost tangible. The rich scent of roasted venison, the warmth of fresh-baked bread, the wood smoke clinging to his skin, all of it anchored him in a moment he'd thought lost forever. Their feast was simple, without the usual pomp and circumstance of his father's keep, yet it was all the more precious for that. For one special day, he had set aside the Wild Hunt to cook beside her, to steal a sliver of normalcy. By whose permission, his memory didn't reveal.

As Creiddylad hummed and kneaded, he remembered deliberately slowing his movements to chop root vegetables at a human speed. They shared the homemade meal with local farmers and their families. Because that was what she did. She took care of the farmers, their crops, helped the women birth their children. That was why she'd been deemed worthy of the power granted to her.

The sparkle in Creiddylad's eyes as she watched the children play, as she listened to the elders swap stories, was more beautiful to him than any secret of magic that was restricted to those of his kind.

The shadows that seemed to follow him everywhere, even in his immortality, retreated for one magnificent evening. Free from the weight of his Wild Hunt responsibilities and the ever-present specter of death, Gwyn felt a lightness in his heart that hadn't been there in years. Only the moon bore witness as they made love in their chamber that evening until she lay exhausted in their bed, her skin faintly luminescent with her growing power.

Gwyn, his stamina undiminished, held her until she fell asleep in his arms. He lingered, watching the rise and fall of her chest, marveling at the moment's peaceful perfection. Knowing it couldn't last, he pressed a kiss to her temple, breathing in the scent of her hair—wild thyme and chamomile. Drawn back to the Wild Hunt, he slipped away.

With a plague ravaging the island and battles popping up constantly, his work was tireless. The memory of their shared warmth, of her smile in the firelight, sustained him as he returned to guide souls to the threshold between this world and the next.

The irony of his duty wasn't lost on him. He helped the newly departed find acceptance in their final journey, yet he couldn't find peace for himself, much less hold on to happiness. His duties were acts of mercy, but they weighed heavily on his spirit as he was faced again and again with the harshest realities of life and what caused that life to end—war, starvation, petty feuds, greed.

Time lurched forward, dragging Gwyn's memory to the moment he'd dreaded—the day Leon had warned him about. Gwyn had returned home, knowing, fearing exactly what he'd find. Because he wasn't granted the privilege of guiding her spirit, he'd been desperately hoping what he knew had happened was somehow untrue.

The sight of her motionless form on their bed made him freeze. She appeared as if she might stir at any moment, as if she might turn over and greet him. But she was cold. Lifeless.

The sound that escaped him wasn't grief. It was devastation given life. An otherworldly wail tore from his throat, shaking the foundations of their home. The wooden beams of the walls groaned in sympathy with his grief as the house and ascended man trembled.

As he kneeled beside her, his hands searched for any hint, however faint, of her magic, to feel the trace of her one last time. But the unique spark that defined her had completely vanished. Magic always lingered in the body for some time, even after the last breath of life escaped. Yet she was as empty as a dry well, as if someone had robbed her of every spark.

When the raw pain of grief dulled to a bearable ache, his mind turned to the only siphon he'd been aware of. Gwyn instantly dismissed the idea that Llefelys could be responsible for this. He was supposed to be in faraway France. Gwyn's guilt and shame for failing to protect her only slightly cooled his anger at the possibility of her murder.

Yet he somehow knew that the idea of Llefelys being her murderer had stubbornly persisted in haunting his few quiet moments.

Time blurred. Whether it had been days or years, Gwyn couldn't say; his concept of human time at that point was weak at best. Rage had honed his grief to a sharper, harder edge. When next he was aware, he was stalking the halls of his father's keep. Nudd was not to be found in the great hall, so he passed the guards unseen, one after another, until he saw the beauty standing outside Nudd's door.

It was Elena. She was years older, not mature, but in the autumn of her life. It must have been several years since Creiddylad's death and yet, to Gwyn, it seemed like yesterday.

Elena's presence tugged at his heart because he missed her too, and yet he so rarely found the time to remind her of how much her friendship meant to him. How many times had she covered for him when he snuck away to see Creiddylad? How many times had she stepped in to soften the outcome of a feud with his father?

He knew that any conversation with her, even a brief one, would derail his single-minded determination. Seeing Elena and leaving without a word was yet another failure to add to his growing collection.

Nudd sat in his study, as composed as ever, his silver-streaked hair immaculate, robes unruffled—his stillness a quiet rebuke. Nudd listened to him intently, his face a mask of serenity, even as

Gwyn painted a picture of what he had found in the aftermath of Creiddylad's death.

Nudd responded with his usual detached authority, his eyes betraying no emotion. "I thought, as you did, that he remained in France... Though perhaps we were both deceived in this matter. If that is the case, he must be dealt with."

Even in their agreement, the air thrummed with the unspoken tension between father and son, building like static energy into lightning, ready to strike at any moment. Duty only made the space between them wider. Always, always, Nudd expected more from his son—more self-control, more quiet dignity, more focus, but somehow less emotion. Even in his darkest moments of grief.

Gwyn left that day without answers.

One memory bled into another, a flood of images and emotions he could barely process. The moment he had one realization, another would pop up, leaving him little time to deal with his feelings as they came to him. If this had happened just a week before, Gwyn would have been furious about how either Fate or Serendipity had unfairly hidden the secrets of regaining his former power and ascension. But now, faced with the threat of far greater potential losses in his waking life, his personal setbacks seemed unimportant.

The next memory confirmed that Gwyn had wrongly assumed Nudd to be uncaring toward his sorrow. Both men sought Llefelys, albeit differently. Gwyn's Wild Hunt commitments left him little time to investigate, but Nudd's resources were considerable. It wasn't long before Nudd uncovered the truth and shared it with Gwyn: Llefelys had ascended immediately after Creiddylad's death—suspicious.

No longer bound by Llefelys' humanity, they were now permitted to interfere with him directly. Typical of Nudd, he already had a plan underway. Llefelys' ascended powers, he discovered, stemmed from malevolent origins.

"We cannot slay all malevolents," Nudd reasoned, his measured tone betraying neither hope nor despair, only a cold appraisal of the situation. "But we c—"

The dream ended abruptly, though Gwyn woke slowly, his body leaden, his mind lost between past and present. A deep despair settled over him like a burial shroud.

His memory. Leon had said that Gwyn came home to find Creiddylad shrouded, but he'd been the one who'd placed it upon her face. Not the servants. A lie. How much more had Leon lied about?

It didn't matter. The light that Creiddylad had brought into his life was gone. Now Abigail was gone. The shadows of hopelessness closed in, their silent pressure a tangible weight on his chest, so heavy it stole the breath from his lungs.

And yet a voice, urgent and familiar, found a way to pierce the shadows to whisper through his mind, like echoes pinging off canyon walls: *Pretend sleep.*

Feeling like a hollow, defeated shell, he basked in the voice's warmth. Paralyzed, his body was unresponsive. His mind, barely awake itself, slogged through reading his senses to realize where he was.

Why he was on Esmeralda's living room floor was another matter altogether. He paused to assess his strength and discovered realized how weak he was. He heard Leon—no, Llefelys hissing something nearby. Since siphoning attacks caused memory loss of differing degrees each time, his collapse onto the floor must be the result of Leon feeding on him.

Then—

Abigail's voice penetrated the fog of memory and despair. Sharp as the talons of a war eagle, it sliced through the failure and grief. *"Esme is awake. Get ready to fight."*

Sunlight. Hope. Fury.

She'd come. She'd woken him. And she sounded angry.

The certainty that the man who had just assaulted him, Esmeralda, and Miles was the same one who had killed Creiddylad bubbled up like boiling water overflowing its pot.

He joined Abigail in her wrath.

CHAPTER THIRTY-EIGHT

RISE UP

Esme

Pain dragged Esme back into consciousness—searing, white-hot agony that burned along her nerves like ice spikes piercing her flesh.

The pain radiated outward from her spine, her body too weak to shiver against the creeping chill of her depleted magic. She could feel infernal energy flowing in to fill the hollows where her own magic had been stripped away. She was uncertain if it had manifested on its own, taking advantage of her weak defenses, or if she had called it forth unconsciously.

The dark magic tugged at her, cold and insidious, whispering promises of power and escape. She liked to think herself strong, but her physical inability to give in to its wishes might have been the only thing that saved her from losing herself to its violent demands.

Paralyzed, the only thing she could do was hold the infernal influence back and endure the pain. If she lost herself to rage, she'd be no use to Miles. Tuning out the whispers of revenge, she could eventually focus on what was being said around her.

Miles. Focus on Miles.

A rare sunny winter day appeared to be on the horizon. Morning light streamed through the windows, casting long shadows across the place that had been her sanctuary. The contrast between her current situation and the happy vision that came to her next, of enjoying a sunny walk by the lake with Miles and Lily, was so stark she would have laughed had she been able.

Slumped on the couch and still unable to move, Esme could only see Miles kneeling, his posture rigid. In front of him, back turned, Leon was bent over, imposing, taking up far too much room. Unable to see his face, she could only read the tone of Leon's voice. It was dripping with venom.

"I don't know if Nudd will come out again." Miles' voice was carefully neutral, but it carried a note of fear she hadn't heard before she'd passed out. "I can't control it."

She couldn't have been out that long. *Nudd, if you're really in there, help us again.*

Leon's voice was a low rumble, barely audible. She couldn't understand a word of it, but apparently Miles, or Nudd, or both, did. Still, the threat in it was unmistakable.

Miles' response was sharp and quick. "Lay another hand on her, and you won't have to worry about cooperation—you'll have to worry about survival. When he comes out, I start doing things I'm personally not capable of."

Even the room held its breath. Leon hesitated. Was he afraid of Nudd? (Was that too much for her to hope for?)

If it meant realizing that threat, Esme would willingly accept Leon draining her again, or worse. This was her fault. Every reckless choice, every ounce of misplaced trust, had led her here.

She'd been so naïve, too willing to see the good in him, with no real reason behind it. Even after Miles had warned her.

Now Leon was using her to coerce him. Gods, how stupid was she, really? Leon had used magic on her again and again and again.

A sinister shadow now darkened each and every one of their interactions. That first warm, fuzzy feeling at the bar? A puppet master pulling her strings. Their heart-to-heart about being a cambion? A spider weaving its web. Even that comforting hug after the redcap attack—she could feel his coercing touch on her skin now, contaminated with the knowledge that every moment had been calculated, every comfort a lie designed to lead her here, helpless on her own couch.

Miles' voice, delivered with a careful casualness, broke the chain of thoughts binding themselves around her neck. He said, "I'm curious—was leaving Sylas the way you did a message or a threat?"

Leon spoke something in Brythonic, the ancient words flowing over Esme like a forgotten memory.

"I'm listening, but your brother isn't," Miles replied, playing dumb. But apparently, only she caught on. Miles was trying to buy time. "Nudd seems to come out when he's pissed, so telling the truth right now couldn't hurt."

His brother?

"The truth?" Leon's voice returned to its well-known, deliberate rhythm, the voice of the "Leon" they knew. "You begged me to kill the person who thought he was protecting you all."

Esme felt her stomach plummet through the floor and drop all the way to the infernal. She couldn't lose herself right now; she *couldn't*. She strained to hear Miles' stunned response.

He said, "What?"

Leon's tone turned smug. "All it took was promising to hurt a few kids, and that leshy was willing to do anything I asked."

"If Sylas was such a useful tool in hunting all of us, hunting Esme," Miles demanded, incredulous, "why did you kill him after forcing him to betray us?"

The warmth that she once thought she recognized in Leon's voice was now so clearly a mockery, twisted and cruel. She'd been so, so stupid.

Leon's laugh was low and indulgent, savoring the moment. "Because you asked me to."

Leon sighed and turned his head toward her slightly. She swiftly closed her eyes to avoid him noticing she was awake. Though he might already be aware, relishing how he could torture her with the information.

His voice held a smile as he continued. "And because it's good strategy to take care of a powerful threat when they've served their primary purpose—to weaken your alliances. Unfortunately, it didn't play out exactly as I hoped. The women were more... understanding of your covertly plotted murder than I anticipated. So I had to get creative. David came along. He served his purpose."

"And what was that?"

"I'll admit, this is satisfying to gloat about. Blaming David for my actions removed Jacob as a threat. He's across the ocean escorting a neutered David Abington to an old folks' home right now. Abby's mom scrambled David's brain because he siphoned her on Christmas Eve and tried to feed on Esme. Those parts were David. Then I drained Abby's mom so I could pull all this off. One after another, the pieces fell in line."

Christi... Gods below.

The barrage of information hit Esme like cannonballs, each one a different killing blow. She cared much less about David's betrayal than she did about the rest. But his disappearance, coming as it did when stability was most needed, had already sent shockwaves of uncertainty through the magical community.

The truth was a grotesque puppet show. Leon hadn't been merely playing them. He'd been pulling their strings for months. Each kind deed, each shared secret, each piece of advice was another thread of control. And she, trusting fool that she was, had stood next to him while he tied the strings to each of them.

Miles said, "You had us all fooled. And then you do this to the one person who had the most faith in you. Put your skills to good use; hunt down the malevolents as you did in the past."

No, don't be as naïve as me.

"It is adorable that she's so trusting, isn't it? Elena wasn't that way. Wonder what changed this time around? No, I have no intention of doing that. Malevolents have been a source of power for me for years. Why would I give that up?"

Leon's soft laughter made her skin crawl. He turned his attention, but not his eyes thankfully, back to her. "Aside from you, she's probably the closest to solving that 'problem.' I saw her use an infernal conduit on that redcap."

Remembering that moment with the redcap—how it had hesitated, only for a heartbeat, when she'd reached for it with her magic—brought her up short. If she hadn't been prepared for this moment by a series of earth-shattering revelations, each one more shocking than the last, she'd mentally be a quivering mess in a corner, muttering incoherently to herself.

Leon continued, "You said Nudd only comes out when angry. Here's some truth that might do the trick. I'm going to drain her dry. I want that power. Good luck getting her soul back here for a third time since there are no ascended beings to steal it from Annwn again. Well," he drawled, the word dripping with sardonic emphasis, "none for now, at least. I still need to take how Gwyn managed it from his mind, but it's all"—he made a sound like disgust and confusion tangled together—"a jumble inside his head."

Third time. What did he mean? He mentioned Gwyn, too, and... her soul? The puzzle pieces wouldn't connect, but dread bubbled up anyway. She wanted to think that Leon was just crazy, but Nudd was inside Miles' head and Gwyn was here in the flesh...

Then, all at once, Esme's blood turned to ice.

Elena. Leon had mentioned her earlier. The name slammed into her, a visceral shock that left her reeling, the familiar world tilting on its axis.

Leon was saying she *was* Elena. The idea was inherently unbelievable, yet it resonated deeply, settling into her bones like an undeniable truth, filling in gaps she hadn't known existed.

Maybe it was that moment of mental weakness, or maybe it was the fact that her best friend was a badass, but Abby's voice suddenly echoed in Esme's mind.

"I'm about to wake Gwyn up."

It was so shocking her body wanted to jump in surprise, though it remained frustratingly frozen.

Of course Abby figured out telepathy, Esme thought with a hysterical edge of humor. Because apparently that was a thing now too.

Another whisper. *"Breathe through your mouth, and don't look at the door. Katia's about to surprise Leon. Then we're coming in. Help me break this paralysis if you can."*

She was unsure if Abby could hear, but she sent waves of gratitude and love her way. Best. Friend. Ever.

Abby had found her. She was smart; Abby wouldn't try to get them out of this alone. Backup must be on its way.

Esme clamped her focus, pushing the infernal magic flooding her to do some good for a change. A spark of her own body's magic flickered to life, weak but determined, joining in.

Then Nudd's voice filled the room—deep, commanding, and eerily familiar. Esme couldn't understand the words, but Miles' ragged intake of breath was all she needed to know they needed to act.

A terrible understanding of Leon, of his intentions, washed over Esme. She knew with bone-deep certainty that Miles had only minutes left. If they didn't make a move right now, she would watch him die.

"NOW!" she shrieked in her mind to Abby.

If there was any justice in the world, she wouldn't have to watch another nightmare unfold before her eyes—wouldn't have to lose another person she loved in such a terrible way. Memories of her mother and father, of Sylas and Juniper, even Philip Luis flashed through her mind. Something primal inside her screamed NO. Not again. *Not Miles.*

She'd tear the house apart before letting Leon take anyone. With the force of her desperation, her paralyzed muscles trembled as she strained against the magical bonds, her will to break free so strong that she was prepared to destroy herself to escape.

CHAPTER THIRTY-NINE

DOMESTIC CHAOS UNLEASHED

Gwyn

If Gwyn didn't know Abigail's strength, her presence in this fight would have terrified him. But she was a war eagle, a harpy who could transform her rage into mental wings that would carry her to victory. With a carefully controlled movement, he turned his head, his neck finally free, the room's details slowly coming into focus. Esmeralda still lay on the couch. Wide-open violet eyes were staring right back at him, burning with... not hatred. Determination.

Brimstone burned there. She gave him a fractional nod, her gaze flicking to his discarded sword. A silent, unexpected understanding passed between them. She, or maybe Abigail, still thought there was some good in him. After his deception, she still expected him to make the good, moral choice. He hadn't told her about working with Jacob, about their failed plan to set up Leon, but her trust meant more to him than he'd realized.

Movement drew his attention to Miles. He was kneeling with his hands clasped before him, head drooping as Llefelys drained him slowly. Gwyn watched, horrified, as a thin stream of golden light flowed in the space between Miles' skin and Llefelys' grasping hand. Sweat beaded on Miles' forehead, his face was pale, and his body was trembling. Miles' shirt was ripped open at the top. Blood dripped from two long parallel gashes that sliced open the skin below his collarbone on one side.

Gwyn had seen this before—the victims too drained to stand, their eyes vacant, their bodies little more than husks. He'd walked in on one horror as a youth, a scene seared into his memory. Condemned for unspeakable crimes, his uncle's victim had been a powerful mage awaiting Nudd's ordered execution. Llefelys was methodical and cruel when he thought he could savor it. He'd been draining the mage slowly, in a way designed to extract every ounce of power from his victim, with as little loss as possible in the transfer.

The cuts were about physically weakening Miles, about how much pain Llefelys could make his victim endure. Watching Miles' consciousness fade stirred that same damned sense of decency back to life. When had he started to care about this recalcitrant man's fate—his feelings, his safety?

Gwyn had stopped his uncle in the past. He would stop it from happening again.

But Leon had drained some of Gwyn's magic, leaving him hollow and weakened. Now Gwyn would have to rely on sheer willpower alone. He clenched his jaw, eyes narrowed to slits as he concentrated on the steel of his sword. The sword responded sluggishly, rising from its resting place with agonizing slowness. His temples throbbed with the effort of shaking off the lingering effects of Leon's magic, even while performing simple telekinesis. Careful not to make a sound, Gwyn slowly float-ed it upward, its movement leaving no audible evidence to betray his intentions.

Leon's focus remained on his victim, his hand tightening as Miles sagged further. Before Gwyn could jump to his feet, hoping to catch Leon unaware, the front door burst open in a splintering crash, sending vibrations through the floor. Heeding Abby's warning about the succubus, Gwyn snapped his eyes to the floor, breathing through his mouth to avoid her enticement.

Gwyn heard Katia step into the doorway, felt her allure rolling off in waves. From the corner of his eye, he saw Leon freeze, his hand dropping from Miles as his gaze undoubted-ly locked onto the succubus. Gwyn could only imagine the smirk on Katia's face as she pulled him under her influence.

Even so, Gwyn worried about her safety. Katia's courage during the jorōgumo fight was without question, yet com-bat was not her specialty.

Gwyn seized the moment. His sword landed softly in his hand. A quick glance to the side showed Esmeralda prepar-ing herself to move as well. In her last life, and this one, she was not the type to give up, regardless of her condition. Katia's distraction must have freed her from the paralysis Leon had placed upon her.

A flicker of movement caught the corner of his eye, but he dismissed it, focused instead on trying to communicate his intentions to Esme with silent hand gestures.

Still, his mind snagged on the familiar tug of Cerys' pres-ence nearby, even though he had left her outside. How? The lack of any other feeling of magic was telling—classic Fae interference. Finn must be cloaking her.

Gwyn felt the wave of magic as Llefelys snarled, shattering his trance and fortifying his mental defenses. In the space of the same breath, he felt the succubus' intoxicating allure drop. When he looked up, Katia tipped her head back, her black hair cascading behind her. She winked at Leon and blew him a kiss with a mischievous glint in her eyes.

That small defiance almost cost her dearly.

With frightening ease, Leon picked up the nearby solid wood coffee table and hurled it at Katia. Gwyn noted the inhuman speed and strength behind the move—magic-enhanced, without question. Katia dodged it easily, her laughter echoing as she bolted away from the doorway.

But Leon didn't pursue her. Llefelys had the benefit of the same strategic education Gwyn had. He understood that she was a distraction from the threat her presence was meant to hide—from the immediate threats remaining within the room.

Not knowing if there was more to Abigail's ploy, Gwyn charged, blade ready to meet flesh. His uncle, the traitor, the torturer, the lowest of humanity, spun to face him.

Magic surged from Leon—then abruptly failed, flickering out before it could take hold. He must have been trying to mist walk, but Jacob's ward had sealed that escape route weeks ago. Though it helped Gwyn that Leon couldn't use that magic, it also meant that he was similarly restricted.

Leon dodged Gwyn's strike with the fluid grace befitting a son of Beli Mawr. Instead, Gwyn's sword collided with the heavy iron floor lamp Leon had grabbed. The lamp's shaft bent and twisted under the assault. Gwyn's muscles burned, and sweat soon dripped into his eyes. He could feel the weight of his depleted magic dragging him down far too quickly, but he didn't stop, launching one attack after another.

His true purpose was distraction—keeping his uncle's attention away from Esmeralda as she pulled Miles to safety, trying to wake him. Sparks flew as metal met metal, and the force of Leon's deflecting parry sent a jolt up Gwyn's arm. His opponent's speed was unnatural, his strength amplified by the magic he had stolen. Each strike was a step in the macabre dance that he hoped would save at least one life and end another.

A growl ripped from the siphon's throat. Leon's meticulously planned, straightforward route to success had failed. His face contorted in a juvenile rage before smoothing out into an expression that Gwyn knew all too well—contempt.

Leon was preparing to toy with them in the worst ways imaginable, and all Gwyn could do was suffer the next blow.

Esme

"Stay with me," Esme breathed, her voice breaking with desperation. As she kneeled beside Miles, her heart ached; his pallor, stillness, and vulnerability were too much.

The warmth of Miles' blood on her hands made her stomach churn. Esme refused to lose him—not now, not with so much left undone. But, gods, they also weren't the only two people in the room.

Battle seemed like a heroic, righteous thing until there was no turning back. When death was truly on the line, battle was little more than raw emotion, pain, and suffering. This was not glorious.

This fight was completely unnecessary, utterly senseless, and driven solely by the avarice of a single man.

A clash of metal drew her attention back to where Gwyn and Leon fought. For a fleeting second, her eyes met with Gwyn's. His will to fight was burning there, but his exhaustion was unmistakable. She'd trained with him enough to recognize the fatigue in his movements; his sword arm was heavy and his footwork was slower than usual.

What caught her attention more, though, was Leon's restraint. He was the man who had decapitated a powerful leshy's head with one strike and dropped it at their feet to sow chaos. He could have been hurling lightning or flames, yet he chose not to. A cruel smirk twisted his lips as he watched Gwyn stumble, a dark pleasure evident in his eyes. Leon was prolonging the fight, delighting in his opponent's slow decline.

And, gods below, from the look of it, they were all running out of time.

Anger had always been her strength. Now, it would be her weapon. Esme reached into the infernal well within her, the magic of her cambion blood burning hot as she pulled from the infernal realm. As her eyes eclipsed, brimstone-laden shadows coalesced on the other side of the room. Oatmeal, made smaller for the confined space, yet powerful and sleek, emerged from the smoke with red eyes blazing like hot coals in the shadows that made her face.

One hand trying to stem the blood pouring down the front of Miles' shirt, Esme split her mind and desperately ordered Oatmeal to take Leon from behind. The shadowcat leaped up with the aim to sink her claws into his shoulders.

But Leon moved with inhuman speed, spinning to snatch the shadowcat from the air.

Esme poured more power into her creation, willing her shadowcat to fight, to claw, to bite. But she could feel her weakening.

It almost seemed like Oatmeal was losing corporeal stability, but far too fast.

Then she felt it.

Her connection to Oatmeal allowed his siphoning to reach all the way to her. Esme cursed and banished her conjuration, her frustration boiling over. Oatmeal dissolved into nothing. With each passing moment, the fight seemed increasingly hopeless. Leon was so strong. Despite her efforts, Gwyn had only received temporary relief, and she paid a heavy personal price.

"No more conjurations," she muttered, her voice bitter.

Dismissing Esme as no real threat, Leon went back to toying with Gwyn.

Then, out of nowhere, Abby appeared, kneeling next to Miles. On Miles' opposite side, a slightly worse-for-wear Finn also emerged.

With a subtle nod in Gwyn's direction, Abby conveyed a silent message only a close friend would understand. A sword materialized in Esme's hand, forged from the same inky black shadows and brimstone as Oatmeal had been.

Trying to remain unnoticed, Esme hissed, "If that asshole's going to drain me, he's going to get cut in the process. Get Miles awake!"

Abby whisper-shouted back, "Fuck him up!"

Finn's hands hovered near Abby, cloaking their presence from Leon while she worked on Miles.

Esme moved toward Gwyn, and her other friends disappeared from sight. Matching her teacher's movements, she waited, anticipating the exact moment they could execute a synchronized strike.

Gwyn lunged. Esme was half a second behind him.

Leon's response was immediate and demoralizing. An aegis that rippled with Miles' stolen power burst into existence around him.

A profound, unsettling wrongness smacked into her chest at the sight. The dissonance was jarring. It seemed profoundly wrong, unnatural even, that someone as cold and heartless as Leon wielded Miles' protective magic, a power associated with empathy and compassion.

Following Gwyn's lead, Esme stepped back, waiting, watching, but held her blade ready. Anything they hit that shield with, magic or mundane, would be a futile effort. Neither she nor Gwyn was adept at wind, water, or ice magic.

For a moment, the room froze except for their ragged breaths and the faint tingling buzz of magic that felt like static electricity on her skin. Leon was waiting to see what they'd try next.

A sudden change swept over the static hum in the room, replacing it with a wild, untamed energy. A blur of fur shattered the tense standoff.

Lily burst into the room with Cerys following, the gwyllgi's presence a dark counterpoint to the god-touched hound's more earthly one. With hackles raised and a low growl rumbling in their chests, both dogs assumed defensive positions in front of Miles.

Still under the protection of his stolen shield, Leon turned his attention to the dogs. Esme's stomach twisted into a tight knot when the darkness of greed clouded his expression, making his reason for stealing Lily that morning horrifyingly clear.

Lily shared some of Miles' divine magic. She was a prize the siphon couldn't resist. Leon wasn't picky—he wanted *everything* from them.

A horrible smile stretched Leon's face as he lunged forward, seizing Lily by the scruff of her neck as she tried to bite his hand. He effortlessly hoisted her considerable weight into the air and held her to his chest. Lily yelped, her legs flailing as Leon began to siphon her magic.

Not wanting to harm Lily, both Esme and Gwyn immediately ceased their offensive.

In that crucial moment, Leon committed his first serious blunder. Lacking in either the experience or the patience to sustain the shield, he let it drop.

Two hundred and fifty pounds of enraged gwyllgi launched at Leon with a wailing howl that made Esme recoil instinctively. Cerys' crushing momentum sent him crashing to the ground, massive jaws finding purchase on his flank.

Lily wiggled free of his grasp and scrambled to her feet. Gwyn must have used their bond to order Cerys away because the gwyllgi also quickly leaped out of Leon's reach.

Abby

Gwyn became a blur of movement, Esme coming up after him to add insult to his injury. The dogs left Miles' side to join in the attack. Leon defended himself with an aegis, his hands, and small bursts of telekinetic magic but went no further than that. Leon's desire to drain them all might have been the only thing keeping them alive.

Throughout it all, Finn was the silent hero, casting his "ignore me" Fae charm over her as she worked on Miles. Now that his bleeding was under control, it was time to wake him up.

Holding his hand, Abby stepped into Miles' mind, his private space opening to her without resistance. His mindscape stretched out like an infinite warehouse, each memory connected to one another by strings of reason, emotion, and sensations. It wasn't like these things had actual form, but she liked to think of them that way, as storage containers, because it helped her to navigate the complex structure of the human brain.

But Miles' mindscape was different. If his healing hadn't convinced her of his ties to Nudd, his mind would. She could practically see the golden glow of his magic illuminating the entire space.

For his age, Miles had an excessive number of the chilling, persistent memories indicative of trauma. Many of them had the telltale markings of tampering.

And just like that, the pieces clicked into place as she understood the mess she'd seen in her father's memories. This tampering, these leftover scraps of memory, must be from David siphoning Miles over the years. To Abby, a master at precisely dissecting memories like a trained surgeon with a scalpel, the effect siphoning had on memory was sloppy and imprecise. She—and all those she trained in the future—would never again misidentify the work of a magic stealer.

If what Miles had shared with them several weeks ago was true, somewhere within this expanse, Miles was trapped in a dream—a dream she needed to pull him out of. Abby had used her magic on sleeping people only a few times, but the experiences were vivid enough to guide her on what to look for. She searched for something like a door.

Time was precious—Leon was still out there, fighting with Gwyn and Esme. Luckily, time passed differently in the mindscape, and things at the top of her subject's mind tended to be, quite literally, top of mind.

She located the door easily. The door, the dream really, exerted a strange, powerful pull on her. This was answered with a profound tug from deep inside herself.

With a steadying breath, Abby opened the dream. Golden light surged, dragging her in like a riptide. She tumbled through blinding light before landing behind unfamiliar eyes, seeing through them as if they were her own.

The wooden floor gleamed under the light of a long stone firepit that stretched down the center of the room—exactly like Gwyn had described.

From her elevated position on the dais, she gazed down upon three figures. She recognized two of them immediately: a much younger Gwyn, barely in his twenties, and Leon, wearing his true face, the one she'd seen in her father's broken memories, but similarly youthful. The third figure was an unfamiliar woman to Abby, yet she sensed immediately that this woman was the force that had drawn her there.

The woman was slight, with straight blonde hair a shade darker than Abby's own, mostly hidden beneath a fine veil secured by a delicate silver circlet. Her light blue peplum dress was exquisitely made, but it was the way she moved that captured Abby's attention—a familiar nervousness in her stance that suddenly transformed into steel-backed resolve when called upon.

"Quiet, Gwyn, Llefelys," Nudd's voice boomed from the throat Abby now shared. "I have heard your complaints. I shall hear it from the lady herself."

Abby felt like a stunned rabbit caught under blinding headlights. The pieces clicked into place with dizzying speed as the woman, who could be none other than Creiddylad, made a small bow.

"Sire, my servant was stopped from her duties this morning by Prince Llefelys," Creiddylad said, her voice soft but resolute. "She refused to tell me the nature of the interference. When I intervened, your brother laid his hand upon me."

Gwyn's mutter about "cutting it off" reached their ears, but Nudd chose to ignore his son's commentary.

"You are my ally's daughter and have become like my own," Nudd said, his tone measured. "Your conduct has been beyond reproach since the day your father and brother brought you to my doors as a symbol of peace. Tell me true, do you seek to weaken the peace now, or uphold it as befitting your station?"

Gwyn's youthful features twisted with pique, his cheeks flushing, blue eyes blazing. Indignant on Creiddylad's behalf, he erupted. "You dare question the truth of her words?"

Abby sensed Nudd's certainty that Creiddylad was telling the truth. He was waiting, she realized, giving her room to spring her trap. Creiddylad was everything Gwyn had claimed her to be and more. No wonder he loved her.

Creiddylad's eyes flicked toward Llefelys. Then she tilted her head slightly, her voice steady, spine straightening further. "Sire, I would never seek to disturb the peace. Perhaps Prince Llefelys could explain why my servant had to take to her bed after a brief encounter with him? And why, when I confronted him this morning, he claimed to have never spoken to her at all?"

Llefelys' face darkened. "I have not spoken to your hand-maids. I would not lower myself—"

"Then how do you explain being seen entering the servant's eating area by Guardsman Glais?" Creiddylad's voice rang clear. "The same Glais who stands watch over my chambers frequently, whom you just claimed to have seen at the training grounds all morning?"

Abby gasped within Nudd's mind at the guard's name—the one Miles had asked her to research months ago. She sensed Miles' sudden focus shift to her—he hadn't known she was there too.

"Abby?" His mental voice, a disbelieving whisper, sounded incredulous.

"We don't have time," she urged. "Leon is fighting Gwyn and Esme. They're tiring. Leon tried to drain Lily. I need to wake you so we can have a chance against him."

It was clear that Miles' mind was immediately and firmly set. "Do it!"

She would have to remove him forcibly from both his dream and sleep. To put it mildly, his transition would be rough.

"Consider yourself warned: waking up will feel like a day's hangover compressed into seconds. It's going to hurt."

"Wouldn't be the worst wake-up call I've had," Miles replied with grim humor. "An air horn and a bucket of ice water simultaneously..."

He didn't truly know what he was about to experience, but words couldn't describe it. So Abby gathered her magic, shaped it into a brutal ax, and swung.

Dream still playing in the background, the world shattered around them both.

Abby gasped as her eyes snapped open. Miles groaned beside her in a way that suggested her magical ax strike felt more like getting hit by an actual truck. She winced in sympathy and pointed at the fight now raging.

"Sorry," Abby said, handing him Esme's dagger she'd found on the porch. "Get in there. And give me a chance at him."

From the look of things, Abby had probably only been in his mind for a few seconds, but she'd come out the other side feeling like an entirely different person. The spectral memory of a woman, seen through Nudd's eyes, who moved in exactly the same way she did...

There'd be another time for Abby to question everything all over again. But now, there was only time to prepare to strike.

CHAPTER FORTY

A HARPY TAKES WING

Miles

Esme's living room, once a sanctuary of laughter and warmth, was now a battlefield. Furniture lay overturned, glittering glass shards littered the floor, and crackling residual magic filled the air. Miles' ears rang from Abby's earlier blow, but he ignored the pain, clutching Esme's dagger. Concealed by Finn's magic, he waited, poised like a spring, to strike.

Esme remained hidden in a different way across the room. She tried to not bring attention to herself, her summoned blade at the ready, her eyes darting between the fighters, biding her time. Gwyn's sword whistled through the air as he attacked, but the immense ocean of magic Leon had available was enough to make him supernaturally fast.

Without warning, Leon seized Gwyn, and the nature of their struggle shifted—he was done toying with them.

Miles stepped out of the circle of Finn's influence, and Leon's attention instantly shifted his way. With a forceful push, Leon sent Gwyn sprawling. Miles noticed the unmistakable glassy stare of enchantment that appeared in Gwyn's eyes only a heartbeat before he turned, against his will, and attacked Esme.

Miles created a shield around her just in time to deflect Gwyn's strike. The blade skittered harmlessly against it as she darted out of the way.

Leon retreated, his grin a slash of malice across his face. He found perverse amusement in watching Esme fend off Gwyn, watching someone else do his dirty work, as she struggled for breath.

Shouldn't this be enough to piss you off, Nudd? Your own brother forcing your son to attack Elena? But whatever lingering presence of Nudd that had shown itself so forcefully before now was dormant.

Miles met Leon's gaze, fury burning in his chest, but Leon only smirked. Of course he wasn't concerned. He didn't need to fight—not when he could force others to do it for him.

Gwyn's attack shifted to Miles with dizzying speed. His blade cut through the air, but Miles reacted instantly, shifting the shield from Esme to himself. Leon was trying to wear him down. Llefelys wanted Nudd's death to come by a thousand tiny cuts.

Still, during his time as Leon, Llefelys seemed to have forgotten Nudd's proficiency in two areas. Nudd had unparalleled defensive magic and an uncanny connection with dogs.

The request was barely formed in Miles' mind when the action began. Lost to Leon's enchantment, Gwyn stumbled as Lily's jaws clamped onto the back of his shirt, yanking him off-balance. One dog might have been enough, but two guaranteed success. Cerys joined the fray, barreling into her master's side with the force of a freight train. Together, the two hounds sent him sprawling onto the floor.

Miles silently barked orders—Lily to Esme, Cerys to Abby. The dogs moved without hesitation, a seamless extension of his will. Memories of the nguruvilu fight from what seemed like so long ago surfaced: the dogs circling, striking in turns, retreating—a practiced dance of teamwork so soon after meeting. Had he been unconsciously directing their harmony for months?

Through all of this, Esme had her own plan in motion. With Leon distracted, she launched herself at Leon. Her conjured sword aimed straight for his turned back.

Leon's sickeningly playful smirk instantly froze into a cold, malevolent expression. He turned.

Miles tried to transfer his shield to Esme with the same lightning speed as before, but Leon had anticipated the move.

A violent gust of wind threw Esme backward into the wall. Her sword vanished as her concentration broke. She landed with a sickening crack and crumpled to the floor.

Leon wanted him vulnerable. He wanted Miles to be reckless. To rush to her rescue.

Except Miles had trained with Esme for months. He knew her tells. He knew that the groan that escaped her lips was a good sign she could hold on until he, until they, could get them out of danger.

Leon wasn't going to break her. He obviously meant to keep her under his power after this battle was won.

Or, equally as likely, he wanted Nudd to rise to the surface and fight.

But Miles was done. His fury was so all-consuming that it completely eclipsed Nudd's presence, pushing it to the periphery of his awareness and consideration. So Nudd did not assist this time.

Miles launched the dagger from his prosthetic hand, hoping its enchantment would siphon away even a fraction of Leon's stolen power. The blade whistled through the air—and missed, clattering uselessly to the floor. *Fuck*.

Miles didn't hesitate. With a flick of his will, the dagger shot back to him like a boomerang, slicing a thin line across Leon's shoulder before crashing to the floor. Blood welled, dark and glistening.

A primal thrill surged through Miles. Leon wasn't invincible. He could bleed.

He could die.

The tendril of hope had barely taken root when Leon's magic cracked outward—a devastating force of raw power that threatened to drown his fragile victory. Miles reignited his shield, but the impact still drove him back several steps.

Overconfidence would get him killed. One paper cut wasn't worth dying over.

From the corner of his eye, Miles saw his backup plan nudging Esme gently. This was a time he hoped Lily's healing ability would manifest. Cerys moved to stand guard over them both, her growl low and unearthly. Miles backpedaled, positioning himself between Esme, the dogs, and Leon.

Leon was clearly trying to remove some of the complication from the fight. He had once again left Gwyn sprawled on the floor, paralyzed, unattended.

Abby stepped out of the shadows.

Leon's attention suddenly swung her way a beat too late. She placed one hand on Gwyn's exposed skin. The leprechaun's magic dissolved as he materialized beside her, expression grim.

With all the magic swirling in the air, there was no warning when Leon staggered as if struck by an invisible sledgehammer.

Hell yes.

Abby had severed his connection to Gwyn using such brute force that the backlash had snapped back in Leon's face with something like a physical blow. Miles smiled as he saw the golden glow of healing magic from Lily on his left and the smiling face of a blonde harpy taking wing on his right.

Understanding his duty to ensure her flight, Miles charged Leon with the dagger again. His plan was half-formed at best, but he'd gladly trade his safety to buy Abby the seconds she needed.

Chaos was their greatest hope.

Finn wasn't idle. With a furious yell of something in Irish, the leprechaun leaped between them all, a torrent of ifrit fire blasting toward Leon.

Leon's shield popped into place, deflecting most of the inferno—but not all. His perfect face was now marred by furious red blisters and seeping sores.

Leon immediately retaliated. A powerful gust of wind slammed into Miles and Finn, knocking both of them off their feet. Miles dropped the dagger in midair. Then he hit the ground hard, his shield flickering but holding. Abby was far enough to the side to avoid the full force of the blast. She maintained her feet.

Burns, particularly facial burns, were intensely painful—a fact Miles was intimately familiar with. Leon turned all of his attention to using Miles' pilfered magic to heal himself as he and Finn reached their feet.

In that perfect moment of self-centered concentration, of vulnerability, Abby struck. Holding Esme's fallen dagger in one hand, Abby extended the talons of her magic as she seized Leon in a firm grip.

The moment she made contact, Leon's movements stilled. His expression shifted to a slack-jawed vacancy, and his eyes glazed over.

She said a single word. "Finn."

They must have had a plan, because the moment she took control, Finn walked over and inexplicably started pouring magic into her. Miles could only watch as the battle shifted from the physical to the mental realm.

Abby

Abby's consciousness lanced out like a white-hot rapier, plunging deep into Leon's mind. Even it was a battlefield. His mental defenses were a labyrinth of razor-sharp barbs and icy walls, each step, each handhold a fresh agony. She gritted her teeth, fueled by fury and Finn's magic, and pushed deeper.

Pain was nothing. Not when justice was within reach.

First, she seized control, binding his consciousness tight, locking his body in place as she delved deeper. What surprised her most was the extent to which Leon's and Miles' mindscapes were both alike and different. Leon's was orderly like Miles', with more of the sticky, cold memories of trauma than she'd seen in others, but his had a distinct gap in it.

When she'd woken Gwyn earlier, her inexperience at casting her power at a distance had meant that her peek inside Gwyn's mind had been quite limited. The obvious gap in Leon's mind had to be where his imprisonment had created a sixteen-hundred-year void, like a chasm in time. But the gap was too clean-cut. Such precision seemed planned. Magic was a natural force, like gravity and electromagnetism. Its effects would line up nicely, but the edges of its effects should be fuzzy and frayed, not laser cut like this.

Also like Miles, Leon had memories that glowed with magic, but his felt... wrong.

Walking by some of them, she could almost taste iron and a sickening sweetness in her mouth, feel burning from cold or heat on her skin. It was uncomfortable even being near them. Was this the taint of magic stolen through violence? Murder? Cruelty? In his mind, she sped past sharp memories that scraped like shattered glass against her thoughts. Ignoring the pain, she pressed on.

She needed answers. Abby had to know for sure if he was the one who'd put her father in the hospital and stolen her mother's magic.

Following the faint, almost imperceptible tingle of her parents' magical signatures, she found the memories touched by their presence all lined up neatly. Abby chose one memory at random and braced herself. While not an expert, she thought the emotional flatness surrounding his memories was a strong sign that he needed therapeutic intervention—if they weren't forced to kill him first.

Abby didn't have time for dawdling. Finn's magic was a fragile tether, and Leon's will was an unbreakable force born of madness. She tore into the memory, letting it swallow her whole.

Through Leon's eyes, Abby watched her father fight like a cornered animal. She sensed he wouldn't kill her father. The inconvenience of covering a murder was simply too great. But her father's defiance shocked even Leon. The meek man had vanished, supplanted by a primal drive to protect his wife.

Sean O'Malley was a very middle-of-the-pack mage when it came to power. Though not a powerful specialist in any particular magic, he showed a natural talent with plants. The garden they'd trampled fighting the Dullahan blossomed into a spectacle every year once the days were long enough in gloomy western Washington.

If their mother mentioned a flower, the next growing season would unfailingly bring forth that very bloom in a spot where she could happily watch it unfurl its petals from her window. By and large, her father was a soft man.

But that morning, Leon saw a side of him that Abby hoped her father would never have to bring out again. With a flurry of blows and bursts of magic, her father desperately tried to fend him off but failed.

Leon only started draining her mother's magic after he'd brutally beaten her father to the brink of unconsciousness. The whole time, he basked in the cruel pleasure of her father's helplessness, relishing his desperate hope, toying with him by giving the impression that he might have a chance of saving his wife.

Abby left this memory before it was over. The gruesome scene was too much; she simply couldn't watch anymore. She remained uncertain about whether he had fully depleted her mother, but even knowing wouldn't affect the end result.

She needed to move on.

Old memories loomed ahead, their glow dimmed by the centuries they had endured. Finn's magic was unexpectedly strong, so she told herself that she could indulge this once. She grabbed one of the newer "old" memories at random and forced it open.

This one didn't tug on her like Miles' dream had, but the memory pulled her in all the same. Suddenly she was seeing through Llefelys' eyes as he hid in the shadows of Nudd's keep. His scrying showed guards on patrol, servants asleep, and life's ordinary flow within the keep.

Abby almost dismissed the memory, but then a female guardswoman caught Llefelys' eye. Abby's breath hitched as she watched Elena stride through the halls, her movements achingly familiar. When she entered Nudd's private chambers, Llefelys' scrying followed.

"The eastern fortification is secured, sire," Elena reported, her voice carrying the same subtle inflections as Esme's through magic's translation. Even the way she shifted her weight was identical—the same build, though Elena's frame was more muscled from sword work.

"Very good," Nudd replied, his eyes lingering on her face a moment too long. A palpable tension hung between them, a familiarity almost intimate—one Abby recognized.

The way she shifted her weight and tucked her hair behind her ear, the guardswoman was Esme's double. First Creiddylad moving exactly as Abby did, and now Elena mirroring Esme in every detail.

Miles and Gwyn, it turned out, had a very specific type. The puzzle pieces of the truth lay scattered before her, but their shapes were unfamiliar and missing... something.

Overwhelmed, Abby fled the memory, deliberately leaving it open to wither and fade. Llefelys, Leon, didn't deserve to keep this private memory. She ran deeper into the warehouse of his mind, her steps slowing as she passed rows of memories saturated with hatred. One, frigid as glacial ice and throbbing with an eerie, sickly red light, drew her in like Miles' dream had.

Time was short. But she couldn't resist opening just one more. Despite the warning in her gut, Abby ripped it open and dove inside.

The scene materialized around her. Llefelys sat beside Creiddylad, the picture of a calm conversation—except for the stolen mental magic holding Creiddylad paralyzed in her chair. Every muscle in Creiddylad's body was tense, her eyes blazing with unshed tears of silent fury.

Abby was sickened when she realized he was using power exactly like hers for his own depraved purposes. Abby watched, unable to tear her eyes away, as Creiddylad's light dwindled, her lively spirit fading like a dying ember.

Powerless to intervene, she witnessed Creiddylad's magic being devoured by the monster who appeared to be doing nothing more than holding her hand. After Creiddylad passed out, Llefelys gently pinched her mouth and nose closed—she didn't struggle or even open her eyes as she suffocated.

A hollow ache of something remembered, something felt, spread through Abby's soul. The grief and rage were so potent she felt her inner self nearly shatter.

But like always, Abby wiped her metaphorical tears and straightened her spine.

If she couldn't destroy Leon outright in the real world, she would incapacitate him with his own horrors.

The force of her emotions propelled her out of the memory and further into the mindscape. Memory after memory she ripped open, each one worse than the last.

Blood. Screams. Power stolen with greedy hands.

She couldn't stop. Wouldn't stop. Not until he was drowning in his own sins.

Hundreds of murders, ancient and recent, had fueled his endless thirst for power. Each poured out in a torrent of images she couldn't stop. The casual callousness and total absence of remorse that surrounded her inside his mind was almost unbearable.

Leon felt owed all the things he stole. He felt entitled to Miles' power. As if someone like him deserved the blessing of healing.

Abby's journey through his memories ended only when she arrived at his earliest ones, still glowing with childhood innocence. She couldn't bring herself to harm them. Even monsters like Leon had once been human.

It was time to return to the real world and end this.

All it took was a thought. Snapping back to her physical body while maintaining her grip on Leon's mind, Abby found her voice.

"Thank you, Finn," she managed, the jagged edges of hundreds of horrors tearing at her throat.

Abby held Leon as his mind crumbled. All that he was, his sense of self, his brain, melted under her control.

As he fell to pieces, she whispered, "This is from my parents and Creiddylad, you sick fuck."

Then she proved to herself, and to him, that she had what it took to destroy him in the real world. Abby plunged Esme's dagger into his throat, right above his collarbone.

Leon's body convulsed as the siphoning blade drank deep, as the stolen magic was ripped from him with excruciating force.

Abby exhaled, the deed done. But relief was a distant, unreachable thing. The blood on her hands was warm. A strange sense of unreality accompanied the guilt that tried to rise in her chest. It was as if her mind had detached itself from the horrific act, observing it from a remote distance, even if his blood was still sticky on her hands.

She remained detached, a numb observer as a sudden impact violently slammed into her.

The world tilted. Blood rushed in her ears. And as darkness crept at the edges of her vision, Abby stumbled...

CHAPTER FORTY-ONE

INTO DUST

Esme

The instant Abby's mind locked around Leon's, Miles bolted to Esme's side. This could be their only opportunity to reorganize—a fleeting, shaky respite in the eye of the storm.

Lily and Cerys crowded around Gwyn, nudging him with their snouts, their whines soft and urgent, trying to rouse him. He stirred with a guttural groan that sounded painful. Yet he still managed a small, reassuring pat on Cerys' head. He was alive and, importantly, recovering.

Miles didn't look up as he worked over Esme's wounds, muttering her name again and again like it was a prayer. But Esme's attention remained focused on the serpent currently trapped in the harpy's talons. Every cell in her body hurt. Though the snake was subdued, she sensed its fight wasn't over.

Then, right before Abby struck, Esme noticed it. Leon's fingers twitched. His hand curled into a deadly gesture. Even through the fog of her concussion, she recognized it. She'd seen

Gwyn make the same motion too many times to miss what it meant.

Abby was deep in his mind, eyes glazed as she straddled two realities. She wouldn't see it. Not in time.

Hours earlier, while paralyzed in the passenger's seat, helpless as Christi and Sean faced gods knew what, Esme had promised to make her offhanded, violent, very cambion response to Leon's question of whether she wanted "more" with him into a reality.

Her answer was and would always be: abso-fucking-lutely not.

Esme made good on her promise.

She moved on instinct, shoving Miles aside as her sword materialized in a burst of infernal shadows. Abby said something Esme couldn't hear because she was already lunging, her blade a black streak aimed at Leon's eye.

Two strikes landed a split second apart—Abby's dagger piercing his throat and Esme's sword, now sharpened to a stiletto, finding his eye.

Leon's head snapped back. Abby went sprawling from the impact.

Then Esme received undeniable proof that her siphoning blade had always functioned correctly.

It drank in Leon's stolen magic.

The house's protective wards flared to life, triggered by the surge of raw magic unleashed within its walls. All at once, each ward screamed in silent protest. Then collapsed.

A loud pop and magical shockwave only the talented could feel nearly rocked them all off their feet.

The flames that had been building in Leon's hand erupted chaotically, amplified by the magical discharge. Instead of a focused jet of fire, thanks to Esme, his intended revenge on Abby missed its mark. The magic exploded outward in a fiery circle, its heat scorching everything around it as Leon's corpse fell backward.

The destroyed couch went up first, its polyester fabric melting like wax. Flames raced up the walls, devouring everything in their path—fueled by mundane materials and the wild magic crackling through the air like lightning.

Chaos erupted. Miles immediately ran to the kitchen, where Esme had a fire extinguisher stored under the sink.

"Abby!" Esme shouted, seizing her friend's shoulder. Abby unsteadily regained her feet, eyes locked on her blood-stained hands. Esme's violent shake jolted her out of her stupor. Without a second glance down at them, Abby immediately started running toward Gwyn.

Thick black smoke, heavy with the chemical smell of burning plastic and magic, filled the air. The temperature was rising fast enough to make Esme sweat.

Miles burst back into the living room, fire extinguisher in hand. He pulled the pin and squeezed the handle, but instead of a powerful spray, only a weak powder trickled out. The extinguisher sputtered and died.

Miles, usually externally calm and composed, let out a rare shout, "Bloody fuck!" and threw the fire extinguisher down in a fit of passion.

Esme turned toward her bedroom, her voice breaking. "My mother's—"

"Gwyn." Abby shook him, but he was struggling to get his bearings.

The wild magic didn't just feed the flames—it warped them. As the blaze neared the collapsing wards, each began to spark, spitting fiery bolts that crackled and hissed.

The fire had only just started, but it had already gained the upper hand.

"Out!" Finn's voice cracked like a whip, cutting through the rising panic. "Everyone out now!" No room for argument, no room for hesitation. His voice carried an authority that seemed impossible from his small frame.

The windows rattled ominously as magic surged again. The leprechaun screamed, "I'll get what I can, Esme, but ya need to move!"

Gwyn stumbled to his feet, using Abby for support. His face was gray with exhaustion, but he managed to push himself forward, Cerys and Lily pressing against his legs to help steady him. Each step was labored, each breath ragged, but he kept moving forward.

The air shimmered with heat, and the smoke was becoming thick enough that it was difficult to breathe, let alone talk. A support beam groaned overhead as the magic-fueled fire licked at it. Finn physically pushed Esme toward the door when she tried to dart around him to grab what she could.

Miles took a step toward Leon's body. Esme could guess that the remnants of Nudd's presence were pulling at him, urging him not to leave his brother behind. The corpse's single remaining eye, so still in death, stared sightlessly upward as the hungry flames crackled and danced closer.

"Don't." Esme's voice was hoarse as she grabbed his arm.

Finn stopped pushing at her and disappeared.

"He doesn't deserve it," Esme snapped.

"His body—" Miles started to protest.

"—is evidence!" Esme finished. Her thoughts had already journeyed two hours ahead, thinking of the implications of what was unraveling, of what she'd done. "We have to go. Now."

The ceiling's collapse, showering burning debris where the couch had once stood, made their decision. Esme briefly considered the discarded dagger before deciding to leave it where it lay. Then Miles pulled her toward the door as Abby helped Gwyn through it.

On the way, Esme stared at the useless fire extinguisher that had rolled to a stop near the door. Sylas had bought her that. For years, she'd held on to everything he'd given her, unable to discard a single item. The irony that her sentimental attachment to an expired safety device had contributed to losing her home, and with it, every tangible memory of her parents, wasn't lost on her.

They stumbled out onto the street, gasping in the clean air. Finn appeared moments later with a small box and a handful of photo albums, his clothes half-burned away by the flames.

In a low voice, he handed them over, saying, "I saved these..."

"I—" She failed to speak for a long moment.

"We're all here, love," Miles murmured into her hair as sirens wailed, growing closer.

Abby half held up, half clung to Gwyn a few feet away. Tears streamed down his face, making tracks in the soot that covered him in a display of emotion that was almost too much for Esme to bear seeing.

He hadn't betrayed them.

She understood that now. He had also just lost a family member, no matter how despicable Leon had been. Esme knew the bitter taste of that experience. His suffering affected her as deeply as her own.

Finn's head darted to the side as a voice called his name down the street. It was Katia, waving her cell phone in the air like a beacon, standing next to her car. She shouted, "Get in before they arrive, imp!"

It made sense. Even if Finn looked human, his differences would draw unwanted attention from the firefighters assessing their injuries.

"Go, enjoy being dinner," Esme croaked out. "You're my hero."

Before leaving, Finn stared intently at the air around Abby, his eyes never meeting hers. His silence was thick with unspoken words and a fresh tension. He walked over to her and nearly choked up as he grabbed her hands and whispered, "Oh, dove... I'm sorry."

He left, shaking his head, walking on unsteady feet toward Katia without another word.

The group watched in helpless silence as the flames engulfed Esme's home. Except for a single semester at college, she'd lived her entire life in that little house. A tremor started in her shoulders, escalating into a shaking that wracked her entire body.

Everything inside, every space holding countless memories, was now turning to dust. Her past was literally going up in flames.

Abby

As the firefighters emerged from the ruins of Esme's home, Abby greeted each one with a grateful embrace, her small frame steadied by Miles. Drained of energy and emotionally raw from the recent trauma, she felt numb as she worked.

Was Abby grateful for their efforts? Yes.

Was Miles helping her stand? No.

He was covertly giving her what little magic he could after pulling his charming strong leader act on the people asking questions. Gwyn was simply too tapped out to be of much use in that regard, magically speaking.

Even after everything they'd done and seen that day, "first things first" applied. The firefighters left without recalling the body inside—thanks to Abby's magical persuasion. Esme's house, the sole casualty of the fire, had been doomed the moment the wards collapsed. Katia's quick call had at least spared the neighborhood.

Abby had gone home to shower after spending the remaining daylight on the fallout of Esme's house burning down, then immediately fallen asleep, still wrapped in her towel. Throughout, Gwyn had provided unwavering support, accompanying her step by step, despite being in worse physical shape than she was.

He'd tried explaining to her, begged forgiveness for the plan he'd cooked up with Jacob in secret, but Abby had barely heard him. She decided she didn't care. She trusted him. She loved him, even if he was concealing the fact that she was his former lover's double.

After a few fitful hours of sleep, she'd left her apartment quietly, leaving Gwyn sleeping and a note on the bedside table explaining her absence. Abby sat in her father's hospital room, her mother on one side, Colin on the other.

Her father's emergency surgery had gone splendidly—not that Abby had been there to support him during it. Guilt came at her in waves as she looked at him, then looked at her mother, presumably stripped of her magical birthright by the monster Abby had killed the day before.

She felt like a stranger in her own skin, her thoughts fragmented, her emotions numb except for the guilt she experienced about not being there for her family. Was it shock? Trauma? Or something darker? Had being in Leon's mind, unleashing his memories, then running through the cloud of his sins permanently affected her?

Only time would tell.

Leon's murder was something she had more trouble dredging up guilt for. Did that make her a monster too? Maybe. Abby couldn't find it within herself to care about that either.

Telling her family the half-truths about yesterday felt worse than any act of violence she'd committed the day before. Her mother listened, tears streaming down her face as she held Abby close, whispering apologies for the pressure Abby thought was on her to protect her family. Colin was jealous that he hadn't been able to wipe "Leon" off the face of the planet himself. Every move he made proved how consumed by his own guilt he was for not doing more.

It wasn't like Abby could tell her family that Leon and Gwyn were more than fifteen hundred years old. She couldn't tell her family that a demigod's essence possessed Miles. It still sounded insane to her, even if she had seen it within two minds firsthand. As far as the O'Malleys knew, Leon was nothing more than a second siphon who'd acted violently in his relentless pursuit of power.

Maybe someday she could confide in them, but first, she needed to fully grasp the situation herself. She needed to make sense of the puzzle pieces spread before her that she couldn't quite fit together yet. An important piece was missing, and she had a horrible feeling that piece had something to do with her.

In a few hours, she'd have to face reality and talk to the others about everything she'd seen inside Leon's mind. She'd have to tell Gwyn that everything would be okay and that she believed him. Hopefully, she'd be able to help her best friend pick up the few spare pieces of her material life that were left. She'd have to give Katia and that ridiculous leprechaun a big squeeze until their eyes bulged.

Later, she would have time to sift through the images and memories in Leon's mind, to untangle the centuries-old web of connections and betrayals. But for now, her family needed her—both the one she'd been born into and the one she'd forged in fire.

CHAPTER FORTY-TWO

THE BEGINNING OF THE END

Jacob

Rain tapped against the office window, the dim afternoon sun casting what might have been a soothing pattern of light across Jacob's desk under different circumstances. He sat rigid, hands clasped tightly, waiting for his guest to break his long-held silence.

Finn paced, fury radiating off him in literal heatwaves. "You right bastard!"

"Fionn—"

"Don't ya even try it," Finn warned, his blazing temper overriding any hesitation he might have otherwise shown. "You kept me in the dark. *Me*. And it nearly got 'em all killed."

Jacob kept his expression impassive, but his fingers betrayed him, drumming against the desk's edge. "I made a judgment call. Gwyn's loyalty had to be convincing. If anyone suspected he wasn't wholly on Leon's side, the entire plan would have collapsed."

"Collapsed?" Finn abruptly halted his pacing, confronting Jacob with blue eyes that shone with suppressed fury. "Well, ya got that outcome, right enough."

"I gamble with lives daily, leprechaun," Jacob said, jaw tight. "I won't apologize."

"Perhaps ya ought to!" Finn laughed bitterly, shaking his head. "Guess I can't blame you for bein' blind to what's right in front of you, since ya can't hear either!"

Jacob dismissed the cutting remark. So what if his sight was dimming? He was almost one hundred seven.

"And what is that supposed to mean?" Jacob's voice carried a dangerous edge. "This needed to stay contained. We were attempting to get Mr. Chan into a vulnerable position."

"Save your political shite for someone else." Finn barked out another resentful laugh. "I'll clarify, red coat. It means yer meddlin' in something far older and far bigger than you."

The insinuation in Finn's tone made Jacob uneasy. "What exactly are you saying?"

"Somethin' a feckin' thousand years in the making is goin' down. I bind my word to that." He slammed his open palm on the table, emitting sparks of light. "Stand outta their way until they come to you, Jacob. Though I suppose plannin' that spans a thousand years was never gonna go down easily."

"Fionn." Jacob slumped in his seat without realizing it. "Your absolute clarity, for once, on this would be most welcome."

Finn's lips curved into a grim smile. "Willin' to make a trade, colonizer?"

Jacob pushed his chair back and opened the small desk drawer hidden in the desktop. He pulled out a bar of solid gold, the size of a stack of cards. "I'd rather pay you off."

Then, more seriously, Jacob added, "You know I want them to have a happy ending. It appears as though I need to understand what you are saying to help them achieve that."

"Aye." Finn's dinner-plate-sized eyes, gleaming with avarice, remained glued to the bar of gold. "Esme'll be in here within three days wantin' your opinion on it, anyway."

Jacob slid the gold bar across the table. "Start talking."

Finn seized it, rubbing it almost lovingly between his hands. "I'll tell you exactly what I told yer golden boy. He had a bit of an existential crisis on the way, but he eventually got there. I'm gonna need you to keep an open mind."

Jacob disliked where this was headed, but he settled in to listen. He'd been right. Esmeralda was making the end of his life very interesting indeed.

Miles

Miles had never been so glad for a Saturday. After the chaos of New Year's Day, he could finally breathe. He lay propped up on one elbow on his bed after sleeping for twelve glorious hours. Esme lay beside him, biting her lip to stifle a grimace.

He kissed the top of her head. "I know that face, lovely. Before you lose your marbles about it—you're moving in with me. This isn't worth you fretting over."

She tried to sidestep the direct conversation they needed to have with an offhanded comment. "It's fortunate I had a few changes of clothes here."

"We'll go shopping."

She looked at him as though he were mad. He understood what that reaction was about, too. He knew exactly why she had been so adamant about not exchanging Christmas presents. She'd been skint because that bastard had fired her. Because their financial situations were unlikely ever to be equal, it was best to address this now.

"Lovely, I have two high-paying jobs." He ticked off each point on his fingers. "No vacations. No nights out. My car's paid off; my house nearly is. I don't live extravagantly. Your bloody house and everything in it just burned down because someone wanted something from me. If I say I want to spend some of my earnings on something that will bring us both joy—allow me to do it."

The curve of her lips in a pout, those big mischievous violet eyes—it was almost too much to bear. A wide grin stretched across his face. "Stop pouting, Morgana."

She hit him with a pillow.

Grabbing the pillow and tucking it under himself, Miles declared, "I refuse to bend the knee."

He'd said it playfully, but his words had the opposite effect he'd been hoping for. She immediately started crying, clinging to him like if she let go, he'd disappear forever. It didn't take him long to realize that the images conjured by his words were uncomfortably close to the events of the previous day.

He was an idiot. Miles held her tight, whispering reassurances neither of them quite believed but wanted to more than anything.

Finally, Esme's tears slowed. "You shouldn't have done that." She pulled back just enough to meet his eyes, her voice rough. "Not for me. Not at all."

Miles was unsure how far she believed he'd been willing to go, but now also didn't seem like a great time to be completely honest with her. Knowing the truth would only make her cry again. So he pulled her closer and kissed her forehead without saying a word.

"Leon said something before he..." Esme swallowed hard. "He said, 'Good luck getting her soul back a third time.'"

"Lovely..." Miles closed his eyes, breathing in the familiar scent of her. He barely understood it himself, and yet he had known this moment was coming. "I only know what I've been told and what my dreams have hinted at." He paused, gathering his courage. "I don't know if it's true, but Gwyn seems to think it might be, and Finn agrees."

Esme sniffled, moving herself back to look up at him. "What might be true?"

He traced the line of her jaw with his thumb, buying time, gathering more courage. *Fuck.* How was this his life?

"Miles?" Her voice was barely a whisper, fragile and unsure.

"There's something I've been trying to understand for months now. Something about my dreams, about why everything with you felt so..." He searched for the right word. "Inevitable. I've mentioned before that I sleep soundly most nights we spend together. I've been reconsidering how I see the dreams I had last spring and summer, after we first met, especially after what Finn told me."

He lowered his voice. "I thought back then that all the new dreams I was having were just coincidental. But I realize they've been more specific, more like they're trying to tell me something..."

He trailed off, trying to put order to his thoughts.

She waited, tension building in the slight tremor of her hands against his chest. She searched his eyes. "What?"

He laughed. He couldn't help it. "Now I know how Finn felt when he told me about it. Why he was so hesitant to say anything. It sounds bloody mad!"

Esme muttered into his chest, "Now you're just making it weird, babe."

"Oh, it's weird," he admitted. He took a deep breath, the skin on his newly healed scars below his collarbone pulling uncomfortably. "Here goes. Finn says you're Elena. That Abby is Creiddylad. That Gwyn stole your soul—and Abby's—from Annwn. From the Otherworld."

In his arms, Esme froze, every muscle tense.

"Sounds mad, doesn't it?" Miles' laughter was shaky; the absurdity of the situation overwhelmed him, turning his worry into mirth.

The hilarity faded as fast as it had come. He'd already spoken the impossible aloud; now it was time to say his truth. "But these dreams I've had my whole life, seeing Nudd's memories play out... they make more sense now. They're remnants of a love that even death couldn't erase. My soul recognizes yours. It's why I was drawn to you from the moment we met..."

He sighed, feeling her body move with his exhale. "Before you ask again—yes, you're my choice, Esme. Always have been. Always will be my first."

Only then did he realize—he'd already proven how far he'd go when he'd kneeled before Leon.

Gwyn

Still wearing his coat, Finn stood in Abby's doorway, his usual mischief replaced by something darker. "My conversation with Mr. High-and-Mighty went just about as well as you'd guess. Thanks for askin'. Now, what did you call me over here for, seeing as though this isn't your domicile?"

"Your loyalty to your friends is as relentless as ever. I intend on waiting for Abigail here, as *she* requested." Gwyn stared the wily Fae directly in the eyes as he drove his point home. "Consider us equals, leprechaun. Though the exposure of your dirty little secret is, much like the reveal of my personal secret to Miles, entirely a consequence of your actions."

Finn shuffled his feet, plucking lint from his coat. "And what'll that be, princeling?"

Gwyn smiled, genuine yet edged with cruelty. This was the type of revenge Fae thrived upon. So using it against Finn should be doubly effective. "In a moment of passion, you slipped up. I'm sure your, oh... I wonder how many times removed—" He tapped his chin, thoughtful.

The tip of Finn's ears had grown pink. Either his conversation with Jacob had him rattled, or he was aware of Gwyn's meaning. In either case, Gwyn was relishing every second of it.

"Stop lollygaggin'," Finn bit out. "I've things to do."

"Apologies, I was attempting to do the math, but I realized I cannot be certain exactly how many generations you are removed from Christi, Abigail, and Colin. I could never understand why you chose Seattle when you had the entire world to explore. Now I know."

"You think you're clever, do you?"

"Of course, I also speak seven, maybe eight, languages. My hearing was unaffected by the paralysis Llefelys had placed on me. 'Not my granddaughter' was easily translated, imp. Though, as you did protect Abigail, I shall refrain from further mention of this matter—for now."

The truth had come out when Finn, while blasting Leon with ifrit fire, had shouted in Irish about protecting his granddaughter.

Gwyn smirked, savoring the smug satisfaction. It all made sense. Her height, her ability to absorb Finn's magic, her brash tongue—all consequences of Fae blood trying to make her mostly human body obey Fae rules.

Finn crossed his arms and huffed. "Well played, Mr. Newman, well played. Though I count your secret as not long-lived from her." He grinned widely, a retaliatory gesture. The only thing that would have made the look Finn gave him more intimidating was if he had grown fangs. "My granddaughter got a good peek inside two skulls yesterday. Hope you're prepared for that conversation when she gets back. In the meantime, I've got a duty to Arawn I've put off for far too long. I've been havin' too much fun."

The pompous grin that had been on Gwyn's face melted away, replaced by a deepest dread. The name Finn had spoken hung in the air like a death sentence. Arawn—the king of the Otherworld. Arguably the strongest of all.

Gwyn shot up from where he had been sitting, grabbing Finn by the collar. He growled, "Speak."

Finn, not caring a bit for the threat inherent in Gwyn's actions, laughed and laughed until he stopped to gasp for air. "I wasn't lyin' when I said I didn't know how ya took their souls, lad. But I know ya made a deal, and it's *my job* to remind you of the price tag attached."

Abby

It was afternoon when Abby finally made it home from the hospital. Her father was stable, thank the gods, but seeing him so fragile, hooked up to machines...

Miles promised to sneak into the hospital at some point in the next two days to help with some "miracle" healing. She'd never been so grateful to have him in her life.

Though distraught by her lost magic, Abby's mother was too preoccupied with her father to deal with it. Facing that loss was an O'Malley family struggle that lay in the future. Colin and Will, in the same vein, were now questioning their move to Los Angeles. Colin wanted to help their parents recover, so he planned to stay for a while. Will was happy to stay too, as long as he could be with Colin. All that meant was that she didn't have to lose either one of them yet.

Abby opened her apartment door to find Gwyn sitting at the kitchen counter, cradling a mug of tea. Her chest ached at the sight of the dark circles and bruises that marred his face. Still, the rhythmic patter of rain on the windows and the comforting hum of the heat running filled Abby's apartment with a cozy feeling—something she wanted more of.

But only if it included his smile too.

"You're still here," she said softly, setting her bag down and moving to the kitchen. "You didn't have to wait this long."

"How could I not wait for you?" he murmured, not looking up. His voice was rough, his usual brand of arrogant confidence stripped away.

"My dad woke up this morning," she said quietly. "He's... He's going to be okay, and Miles is going to help..." She trailed off, gripping the edge of the counter.

"I'm sorry," Gwyn said hoarsely.

"Hey," she whispered, standing across from him. "You okay?"

The second it was out of her mouth, she realized how stupid the question had been.

Gwyn huffed a bitter laugh, shaking his head. "No. I rarely am, actually." His answer felt packed with subtext, like he was alluding to several things at once. He glanced at her, his sapphire eyes filled with the same raw pain she'd seen on New Year's Eve.

Not knowing what to say, she fell back on her trademark blunt honesty, hoping it would get one of the many conversations they needed to have out of the way. "I'm sorry I killed your uncle."

He tented his hands, rubbing at his nose and stubble. Gwyn gave a tiny shake of his head. She imagined him standing up and walking out her front door, having realized that she wasn't the type of woman he wanted to be with. That he wouldn't be able to look at her without seeing his family's blood on her hands.

Instead, he dropped his hands and met her eyes. "I am grateful for it. Thank you. I expected to do it myself."

Silence stretched as she absorbed what he'd said.

Then she filled the silence with more brutal honesty. "I looked at a few of Leon's memories while I was inside his head.

I know you're telling the truth about who you are. Actually, I don't think I've ever not believed you. I don't know why, but the second I read about Nudd and you in Esme's car as we traveled to meet you at my parents' house that first time, everything just sort of clicked, and I barely stopped to question it."

Gwyn's eyebrows inched upward slightly.

Abby continued, "And I got pulled into one of Miles' dreams when I tried to wake him up. So I know what you mean about him being just like Nudd, too. Because I've seen Nudd, I've seen you, Elena, and… I've seen Creiddylad. I get it now. I get why you called me her name."

His hands flew back up to his face, this time to cover it entirely. "Abigail—"

"Stop. Gwyn, just let me get this out. This is important. I'm not angry anymore." Abby took a reinforcing breath. "I watched her die, Gwyn. You told me you couldn't remember what happened to her. Do you… do you want to know?"

"I think—" His voice broke. Years of meticulous self-control crumbled under the crushing weight of all the guilt he was carrying around.

The fearless, infuriatingly arrogant ancient prince who faced down monsters with a smirk crumpled in on himself. He tucked his face into his hands again as deep, soul-wrenching sobs wracked his body. When he glanced up, tears were streaming down his face.

For a long moment Abby stood frozen, struck by the raw humanity of his grief. Gwyn didn't adhere to modern society's restrictive standards for masculine emotional expression. She'd seen Gwyn fight, seen him laugh, seen him in moments of passion—but this? This complete dissolution of his carefully maintained control shocked her to her core.

He was unfettered.

Abby watched as a storm of emotions—anger, guilt, and deepest hurt—swept across his face. Overcoming her hesitation, she moved to him. She felt his warm, ragged breath ghosting across her skin as his tears fell.

At long last, his reply came, a low murmur barely audible as he spoke into her chest. "I think... I think I already know how it happened. It was my fault," he choked out. "I wasn't there. I failed her. I failed everyone."

Still holding him, she talked into his hair. "You didn't fail her, Gwyn. Llefelys was a monster. I'm so sorry. Listen."

She created distance between them, wanting him to see the seriousness in her eyes as she delivered yet more honesty. "But I also watched her live through Nudd's eyes. She was a force. You were right to love her. I should count myself lucky that you confused us."

Gently, she cradled his face in her hands. Her thumbs brushed away the tears that lingered on his cheeks. The sensation struck her again—an echo of motion and posture that seemed like it belonged to the woman she saw in memories.

"Gwyn," she whispered, "what's my connection to her? Why did it feel like I was watching myself in those memories?"

Gwyn's shoulders slumped. A sigh escaped his lips as he stared blankly ahead for a long moment, seeming utterly lost. Then he turned his stare on her with eyes filled with anguish.

He whispered back, "Abigail, you *are* her."

***

Hours of conversation later, Abby stood before her bathroom mirror. With Gwyn home caring for Cerys, the isolated quiet gave her time to indulge her curiosity. Waking up that morning, she'd felt like a completely different person, a feeling Gwyn later confirmed by explaining just how different she was.

Right after she'd gained Colin's gift of magical sight, she'd spent a long time gazing at her reflection as she practiced simple magic. It had been a great way to learn what all the different colors meant, to learn how magic traced back to its source. But now, a powerful premonition, a feeling deep in her gut, hinted that once she saw herself, there would be no going back, no chance to undo what she'd seen.

But she did it anyway.

Abby gasped, stifling a scream that wanted to tear its way from her throat. Waves of shimmering gold light danced and flickered in the air, surrounding her head like a halo. The golden light wasn't only around her head—it was inside her too, swirling and pulsing exactly like it did within Miles.

***

What Esme, Miles, Gwyn, and Abby had thought was the conclusion of their worst problems was actually the beginning of the end. But only one troublesome leprechaun knew this, and he was enjoying himself far too much to spoil the surprise. But he was also digging a grave and hiding the weapon. A bit of sweat and magic was all it took to secret the bones and stored power of one potent magus away for later use.

CHAPTER FORTY-THREE

THE VIPER

Seren

Half a world away, a middle-aged woman, her winter-honey-colored hair still vibrant and untouched by gray, sat brooding over the information displayed on her laptop screen. Pages of description detailed what she'd waited a lifetime for, yet also dreaded.

A picture, one of a young woman with hair exactly like hers holding a siphoning dagger, made her stomach clench with sudden recognition. The viper wrapped around her neck like a living necklace shifted under her skin in a way that mirrored her rapidly changing thoughts. Half were dark, half were nostalgic, but none were settled.

By nature, Seren Lewis was an impatient woman. But, then again, it had been nearly two millennia since she'd heard news that drove her to such agitation. Not since *her*.

Fate, it seemed, delighted in irony. A reunion between them was inevitable, but did it really have to be in bloody Seattle? Of all the places in the world, why not Mykonos or Nice? Somewhere with sun and sandy beaches and the faintest hint of joy. But no. It had to be there, in the rain-soaked city where moss clung to every surface.

Or perhaps it wasn't fate at all.

Seren's lips curled into a bitter smile. This reeked of Arawn. The King of Annwn had never forgiven her for meddling.

Seren picked up her phone and dialed her old mentor. "Jacob, is your vote still a 'no'?"

His confirmation was immediate. He was adamantly against arming the magic users of the world with the knowledge they needed to protect themselves against the malevolents.

Nearly every member of the International Assembly had refused to believe how bad things had become. Seren had known that it was getting worse for years, but the proof coming out of Seattle made how close they were to catastrophe undeniable.

If they wouldn't help, she'd have to solve the problem the hard way. What was ten, fifteen more deaths on her conscience at this point?

Her fingers hovered over the keyboard, the viper at her neck relaxing with her decision made. With a sigh, she opened a new tab and booked a flight to Seattle. *Merde.* She loathed the idea of stepping into another mess, but some things couldn't be avoided. Not when the stakes were this personal.

Change was coming whether they liked it or not. And if a few heads had to roll—figuratively or otherwise—well, that was just the price of doing business.

The End

SNEAK PREVIEW OF BOOK #4

Seren

The smoke had already begun to clear by the time Seren emerged from the unmarked SUV.

To mundane emergency crews, it would appear to be a mundane explosion. The French authorities would conclude that a minor leak from the farm's propane tank had ignited into a devastating fire, claiming only one life. A few well-placed illusions would ensure that the news would spread the lie by morning.

Magic had to be hidden. Even when it cost a seated member of the French Assembly's life.

Seren stood at the edge of the Montsauche copse, her coat fluttering gently in the spring breeze. She was careful not to step on shards of scattered glass as her boots crunched over gravel and burned leaves. The countryside was no place for heels, but she had an image to maintain.

Thibaut Robail's corpse lay with limbs splayed at awkward angles, the scorch marks of his magic surrounding him in a perfect circle of destruction. Nearby were twenty more bodies, half-destroyed and burned to a crisp, their wings either folded beneath them or shattered. The fight must have been magnificent to witness; Thibaut had lasted until the final one fell.

Only after seeing the other casualties did the English expression Seren was searching for come back to her. *Two birds with one stone.*

Thibaut was a strong mage. That power had been his undoing. Yet he had died a warrior; he deserved her respect.

Again and again the International Assembly voted for their own destruction. They voted for the hard way of fixing the problem, which would tear civilization apart if something didn't change immediately. So Seren took it upon herself to make a solution.

Just as she leaned over to brush a lock of hair from Thibaut's eyes, she heard a soft footfall behind her. It was one of the field operatives from the Assembly's Paris Corded Brotherhood. The woman wore clothes more suited to the countryside, but her aura was all combat readiness and barely suppressed grief.

With arms tightly crossed, she accused, "You expected this." Though she stood perfectly still, there was a waver in her voice. "But you didn't stop him."

"He made a choice," Seren replied without turning. "His final one."

"You could have ordered him."

"I *could* have ordered him. But then we would be covering up the slaughter of an entire town instead of one corpse!" Seren did turn around then, raising an eyebrow. "*You* could have joined him in the fight!"

The woman's breath hitched, like she wanted to argue but couldn't find the fault in the logic. Seren shamelessly exploited the Corded Brother's guilt, ensuring her own insecurities prevented her from fully considering the predicament Thibaut had found himself in at his end.

Seren was cold because the world required it. The safety of the many over the lives of the few. It wasn't cruelty. It was balancing scales.

The woman's eyes flared, tear-bright and furious. "We didn't think it was this bad."

"None of you do until someone else dies!" Seren snapped.

"You're a monster."

"I've been called worse." Seren stepped forward, past the scorch circle that delineated one man's final stand against true monsters.

A quiet whimper startled them both. Seren turned sharply, hand half-raised in reflex before she saw the source.

A teenager—no, younger. Maybe eleven. She was hunched, trembling, holding a phone in her hand like it could ward off spirits. Thibaut's daughter. The girl had likely hidden as instructed when Thibaut had sounded the alarm. Smart. She had her father's stubbornness in the set of her face.

The girl studied Seren like *she* was the creature who'd killed her father.

The grieving child was only half-correct.

Seren stepped closer. "I'm sorry, darling. We did not know you were with him."

The girl didn't speak. Her red-rimmed eyes glared up at Seren.

Seren crouched, careful to keep her distance. "You'll be looked after. The Assembly will see to that."

"I don't want them," the girl whispered, voice hoarse from smoke or grief. "I want *him*."

Seren's face didn't change, but something in her chest pulled tight. She knew this pain. She'd lived it.

"I know," Seren said. She stood, unable to offer comfort, yet unwilling to be cruel. "Wishing doesn't stop the world from ending. Doing something does. He did *something* important."

With the arrival of another car on the gravel road, she left the girl with the Corded Brother and the Assembly's cleanup crew. By the time she was back in her SUV, Seren's phone was already blowing up with notifications. Assembly members were demanding answers she'd already given.

She was playing the long game. The game they were too scared to acknowledge even existed. The Assembly would argue over silly things like how best to bury Thibaut, how to eulogize him. Then they'd waste hours pretending this was a tragedy no one could have predicted.

But Seren understood the truth. This had been necessary. She wasn't finished doing things the hard way, exactly as they had voted for.

It was the cost of keeping the malevolents contained. Magic required balance, and his death wasn't enough.

Thibaut had made the right move.

Sometimes being a hero meant dying when the world needed you to. And sometimes being a villain meant letting them.

Esme

Three months later

At the Sanctuary of Spirits, regulars knew the seat in front of the garnish station was one of last resort. The cramped space, along with the lingering scent of bitter orange zest, muddled mint, and the cloying sweetness of maraschino cherries that clung to everything within a three-foot radius—it was a sensory assault and a logistical nightmare for both bartender and guest. So when Maureen Mitchell claimed that spot, Esme's internal alarm bells started ringing.

With a flick of her fingers, Esme summoned a sticky pint glass. It skidded across the bar top and into her hand. The sour tang of stale hops hit her nose as she caught it with a practiced motion. *Nope*, she decided, *not tonight*. She was not going to fight with Maureen. She'd let anything Maureen said go and move on.

It had been three months since the new year had turned their lives inside out, and Esme was still reeling from the emotional aftershocks. Finding out she was probably Elena reborn, with Abby as her counterpart Creiddylad, should have been empowering. Instead, it terrified her.

Revelations, as it turned out, came with consequences.

Her house had burned to the ground, forcing her to move in with Miles permanently, along with Lily, who had appointed herself Esme's furry emotional support system. It wasn't the fact that the paintings her mother had made were ruined or even the ashes leftover from her childhood stuffed animals that bothered her most. It was the betrayal.

Sylas, misunderstood and maligned, had tried to protect them, especially the most vulnerable in their community. While Leon, smiling, affable Leon, had orchestrated the whole murderous scheme.

And as if the ancient Welsh soap opera unfolding around them wasn't enough, Finn had decided to drop their shared mythological baggage straight into Jacob's lap. The information had sent him spiraling down a path of obsessive research. He barely slept, ordered every single piece of literature on the subject, from *The Mabinogion* to scholarly articles on the Welsh afterlife, and muttered constantly about "breaking the laws of magic."

Meanwhile, Abby and Gwyn had grown closer. They were practically cohabiting, still debating whether to set up house in his cramped downtown apartment that was right next to her work or her cozy space with more room but a longer commute. And Colin and Will? Off to L.A. in pursuit of sunshine, leaving Esme short one work bestie.

Throughout this, there was one constant: Finn hadn't changed at all.

Esme took a deep breath, squared her shoulders, and plastered on a smile, ready to play nice with Maureen. She waved as she finished the cocktail she was working on. Recently, the powerful evocation mage and Esme had been getting along surprisingly well, a change from the past when Maureen's hateful bullying, because of Esme's demon blood, had made things unbearable between them. So maybe this interaction wouldn't be so bad.

Esme was psyching herself up to take Maureen's order next when a newcomer walked in and claimed the spot directly next to her former nemesis. Esme froze mid-step, then pivoted smoothly to polish a glass she'd already cleaned twice. Esme might have brushed it off as a friend dropping by because Maureen and the newcomer were about the same age, but Esme didn't miss the way Maureen's expression changed.

Maureen Mitchell, outwardly prim and proper but inwardly venomous and icy, stiffened in fear. As she clutched her glass, her knuckles whitened, and her face lost color. Even a tray of the world's best chocolates wouldn't have been able to distract Esme from eavesdropping on *that* conversation.

Maureen Mitchell was not afraid of people.

Maureen's companion was the picture of understated wealth with an edge, like old money dipped in danger. Her black cashmere cardigan, dress slacks, and impeccably styled light brown hair were traditionally professional in every way. But the tattoo of a detailed serpent, its scaled body wrapping around her neck like a living choker, and ears full of expensive-looking piercings gave her appearance an edge that Esme couldn't help but admire.

Hands now clasped too tightly in front of her, Maureen stood and greeted the other woman. Esme grabbed a rag and made her way down the bar, wiping surfaces that didn't need cleaning. She detected a subtle European accent in the stranger's voice, vaguely reminiscent of Gwyn but softer, perhaps from somewhere near France.

Esme missed the woman's name but caught onto the conversation mid-sentence thanks to her improved cambion hearing.

"—because it's my first visit," the woman was saying. "Though I see some people remain consistent."

"—hardly the most welcoming climate," Maureen muttered, her expression carefully neutral.

The other woman hummed, tipping her head as though amused. "That's a matter of perspective. Adaptation can be... messy."

Esme reached their section of the bar, noting how Maureen was fidgeting. Leaning against the bar, she flashed her usual work-friendly smirk. "Hello! I'm Esme. Can I get you ladies anything?"

With a cursory glance and a mumbled, "The usual," Maureen kept her attention wholly on the other woman. Catching herself, Maureen added, "Esme, this is Seren. She's... visiting."

"A pleasure," Seren said, studying the drink menu. When she looked up, Seren's gaze on Esme triggered an instinctive warning in her gut. "I'll try 'The Last Word.'"

"That's my favorite!" Esme said brightly, trying to shake off the strange sinking feeling. "Okay, I'll have those out in just a—"

Something about the way Seren looked at her as she said it made the hair on Esme's neck prickle. Or maybe that was—

The air shifted—sudden, nauseating, *wrong*.

The fine hairs on Esme's arms rose, a crawling sensation creeping down her spine. A sickening, wrong cold slithered from less than ten feet away, making the temperature plummet. Esme felt the distinctive magical signature that harbingered trouble of the tooth-and-claw variety.

Malevolent magic. In her bar. In front of *civilians.* If anything happened to the Sanctuary—her sanctuary—she'd never forgive herself.

She didn't know why she was surprised. Three months into the new year, they'd already endured more fights against malevolents than in all the preceding year.

Esme tensed, calculating the best way to act without drawing attention. She watched both women stiffen in recognition.

"Brr," Esme said loudly, shivering for effect. "Do you feel that? Must've left one of the refrigerators open in the back."

Fuck, fuck, fuck.

Maureen's gaze snapped to hers, sharp and knowing. Seren let out a sigh, not of fear or shock, but sounding like something close to resignation.

"Maureen." Seren's voice was barely above a whisper, but it carried the kind of authority that expected immediate compliance. "Weave an illusion of normalcy around the empty table to my left. Thank all the magic that it's not busy in here. Whatever is coming out is small. I'm slowing its emergence." Her violet eyes, starting to fill with shadows, locked onto Esme's. "I see that you know about our situation. Grab a towel and be ready to act if my aim is off."

Esme's mind reeled. The woman was aware of the malevolents. And she was slowing its emergence? *How*? Beyond that, she was clearly accustomed to unquestioning obedience.

Before Esme could decide if she should carry out the stranger's orders, she found herself moving.

She darted to the bar and grabbed the largest towel she could find, along with a mop bucket. By the time she reached the empty table, the feeling of Maureen's magic around her was strangely blunted, as if something or someone was cutting off everyone's perception of the magic being cast.

Who was this woman?

Esme had only witnessed a few malevolent emergences with her own eyes before that moment. They had been violent and fast. This was altogether different.

The same cold was there, chilling her feet through her shoes. The same wrong, nauseating feeling of malevolent magic was there too. But Seren's intervention had slowed its emergence and weakened it.

Sprawled beneath the table on the bar floor, the creature appeared dazed and immobile. It had skin that was more green than brown, needle-sharp fangs, a heavy brow, and sparse tufts of black hair sprouting from its head. Though small enough to be a child, it radiated malevolent magic and was damned mean.

Whatever magic Seren was working on it was powerful. The creature's feeble attempt to hiss and lunge at Esme resulted in a slow, awkward flop onto the floor. Esme averted her gaze. Staring would only make people more aware of the impossible event unfolding right before their eyes. *Double fuck.*

Esme nervously scanned the room, but the chattering, laughing patrons were oblivious. A selkie and a human man, the nearest couple, leaned in close to each other, blissfully unaware of the supernatural danger so near. Maureen's illusion was holding—for now.

Thank goodness it was after food service hours. Wexley, the Sanctuary of Spirit's púca chef, sensed malevolent magic even if he didn't know that monsters were a true possibility. He would have had a coronary event had he been serving somewhere nearby. Esme's immediate instinct was to squish the nasty goblin thing with her heel, but she held back, feeling a second surge of magic around the creature.

The shadows along the edges of the table moved as she pretended to be cleaning up a mess with the broom. Tentacles of inky blackness, stinking with the scent of brimstone, slithered up from the floor.

Esme barely stifled a gasp. The tentacles—they looked exactly like her infernal creations. Like her conjured blades, like her summoned shadowcat, but most of all like her eldritch abomination. Seeing her most private magic, perfected by a stranger's hands, chilled her in a way that went deeper than mere recognition.

Three strikes of the tentacles were all it took, flawlessly executed: one down the creature's throat to silence it, two through its nostrils to end it, one wrapped across its arms and legs to bind it. It thrashed weakly, trying to claw and bite down on the tentacles. Within seconds, its struggles weakened and finally ceased.

Snapping back to reality, Esme felt the sweat beading on her back and her rapid heartbeat.

That was... holy hell. What had she just witnessed?

Esme forced herself to move, to act like everything was normal. Fighting the urge to stand there, she wrapped the goblin in the towel, making it appear like she was soaking up a mess. Esme glanced at Maureen, whose hands trembled slightly as sweat beaded along her hairline, her eyes slightly narrowed in concentration. While Seren examined her nails as if waiting for Maureen to finish her thought, not the least bit ruffled. Esme tossed the body into the mop bucket, its wheels squeaking in protest as she shouldered her way through the swinging kitchen doors.

The corpse was a problem for later. Figuring out who the hell Seren was had become Esme's immediate priority.

As she exited the kitchen, Seren was waiting, already smoothing her elegant coat and leaving money on the table.

"Enough bullshit for what was supposed to be a relaxing night," Seren muttered to Maureen, then added with a slight nod to Esme, "Passable. Let's see if you survive."

Esme scowled. The door's magic hadn't finished buzzing with Seren's exit before Esme was back at Maureen's side. "What the hell was that? Who is she? *Passable*?" With each question, her voice climbed an octave higher.

"That," Maureen said, gesturing with her glass, "was some sort of test for both of us. You passed." She pushed away from the bar. "Barely."

Maureen exhaled, draining the last of her drink while standing. "Could've been worse, Charity Case. She's... not someone you want to cross," Maureen said tightly. The glance she cast at the door wasn't fearful; it was reverent in the way one might show a vengeful god.

And, for once, her words contained no venom; only a weary sigh hinted that Seren hadn't finished with any of them.

If you enjoyed this book, I'd be grateful if you could take a moment to leave a review. Your support means the world to indie authors like me and helps other readers discover new stories.

Want more? Sign up for my newsletter to receive a free copy of the prequel novella, plus exclusive previews and updates on upcoming releases. www.stellahopeauthor.com

ABOUT THE AUTHOR

Fantasy author Stella Hope blends myth, romance, and non-stop action in each of her novels. Her favorite stories feature strong female protagonists, their loyal companions, and a generous sprinkle of humor.

Before embracing her passion for writing, Stella embarked on an academic journey that began with bachelor's degrees in Latin and geography. Afterwards, she pursued a graduate degree in environmental science and worked as a scientist for a few years. Stella's love for books eventually led her out of the forest and into the world of libraries, where she had the pleasure of running two public school libraries.

She lives in the PNW with her family, where she occasionally has to leave her writing cave to thwart the neighborhood bear's attempts at pilfering food from her bird feeder. When she's not writing, she's doing her best to stay away from bears, bobcats, deer, and sometimes coyotes during her trail runs and hikes. Her efforts are frequently less successful than one might suppose.

If you'd like to receive sneak previews, updates from Stella, and free content available only to subscribers, please join her mailing list at stellahopeauthor.com